# A ROGUISH CHRISTMAS

## Steamy Regency Romances

---

## By Georgette Brown

Georgette BROWN

A DECEMBER TRYST

# A DECEMBER TRYST

## By Georgette Brown

# Chapter One

Settled into his seat, the Viscount Carrington stretched his legs as far as he could in the confines of the carriage and observed the only other occupant in the vehicle seated across from him. Adeline, a young woman and his ward, had not spoken to him the whole of their ride to the first of many Yuletide gatherings and stared rather anxiously out the window. He would have much preferred to skip the festivities in favor of spending a sennight at Château Follet, his favorite den of debauchery. But as Lady Bettina, their grandmother, nursed a cough, it fell to him to accompany Adeline to the Moorington ball.

"Am I such tiresome company these days that you cannot find two words to speak to me?" Arthur tried in a teasing tone.

Startled, Adeline turned her large blue eyes toward him. With her dark golden curls and petite frame, she presented a contrast to him.

"You? Tiresome? Never!" she assured. "I was preoccupied—worried that the snow might make us late to the ball."

She glanced out the window once more. He followed her gaze and noted the ground bore a light coat of white beneath the bright moonlight, but the carriage continued easily upon the road. He looked back to Adeline, who continued to look silently out the window, unsure what to make of her taciturn mood. Perhaps it was customary for young women of her age, seven and ten, to vacillate between reticence and loquacity. He had assumed guardianship of her just prior to her come-out, and though she spent more time in the company of Lady Bettina, than in his, he felt he knew Adeline well enough to detect that something was amiss. Adeline had been distracted ever since returning from Bath with Lady Bettina.

"If anything, I think we shall be early," he told her.

She seemed not to hear him and made no response. He eyed her more keenly, looking for signs that she might be unwell, but she had a healthy glow to her countenance. Beneath her coat, she wore a gown of silver and white that perfectly displayed her slender arms. Her hair was perfectly coiffed with just the right amount of tendrils curling loosely about her physiognomy to provide a diaphanous appearance. Were he not seven years her senior and her guardian, he might have considered her worthy of conquest.

His observation took in the small but simple necklace with a single opal solitaire, and he was rather surprised that she had not chosen to wear the diamond and sapphire he had gifted her for her birthday.

"Is that new?" he asked.

She turned to him with raised brows.

He pointed to the necklace.

She put a hand to the opal and flushed. "Oh. A trinket from a...friend. In honor of St. Nicholas Day."

The scenery outside the window seemed to captivate her once more.

He raised his brows. "A friend?"

She glanced briefly at him, nodded, then returned to the window.

"What friend is this?" he prodded.

"I can see the Moorington estate!" she cried.

Either she had not heard him or she needed a diversion. He wagered it was the latter.

"Do you think they will serve apples *a la parisienne*?" she continued, her earlier reticence gone in an instant. "I found it such a wondrous dessert when they had it for Twelfth Night last year. As much as I love plum pudding, it was quite exciting to try something new."

He allowed her to prattle on, but as the carriage drew nearer to their destination, she fell once more into silence. Her body, however, was hardly quiet. Her hand tapped her fan against her reticule. Her feet shifted restlessly.

Something was afoot with Adeline, Arthur decided. Something having to do with the Moorington ball. And he determined that he would uncover whatever it was she was keeping from him before the night's conclusion.

PHILIPPA GRAYSON NEARLY toppled over in her attempt to look around the gentleman standing in front of her, blocking her view of her son, George, who stood on the other side of the ballroom with his twin sister, Honora. Her children were speaking with the Moorington girls, Emily and Jane, and though Emily giggled often at what George had to say, the interest seemed to flow primarily in one direction. It would not be Jane Moorington who had captured her son's heart for she had a beau. Though Philippa supposed it was possible for George to have fallen for the flaxen-haired beauty, she prayed he had enough sense not to pursue a woman already spoken for. But the fact that George would not reveal the name of his lady of interest did give Philippa pause.

"La! I suppose you have been here all night," mused Melinda St. John as she took a seat beside her friend and fanned her ample décolletage with an ornate fan. "I have been thrice down the dance floor despite being a full ten years your senior. You cannot claim to be forty years yet but sit about as if you were an eighty year old widow."

"I am indeed a widow," Philippa replied as she watched George greet and smile at a redhead. Was this young lady the one?

Melinda followed Philippa's gaze. "Who are you staring at? A handsome rogue, I hope."

"He has asked her to dance," Philippa murmured to herself. To her friend she asked, "Who is that dancing with George?"

Melinda frowned. "Have you only eyes for your children?"

Philippa made a face. "Who else would I have eyes for?"

Melinda poked her in the arm with her fan. "Yourself, of course."

"Me?"

"La! Why not?" Melinda looked Philippa over. "The years have been kind to you. You have a decent figure. No one would condemn you as it has been years since your husband passed. God rest his soul, but you are a living woman, with, dare I say, *needs*. La! *I* have needs, and, alas, my husband is very much alive."

"I should see my children settled first. They are both of them twenty and, till they are married, they are in my care."

"Why do you worry? Honora has more suitors than she needs. I thought it quite grand that she had the eye of an Earl last season."

"While there are many men who seek her attention, not all of them have matrimony in mind. They cannot for we have not breeding, and our wealth is not what it once was. But if George were to make a good match, I think his sister's might improve. And he is besotted. He confessed that he has never been more in love. In *love*. My George has never used the word before, and I have never before seen him in such gay spirits. But he will not tell me who she is. Of course I was quite disappointed that he would not, but he assured me that it was not because he was critical of me and that he would provide her name as soon as he had permission to grant it."

Melinda furrowed her brow. "And why would she not grant it?"

"I know not. But young people these days prefer their independence. They are not as accustomed as we were to being watched and scrutinized. Honora knows her name but is sworn to keep her brother's secret."

"That is what comes of having twins." Melinda tapped her fan on Philippa. "Look! There is Sir Tallmadge. What do you think of him? Not bad for a widower of fifty, eh?"

"I could hardly aspire to someone of his stature," Philippa dismissed, keeping her gaze upon George and his dance partner as they came down the line. Her late husband had come into wealth through trade and, thus, considered common stock.

"I would agree if you were seeking courtship with him, but for a lover, I think he would as likely take you to bed as anyone."

Philippa blushed to the roots of her hair.

"Or, look there, Mr. Gregory. Always proper. A bit dull for my taste, but he might suit you. He's not married as yet, though I wonder why. He has property that brings him five thousand a year."

"Mr. Gregory is but thirty years of age!"

"For a lover, the younger the better! Now *there* is one whom I should very much like in my bed. I should not care if he had any skills in lovemaking but would be content to stare at his naked form for most of the night."

Philippa looked across the room for this Adonis. It was a gentleman she did not recognize. He had raven locks and a charming smile that had both the Moorington girls flushing and twittering. His coat tightly hugged a broad chest and wide shoulders while his trousers molded a tapered waist and long legs. She understood why Melinda might be content with ogling the man in the buff.

Goodness! Why was she contemplating a naked man? She was spending far too much of her time with Melinda.

"Though I suspect Lord Carrington could not be so very bad in bed or he would not have had as many lovers as he had, including that courtesan Harriette Dubouchet."

"You wish to consort with a rake?"

"La! Of course! I am not seeking a husband—I have one of those, and he is about as exciting to make love to as beefsteak. I want a man to satisfy my *carnal* desires. And I think the Viscount Carrington would do quite nicely."

Philippa stared at Melinda. For the most part, she chalked her friend's ramblings to an amusement Melinda derived from shocking her friend with such talk, but Melinda was practically drooling.

Melinda snapped her fan open and waved it furiously. After a moment, she turned to Philippa. "Why do you look at me like that? You cannot pretend you have no fantasies of your own."

"I beg your pardon!"

"La, Philippa! You need not be ashamed when speaking to me. You know that I will not censure you for your honesty. The younger generation has a much better appreciation of such matters when it comes to the gentle sex. Not like our husbands who came of age in the last century and still hold to the belief that women have *none* of the same desires that men have."

"But perhaps they have *more* of those...desires. It is more in their nature."

"La! My eros could run circles around my husband's. Men may come into it with greater verve and fire, but their flame dies easily whereas *ours* continues to burn. Hence, it is quite reasonable to seek a younger man as our appetites are better matched."

Philippa was surprised that she could not fault Melinda's reasoning. Nevertheless, she was hardly won over.

The dance having concluded, George made his way to his mother.

She could hardly wait for him to finish greeting Melinda when she inquired, "Is that the young woman who has captivated my son?"

"No, mama," he replied with a broad smile.

"Is the object of your affection not here tonight?"

"She is here, but I have not had a chance to speak with her yet."

"I pray you will do so soon as I am quite eager to meet her."

"I pray it will happen as well."

Melinda interceded, "Let me try with your son. I will know his mystery lady as there is hardly anyone here I do not know. Come, young man, escort me to the refreshment table."

Philippa watched Melinda take George's arm and lead him away. As she rose to her feet to stretch her legs, she spotted Honora, who, not minding where she walked, bumped into a gentleman and dropped her packet of lemon drops. He turned around, and Philippa saw that it was the Viscount Carrington. He picked up Honora's confections and handed it to her. They exchanged pleasantries. Honora's cheeks colored, and she lowered her lashes demurely. Philippa had never seen her daughter respond in such a fashion. What had the man said to her?

This would not do. Philippa made her way to Honora.

"Your pardon, I have need of my daughter," Philippa said to the man as she grabbed Honora's arm and led her daughter away.

"What is it, mama?" Honora asked.

"Hm? Oh, well," Philippa stammered. "What was it that Lord Carrington said to you?"

"You know the Viscount?"

"Only by name. Melinda warned me of him."

"Is that why you came to get me?"

"What did he say to you? Nothing inappropriate, I hope."

"He quoted Shakespeare when returning my lemon drops: 'sweets to the sweet.'"

"Is that all?"

"Yes, mama."

Philippa looked over her shoulder and noted that the Viscount now spoke with another young woman of beauty.

"You fibbed to Lord Carrington," Honora accused but without anger. "You had no need of me at all."

"I have a need for my daughter to be safe from rogues."

Honora laughed. "You have no proof that he intended anything with me. And while I understand Mrs. St. John is your dear friend, I wonder that she is always correct?"

Philippa had to agree with Honora's assessment. Melinda tended to enjoy gossiping and reveling in the scandalous.

"Do you think I cannot fend for myself?" Honora asked.

"Well, you do possess a maturity beyond many of your peers, but why give a man like that more opportunities than he needs?"

"A pity as he is quite handsome, is he not?"

Philippa shook her head at her daughter before turning the conversation to other topics. There was no need to talk of Lord Carrington further.

AS THE WOMAN BEFORE him was the daughter of his banker, Arthur had to endure her conversation for longer than he would have liked. As she prattled on about the drudgery of charity work, his mind wandered to the striking young woman who had bumped into him. He preferred to spend his time in London but was surprised he had not crossed paths with her before, especially if they had the Mooringtons in common. She shared many of the same features as her mother: light brown hair that caught the glow of the candle lights, luminescent sapphire eyes, and a general softness to her features. He shook his head to himself, remembering how the mother had swooped in and carried her daughter off with such haste that he could not be faulted if he took offense. Which he did not. The woman had sounded polite enough, though she could not hide her look of doubt when their gazes had met. She must have been young when she had her daughter for the blossom of beauty had not faded in her. She was nearly as pretty as her daughter.

"...and they have not enough appreciation for the philanthropy they receive," the woman continued.

Arthur looked past her, evaluating the other women present at the ball. He wondered if any of them would make a good candidate to take to Château Follet, dubbed the Château Debauchery by some. There was Agnes Fairchild. He and she had had a brief but passionate affair when they were both eight and ten, before she married an Earl thrice her age. But she was a widower now, and if she possessed the same verve and sense of adventure, she might be more than receptive to renewing their prior acquaintance.

He had nearly settled on Agnes when he spotted Adeline. A young man had approached her, and it seemed her whole being sparkled. This then was her secret and most likely the 'friend' and source of her opal necklace. Arthur was immediately inclined toward skepticism and the young man's true intentions, for an upright gentleman would have spoken to Adeline's guardian before commencing a courtship that involved the gifting of baubles, but Arthur saw that the young man's countenance glowed as much as Adeline's. Where had Adeline met this young man? In Bath, perhaps. But without the knowledge of Lady Bettina?

Arthur recalled that his grandmother had been ill for a good duration of her time in Bath, but Lady Bettina had assigned a friend of hers, Mrs. Patterson, the wife of a pastor, to chaperone Adeline.

The young man, who could not have been much more than twenty or so in age, was familiar to Arthur, though he prided himself on remembering faces. Upon closer inspection, Arthur realized why he thought he might have met the man before. Though the young man's hair was a darker brown, he very much resembled the young lady with the lemon drops.

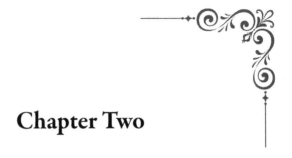

# Chapter Two

Arthur looked about for Adeline with the intention of asking her to dance and inquire after the fellow she had been speaking with, but he had lost sight of her when the host of the ball had come to speak with him and ask him if he wanted to join the older men in cards.

"After I have fit in another dance or two," Arthur answered.

Richard Moorington patted him on the back. "Have at it, young man. Enjoy the merriment while you can. Dancing loses its luster when you are my age."

Arthur scanned the room for Adeline. He did not find his ward, but, spotting the young woman of the lemon drops, he asked Richard to introduce them.

"That beauty there in the lavender gown?" Richard asked.

"Yes, who is she?"

"Miss Grayson. I cannot recall her given name. They are close friends of Melinda St. John. She is my wife's cousin."

Richard was too much the gentleman to speak blatantly ill of someone, but his tone suggested that he was not partial to Melinda.

The men made their way to Miss Grayson. Richard provided more than an introduction. He audaciously proposed that Miss Grayson dance the next set with Arthur.

"I hope you will forgive my earlier clumsiness," Miss Grayson said as he led her onto the dance floor.

"There is nothing to forgive," he replied as they took their positions. "It was a mere accident, and no harm came of it."

"Accidents are a pattern with me, I fear. You have been warned, my lord."

Despite her self-effacement, she danced well, indicating she had had lessons. He complimented her on her grace.

"I think it *your* skills that have inspired me, my lord," she said, "but much remains in the dance. I have many opportunities yet to step on your feet."

"You are modest."

"Indeed, I am not. I know that I have inherited the trait of clumsiness from my mother."

"Is that why I have not yet seen her dance tonight?"

"Perhaps. She danced more when my father was alive."

"He has passed? I'm sorry to hear it."

He tried to remember if he had ever heard the name of Grayson before. "Is it just you and your mother then?"

"And my brother."

"I do not think I have met him. What's his name?"

"George."

Arthur doubted not but that Adeline's friend was George Grayson, but he wanted Adeline to confirm his conclusion.

"Our host tells me your family is a friend of Mrs. St. John," he said.

"My mother and she are good friends."

By the time the dance had finished, he had collected a fair amount of information. His dance partner was not related to the Graysons of Staffordshire, George was finishing his last year at Cambridge, their father once had shared investments with Mr. St. John, and Mrs. Grayson was even more modest than she was clumsy.

He had been tempted to ask a few more questions about Mrs. Grayson, whom he had seen halfway through the dance, looking upon them with grave concern, confirming his earlier suspicions that she did not approve of his attentions toward her daughter. Although he found Miss Grayson had proper manners and the family clearly had enough finances to fund a dance instructor as well as a French tutor—in their course of their dialogue, he had sprinkled in a few French phrases, which Miss Grayson had responded to without trouble—he gathered they were not a family of note or he would have known them before and Richard would have commented on such. Who was she, then, to disapprove of him?

After thanking Miss Grayson for the dance, he returned to looking for Adeline. A few minutes later, Mrs. Grayson appeared at his elbow.

"Lord Carrington?"

He turned and bowed.

"May I have a word?"

From her tone, he knew full well what that word entailed, but he bowed.

"Shall we walk to the refreshment table?" he suggested. "I fancy a glass of port."

Flustered, Mrs. Grayson looked as if she could use one herself. A little wine would help round her edges and might stay her from tearing his head off. She headed toward the refreshments before he could even offer an arm.

Once at the table, adorned with fruits and holiday favorites, he offered her a glass of ratafia. Preoccupied and nervous, she appeared to mindlessly accept the drink. Arthur thought about engaging in small talk but sensed she was eager to speak her mind.

"To whom do I have the pleasure of speaking?" he asked.

"I realize it is quite unorthodox of me to request an audience with you prior to a formal introduction," she began as they made their way toward a more private corner of the room, "but, you see, you were dancing with my daughter."

"Just now," he acknowledged, not intending to make this easy for the woman if she intended some manner of set-down. "My compliments to her dancing instructor."

"Do you intend another dance with her?"

He thought for a moment. "I had not made a list of whom I intend to dance with and how often."

Mrs. Grayson nodded. "Honora is polite, but she is less fond of dancing than it appears."

"She seemed to enjoy herself. If I am not mistaken, she is on the dance floor as we speak."

Mrs. Grayson sucked in her breath. "Because she feels it impolite to refuse, but I hope you, my lord, will have the courtesy to save her the trouble of accepting when she would prefer to decline."

He risked coming across impertinent, but it was no more than she was in speaking to him. "Does she by habit attend activities she dislikes?"

Mrs. Grayson frowned. "She enjoys the company of friends, the discourses that can be found at functions such as this. And the music. She is not stupid, my lord, if you are suggesting that she deliberately seeks out discomfort."

"Then do you, as a matter of course, have this conversation with every man who dances with your daughter, or am I singular?"

She bristled. "If you must know, you are unique. And I would not normally speak with such bluntness, but you seem to me a man who does not need statements disguised in sugar."

"You know this of me after a few minutes of conversation?"

He knew not why he provoked her. It was not in his nature to be mischievous, but this woman had formed a bias against him without knowing him.

"Perhaps it is my hope that you are such a man," she snapped.

He imbibed his port and wished that she would do the same, but she had not taken one sip. A part of him was ready to be done with her. Another part was amused by her disdain of him and curious how she would react if he refused her request.

"Perhaps I am. Perhaps not," he said. "Or perhaps it depends upon the circumstances."

She knew not how to respond at first, finally settling on a question. "May I speak plain, my lord?"

"Am I capable of preventing you from doing so if you so choose?"

She knit her brows. Perhaps the port had gone to his head, but he found her rather charming when ruffled.

"Perhaps not," she conceded. "I hope that we have an understanding with regards to my daughter."

"Do we?"

"Yes, I have explained that my daughter does not favor dancing as much it seems."

"But she does enjoy conversing."

It was wretched of him to tease the woman, but if she was going to disapprove of him, she would have to come out and say it.

"If you must know, my daughter is not the kind of woman for a man such as yourself."

"A man such as myself? You purport to know me well, madam. Tell me, what kind of man, am I?"

Her bottom lip dropped but no words came out. While she pondered how best to answer, he took in her appearance. Though she had not the flush of youth, he liked how her form filled her gown. Her body had not the scrawniness that many younger women possessed but offered a fullness that he found inviting. Her stays certainly presented her breasts in a most pleasing manner.

"I think you know to what I allude," she said in a lowered voice.

"I have an inkling, but how can I be sure I am correct lest you enlighten me. I am particularly intrigued how you have come to form a judgment about my character prior to having spoken a word with me?"

She blushed. "Your reputation precedes you."

"My reputation in what? Fencing?"

"You are deliberately being difficult."

"And you presumptuous, madam."

He expected her anger to double. Instead, she looked a little sheepish.

"Fair enough," she conceded. "I am glad we can each of us claim our stripes."

"Aside from impudence, what stripes am I claiming?"

She frowned but finally spoke the accusation she had been alluding to since the start of their *tete-a-tete*. "Of being a rake. My lord."

"That is no lighthearted allegation," he said. Though he worried little that he had such a branding, his stern tone made her shift uneasily.

"Forgive me if have I insulted you," she said, "but you see my position. Surely you would not fault a mother for wishing to protect her daughter."

"I would not fault a mother, but you make a bold assumption, madam, to charge me of having ill intent toward your daughter."

"Do you not?"

"In truth, while your daughter is very comely, I did not ask her to dance so that I may seduce her."

"Then, pray, why did you ask her to dance?"

"That is my affair."

"I am her mother. Thus, it is my affair as well."

He passed his empty glass to a footman with a tray before turning his full stare upon her. "Mrs. Grayson, I have permitted you to speak with impunity in such fashion that, were you not of the fair sex, might land a glove in your face. I understand that Mrs. St. John is a dear friend of yours—"

"What has she to do with this?"

"—but you are too quick in your judgments."

"Do you deny being a rake?"

He took a step toward her. "I wonder who is the rake here? Whose mind is turned toward guilty pleasures?"

Her mouth dropped open. She quickly looked about to see that no one was within earshot.

"I know it is not I who voiced the matter," he murmured, his gaze momentarily fixed on her lips.

"I merely—you are wrong to blame me—you are the one with the reputation!"

"I admit I know not *your* reputation."

"It is a sterling one!"

"A shame, then. I had thought it might prove more interesting."

"There! You are a rake, sir!"

"If I claim to be one, it is because I do not hide beneath the mantle of sterling qualities."

"Do you mean to suggest that I do?"

He cocked a brow at her. "I don't purport to know whether you do or don't, but I would not censure you should you admit to being rake."

She gasped. "I certainly would claim no such thing!"

"Why not?"

She looked at him, flabbergasted, before straightening. "That you ask such a question indicates your true character. I have not the slightest inclination to—to—"

Finding this all too amusing, he pressed again, "Why not? All humans, man or woman, are imbued with certain base instincts, with similar longings and desires—"

"This is most inappropriate," she scolded.

"It is the truth, is it not? You, Mrs. Grayson of the irreproachable reputation, have such desires. Perhaps you have a paramour—"

"I most certainly do not!"

"You need not feign shame with me. You are a widow and entitled to one."

"I feign nothing. I have never considered taking a paramour."

He raised both brows. "Never? Why the devil not?"

"Because...because it is not in my nature!" she replied, aghast. "And I will thank you to speak no further of this. It is highly improper."

"I remind you that it was *you* who sought a conversation with me, madam."

"Not for—for *this*!"

He nearly said something to the effect of living up to her expectations of him as a rake, but he held his tongue. The poor thing was flustered enough.

"And I have had enough," she pronounced. "You are beyond impertinent. Abominable would be too modest a description."

With lifted chin, she intended to sweep past him. But her regal or condescending departure was cut short. Her foot slipped from beneath her, sending the wine in her glass splashing. A good portion landed upon his waistcoat of cream brocade. She put a horrified hand to her mouth upon seeing the stain of red.

"Your pardon!" she cried before waving down a footman. "Salt, linen, and some mineral water."

Arthur pulled out his handkerchief and attempted to rub the stain. Miss Grayson was not wrong when she said she shared her clumsiness with her mother.

"No, no, you will spread the stain," Mrs. Grayson admonished, taking the handkerchief from him.

He would not have been surprised if she had left him, deeming that the spilt wine was nothing less than he deserved for his impudence. Instead, she stayed until the footman returned with her requested items. First, she rubbed salt into the stain, then applied the linen. After several applications, she dabbed the cloth into the water and blotted his waistcoat. In order to attend to his waistcoat, she had to stand very near him, and he could have kissed the top of her head if he lowered his enough. He could also smell her. Not the pungent sting of perfume, but a fresher fragrance. Light and pleasant. He liked it.

"You will want to wash the garment sooner rather than later," she said, stepping back to assess her handiwork.

To his surprise, the stain had faded significantly. In dim lighting, one could hardly discern it. She must have spilt a fair share of wine to know such a trick.

"I would I could completely restore your waistcoat to its prior condition," she regretted.

"It is remarkable that you were able to address it at all," he marveled. "Thank you."

His lack of anger seemed to surprise her.

"You are welcome, my lord. Perhaps if you had not riled me..."

"Of course."

"But I am prone to awkwardness."

Remembering that she still held his handkerchief, she returned it to him. Their fingers brushed in the exchange.

"I had best take my leave before I damage your attire further," she said.

He watched her retreating back with new interest. He suddenly knew whom he wished to take to the Château Debauchery.

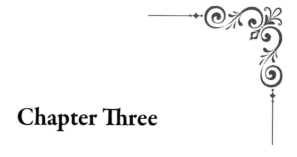

# Chapter Three

Her conversation with Lord Carrington could not have gone worse, Philippa decided as she made her way down the corridor. Still rattled, she hoped she would never have occasion to speak another word to the man. He was truly horrid, accusing her of licentious thoughts and finding fault in her lack of a paramour.

"La! And I thought you too fastidious to consider a younger man," Melinda said, catching up to her. "I saw you and the Viscount Carrington in that corner together."

"Do not suggest such a thing to me," Philippa replied. "That man is odious. The worst reprobate I have ever come across."

"Goodness! For you to speak such words, one would think he had assaulted you. Did he touch you inappropriately? Are his hands large and strong?"

"Melinda!"

"I should not mind it at all if he wished to have his way with me."

"You shock me. A man has no right to impose himself on anyone merely because he is blessed in appearance."

"Ah! So you do think him handsome!"

"I think that is one of very few redeeming qualities he has."

"And what are the other qualities?"

"I would have said none, save that he showed surprising patience and forbearance when I spilled my wine upon his waistcoat, which was a very fine garment."

"How was he odious?" Melinda asked, her eyes sparkling with intrigue.

"He talked of the most inappropriate matters and dared suggest there was something wrong with me because I had not a paramour!"

Merely recalling the conversation disconcerted her. She continued down the corridor, though she had no destination in mind.

"Indeed! How did he come about to say such a thing?"

"I haven't the faintest! I had intended to ask him not to dance again with Honora, and he was quite tiresome in not honoring my request from the start. I had to explain that he had the reputation of a rake!"

Melinda's eyes widened. "You called him a rake to his face?"

Philippa cringed. "I had to! And for that, he called me presumptuous!"

"Well, you cannot fault him for that. I cannot believe you accused a Viscount, Philippa. Have you lost your senses?"

Philippa bit her lip. "He had me unsettled. But it was wrong of me."

"I am surprised he was not furious with you—and especially if you had ruined his waistcoat!"

Philippa's shoulders dropped. She had made a mess of things. But, truly, she had never in her life had such an outlandish conversation with anyone. She ought to have behaved better, but how else was one to respond to his statements?

Melinda tapped Philippa with her fan. "What else did he say of paramours?"

"I can scarce recall."

"Was he offering himself as one?"

"Melinda!"

Philippa stopped walking. "I must find Honora and reiterate my cautions to her in regards to Lord Carrington. He is far worse than I thought!"

She turned around and headed back to the ballroom.

"Mama!" George called while she was still in the corridor. Beside him stood Honora and a petite young woman with delicate curls and long lashes.

She must be the one, Philippa felt. There were small cues such as the small smile on Honora's face, the hesitancy of the young woman between them, and the glow upon George's face.

"Mama, I should like to meet you Miss Adeline Hartshorn."

Miss Hartshorn bobbed a curtsy. "A pleasure, Mrs. Grayson."

She has pretty manners, Philippa deemed.

"Mama, Miss Hartshorn is the one—the one I spoke of, rather."

"At last," Philippa exhaled.

George introduced Melinda, and they started with small talk. Miss Hartshorn provided that she was from Derbyshire; that she had lost her father, a Lieutenant General in His Majesty's Army; and that while she enjoyed the sights in London, she preferred the quiet of the country. Miss Hartshorn inquired politely after Melinda and Philippa.

"I reside with my grandmother," Miss Hartshorn replied to Melinda's question. "Lady Bettina."

Melinda furrowed her brow. "Bettina? The dowager—"

Just then, the music began to start anew, indicating the musicians had concluded their reprieve.

"George, you should ask Miss Hartshorn to dance," Honora said with a mischievous smile.

George turned eagerly to his mother.

Philippa waved them away. "By all means."

George led Miss Hartshorn to the dance floor. Philippa followed to observe them.

"Is this a waltz?" she asked, seeing the men put arms about the women.

"It is quite the fashionable dance among the beau monde," Melinda replied, "though I am surprised Mr. Moorington would have agreed to it."

"I think Emily had requested it," said Honora.

"Miss Hartshorn seems a nice young lady," Philippa said to Honora. "I should like to be better acquainted with her, especially if George loves her as much as he declares, though I wonder that he could have such a strong attachment from having known her but three months in Bath."

"He wrote to me nearly every day. I could count on my hand the number of sentences that did not contain her name."

"And you said not a word to me."

"I told you he had met someone."

"You said nothing of the depth of his feelings."

"He was concerned for her sake, given that he described Miss Hartshorn's grandmother to be quite disapproving "

"If it is the Lady Bettina I know—" Melinda began.

But she was interrupted by the Viscount Carrington, of all people.

"Mrs. Grayson, may I have this dance?" he inquired.

Philippa stared at him, appalled. He dared have the affrontery to ask her daughter to dance after she had made it plain she wanted none of his attention bestowed upon Honora.

"My daughter is engaged at the moment," she said sternly, almost asking him if he wanted to risk another glass of wine spilt upon him.

But her daughter and Melinda were staring at her. As was the Viscount.

"He asked you, mama," Honora said.

Puzzled, Philippa looked from Honora to Lord Carrington, who presented his arm.

"May I?" he asked again.

Was this some kind of jest?

"She would love to," Melinda answered for her, practically shoving her into the viscount.

"No, not I," Philippa cried. She had never danced the waltz in public and only a few times with George when he had wanted to practice. "I should not be very good."

"I am sure Lord Carrington is good enough for both of you. Go! I have need of your daughter in a round of whist."

Philippa supposed she should be grateful that Melinda was taking Honora out of reach, and it was better that Lord Carrington dance with her instead of her daughter. With a nudge from Melinda, she took Lord Carrington's arm, which felt strong and muscular beneath his coat and shirtsleeve. Her cheeks burned to notice such a thing. When he put his hand upon the small of her back, she feared her entire face would turn crimson. This was highly unusual, to be dancing with a man barely older than her son. It was not as if he was a friend of her son or some relative. He was a man she barely knew. If only he had not chosen the waltz. The constant turning made her dizzy, and she was not accustomed to the three-quarter beat. Most of all, it was unnerving to have his hands upon her, his body so near to hers for the entire dance. She tried her best not to look a complete imbecile and to find the right footing.

"Look at me," he directed, "and worry not of the footwork. The grand thing about waltz is that you need only repeat your steps over and over."

"Not mind my footwork?" she asked, incredulous, as she continued to look down at her feet. She lost track of whether she was to step back on the right or step forward.

Another couple bumped into them as they whirled by, sending the viscount into her. His scent, evergreen and laced with the woodsy notes of wine, filled her nostrils.

"Your pardon," he said, stopping.

"Did I not say I could not dance?" she asked, relieved that it was all over. She would leave George alone to spend time with Miss Hartshorn while she joined Melinda and Honora in whist.

"I will dance for the both of us," Lord Carrington told her. "You need only surrender to me."

She was still reeling from his choice of words when he, his arm still about her, swept her back into the throng of dancers moving around the room.

"Keep your eyes on me," he reminded her.

She noticed his grip was tighter, and his steps more pronounced. Gently but firmly he pushed her back as he stepped into her, then pulled her around his left hip as he stepped around to his right, then pulled her toward him as he stepped back. There was so much turning, she quickly gave up on minding her foot steps and did as he told, keeping her gaze upon him and letting him guide their direction.

"You have improved already, Mrs. Grayson," he noted. "All you had to do was follow my command."

She bristled at his choice of words again, but having settled into the rhythm of the dance, having ceded control to him, she was better able to enjoy the thrill of spinning about the room.

"I have not had the pleasure of meeting your son," he said. "George, is it?"

"Yes," she replied.

At that moment, they passed George and Miss Hartshorn, both of whom looked at her in surprise, even a little concern. She did not fault them. Even with Lord Carrington's superior dancing skills and his grace, she must have looked awkward. And it must have been a rather uncommon site for George to see his mother dancing, with a stranger, no less.

She turned to Lord Carrington. "If you think you can persuade me to approve of your attentions to my daughter, it is a fruitless endeavor."

"I have no such motivation. Can a man not enjoy dancing with a pretty woman?"

She refrained from rolling her eyes as it would have been unladylike, but she replied, "Empty flattery will not work on me."

"It is not empty flattery."

In discomfort, she cleared her throat. "You had better try your charms on one much younger."

"Are not women of your age just as deserving of compliments?"

"I would sooner not receive them from men such as yourself."

"You wound me."

"Hardly. You cannot pretend that anything I have said matters at all to you."

"You had rather I take your insults to heart."

"I am not given to disparaging men I hardly know."

"I am exceptional then? Should I be flattered?"

She could not resist an unexpected chuckle. What a trying man!

Seeing that they were near to colliding with another couple, he drew her closer to him to avoid the collision. Her breath left her, and her face grew warm. She prayed the waltz was nearly over. This man had more of an effect upon her than she liked.

Silence momentarily fell between them before he said, "My intention in asking you to dance, Mrs. Grayson, was to ask your pardon. I behaved rather abominably when last we spoke. That your prejudice perturbed me was no excuse for my behavior."

Surprised, she searched his countenance for evidence of his sincerity.

"Well..." she began, "I behaved rather abominably as well."

"You had a noble incentive: the protection of your daughter."

Did he speak honestly or did he have some ulterior motive? Was he truly remorseful and, most importantly, would he heed her appeal to him?

"I thank you for your understanding, my lord."

"It is better to be too careful than not. It is the duty of a parent or guardian to look after their children, even into adulthood if needed."

"Indeed."

"At times, a parent or guardian must overrule the desire of the child for, more often than not, the parent knows better than the child."

"Yes."

"Especially in matters of the heart."

Surely he did not mean to suggest that Honora had tender feelings for him? He would be beyond bigheaded to think that a woman he had but just met could fall for him. He was a rogue and presumptuous, but she did not think him narcissistic.

"Our years provide a maturity they have yet to attain," she acknowledged.

"And youth can often inflate emotions that have not perspective lent by experience."

"Do I dare believe, my lord, that you appreciate my position?"

"I do."

"Then you will not be seeking my daughter's company?"

"I will not."

She sighed in relief. She had misjudged him. It was magnanimous of him to honor her request after all that had happened.

"You make me happy, my lord. I think we had got off on a poor footing, and I apologize once more for my transgressions."

The waltz came to an end. They separated and bowed to one another.

"It pleases me that you are happy," he said, leading her off the floor. "Thank you for the dance."

"And I thank you, my lord."

He bowed once more and parted ways. As soon as he was gone, Melinda pounced upon Philippa.

"My dear, you looked lovely in the waltz," Melinda praised.

"All credit must go to Lord Carrington," Philippa replied, recalling how he took command of the dance.

"And how was it to be in his arms?"

Philippa flushed. Disarming. Unsettling. And rather pleasant.

"I thought you were playing whist?" Philippa returned.

"La! I had something important to share. Remember that Miss Hartshorn had mentioned her grandmother was a Lady Bettina? Well, I made some inquires, and her ladyship *is* whom I thought she was."

Philippa raised a brow.

"Lady Bettina is also *his* grandmother! And he is her guardian! Miss Hartshorn, that is—not the grandmother."

Philippa narrowed her eyes. "Who? Who is Miss Harshorn's guardian?"

"Lord Carrington!"

# Chapter Four

She had felt quite delightful in his arms, Arthur recalled of his waltz with Mrs. Grayson. Still soft and supple, but she held her frame with sturdiness, which might have been the result of her feeling ill at ease in his arms. Nevertheless, he believed her body would do quite nicely.

She had blushed in his arms. And it was not because of anything impertinent he had said. She had laughed, too. And gasped. He wondered what other delightful sounds he could draw from her.

Fixed on keeping her daughter from him, she did not appear to know that the object of his son's affection was his ward. He had watched them from afar, and there was no doubt in his mind. He only needed to confront Adeline with it.

"You owe me a dance," Arthur said to his ward with a bow, noticing that she glanced away—or at someone else, rather—before she curtsied and took his arm onto the dance floor.

They took their position and acknowledged the other couple before them. The music began, and after going through the first set, Arthur began his inquiry.

"Do you wish to tell me who that young man was you were dancing with?"

Adeline flushed as he guided her in a circle around him. "A friend."

"The same friend who gave you that necklace."

Her eyes widened. "Not—not necessarily."

"Come, Adeline. Do you truly wish to lie to your guardian?"

Her face fell. Lowering her gaze, she shook her head. "Forgive me. You have been nothing but kind and altruistic to me."

"I should say I deserve the truth."

She nodded with genuine remorse. Upon seeing the misery in her face, he could not help but feel badly, though it was not he who had committed the wrong.

"Adeline, I am not vexed with you, but I should like to know who this young man is. As your guardian, it is my responsibility to know."

Biting her bottom lip, she nodded again. "His name—his name is George Grayson. We met in Bath. He was there with a friend from Cambridge. And—and..."

"And you are quite taken with him," Arthur finished.

Her cheeks darkened in color, but a part of her seemed relieved that he knew the extent of her affections.

"Why did you not speak of him before?"

"I worried that you might not approve. Grandmother met him briefly, and I could tell she thought him nothing."

"Is he nothing?"

Adeline returned a tortured look. "He is the most courteous, considerate, caring gentleman I have ever met!"

"That is high praise, though, as you are but eight and ten, you have not dealt a great deal with gentlemen."

"I know enough of *people* to know that he has a good heart and kind disposition."

He raised his brows. "How long have you known this fellow?"

"Three months. Three fortnights during my time in Bath, and we corresponded thereafter."

"And you kept all this from me as well as your grandmother?"

She looked devastated. "It was wrong of me, I know."

"And him. No man of honor would court a young woman in secret."

"No! It's not his fault. I begged it of him."

"He should have, at least, come to see me tonight."

"That was my doing as well. I told him not to till I had had a chance to speak with you first."

Arthur was silent as they traded partners. He did not like the extent to which Adeline and Mr. Grayson had kept their friendship secret from everyone. He had seen the adoration in the young man's face when he gazed upon Adeline, and the happiness in hers.

"Why do you think your grandmother would disapprove?" he asked when he had rejoined Adeline.

"She thinks quite highly of our family, of our breeding," Adeline answered. "He is more...common."

He had known the answer but was testing Adeline to see if she knew.

Adeline lowered her eyes and asked in a small voice. "Do you think so?"

"I know very little of the Graysons. Of what I know, I would say that our grandmother is correct."

Her face fell. "But you were speaking and dancing with Mrs. Grayson."

"A dance is nothing. You are seeking a suitor, and that is significant."

"But..." she struggled, "but do you not want a man of decency, of intelligence—he is attending Cambridge—"

"You can find such qualities in men of much greater standing."

"But—will you not give him a chance?"

She looked ready to cry, and that he could not bear.

"I will meet your Mr. Grayson, but it is my duty to see a proper match for you."

But Adeline was too overjoyed to hear the second half of his statement. He was glad to bring her such pleasure, but it would only forestall the inevitable sorrow when he refused Mr. Grayson.

YOUNG GRAYSON APPROACHED Arthur in the cardroom. Arthur had just finished playing several hands of brag when Mr. Grayson asked to sit with him.

Arthur picked up the decanter of burgundy and offered it to Grayson, who politely declined. It was a minute mark in the young man's favor that he did not avail himself of wine too readily.

"My lord, it is a great pleasure to finally meet your acquaintance," Grayson said, a touch exuberantly.

"I take it my ward has finally given you permission to speak with me," Arthur remarked as he appraised Grayson more closely. The young man was sharply but modestly dressed. Here was no pink of the ton.

Grayson laughed nervously. "That she has."

"You do not mind being restricted by one of the gentler sex?"

"I choose to honor Adel—Miss Hartshorn's request. I have no wish to cause her pain in any way."

"No? I think it behooves us to speak frankly with one another."

He stopped for Grayson's reaction.

"By all means, my lord."

"I am aware of my ward's feelings, and it would seem her affections are reciprocated."

"Twofold!"

"That the two of you have conducted a furtive courtship, without my knowledge or that of her grandmother, does not speak well."

Grayson had the same crestfallen look Adeline had had earlier, but he mustered his courage and forged ahead. "I understand."

Arthur leaned back in his chair. Here was a chance for Grayson to place the blame at Adeline's feet, but he didn't.

"I can only ask your forgiveness," Grayson continued. "We have every wish to be above board and to earn our way into your good graces."

"Why now?"

Grayson paused before saying, "Because I wish to ask for her hand."

Arthur rose to his feet. "You what?"

Grayson looked worried and appeared to swallow with difficulty. "Please know that I love Miss Hartshorn, and I have every intention of being the best husband—"

"You've known each other all of three months and wish to be married?"

"Does love have a prerequisite set of time?"

"What can you know of love? You are but twenty, and she eight and ten years of age."

"Many have married at our ages. It is hardly unusual."

"But it is unusual to ask me for my blessing when you have known me all of five minutes."

"Adeline told me much about you, of your kind temperament and generosity."

"And she has told me nothing about you. You said you have no wish to cause Adeline pain, but surely you know that you are hardly the best match for her, the pain it would cause her family."

Grayson straightened. "While I may not have the wealth and breeding she deserves, no man could treat her better. She will want for nothing for I have sworn that my first purpose in life is to see to her happiness."

Arthur was glad to see that the young man had some backbone, but he was not ready to concede. "You think highly of yourself, then, if you think she would be happiest with you."

"It is not born of conceit, my lord, but the depth of my devotion. I have seen in my parents' marriage that there is much happiness to be had when there is love, respect and friendship. A foundation in these qualities can weather anything."

"That is a lovely sentiment but naive. What does your mother think of all this?"

"She is happy for me."

"She knows and condones your desire to marry?"

Grayson hesitated. "I had thought to have your approval before I told her the happy news."

"Even had you the sort of background that would befit Adeline's hand, I know not that I would approve of so quick a marriage."

"What length of time would comfort you?"

Arthur sat back down. "I know not. I would have to give it some thought. At least a threemonth."

Grayson paled.

"If your love is as grand as you claim, you will wait for her."

"My love is true and steadfast, but we see no reason to wait when both of us are ready."

Arthur shook his head. Mrs. Grayson had not seemed the sort of woman to raise a frivolous child, but perhaps the absence of a father had consequences upon the son. Not knowing Grayson well, it would be unwise to forbid the marriage outright. He might run off to Gretna Green with Adeline.

Arthur's thoughts turned back to Mrs. Grayson. Here was occasion to speak with her again.

# Chapter Five

"My dear, why so glum?" Philippa asked George in the carriage ride home. She glanced over at Honora, who shrugged her shoulders. How could he have gone from elation to sorrow in the course of a single ball? Had he quarreled with Miss Hartshorn?

"I met the Viscount Carrington," George replied.

Philippa's heart sank. She guessed, "He did not approve of your suit?"

George kept his gaze downcast.

"Melinda said Lady Bettina is quite high and mighty, but it does not follow that Lord Carrington must be the same. What did Miss Hartshorn say of her guardian?"

"She thought he might be more amenable to us as he is nearer our generation than Lady Bettina's."

"Did he forbid you from seeing Miss Hartshorn?"

"No."

"Then what did he say?"

"He did not think it a fitting match, though I don't think he was against me entirely. But he did disapprove of my request for her hand."

Philippa's eyes widened. "You requested her hand in matrimony?"

"I had not thought to do it tonight, but I love her, Mama."

"Marriage need not follow the instant you fall in love."

George looked more miserable.

"You should tell her," Honora encouraged him.

Philippa sat at attention. "Tell me what?"

"You like her, do you not?" George asked of his mother.

"Miss Hartshorn? She seems delightful, but I barely know her."

"I know her well, and she is the most gentle and sweet creature. And I will do what it takes to marry her."

"But why the rush? And with Christmas yet to pass."

"We met in Bath at a dinner party of Colonel Worth, who is an uncle of Harold's," George explained.

Harold was George's bosom friend from Cambridge.

"I came across her crying in the gardens," he continued. "I made her laugh. She would not tell me why she was crying, but we found we enjoyed each other's company. When I was not with her, I spent every waking hour thinking of her. Mama, I have never had this happen with anyone."

"Not even when he courted Josephine," Honora added.

"I could not be happy without her."

"That is a drastic claim," Philippa said. "Youth has a way of coloring love, making it more grandiose and devastating—"

"But you and Father married when you were our age."

"That was a different time."

"It was not so long ago."

"Is it your wish or hers to marry soon?"

"It is both our wishes. And if Lord Carrington will not give his approval, we will go to Gretna Green."

"You must not! That is the absolute wrong thing to do. You will only upset her family more. They may even disown her."

"That could not be worse than..."

"Than what?"

When George did not answer, Philippa looked to Honora, who looked down as well. She turned back to George.

"Adeline thinks she may be with child."

Philippa felt the world spinning about her in worse ways than waltzing.

"Have I done so poor a job in raising you?" she cried.

He clasped her hands. "Mama, it is not my child. I would never have compromised her."

This was too much, Philippa decided. She looked to Honora for some sense.

"Adeline confessed to me a month later why she had been crying that night at the home of Colonel Worth. Her lover, a lieutenant, in Colonel's Worth regiment, was engaged to another."

"But it ought be this lieutenant who should marry her."

"She wants nothing to do with him."

"How very convenient that she should then fall in love with you!"

"She is not like that, Mama. There is not a duplicitous bone in her body."

"Are you quite sure?"

"I am. Just as sure as Father was when he married you."

Philippa paused. She and Francis had had a relative quick courtship as well, marrying within four months of their introduction.

"Are you certain she loves you? Perhaps her broken heart lends her to falling in love with the next man to come along."

"You think I cannot captivate a woman on my own merits?"

"I would not question any woman who falls for you."

"Mama, even if she did not love me, I love her. And I will do whatever it takes to guard her reputation."

Philippa let out a long sigh. She could see the determination in her son. He would go to Gretna Green, and there was little she could do save warn Lord Carrington, who might then send Miss

Hartshorn to a nunnery. But she could not betray her son, nor break his heart.

She spent most of the night awake, mulling over the situation. A part of her could scarcely believe it. What an absolutely daft night it was! She thought of Miss Hartshorn, who had seemed rather innocent, and perhaps she was. Philippa recalled how close she herself had come to giving her maidenhead to her husband before they were married. And she could not fault George for wishing to have as happy a marriage as he had witnessed.

She thought of her exchange with the Viscount Carrington, of his words about shielding children from their own folly. Had he known then that his ward and George desired to marry? She would have to speak with Lord Carrington.

The prospect made her groan. The man was not easy to talk with, and now she had to present an even more delicate subject.

When sleep came at last, she dreamed of whirling about the ballroom with Lord Carrington. She dreamed that he held her close, lowered his head, and kissed her.

She awoke with a gasp and a disconcerting warmth in her belly.

She stared up at the canopy of her bed. "Heaven help me."

"DID YOU KNOW HE INTENDED to ask for your hand?" Arthur asked Adeline as they took tea in the drawing room of his townhome. He had specifically invited Adeline over when he knew Lady Bettina to be occupied elsewhere. He would have spoken with his ward earlier at the conclusion of the Moorington ball, but they had offered to share their carriage home with two friends of the family.

Adeline's hand shook as she reached for a biscuit. She gave a small nod.

"He is very hasty."

She looked up at him. "He is very—we are very eager. When there is no doubt as to how fond we are of one another..."

"Yes, he professed his love most emphatically."

"Did you not like him?" she asked with great worry.

"I liked him well enough, given I know so little of him. As such, you cannot expect that I would so readily approve his suit."

He hated the crush of disappointment upon her face.

In a small voice, she asked, "How much longer would you need to feel you know him well enough?"

"I know not, but it seems he would have it as soon as possible, this month even, though you both know no proper wedding can be had during Christmas."

"In January then?"

Arthur rubbed a temple. "I know not that I wish to give him encouragement if I am to reject him later. Our grandmother would never sanction a relationship with someone as common as George Grayson."

"That is because she is of another generation. Surely you are not so old-fashioned to think so?"

Silent in thought, he considered a handful of relationships he knew in which a family friend or acquaintance had married beneath their station. There was Lady Katherine, a once frequent guest of Château Debauchery, who had taken for her second husband a man of vastly inferior background, but he understood them to be very happy. There was also the marquess who had married a mulatto.

"While I would not censure the joining of two people from vastly different backgrounds," he replied, "society will make it hard upon you."

"We care not what society thinks. We know we shall be happy together."

"You think so now, but in hindsight, you may feel differently."

"I thought you possessed a more progressive mind! Are society's norms more important than my happiness?"

"It is your happiness I'm trying to guard."

"Then let us marry!"

Arthur shifted in his seat. It was one thing for a titled nobleman to wed beneath himself. It was different for a young woman like Adeline. He glanced over at her. He could not gaze upon her pained expression for long. He rose to his feet.

"If we cannot have each other, I know not what I should do," Adeline cried. "I cannot even conceive of the despair I should be in."

He considered discussing the matter with Lady Bettina, but he knew exactly what his grandmother would say, and in no uncertain terms. His thoughts were interrupted by the appearance of a footman, who presented him with a card, a request from Mrs. Grayson to call on him.

# Chapter Six

Philippa paced the drawing room as she waited for Lord Carrington. The man whom she had offended and spilled wine upon held the happiness of her son in his hands. She was glad she and the Viscount had buried the hatches before the night at the Moorington ball had concluded, but how would he receive her now? George had said that though his lordship had not been unkind, it was clear he did not regard her son's suit highly.

Two days had passed since the Moorington ball, and though George had been devastated by Lord Carrington's disapproval, he had become more resolute to marry Miss Hartshorn. Philippa could say nothing to dissuade him from taking Miss Hartshorn to Gretna Green if needed, and she knew her son would do it. He had his father's determination. She recalled when George was eight and deathly afraid of heights, he had determined that he would climb to the top of their fir tree because a friend of his had dared him to. Through much trembling and perspiring, George had made it to the top.

Yesterday, Philippa had met with Miss Hartshorn, who had arranged with George that she would be at St. James' Park with a friend. Miss Hartshorn was as polite and deferential as before. She had acknowledged that running off to Gretna Green was severe, but she could think of no other solution. Philippa could see the poor thing was petrified. She also saw that Miss Hartshorn seemed to worship George. Perhaps the young woman saw him as her savior. Her temperament might do nicely for him, Philippa decided.

She would support their desire to marry and do what she could to prevent their running off to Gretna Green.

"Mrs. Grayson," Lord Carrington greeted.

"Thank you for agreeing to see me," she said, catching her reflection in the looking glass behind him. She had taken more pains than usual in her toilette. For such an important conversation, she would have wanted to look her best. But she had chosen to wear a pelisse trimmed with swansdown that was perhaps a bit small on her but had a more youthful color than her spencers or redingotes.

"Of course. Would you care for a glass of mead? Or a cordial perhaps?"

"Thank you, no. I think, despite our inauspicious beginning, that we deal well with one another. Although our acquaintance has been short, we have been able to speak frankly."

"That we have, Mrs. Grayson."

As she had not yet taken a seat, he remained standing, but she was too anxious to sit. "Perhaps you know why I have come?"

"I take it, it is in regards to your son."

"He is very much in love with Miss Hartshorn, and I believe she feels the same for him."

He drew in a long breath. "Yes, that would seem to be the case. And I believe we had discussed how a parent or guardian must sometimes overrule the desires of the young."

"You are young yet, my lord."

"But in my capacity as Miss Hartshorn's guardian, I must assume the mantle of one much older."

"Have you ever been in love?"

"Me?"

She nodded.

He seemed skeptical of her question but humored her. "I have had tender feelings for another."

"Then you understand the pain that can come with that most potent of emotions."

"Are you saying we should indulge them in this love affair of theirs?"

Taking a fortifying breath, she nodded.

He frowned. "While it may be no small matter for your son—indeed, it is to his advantage—to court Miss Hartshorn, you surely see that it is not in her interest?"

She hesitated before forging ahead. "I think it is in her interest."

He looked astounded. "Because she is in love? I had not thought you a sentimentalist, Mrs. Grayson."

"I am not so very, but the children are deeply in love. It is plain to anyone."

"There are other practical considerations to be had."

"Our background may be modest and humble, but my son will treat your ward as well as anyone. They may be young, but I have confidence they will survive what hardships may be thrown their way, and especially if they had the support of their family."

"Of course a mother would see her own son in such favorable light."

She lifted her chin. "It is true that I am partial, but I am not so naive nor so biased that I would not see his faults. If I had not thought him capable and up to the task of marriage, I would not condone it."

He raised his brows. "You approve their *marrying*? They have barely had a courtship."

"I see no reason to wait."

"Mrs. Grayson, you surprise me," he said before turning from her.

Without thinking, she placed a hand upon his arm. "I know we have but just met, but I entreat you to trust me. I have seen many marriages in my time. I have seen those that have prevailed and those that have failed. I urge you to reconsider."

He gazed down upon her hand. Realizing she still touched him, she started to withdraw, but, to her surprise, he placed his hand over hers before she could pull away.

"I will reconsider on one condition," he said.

She barely heard his words, her focus being on the hand that trapped hers.

"I wish you to accompany me to a place called Château Follet," he finished.

Château Follet? Where had she heard that name before? And why would he wish her to go there?

"What has this Château Follet to do with my son or Miss Hartshorn?" she inquired, trying to still the quickened pulse his touch caused. Why did he still hold her hand?

"It has no direct connection to them, but it is an opportunity for you to persuade me to their cause."

Melinda had once mentioned a Château Follet, Philippa remembered. Had Melinda dubbed it the Château Debauchery?

"But why there?"

He took her hand in his and drew her to him, as close as when they danced. No, closer. Her heart rate spiked and her head spun now just as much as it had during the waltz. This was just as in her dream, only it was real. But it made no sense. What folly was he up to?

"Because I wish it," he murmured. "Because there you will surrender yourself to me."

She pressed her hands against his chest to ensure some distance between them. His other hand had snaked around her to her lower back, holding her in place. She found herself caught in his gaze, but surely he could not desire her. This was some charade, perhaps some test of her virtue to see if George had a good mother.

"Lord Carrington, pray, unhand me," she told him.

He brought her closer, making it extremely difficult to think.

"I protest this mockery of yours," she tried, pushing against him harder.

"Three nights, Mrs. Grayson. I promise you will enjoy it."

"You are mad! Unhand me this instant!"

He released her, and she scrambled a safe distance from him. She should take her leave. Now.

"You cannot be in earnest," she said between difficult breaths, stalling for time to piece her thoughts together, "and I will not be a source of ridicule for you."

"I am deadly earnest," he said calmly.

"You desire my company at this Château Follet?"

"I desire more than your company," he replied with a devilish grin that only made him appear more charming, though she should be furious at him for his audacity.

"Surely there are other women who can accompany you."

"There are. At present, it is you I want."

Her legs grew weak. She did not like this at all. She was a woman of maturity, not some trifle young thing he could toy with.

"You disrespect me, my lord," she admonished.

"Do I? There are no shortage of women who would be flattered by my interest."

"Then turn your attentions to them!"

"We talked of dispensing with pretenses. You acknowledged that you had no paramour. I should be flattered to be yours for three days."

This was madness. If he knew the desperation his ward was in, he would not use this opportunity to serve his own purposes. But Philippa could not bring herself to reveal what had been told to her in confidence by her own son.

"Come, my lord," she attempted, "let us talk like reasonable, civilized people."

He took a step toward her. Every nerve jumped to life.

"Hang civility and reason."

"Think of Miss Hartshorn! Would you treat her desires so cavalierly?"

"If I thought only of her interests, I would tell you that your son is not welcome to court her and ensure that she not see him again. There should be nothing more to say betwixt you and I."

Philippa closed her eyes. When she opened them, she gave him a stern stare. "How will I know that, at the end of three days, you will reconsider your stance on their marriage?"

"On their courtship. Marriage is out of the question at the moment. And I make no promises. But your one chance to advocate further for your son is to accompany me to Château Follet."

# Chapter Seven

Arthur had little doubt, as he watched Mrs. Grayson depart, trembling from head to toe, that he would soon have her writhing beneath him. He had detected her response to him during the waltz and confirmed it when he had held her in his arms just now. His touch discomposed her, but she did not push him away as hard as she could have. Far from it.

He regretted coming across so roguish. He had never had need to be so bold with a woman before, but Mrs. Grayson's resistance was high despite her attraction to him. Despite balking at his proposition, she had not refused him outright. Perhaps she had a greater interest in him than he had thought, but he suspected it was her love for her son that provided her primary motivation in entertaining his invitation. Regardless, he intended to make it worth her while.

She would not be the first widow he had taken to bed, though Mrs. Richards had been quite a few years younger. But he enjoyed all manner of women. Their varied qualities and experiences made every encounter novel.

It had been rather ruthless of him to exploit her situation. An intelligent woman, she must know she had few cards to play, and he would wager that she would sacrifice her irreproachable reputation for her son's happiness.

Two days later, he received a cursory note from Mrs. Grayson that she would accept his invitation.

He did not reveal to Adeline that he was going to the Château Debauchery, but he did assure her that, during his time away, he would make inquiries into the Grayson family and give more thought to Mr. Grayson's suit. He also arranged for Mrs. Williams, a ladies' companion, to look after Adeline should Lady Bettina be unavailable. Happy that her guardian was giving her love a chance, Adeline made no complaints.

Mrs. Grayson had refused to be seen in his carriage and told him she would meet him at a posting inn outside of London. He found her there, wearing traveling clothes of the blandest color. Of course she had no wish to call attention to herself. And she had no need to impress him. He cared not what she wore, only that her garments would come off.

In his carriage, she sat as far from him as possible. If she sat any closer to her side of the carriage, she would be outside the vehicle. After inquiring into the length of the journey and the number of stops to change the horses, she asked, "I suppose now would be as good as any to present my case in regards to my son and your ward?"

"I will uphold my end of the agreement," he answered.

"While I know you cannot take as truth the praises a mother would sing of her own son, I will tell you, nonetheless, that my son is a determined young man. You may deem it stubbornness, and I would not disagree. He is loyal to a fault, especially to those whom he cares for. When his father was ill, he returned from Cambridge, forsaking his studies so that he could be present to look after us."

"That is commendable."

"A few years ago, when Honora was most distressed that she had left behind her most prized scarf, one her great grandmother had bequeathed her, George rode three hours through heavy rains to retrieve it for her. He would do no less for Miss Hartshorn."

"Mrs. Grayson, I am inclined to believe your son a very fine man, but he could have the qualities of a saint and still be unsuitable for Adeline."

She exhaled a long breath before saying, "He is determined to marry her, my lord, and I fear they may run off to Gretna Green."

"The concern had crossed my mind as well. I will not hide the fact that my ward seems quite devoted to your son as well. But we cannot allow such a fear to force our hand."

She opened her mouth to speak, but then closed it.

"Pray, speak your mind," he encouraged.

She pressed her lips together, looking down and away from him. What had she meant to say?

"Has he revealed plans to take her to Gretna Green?" he guessed.

"George does not keep secrets from me."

"But it seems you were unaware of Miss Hartshorn till the Morrington ball?"

"That was because—"

She stopped herself and stared at the window. He watched her bosom rise and fall with uneven breaths. Was there something she wasn't telling him?

"He confided their willingness to resort to Gretna Green if they cannot have your approval," she said after some silence.

Arthur shifted in his seat, not pleased yet unsurprised that his ward would defy his wishes.

She turned to him, her expression solemn. "And I think they will do it, my lord. You can take all the precautions that you wish, but they will find a way. Consider yourself: I doubt not that you could move mountains if you wished to attain your heart's desire."

He inclined his head to acknowledge her compliment. "That may be, but it is my duty to do all in my power to prevent that. I cannot capitulate before trying."

"And if they were to succeed? Would you reject them still?"

"I know not."

"It would devastate Miss Hartshorn if you did."

"She must take that into account if she wishes to choose your son over her obligations to her family."

"We could spare her such pain if you were to approve their courtship."

He became silent in thought. Of course he had no wish to distress Adeline, and the guilt would not sit easily upon him, but he had to believe he could bear the unhappiness knowing that he acted in her favor.

He held Mrs. Grayson's gaze as he said, "Your son is fortunate to have such a compassionate and articulate mother."

Her cheeks colored a little. "And I commend you for taking your role of guardian so seriously. It is not often a man of your youth would have such a responsibility."

"It pleases me that you can approve of a rake such as myself."

"Well, if you must know, you are far worse a rake than I thought at the Morrington ball."

"And yet your anger seems to have dissipated significantly since our last meeting."

"That is only because I have placed my son's needs above mine own."

"Do you never indulge your own needs?"

"I am a mother."

"You are a woman."

She let out a shaky breath and looked away.

"Your stay at Château Follet could serve two purposes. Your son's as well as your own."

"Mine?" she cried.

He left his side of the carriage to sit nearer her. She immediately straightened.

"You have leave to shed your matronly shackles," he told her. "When you surrender to me, you will exalt your desires. Do as I say, and I promise pleasure shall be yours for the taking."

Her lashes fluttered quickly, and she looked out the window. "You mean your pleasure."

He pressed the back of two fingers against the far side of her chin and turned her face toward him. "Why resist? You have already agreed to spend the three nights at Château Follet—"

"I have heard it dubbed the Château Debauchery."

"Have you now?"

"Do you deny it?"

"Not at all. Its sobriquet is well deserved. Scandalous affairs occur there, and there are parts of the Château that are not for the faint of heart, but we will only venture where you are comfortable."

"Comfortable? You think I shall find any aspect of this situation *comfortable*?"

"Do you not wish to make the most of your predicament?"

She had no reply, and he suspected that were he to kiss her now, she would permit it. Instead, he let go of her chin. Ardor simmered in his veins, but he would not rush matters. Before the end of their stay, she would no longer deny her desires but beg for him to fulfill them.

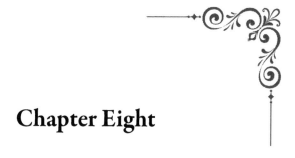

# Chapter Eight

A part of Philippa was quite disappointed when Lord Carrington released her. It had been years since she had been touched like that. The more sensible part was relieved. It had seemed he might kiss her, and she had not been kissed by a man since her husband had passed. She had feared she would not refuse him if he did, and if she allowed it, then he might think her every bit as wanton as he.

He slid over, providing her more space. She wanted to speak, to indicate that his effect upon her was not so significant, but she knew not what to say.

He broke the silence. "Tell me more of your son."

Surprised but grateful for the solicitation to speak further of George, she told him of how cautious George often was as a child. His twin sister was more wont to take risks. Honora had learned to crawl first, walk first, and ride first. But he never bore any resentment toward his sister.

"Having grown up with a sister who was also a close friend of his, he possesses a sensitivity that other men may not come by as readily," she told Lord Carrington.

His lordship inquired politely into her husband and the rest of her family. She asked him about his, and they fell into an easy conversation. If she had not known him to be a rogue of the first order, she might have enjoyed their *tête-à-tête*.

At the posting inn, they sat together for lunch. Having talked of George's childhood, she inquired after his.

"Unlike your son, I was a rapscallion," Lord Carrington admitted. "I had a younger brother not two years my junior, and we were quite the handful for our poor governesses. One year, we had no less than three different governesses."

She had then proceeded to smile and laugh at some of the escapades he described.

"If you had been my son, I would not have tolerated your mischief," she told him.

He grinned. "And what would you have done?"

"My husband would have administered the discipline. I would have admonished you and your brother."

"And taken away our biscuits?"

"Perhaps, but I think children have a natural inclination to please their parents, and I should have praised you when you did, which would encourage more behavior of the same."

He thought for a moment. "A rather novel approach. I cannot remember a time when my mother or father had praised me. I do remember much scolding, though."

It was her turn to grin. "I'm sure it was much deserved. I think they did not scold you enough."

He laughed, a sound she found she enjoyed. She inquired after Adeline next. "While no case need be made for her—I trust my son's judgment—it would be comforting to know more of her and how she might be a good wife for George."

"I cannot guess as to whether or not she would make a good wife," he replied. "It would seem many fine persons do not a fine couple make."

"That is true," she acknowledged. "Temperaments must suit, some interests must be shared. Mutual respect is a must."

"And is passion required?"

She hesitated. "It is not required, but I think it can benefit a marriage. Passion is more a requisite for mistresses and paramours."

"For the likes of you and I."

"I am not your mistress, and you are not my paramour."

"For three nights, we are lovers."

She cleared her throat and quickly turned her attention to the food and drink before her.

"Who knew you for a lightskirt!" Melinda had teased when she had confided in her friend, whose assistance she needed to maintain her alibi for leaving town unexpectedly.

Philippa had felt horrible lying to her children, but she did not want George to know the lengths she would go for his happiness, or for him to be so incensed with the Viscount that he challenged the man to a duel.

"Be sure to shed your prudish qualities," Melinda had advised. "Behave as abominably as you can! Be wanton. Be licentious. Be free. How I envy you!"

Philippa supposed she could be glad of the opportunity to take a man as handsome as Lord Carrington to bed. As a widow, she had not the cares an unmarried woman would have if anyone found out. That a man such as he desired her enough to want her company for three nights had stroked her vanity. But could she do as Melinda urged and be wanton and licentious?

THE HOSTESS WAS A MAGNIFICENT creature. Philippa would not have thought Madame Follet more than but a few years her senior, but the woman radiated with the vigor of a woman much younger. She also dressed in the style of a younger woman with a diaphanous gown that clung to her slender body.

"Lord Carrington, a pleasure as always," Madame Follet said as she received them in her drawing room. "I have rooms arranged for you and your guest in the East Wing."

The Viscount frowned. "I should prefer the West Wing this time."

She appeared surprised. "But you have always favored the East Wing."

"If it is no imposition, the West Wing would be more fitting this time."

"*Bien sûr*."

After they had sat with Madame Follet a while and their rooms were ready, Philippa turned to Lord Carrington, "What is the difference between the West Wing and the East Wing?"

"The East Wing is more...ribald," he replied. "As this is your first time here, you will find the West Wing more comfortable."

As they had few servants to spare, Philippa had not brought a maid with her, but Madame Follet graciously provided one of her own, a young Indian maid named Bhadra.

The bedchamber Bhadra showed her was nicely appointed with walls adorned with silk, oil paintings, and golden sconces; polished furnishings; and sumptuous linen covering the four-post bed. Bhadra assisted Philippa into her evening gown.

"Lord Carrington thought you might prefer to take supper in the privacy of your chambers," Bhadra said. "I can have the food brought up when you are ready, madam."

The Viscount was more thoughtful than she would have expected, Philippa mused. She gazed at herself in the looking glass. Though she had a pleasant shape, she nevertheless wished she had the form of her earlier years. The gown she wore had a lower neckline than most of her other gowns, but the dark burgundy hue was not a hue that would have been worn by younger women. Would Lord Carrington like what he saw?

"Is Lord Carrington a frequent guest here?" she asked of Bhadra.

"He has been here twice before this year."

With much younger women, no doubt, Philippa thought to herself.

"But I think this is the first time he has come during the season of Christmas," Bhadra finished.

Philippa had noticed the festive decorations of ivy and tinsel about the Château, reminding her that she had much left to do in the way of Christmas, including the preparation of the boxes for the servants, though Honora had assured her mother that she would oversee that task.

"Shall I have supper brought up, madam?"

Philippa nodded. Bhadra departed just as Lord Carrington arrived, looking quite dapper in his silken waistcoat, sharply tied cravat, and buff colored trousers. His gaze settled upon her, with appreciation, it seemed.

"Was I right to assume you prefer supper in your room?" he asked.

"For tonight, though I did find Madame Follet a gracious hostess."

She sat on a divan in the sitting room. Lord Carrington took a seat opposite.

"It was kind of you to see to my comfort," she said.

He smiled. "I am not all cad."

She had very little experience with rakes and scoundrels. They had never seemed interested in her when she was young. How odd that one should want her now that she was much older.

She returned his smile. "I had my doubts."

"Considering you called me a rake with nothing but the word of another, I think I had behaved well in our first encounters."

"You most certainly did not! You suggested I had a paramour. What did you know of me to speak such a thing?"

"Is the thought of a paramour truly so horrible? Do you intend to spend the rest of your life without the touch of man?"

She drew in a sharp breath. "You overestimate the value of such a thing. There is more to life than carnal satisfaction, especially this time of year, when our minds should be turned to family and Christ."

"Perhaps you would not *under*estimate the carnal if you allowed yourself to revel in its pleasure. Do you, Mrs. Grayson, take pleasure in the carnal?"

"Lord Carrington—"

"Arthur. As we will shall know each other in the biblical sense soon enough, there is no reason for formal addresses."

"Lord Carrington, you are impertinent."

Instead of being offended, he appeared amused. "Your refusal to answer makes me question whether you ever have? Did your husband satisfy you in bed?"

Her mouth dropped. "That is absolutely none of your affair!"

"You need not be ashamed if he did not, and I do not ask to condemn the man."

"You ask to rile me and indulge your insolence!"

"I cannot deny I very much like the rise of color in your cheeks when I vex you. It's quite becoming."

Once more she found herself torn. She was flattered and upset all at once. Never was there a more exasperating man!

And the hunger with which he gazed upon her took the words from her, so that she had no response for him. Her legs trembled, as if he had caressed her rather than just stared at her.

Thankfully, supper was served.

"I wonder if you will curb your impudence when you are ready to seek a wife?" she asked as they tucked into meat pies, root vegetables, bread and cheese.

"I have time," he replied, pouring wine into her glass.

"The years will pass faster than you realize. You ought to begin practicing as soon as possible. Starting now, perhaps."

He chuckled as he raised his wine glass. "To you, Mrs. Grayson. To your candor, your wit, and your beauty."

"You can save such sweet talk for your other conquests. I am compelled to submit to you."

He lowered his voice. "I merely speak the truth."

"What do you hope to attain with flattery?"

"Nothing. As you said, you are compelled to submit to me."

He had that look once more, the look that stalled her breath and now took away her appetite.

"And I will wait no longer to taste of your submission," he said, moving to sit beside her.

He brushed away a tendril from the side of her face.

She stifled the groan that formed in her throat. "We have not finished our supper yet, Lord Carrington."

"You will call me Arthur, and I shall call you Philippa."

She nodded for when he addressed her as Mrs. Grayson, she was reminded of how much older she was.

His hand moved to caress her cheek. "You will enjoy the feast I am to provide more than the meat pie."

A soft moan escaped her. How quickly her body responded to him, as if famished for his touch.

"What a lovely sound," he murmured. "I will draw all manner of sounds from you tonight. Before we are done, I will hear you scream my name and know how you tremor in ecstasy,"

That he could so easily seduce her made her tremble with fear and delight. She wanted this. She wanted to do what Melinda told her and abandon her guard.

As if knowing she had come to this conclusion, he smiled, such a grin of satisfaction brightening his masculine, strong features that the urge to please him, to see him smile like that at her again and again washed over her, pooling between her legs.

He pulled her to her feet. Then, cupping her cheeks, he brushed his lips over hers before claiming her mouth with such force that she thought she might suffocate. He drew her into him, and she felt his hard desire, the long length of him against her. She parted her lips to let him in, and he responded with a groan, his tongue darting in, finding hers, leading her in a dance more seductive and dizzying than any waltz.

She met his exploration with little whimpers of delight. His lips alone had the power to lead her to the precipice of pleasure, where she longed to hang. He deepened the kiss, his hands roaming over her. His fingers tangled in her hair, caressed her back, cupped her arse, dug into her hips.

The kiss went on and on, easily the longest kiss she had ever known. As his mouth roamed over hers, he began unpinning her gown. Panic rose within her. She had never been naked before any man save her husband, but she did not wish for Arthur—Lord Carrington—to stop.

After pulling the gown down her shoulders, he kissed the parts he had bared, leaving her breathless. He untied her skirts easily, then turned her around to unlace her stays.

*God in Heaven*, she thought to herself. This was truly happening? She was to lay with a man, a rake and one so much younger?

Once she stood in nothing but her shift, garters, and stockings, he wrapped an arm around her waist and pulled her to him. She blushed to feel her backside against him. Cupping her jaw, he turned her face up toward him, and his mouth descended upon hers once more. She gasped against his lips when his hand moved to her breast, palming an orb. Her nipple hardened beneath his hand. He groped her harder, and need swelled between her thighs. She closed her eyes, allowing his kiss and touch to fill her senses.

He yanked her shift down, baring all. Her eyes flew open. He spun her around and beheld her at arm's length. She tried to cover herself for she stood in nothing but her undergarments.

He shook his head. "You are not to hide from me. You are mine while we are here, and I will drink in your full beauty."

His trousers tented but he did nothing that indicated he would take care of his own desire, as she had expected. His gaze did just what he had said, his expression full of thirst, like that of a parched man who had been in the desert too long and found an oasis.

"And drink of you I shall."

Desire strummed through her, and she was at once that burning desert and the watery, shimmering oasis. He claimed her again and again, devouring her, his lips pressed to hers. He swept her into his arms, and her slippers came off as he carried her to the bed.

"It has been a long time..." she began, but words failed her as he pinched her nipples, rolling them between his strong fingers until they hardened into peaks, as if trying to move closer to his touch. Why was her body betraying her in this shameful fashion?

"I will have you now," he said, his voice rough.

He ran his hands along her sides, then cupped her breasts, working his tongue over one until her thoughts became a jumble and the wetness between her thighs slicked.

There was no struggle left, only surrender. He kissed his way down her belly, his tongue flicking over her heated flesh, leaving a burning path.

She tried to resist again and pressed her legs together; surely he did not mean to kiss her down there? No man had ever...

He played with the curls of her most private place, gently, moving his hands down, parting her thighs.

"Please, Lord Car—Arthur—"

"Has no man ever pleasured you in this way?" he asked as his fingers caressed closer and closer to her bud of pleasure.

She shook her head.

"I am honored to be the first then."

Before she could respond, he fingered her opening, swirling her own excitement until he reached that bud of delight that she had found was the way she could pleasure herself better than any man could.

But not better than this man. He stroked and caressed, back and forth, then in circles until she panted and emitted a low scream.

"You will spend for me. Again and again."

She almost laughed at his certainty, his arrogance.

"Do you touch yourself thus?" he asked.

How wicked of him to ask! She lay back in the bed, the soft linens surrounding her, and clamped her lips shut. Removing his hands, he stood and looked down upon her.

"Do you?"

She glanced up at him, pleading with her eyes for him to resume his touching. Moment by agonizing moment, he stood still, watching her with a determined brow.

"Tell me, or you shall lie here while I have an ample glass of port."

"Yes!" Truly, he was an insufferable man.

"Good." His fingers began again and she almost cried with relief. Then he removed them, only to replace them on her breasts. She thrust her hips at him, silently begging him to satisfy her deepest cravings.

He ran his tongue along her thigh, moving slowly to her seam. Her hips sprang up again, her body possessing its own mind, one that was at one with his. He licked and kissed her before sucking that bud of delight in and out of his mouth, using his able tongue, swirling and swirling until she gripped at the bedclothes, arching into him, her body aflame. He grasped her hips to keep her steady, to keep her from moving away from his hot mouth.

She came apart, crying out again and again, words that had no meaning, but he did not relent. Oh, lord, she would not, she could not go on. But she did; he wrung spasm after spasm from her, her body bucking against him, as he sucked and licked her while she—and the world as she knew it—exploded in flashes of light and heat.

# Chapter Nine

Good God, she was beautiful, and still coming, her juices coating his tongue and chin. She was even more spectacular than he had imagined—and he had thought of her many times these last days, since she had softened in his arms. Those thoughts of her had stretched his cock, which he had had to relieve several times. And now he would have her, and find the sweetest of relief in her warm, wet cunnie.

He lifted his head, to watch her as she came down from the heights of her ecstasy. A more beautiful sight he had never seen, indeed. Her hair had came undone, its golden strands framing her blushing cheeks, her curves nestled in the white linens, her pale skin glistening.

His cock strained against his trousers. He slid his fingers through her slickness once more, and her body shuddered. With a smile she couldn't see, he gazed at her face again, her head lolling, eyes closed. She breathed more steadily now, but she seemed to be out of consciousness.

He divested himself of all his garments, setting them upon the other chair. His cock now freed, it pointed toward the object of his desire. But he would not take her, not yet. Not till she was aware of what they did. He wanted her to see him over her, to scream out his name as she fell into bliss over and over again.

She shifted. Her breasts moved invitingly, so he grasped them. They fit perfectly in his hands, and he squeezed and played with them until her whimpers turned into moans once more.

"It is my pleasure to watch you, but my cock would prefer to be buried inside you." He climbed onto the bed and kissed her. She tasted of sweet wine and desire.

"Are you ready, my love?"

"Yes," she groaned. She parted her legs and he rewarded her with more kisses on her plump, red lips, and caresses to her clitoris. He felt her body tremor again, those sweet shudderings of ecstasy.

Positioning himself over her, he rubbed his length through her wetness. She bucked toward him. He pressed her down and held her in place. With a grunt, he speared her, his hard member making her his.

Her silken walls contracted around him, and he had to steel himself from releasing his seed in her. He would last, for her, to show her what pleasure a man could inspire in her.

She moaned, low and long, as he set a steady pace, rocking in her, tensing his upper body to keep from joining her in the pool of bliss she seemed to be swimming in. He took one of her legs and wrapped it about his hips while her hands roamed his chest before falling to her sides as he stroked inside her with renewed vigor.

Meeting his movements, she then stilled, the calm before her storm.

His own was imminent, but as he had no sheath, he would not be able to come to completion inside her. He gave several long, deep thrusts until he felt her insides begin to shake, and pulled out. With one hand, he circled her clit while his other stroked his cock. She came against his hand; he slid his fingers inside her to feel her while he spilled his seed across her belly. The beads of his ejaculate joined her own glow and he groaned with her and collapsed beside her, cradling her to him.

He kissed her perspiring brow before falling into slumber.

Her whiffling breath and breasts moving against his chest awoke him some time later. Early morning light, soft as her body against him, filtered through the window curtains.

He rose and found the sheath he had intended to use before. He glanced at the naked beauty curled in the bed. As if sensing his stare, she opened her eyes and started.

Grasping at the bedclothes, she tried to cover herself. He shook his head.

"No, leave them off."

"But—"

He strode to her and silenced her with a fierce kiss. Her tongue tangled with his and soon their limbs did the same, their bodies pressed together, moans echoing in the morning stillness.

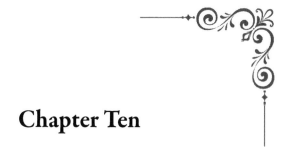

# Chapter Ten

Philippa shifted under him. The weight of him upon her renewed the sparks that had died to barely glowing embers in the night. Never had a man affected her thusly. She stiffened—was she somehow disloyal to her beloved husband? He would want her to be happy, she knew, but somehow enjoying this much pleasure with another man seemed wrong, though Francis was many years gone.

"Do you wish to stop?" he asked between kisses, his mouth so near hers, she could still taste him, a musky, salty savoriness that was all things carnal.

"No, yes, I..." She could not continue. He was a man of great perception; he had felt her tension as quickly as she had thought of it.

"You have yet to scream my name," he said. His strong, lean body next to hers did things to her she had not known possible.

"Why would I do that?" she gasped out as he tweaked her nipples, which stood to attention at his touch. Her body seemed his to command, for she flowed again under him, waiting for him to take her again, as he had last eve.

"Because I shall make you so ecstatic that you'll wish to thank me."

"Indeed?" she replied half-heartedly. She had no doubt that this man could make her do such a wanton thing, and more.

He grunted a response. His member rested on her mons, the tip dipping dangerously close to her opening. Her body betrayed her yet again as her legs parted for him. He slipped inside her and she gasped at the pleasure of him filling her. Inch by glorious inch he claimed her, but still he was not buried to the hilt. She wanted him to ram himself as deep as he could, as he had last night, when she had come undone so completely. And yet, she shouldn't want that.

"More," she whispered.

He growled, a satisfied sound, and gave her another inch of his cock. It pulsed in her, or was that herself? She shivered when he withdrew, tugging upon some sensitive spot within her, and sighed when he sank once more into her. The back and forth motion ignited the fire till bliss ripped through her.

"Arthur!"

He grinned and shoved himself into her with such force that her breath caught in her chest for a moment.

Heaving in air, she dug her fingers into his broad back. Their gazes met and she could not look away. His determined focus and admiring intensity made her continue spilling over and over into ecstasy.

And then he spent. She gasped as he shuddered in a powerful release; for a moment her vision went hazy, so great was the pleasure of their climaxing together.

They lay entwined, their breaths still loud from exertion, their skin hot against one another. He kissed her brow before easing from her. A soreness remained where he had stretched her.

Glancing over at the sitting area, she remarked, "Oh, dear. Our supper. It has gone to waste."

"I can ring for breakfast," he murmured as he lay sprawled upon his back.

She rose from the bed and found a robe to slip into. "There is no need. Not everything will have spoiled."

"I will ring for breakfast," he restated. "I shall want coffee."

"Oh, yes, coffee would be nice."

As they waited for breakfast, Philippa picked at some bread from supper. She still felt the glow of her congress, but she had a task of greater importance to tend to.

Arthur had collected his clothes and began dressing. She decided to serve as his valet and help him.

"If you could choose any man for Miss Hartshorn, what sort of qualities would you wish for her husband?" she asked. "Aside from his standing and breeding."

"I should wish for a man who cherished her and treated her well without spoiling her."

"I must admit that my George might not have as firm a hand. Miss Hartshorn has quite the influence over him."

"I suppose it were better he care too much than too little," he said after pulling on his trousers. She watched him button his fall and slip the braces over his shoulders, then handed him his waistcoat.

"Would integrity matter to you?" she asked.

"Of course. As well as constancy or loyalty."

"And what if a man were not of high character but had blood bluer than the sea?"

"I should not approve."

"Then it would seem character trumps breeding."

"If there were but two sorts of men, but Adeline is not limited in her choices."

"Nor are the prospects for my son limited. Any woman would be lucky to be his wife."

Arthur smiled at her. "So says his mother."

She assisted him his collar and then his cravat.

"The chances of meeting someone who is possessed of all the qualities you wish for and with whom you find a rapport are not as great as you would think."

He watched as she folded and tucked his neckcloth. "Was it not so with you and your husband?"

"It was, though my father was not overjoyed with my choice, given that Francis was near penniless at the time. But I saw promise in Francis. I knew his devotion would imbue him with perseverance and determination. George is no different."

"But why should Adeline not have the best from the very beginning? She need not wait as you had."

"It was a sacrifice I was willing to make to marry the man I loved. Believe me, I have seen many marriages of far superior situations be nothing but a source of misery for both parties."

"Adeline is accustomed to certain privileges. Pin money, even. She may not come to terms with receiving less, and that would put strife upon their wedded bliss."

"At present there is more at risk than..."

She blanched for she had been about to say more than she ought. She kept her gaze on his cravat, hoping that his lordship had not noticed her slip of the tongue.

# Chapter Eleven

"More at risk?" Arthur echoed, sensing concern in Philippa's demeanor.

"I meant to say that she risks at all and more if she were to run off to Gretna Green," she said.

Was that what she had intended to say? he wondered.

"Not all the riches in the world can buy love," she quickly added.

"You are sentimental."

"Because I am blessed to have had it, and I would caution both my children to marry without it. Even were Francis not to have come into any money as he had, I would still wish to marry him."

Seeing the look in her countenance when she spoke of her husband, Arthur suddenly felt envious. No woman had as of yet claim to hold such tender feelings toward him. And this Francis Grayson, with no wealth and no breeding, had won the affection of a rather remarkable woman.

"There," Philippa pronounced, finishing the cravat.

He looked down at her handiwork. "Impressive. As good as my valet would have done."

She smiled up at him. "Francis had not always had the funds for a valet, so I served in that capacity for many years."

He suddenly wanted to crush her to him and undo all that she had done. He wanted to be naked against her.

But a servant bringing breakfast knocked. They dined on ham, beans, and toast.

73

Afterward, he said, "I cannot claim to have the skills of a dressing maid, but if you wish, I should be happy to assist."

He would just as likely *un*dress her, he silently added.

"I most certainly prefer a dressing maid," she remarked.

"I see there to be some sunshine peeking through the clouds. Would you like to tour the grounds on horseback?"

She perked at the thought and nodded.

Leaving her to her toilette after breakfast, Arthur returned to his own chambers. He pondered all that Philippa had said. Would Adeline feel about George the same as Philippa did about her husband? If she did, perhaps it would be better than being married to a man who could give her the world but who could not make her happy. Even if she should be *content* with such a man and he did not treat her poorly, was it better to be married to a man she loved?

Prior to his departure for Château Follet, he had made inquiries into the Grayson family. He had heard nothing ill of them save that they were *bourgoise*. Those who knew of Mr. Grayson considered him a modest and ethical man. If the maxim that the apple did not fall far from the tree held true, then Adeline could do far worse than George Grayson.

His valet handed Arthur his crop. Prior to deciding that he had wanted the company of Philippa Grayson, he had looked forward to wielding one of his favorite implements against a pretty backside. He imagined applying the crop to Philippa's supple derriere. The thought stirred the heat in his loins. Could Philippa be persuaded to suffer a more wicked form of submission?

He met Philippa downstairs. Her riding habit of dark grey was likely not the latest fashion, but it fit her smartly.

"We need not ride for long if it is cold," he said.

"I have gloves and scarf. I should last a decent spell," she replied.

Their horses were brought around, and they rode toward the hills.

"What a lovely view," she commented when they had ascended the highest hill overlooking the Château with its two pointed towers serving as bookends of the perfectly symmetrical façade. The steep hip roofs of zinc contrasted with the ivory stones. One would have thought the chateau plucked straight from the French countryside. "How did Château Follet come to bear the moniker of Château Debauchery?"

"Madame Follet and her husband, when he was alive, believe there ought be no shame in indulging our prurient inclinations. These were instilled in us by our Good Lord."

He did not reveal that Monsieur Follet had once consorted with the likes of the Comte de Mirabeau and the Marquis de Sade.

"Would you claim that avarice and other unsavory qualities that exist in man were also placed there by God and should thus be indulged?"

"The desires of the flesh are universal to all. Every creature, even. That is not the case with avarice."

"It is our duty to go forth and multiply, but I suspect that is *not* the purpose at Château Follet."

"Good God, I hope not!"

"The last thing the world needs is more Lord Carringtons in the making!"

He laughed. "I do not disagree, Mrs. Grayson."

"Philippa."

He met her gaze. Mirth made her fetching. Extremely so.

"Philippa," he repeated. His horse stood near hers, and he could easily reach over and kiss her. And that is precisely what he would do.

But their moment was interrupted by a man calling his name. He turned and saw a man and woman on horseback trotting their way toward them.

"Devon," Arthur greeted of the man.

Once the other couple had drawn near, introductions were made. The Viscount Devon, the son of an Earl, was a frequent guest at Château Follet, but his guest was a young woman Arthur did not recognize. She appeared quite young, not much more than eight and ten, but very pretty.

Devon introduced her as Miss Collingsworth, and Arthur introduced Philippa as Mrs. Gray.

"I thought I saw you headed to a corridor in the West Wing," Devon said to Arthur. "What the devil are you doing there?"

"That is where our rooms are," Arthur replied.

"But you once told me you found the West Wing deadly dull."

"I had a change of heart."

"Truly? That surprises me greatly. I thought you and I had much in common. You should never find me in the West Wing."

"We had thought to ride a bit further. Would you care to ride with us?"

Miss Collingsworth, who had been conversing with Philippa, glanced up. "The air is rather chilly now that a cloud has come across the sun."

"Riding will warm you," Devon assured her.

The four turned their horses toward a field where the men urged their horses into a full gallop.

"Are we to turn back now?" Miss Collingsworth asked hopefully when the men rejoined the women.

"Not yet," Devon replied. He turned to Arthur. "Did you know the Marquess of Alastair was here a few months back with the plainest looking bird? And before him, the Earl of Carey had with him a young woman who looked as if she belonged at a nunnery instead of Château Follet. It is as if they have partaken of tainted waters. Or perhaps they are in need of spectacles."

"I think Miss Collingsworth is feeling cold," Philippa interjected.

They all looked to see that the young woman was shivering.

"A few minutes more, then we shall turn back."

"I can accompany her back to the Château," Philippa offered.

Though Arthur would have preferred she stayed, he would not prevent her. He and Devon rode further.

"I never would have thought you one to develop a taste for older flesh," Devon remarked. "Is she a widow or are you in the business of cuckoldry."

"She is a widow."

"For a widow, she is fairly handsome, but you could have far prettier at your beck and call."

"She intrigues me. Perhaps I tire of young pretty things at my beck and call."

Devon sniffed. "That I cannot imagine ever tiring of."

"I had thought so, too."

"But do you not prefer the slender, nubile body of a younger woman?"

"Mrs. Gray has a fine figure."

"Surely her belly is not as taut? Perhaps her breasts hang in the wind?"

"Her body may not have the firmness of her youth, but a naked woman is always a thing of beauty."

Devon nodded. "I take it this is her first time here or you would not stomach staying in the West Wing?"

"That is correct."

"Do you intend to venture into the East Wing?"

Arthur considered it for a moment. "I think not."

"Truly? I would think an older woman more game and less shy than a younger one."

"She has not been with a man since her husband passed."

"Then it is like bedding a virgin?"

"Without the bloody mess."

Devon raised his brows, appearing to have a new perspective. "I have never lain with a woman older than myself."

"I would recommend it. They have a greater level of appreciation born by experience and possibly disappointment. And they have not the arrogance of many younger women who expect to be treated as if they were princesses."

"That does sound inviting, but I like the wonder of virgins. There is a certain satisfaction in sowing fields untouched by any other."

Arthur shook his head. And Philippa thought him a cad.

During the rest of their ride, they reminisced of prior visits to Château Follet and ended with Devon urging Arthur to join him and Miss Collingsworth in the East Wing.

"I hate to think of you languishing in the West Wing, my friend," Devon said before they parted ways in the foyer of the Château entrance.

Philippa came upon them just then. "Lord Devon, Miss Collingsworth is asking for you."

Devon rolled his eyes. "Does she expect me to watch over her every minute that I am here?"

"I think she is feeling unwell."

"You had best go to her," Arthur suggested.

Devon bowed to them, then took his leave. Philippa watched him depart with a frown.

"Is he a good friend of yours?" she asked.

"A friend," Arthur acknowledged, "but only through our shared interest in Château Follet. You do not appear enamored of him. Why?"

"I think he is self-indulgent and could be a better host."

"Indulgence is the purpose of Château Follet."

"Nevertheless, he seems arrogant to me."

"That is a rather quick judgment you have formed. You have been in his company for but an hour and barely spoke with him."

"He barely spoke to me."

"Is that it? He did not show you enough interest?"

"Not at all! You think I care for the attentions of every man? There is something in his carriage and the way he speaks...it is hard to describe."

"The intuition of a mother?"

"Well, why not? I did have a chance to speak to Miss Collingsworth. Frankly, aside from his very fine hair and pretty lashes, I know not why she is fond of him. And why does he disparage the West Wing so?"

"You had rather not know."

"What do you mean?"

"Trust me."

She narrowed her eyes at him. "But he and Madame Follet assumed you preferred the East Wing. Why?"

"Perhaps we can stay in the East Wing the next time we come to Château Follet."

"You know full well there will be no second time. What is in the East Wing?"

"I have yet to change, Philippa."

"Perhaps a quick look—"

"I smell of horse."

"I do not mind it."

He stared at her. He supposed one look and she would want to turn on her heel and flee. But would she also then think him a monster for enjoying what transpired in the East Wing?

"The East Wing is not for the novice," he told her.

"How can I be a novice? I am a widow."

"A widow who, till yesterday, had no lover other than her husband."

"Are you going to show me the East Wing or not?"

He still hesitated. She studied him more closely.

"What secret hides in the East Wing that you are so reluctant to share?"

"It is your comfort I have in mind, a desire to protect your sensibilities."

She arched a brow. "You are the younger–"

"Not in this subject."

"I think it impolite of you to keep secrets from me when I am risking my reputation to be here with you."

"But it is not for my benefit that you do so."

"True, but it is your fault that I am here."

At that, he could not help but chuckle. "Very well. I did give you fair warning. It will not take me long to change."

"That is unnecessary. I can tolerate the smell of horse. And the delay may only serve to give you time to change her mind."

She began walking in the direction of the East Wing, leaving him little choice but to follow her.

"As I said," he said as he matched her quickness with his longer strides, "the guests in the East Wing have very little to no reservations. You will think them beyond wild and wanton. The debauchery that occurs here is wicked, sinful, taboo."

"And that is your preference?"

His grip tightened about the riding crop he held. "It depends upon my mood."

In the West Wing, paintings of nudes abounded, but they were more benign. One might find a painting of a naked woman reclining in a pastoral setting or a scene of satyrs chasing nymphs. In the East Wing, the art took a decidedly bawdy turn. The first painting they came across in the corridor was of an orgy involving many couples.

Philippa gasped. "Do you do that in the East Wing?"

"It has been known to happen

," he murmured, looking away from the provocative painting in the hopes that his fast stiffening cock would return to its sleeping state.

They moved on to a painting of a naked man, holding his rigid member between his hands, his countenance contorted in lust.

They came next to the doors of an art gallery which housed Madame Follet's extensive collection of erotic art from statues and marble carvings to prints and tapestries. He wondered if Philippa might be intrigued by the copper moldings depicting various positions of Congress. But when he opened the door, all they could take notice of were two guests of the château. The woman knelt before a man, her mouth encased over his erection. They looked up upon hearing Philippa gasp but returned to what they were doing without acknowledging their presence.

Arthur closed the door and noticed Philippa's eyes nearly bulging nearly bulge from her head. Her entire face had turned color.

"Thus far, how what think you for the Easty Wing?" he asked

She collected her breath. "This place is scandalous...but tolerable."

He was glad to hear it but wondered if she spoke with complete conviction.

"What was that poor woman doing?" Philippa asked after they had resumed walking.

"Poor woman? It looked to me as if she was enjoying herself."

"But that man had forced his member into her mouth!"

"Did you not see the ravenous look upon her face and how her eyes begged for his cock?"

She was silent for a minute before saying, "She can enjoy such a thing?"

"Yes, though, admittedly, his enjoyment is probably the greater."

She was quiet in thought once more. His ardor was stiffer than ever now.

Looking at him sidelong, she asked, "Have you enjoyed such manner of activity?"

They stopped in front of another painting. This one was of a woman bent over the back of a chair, her skirts thrown over her waist to display her arse, while a man prepared to penetrate her from behind.

"Oh my," Philippa murmured as her gaze took in every detail of the painting.

Arthur imagined Philippa bent over the back of a chair, ripe for the taking. He could take no more. He had questioned the wisdom of coming into the East Wing, and now she had to understand that consequences would follow.

# Chapter Twelve

Philippa had imagined to find more bawdy works of art in the East Wing, but she had not expected this. And she had not expected to walk in on guests engaged in prurient acts before her eyes. Did Arthur speak true? Did that woman enjoy herself?

The sounds of the woman grunting and groaning lingered in Philippa's ears. After the initial shock and embarrassment, she found that recalling what she saw had begun to arouse her. And though she found the first two paintings disturbing, the one she studied now was different. The young woman baring her rump seemed to be smiling at *her*, inviting her to share in her titillation.

Walking on, they passed by another set of doors. This time Arthur knocked before opening them. Philippa entered the chambers, dark for the curtains had not been drawn aside.

Arthur closed the door behind him, and before she could ask what room they were in, he had yanked her to him. She collided into his body. He whirled her around, trapping her between the hardness of the door and the hardness of his body. And then his mouth engulfed hers, his lips crushing hers in almost bruising fashion. She needed to protest. They were not in the privacy of their own bedchamber. What if someone were to open the doors upon them as they had to the trio in the art gallery?

But his kiss was too encompassing, too powerful, too exciting. She could do nothing but drown in the force of it. His tongue invaded her mouth as he pressed her into the door. She could feel the length of desire hard against her belly, and her body responded, her desire flaring like dry grass catching fire.

She was able to draw in air when he moved his mouth off her lips to sear her neck with hot kisses. A moan took the place of the words she had meant to say earlier. He grabbed a buttock of hers and ground her pelvis against his erection.

Her self-consciousness made one final attempt to master the situation. "Surely you are not thinking to—"

"Perhaps next time you will heed my warning," he growled against her neck.

He took her mouth once more in his, and she knew further protest would prove futile. The craving between her legs had grown hot and heavy. She wanted an encore to last night and this morning.

Of her own volition she ground her hips at him and attempted to return his ardent kisses. She had never thought she could desire a man more than she desired her husband, yet here she was, wanting this man, craving this man. It was he and he alone who could satisfy the longing in her body.

Grabbing the back of her thighs, he hoisted her legs over his hips so that she straddled him. Holding her aloft, he slammed his hips into her. Her head bounced against the door, but she paid it no heed. A greater need called to her. She wrapped her arms around his neck as their bodies pulsed and undulated against the door. She could feel her desire moistening her petticoats.

He carried her deeper into the room and sat down on what seemed to be a bed. Their mouths still joined, he pulled at her skirts where they were caught between them, then slid his hand up her leg to where she was most wet. She moaned when his digit connected with that most sensitive bud below. He fondled it till her desire soaked through her petticoats and into her gown.

He stopped only to unbutton his fall and pulled out his member.

"Have you a sheath?" she managed to ask above the screams of her ardor and the temptation to throw caution to the wind.

"I will withdraw in time."

She prayed that would be enough and said nothing further when he lifted her and speared himself into her heat. She shivered as she slid down his length.

"My God," he breathed, throbbing inside of her.

As if savoring the moment, he did not move. It was she who stirred. Grabbing her waist, he rocked her to and fro on his erection, grinding her womanhood against his pelvis. She whimpered and sighed, then grunted and gasped as the promise of rapture crept nearer and nearer. From the tension in her loins, euphoria bloomed. She assisted in the exertions till she could feel the perspiration between her breasts. Despite her fear of someone walking in on them, she let out a loud cry when ecstasy crashed down upon her, shaking her, ringing her body with bliss from head to toe. He pumped himself into her throughout her eruption, stopping only after she slumped against him, spent. He lifted her off him, took out his handkerchief, and spilled his seed, his hips bucking and his body trembling.

After he had cleaned himself and replaced his fall, he turned to her, took her chin between his thumb and forefinger and pulled her into a brief kiss

"I fear you smell of horse, too," he said.

She smiled. "I should take a bath then."

She smoothed her skirts while he retrieved the riding crop he had dropped, and they took their leave. She was sure there was much more to see of the East Wing, though a part of her felt she had seen enough. Nevertheless, a plan formed in her mind, and it involved the East Wing.

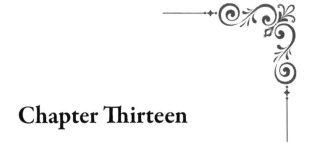

# Chapter Thirteen

Philippa desired to join the other guests for dinner and promptly took a seat next to Miss Collingsworth. Arthur took a seat opposite the women and next to Devon. The meal comprised several yuletide favorites of Madame Follet, marrons glacés and ham with candied apples, as well as more English dishes such as mince pies and Christmas pudding.

Arthur had hoped to converse mostly with Philippa, but she was rather engaged with Miss Collingsworth. It was not till Devon asked Arthur if he had ever done a "round robin" with his guest and others that Philippa glanced up.

"Is that a common activity in the East Wing?" she asked.

"Quite common," Devon replied, then turned to Miss Collingsworth. "Shall we give it a go tonight? It shall be quite enjoyable!"

Miss Collingsworth made no reply and only stared into her soup.

"For you certainly," Philippa said.

"For everyone involved."

Miss Collingsworth blanched.

"Do you mean to exchange women as if they were cricket bats or horses?" Philippa accused.

"I would never exchange a good horse."

Seeing the stern look across Philippa's face, Arthur intervened. "You need not worry. We shall remain safely in the West Wing."

"What of Miss Collingsworth?" Philippa pressed. "Perhaps she should remain in the West Wing as well?"

Devon frowned. "Now why the devil would she do that?"

Philippa turned to the young woman. "My dear, would you prefer the West Wing?"

The question clearly distressed the poor creature.

"I-I know not," she stammered. "What is the West Wing?"

"A place for cowards," Devon replied. He turned to Arthur, "Your pardon. I mean you no disrespect. I meant to say that the East Wing is for the more adventurous."

"She may be more comfortable in the West Wing," Philippa insisted.

"But find the East Wing more exciting," Devon countered.

"Perhaps we should ask her what she prefers? Comfort or excitement?"

Devon stared at Philippa, clearly displeased at her interference, but he asked his guest, "Well, Miss Collingsworth? Comfort or excitement?"

"I suppose..." she responded, "excitement."

Devon smiled. He raised his wine glass. "To excitement."

Now it was Philippa's turn to appear displeased.

After dinner, the guests separated. Some, including Devon and Miss Collingsworth, headed toward the East Wing.

"I worry of her," Philippa confided to Arthur as she took his arm, and they strolled in the direction of the West Wing. "Lord Devon pays her no heed, and I think her too timid to speak her true thoughts and feelings."

"You wish to tell Devon what he can or can't do with his guest?"

"He would not listen to me. Would you have a word with him?"

"He will pay me no heed either. Our friendship is limited."

"Will you, at least, make an attempt?"

He looked down at her—a mistake for her imploring eyes left him with no choice.

"I will make an attempt," he agreed.

Her face brightened, making it worth his while.

"There is good in you," she said happily.

"How is that possible? Am I not an odious rake?"

"You are that as well."

"Such impudence would land you a sound thrashing in the East Wing."

She was quiet for a moment before asking, "Have you given more thought to my son's suit?"

"I have not changed my mind if that is what you ask, but I am more encouraged that your son may be a good man."

"And if this were to prove true to you beyond doubt?"

He hesitated. "It does not change his background."

"Are there no extenuating circumstances in which you would approve marriage between Miss Hartshorn and George?"

"Such as?"

She grew quiet once more. They came to the stairs that led upstairs to their chambers.

"If her health depended upon it," she suggested.

"Her health? How?"

"I cannot speak to particulars, but let us assume she risks more than her current situation."

"I fail to conceive—"

"What if they were compelled to do something more drastic than Gretna Green if they cannot marry?"

"Why this exercise in hypotheticals?"

Philippa struggled with something in her mind. "Do you find the West Wing dull compared to the East Wing?"

"Not at present."

"But if you did not worry of my comfort, you would choose the East Wing."

What was behind all these questions? he wondered. Here was a clear difference between the sexes. Men did not engage in so many inquiries before stating what occupied their minds,

"I suppose."

"Then I have a proposition of mine own."

"Indeed?"

"I will go with you into the East Wing if you promise to delay your decision on my son's suit for a fortnight."

He stared at her in disbelief. Had he heard correctly?

"You would go into the East Wing?" he asked.

She nodded.

"We have been there already," he noted.

"I would...I would surrender myself to any activity you wish to engage in, even the ones more suited to the East Wing."

He could hardly contain the thrill that went through him. Of course he believed her. Her love for her son was steadfast. She had risked her reputation to come here with him. Why should she not risk more?

"You impress me, Philippa."

"Then you will accept my proposition?"

He wondered that she only asked for a fortnight. Why not longer? He would have accepted if she had requested a month.

"In the East Wing, you not only surrender yourself to me, you *submit* to me," he told her.

She lowered her eyes. "Yes, I understand."

"You are prepared to allow me dominance over your body?"

"For a fortnight," she insisted, "you will give my son's suit genuine consideration. I want your word as a gentleman. It would be too easy for you to default on your end once the night is over, but I trust you."

"You would trust a rake?"

"You surprise and impress me as well, Arthur."

He pulled her closer to him. "Madam, you have my word."

THEY RETURNED TO THE room they had occupied earlier that day in the East Wing. The servants had lit the candles of the room, which was one of the less intimidating rooms in the East Wing, such as the one modified to resemble a medieval torture chamber. This one had a four post bed covered in silk linen, a Persian carpet, and gilded candelabras.

He left her in the room while he went to seek out Devon. Unsurprisingly, after Arthur spoke his peace, Devon assured him there was no cause for concern.

"It surprises me not that Mrs. Gray should be afraid," Devon told him, "as she has never experienced the enticement of the East Wing for herself. Miss Collingsworth likes to play the shy one to others, but she is another person entirely in bed."

With no more to say, Arthur returned to Philippa.

"What happened?" she asked after he had locked the doors behind him.

"He heard my concerns—our concerns—though that may not alter his actions. But we can see how Miss Collingsworth fares in an hour or so."

Philippa appeared somewhat mollified.

Looking down at her, he nearly asked if she was certain *she* wished to proceed, but he didn't want to give her the chance to change her mind. Gently, he cupped her face in both hands.

"How fortunate I am that you love your son so much," he murmured.

"You cannot now accuse me of being a dowdy old widow," she replied.

He chuckled, "Far from it."

"You will take some mercy on me, my lord? As I am a novice."

"Of course.

He studied her lips, then lowered his head to claim them. They were soft and yielding beneath his own. He kissed her tenderly as he breathed in her scent. He felt he could taste the flavors of the holiday upon her. There was no holiday as special as Christmas, and tonight he added another reason why. He slid one hand up the back of her head, his fingers entwining in her hair. He held her head in place as he deepened his kiss, taking larger mouthfuls, prying open her lips to plumb the depths behind. His other hand went to her back to urge her closer to him. Ardor roiled in his loins. He could not, for the moment, imagine lusting more for a woman.

He trailed kisses down the side of her neck as he began removing the pins in her gown.

"You do not mean to undress here?" She asked.

"Why not? I have locked the doors, though I could open them if you prefer."

She huffed, "Of course I would not!"

He grinned. "Perhaps one day you will."

She stared at him before shaking her head as if faced with an incorrigible child.

The skirt of her gown slid to the floor. He untied her petticoats, allowing them to pool at her feet, then pulled the sleeves of her gown down next. After removing the top of her gown, he leaned down to kiss the swell of her breasts. He remembered one guest describing the orbs of young women as peaches and the bosom of older women as melons. That man preferred the latter. Arthur appreciated both types of fruit.

Reaching over, he pulled over a ladder-back chair with a silk cushion. "Have a seat."

She sat down, her posture prim and proper. He shook his head and pressed down on her shoulders so that she slumped in the chair instead. He took one arm and bent it toward the back of the chair.

"Spread your legs," he directed.

She colored.

"Madam, I have seen everything of your body. I have touched everything."

With lowered lashes, she parted her knees.

He pulled her shift up to her thighs, then took her other arm and positioned her hand between her legs. The color in her cheeks deepened.

"Touch yourself."

She glanced up at him.

"This is highly irregular," she demurred.

"Do it."

With reluctance, she brushed her hand against herself.

"I think I will follow your example of using incentives in favor of punishment. If you please me, I will allow you to retain your undergarments."

She touched herself again.

"Very good," he said as he removed his coat. He preferred not to be constrained by garments when in the East Wing. "I want you to fondle yourself till you're wet."

He worked on loosening his cravat next.

"I know not that I can arouse myself in your presence," she said.

"Try."

As he removed his cravat and collar, he watched her tentatively moving her fingers along her flesh. If he were a painter, this was the pose he would paint her in, lounging wantonly in that chair, her legs spread wide, pleasuring herself. He shed his waistcoat and pulled down his braces.

"You are a lovely sight, Philippa."

She flushed and said nothing, but he was pleased to know his hunger was reciprocated for she had unconsciously licked her bottom lip when he pulled his shirt overhead. Her gaze traversed the ridges of his chest muscles.

"Are you wet now?"

She moved her fingers lower. "A little."

He walked over and knelt beside her. He reached over to join his hand with hers. Taking her digits in his, he guided them along her clitoris. She let out a soft moan. After several minutes of stroking, he dipped his fingers down.

"How nicely your cunnie weeps for me," he told her.

Together, they fondled her till she showed evidence of straining toward her climax. A minute or two more and she might spend, so he stopped and pulled her hand away. Her lower lip dropped. She looked at him in a confused daze.

"On your knees," he commanded.

She did as he bid.

He went to stand in front of her. "Now we will attend to my pleasure."

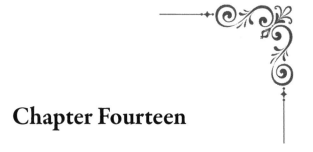

# Chapter Fourteen

Philippa found herself staring at his cock. She had never beheld one so close before and was somewhat mesmerized. This extension of him had been inside her, had lengthened and hardened till it felt of stone. She eyed the veins, the flare of the head, the slit at the top, where a drop of moisture glimmered.

"Taste it," he said.

She balked.

"You've not tasted of a man's member before? Not even your husband's?"

"I have not."

Taking his member in hand, he presented it to her. She grimaced. This was irregular, deviant and wanton.

"Come, Mrs. Grayson," he urged, placing the tip of his rod upon her lips. "Lick it first."

She flicked her tongue over the slit and tasted the saltiness of his seed. Her cheeks warmed. Was there a special place in hell for those who engaged in perversions?

"Now open your mouth."

She parted her lips for him to insert himself into her. She gagged when he touched the back of her tongue.

"Try again."

Straightening, she opened her mouth once more, and once more she gagged when his flesh grazed her tongue.

"It takes practice," he admitted. "Luckily, we have all night."

She frowned at the prospect, and this time, when he inserted himself, she ignored the reflex to gag.

"Now close your lips, but not your teeth," he instructed.

She did as he bid

"Well done," he praised. He entwined his fingers into her hair. "You have such pretty lips. They are a thing of beauty about my cock."

Cupping the back of her head, he urged her forward onto his cock. She gagged at the additional inch. He let her come off his member, but she knew he was not yet satisfied. She prepared to take his length inside her mouth once more. He slid himself into her and groaned as he settled his length upon her tongue.

"Now suck."

Obeying, she closed her lips about him, trying not to bite him, and sucked. He grunted. His hips moved, sending more of him into her mouth. She started to gag, but he held her head in place this time. He pistoned his hips several times before pulling her off him so that she could catch her breath and recover.

Philippa knew not what to think of this. She felt depraved, naughty, and somewhat titillated, partly because his enjoyment was evident. For that reason, she opened her mouth to receive him.

She controlled her reflexes better this time, and he was able to shove himself deeper into her mouth, but when he tried to fit all of him into her, she choked. With his member still filling her mouth, she coughed and gagged. She desperately wanted her hands free to push him away.

He pulled out. "You are a delight, Philippa."

Picking her up, he walked over to the bed and placed her upon it. He spread her legs and positioned himself between them. After gathering her shift past her waist, he brushed his fingers through the hair he had laid bare before grasping his member. He stroked her pleasure bud with his tip. She marveled at how he wielded this instrument of his, this steel wrapped in velvet. Currents of delight flowed from her clitoris, rippling through her loins. She sighed in contentment till gradually, the pleasure built to a frenzied pitch, then her sighs became pants. The tension coiled in her belly needed release.

As if he knew this to be the case, he stopped. She groaned at being left bereft. Her climax had been near. Why did he stop?

He flipped her onto her stomach and pulled her to her knees. He could not mean for her to be in such a position? She had to turn her face to the side to breathe. He threw the hem of her shift toward her head, revealing her derrière. With both hands, he caressed her buttocks.

"You have so many assets," he murmured before giving one buttock a playful swat.

She flushed. She knew not what to say. He groped her bottom cheeks, sinking his fingers into the flesh, grasping and kneading. He stopped to playfully smack one side, then the other. She cried out, more in indignation then pain. The indignity of it all! She had never felt so embarrassed. She was a grown woman, not a wayward child, but she said nothing when he spanked her again.

She yelped, though it barely stung. "Lord Carrington, this is highly irregular!"

He chuckled before acknowledging, "Indeed, though I can think of better descriptives."

"Am I to be let up now?"

"No."

At first she thought he intended to spank her more, which, to her surprise, did not dull the desire humming in her body.

She heard what she hoped was him putting on a sheath. It was, for she felt the difference when he pressed his member against her folds and sank into her. He rolled his hips at a leisurely pace. Despite the discomfort of her position, the waves of bliss continued to build, larger and larger, higher and higher. Until they crested, drowning her in rapture. As she wailed in relief, he shoved himself into her repeatedly. He would have sent her across the bed if he had not a firm grip upon her hips, holding her up. With a few more forceful thrusts, he spent with a roar.

He collapsed beside her while she gingerly straightened her stiff legs.

He reached over and untied her arms. "How do you fare?"

"You were quite merciful with me, I think. And I had come to expect something dreadful."

"In truth, you have seen but a small portion of the East Wing, but I want no horrors to taint you memories of the Chateau."

He gathered her into his arms. As she sighed against him, she found herself fortunate to have been propositioned by a man she had once considered a libidinous rogue. As it turned out, perhaps she was one as well.

PHILIPPA PURRED AS she felt the warmth of Arthur's arms about her as they lay in bed. She blinked at the light slicing between the curtains, ready to nestle further in his embrace when she sat up with a start. They had slept through the night!

"Miss Collingsworth!" she blurted. "Lord Devon!"

Half asleep, Arthur grunted, then pulled himself up in bed. They dressed quickly and went in search of the pair. Not finding them in any of the common areas, Philippa and Arthur split up. Philippa came across a maid and asked where Miss Collingsworth's chambers were.

Coming up to the doors, Philippa could hear crying. She knocked. The crying stopped.

"Miss Collingsworth? It is I, Mrs. Gray."

After a few moments, a trembling voice uttered, "Come in."

Philippa opened the door to find Miss Collingsworth in her bed, shaking, her face covered in tears. Philippa quickly went to her.

"My dear, what has happened?"

Miss Collingsworth lifted the bedclothes, revealing her blood-stained night shift.

"It won't stop," she cried.

"When did it start?"

"Last night when I gave up my maidenhead."

"Could it be your flux?"

"Perhaps, though I had it a fortnight ago."

"Does it hurt?"

"It hurt so much last night I thought I would die. It hurts still, though not nearly as bad."

Philippa pressed Miss Collingsworth's hand. "I think all will be well, but I should like to send for a doctor."

Miss Collingsworth nodded.

Philippa went in search of a maid to bring Miss Collingsworth some tea and breakfast. She came across Arthur.

"Find Madame Follett and request a doctor," she told him.

"She is as bad as that?" he asked. "Is she hurt then?"

"I know not the extent, but she is terrified. Where is the Viscount Devon?"

"I found him asleep in the Inquisition Room."

"Inquisition Room?"

"It is one of the harsher rooms."

Philippa paled. "Poor Miss Collingsworth."

Arthur went to talk to Madame Follet. After finding a maid to request sustenance for Miss Collingsworth, Philippa returned to the young woman.

"I am such a fool!" Miss Collingsworth wailed. "Château Follet is nothing like what my friend Anne told me!"

"You said your family was back in London?" Philippa asked.

"Yes, but they think I am with Anne and her family!"

Miss Collingsworth burst into a new set of sobs. Philippa put her arms around the young woman. After she had quieted some, Philippa asked what Lord Devon had done? It took several minutes of coaxing, but Miss Collingsworth finally described clamps that had been attached to her nipples, being lashed upon the legs and backside with a cane, and penetration, first by the Viscount and then by a wooden dildo.

One of the guests at the château happened to be a doctor, who, after examining Miss Collingsworth, said there might be a sizable tear inside but that it should heal.

"Dry your eyes, my dear," Philippa said. "The doctor says you shall heal, and I shall see you safely back to London today."

From the corners of her eyes, she saw Arthur, who stood near the threshold, straighten. She turned to him. "We must."

He nodded.

Philippa released a sigh of relief. She knew not what she would've done if he had refused. She supposed she could appeal to Madame Follet to lend her a carriage, but it was much nicer returning with him.

While their things were being packed and Lord Carrington's carriage prepared, Philippa stayed by Miss Collingsworth's side as much as possible. They did not come across Lord Devon till they had put on their coats and were ready to enter the carriage.

"I say!" Devon protested. "What is happening?"

Philippa went up to him. "If I were your mother, I would have such words—no, I should do more than have words with you!"

Devon turned to Arthur, who returned no sympathy and said, "I have spoken with Madame Follet, and she wishes to have a word with you. I would not keep our hostess waiting."

Flustered, Devon looked at them all before whirling on his heels to find Madame Follet.

During the carriage ride, Arthur made several attempts to cheer up Miss Collingsworth. At the posting inn, Philippa assisted in changing Miss Collingsworth's linen and petticoats. The bleeding had subsided.

"I shall forever be grateful to you both," Miss Collingsworth said when the carriage pulled up to the Collingsworth household.

"I think perhaps I should go with her," Philippa told Arthur. "I will send for a chaise to bring me home."

He looked disappointed but nodded. He declined Miss Collingsworth's offer to join them for tea and returned to his carriage. Philippa watched the vehicle pull away, realizing that she missed him already and wishing they had had their full time at Château Follet.

# Chapter Fifteen

"Devon? I would challenge him to a duel and blow his head off if I could," the Baron Rockwell had said.

Arthur had come across his friend at a coffeehouse the day after returning from Château Follet.

"The bastard cut my time at Château Follet short as well," Rockwell continued. "I have told Marguerite to ban him. He is no good and makes prey of virginal young women."

"I wish I had known better," Arthur said. "He had with him this poor young thing. She reminded me a little of Adeline, and I thank God it was not Adeline who was with him."

Which made someone like George Grayson a relief. True to his word, Arthur had given more thought to Grayson's suit. He was disgruntled that he did not have the full three nights he had expected, but he would uphold his promise to Philippa.

Back in his townhome, memories of Philippa filled his head. During their carriage ride back to London, he had noticed her gloom and had asked her about her marriage as that seemed a happy subject for her. He did not doubt that George Grayson had had as good an upbringing as could be had. In many ways, Grayson's lack of wealth meant that George spent a good deal of his childhood with his mother instead of a governess. And to receive such love and devotion from a woman such as Philippa must have been glorious. Arthur felt both sad and envious.

But he had had Philippa in a way George never would. Arthur could see with vividness her delightful backside rounding the bed, hear her cries as she came undone, and feel her heat wrapping his cock.

A visit from Adeline interrupted his reveries. She had come to request more pin money.

"Your current amount is insufficient?" he asked as he sat down at the writing table in his study.

"I need new gowns or, at the least, my old ones altered," she said, staring down at her feet.

"You had new gowns sown last month."

"Yes, but I—I think I have indulged in far too many yuletide sweets."

"That is a shame."

He looked more closely at his ward, noting that her face appeared rounder. Had Philippa remarked on the state of Adeline's health? What precisely had she said? Did Philippa know something?

*Are there no extenuating circumstances in which you would approve marriage between Miss Hartshorn and George?* Arthur remembered her asking.

*"If her health depended upon it."*

*"Her health? How?"*

*"I cannot speak to particulars, but let us assume she risks more than her current situation...What if they were compelled to do something more drastic than Gretna Green if they cannot marry?"*

Arthur leaped to his feet. "Adeline, is there something you've not told me?"

Adeline, taken aback, stared at him with widened eyes full of fear.

He felt a pit in his stomach. "Did you—Did he—My God."

So that was why they wished to marry with little delay. And Philippa knew it. She knew it this whole time and had said nothing to him!

"I will have the truth, Adeline," he said sternly. "I thought better of you, but to repay my kindness with falsehoods and pretenses—"

Quaking, she burst into tears. He bit back an oath. This was too much. He was not equipped to handle the guardianship of a young woman.

Her sobs tore at him. He wanted to storm out of the room, but he could not bear her crying. He pulled her into his arms.

"I would you had told me earlier," he sighed.

"F-Forgive me," she wailed. "Please do not disown me! Please!"

He could not find it in his heart to do such a thing, but he would have a word with George Grayson. And he had come round to thinking the young man might be worthy of Adeline!

After sobbing for longer than Arthur thought it possible to sob, Adeline calmed down.

"We will discuss the matter tomorrow," he said as gently as he could despite the anguish he felt. He saw her home to their grandmother's and told Mrs. Williams that, under no circumstance, was she to let Adeline out of her sight.

He then went to call upon the Graysons and was told that Mrs. Grayson was out but that George was home. He was shown into the drawing room, where he promised himself he would not wring George's neck.

"Lord Carrington, to what do I owe the pleasure—" George began upon entering.

"It is without pleasure that I come here," Arthur seethed. "You are a blackguard and a deceiver."

"My lord?"

"Do you deny having taken advantage of Adeline?"

"My lord, I have the utmost respect and love for Miss Hartshorn!"

"If you love and honor her as much as you claim, you would not ruin her!"

George blanched. "Ruin her? I would sooner die than see her pained!"

"You lie! I will see you run out of town. You'll not have the slightest opportunity afforded to you."

"What is this?" came a cry from the threshold.

They turned. It was Philippa, still in hat and bonnet, having just arrived home.

"Ah, the source of your skills in deception," Arthur remarked.

Philippa stared at him agog. "What is the purpose of your visit, my lord?"

"To inform you that I do not need a fortnight to consider your son's suit. He is a scoundrel. And you, too, madam!"

"My lord, I own I made a mistake," George said, "but it does not change the fact that I love and adore Miss Hartshorn and pledge my life to her happiness!"

"You placed your own carnal desires above her needs."

"You are one to talk!" Philippa accused.

"I have never deflowered an unmarried woman."

"Nor has my son!"

Arthur started. He turned to George. "Adeline is with child. Do you deny that you are the father?"

George hesitated, then looked him square in the eyes. "No, my lord!"

Deciding he would wring the man's neck afterall, Arthur lunged toward George and grabbed him by his collar.

"Stop! Stop this!" Philippa exclaimed. "Leave my son be! He deserves not your censure!"

"He deserves an early grave," Arthur snarled.

She tried to pull him away. "All he says and does—all of it—is for Adeline's sake! To protect her!"

"I am done with your deceit and dishonesty. You and your son's."

"What of your family's?"

"Mama, pray do not!" George shouted. "Say no more!"

Philippa looked ready to cry. "It isn't fair!"

George gave her a silencing look. She stepped back, her face full of misery.

Observing the interaction between mother and son, Arthur paused. "What further truths do you mean to hide from me?"

Philippa sank into the nearest settee and covered her mouth. Her whole body trembled.

"I will suffer no more falsehoods or lies of omission," Arthur told her.

She turned and glared at him. "The only scoundrel here today is you, my lord!"

He stared at her, taking in the passion that flared from her eyes, the conviction in her voice. This woman, though he knew her but a short time, could not be guilty of the duplicity he accused her of.

"What did you mean when you referred to my family?" he asked quietly, staying his anger.

She looked away.

"Nothing," George answered.

"Philippa?"

George raised his brows at the familiar address he used.

Still avoiding his gaze, she shook her head.

"My lord, I admit to an egregious error in judgment," George said. "I fully comprehend and deserve your wrath. Nevertheless, I still wish to marry Miss Hartshorn and vow that I will make her happy."

Arthur studied the young man, who spoke with the same passion and conviction as his mother. Arthur looked to Philippa, who still trembled. How he wanted to comfort her and wipe away her tears!

This was not the sort of response he expected from a family trying to further its own standing by worming its way into a better one. He recalled how Philippa had taken the concerns of Miss Collingsworth in hand. Her compassion was genuine. It was as if Miss Collingsworth was her own daughter. She would regard Adeline similarly and go to even greater lengths—

Arthur whirled his attention back to George. "Are you truly the father of the unborn child?"

George straightened his shoulders. "I am."

Arthur turned to Philippa. "Is he?"

She trembled harder.

"I will have a word with your mother," Arthur said to George. "Alone."

George looked at his mother. "I think not, my lord."

"You wish me to approve your suit yet choose to defy me?"

George looked abashed. "Your pardon."

With one last look at his mother, he withdrew. Arthur turned his full gaze upon Philippa.

"Is George the father?"

She rose to her feet. "I have nothing to say to you."

She made for the doors but he caught her. He searched her eyes. Like his earlier, they burned with anger.

"Tell me, Philippa—"

"I would I had never gone with you to Château Follet!"

She tried to struggle out of his grasp, but he only held her tighter.

"He's not the father, is he?"

"No! I will not have my son's wrath upon me because of you!"

"I have only to ask Adeline. She cannot deny me the truth."

At that, her strength seemed to leave her. He wrapped his arms about her.

"Philippa, how could you? Why did you?" he murmured into her hair. "Had you told me in the first place, I would not have charged into your home to wrongly accuse you and your son—and now I must beg your forgiveness. You must think me a brute."

"That you are," she mumbled into his chest.

He held her in silence for several minutes before saying, "You owe me one more night at Château Follet."

She pulled away from him to stare at him. "Is there no end to your—"

"But I shall not claim it till after the new year as you have much to plan for."

"I have not agreed to anything, but there is much to be done still for Christmas."

"There is Christmas. As well as a wedding."

Her mouth dropped. "A—a wedding?"

"I think your son will have no room for wrath when there is joy to be had."

She grasped his lapels. "Do not dare toy with me. Do you speak the truth? Do you approve?"

He took a hand of hers and kissed it. "I do."

She cried out. Delight replaced misery in her countenance. "A better Christmas could not be had!"

He grinned. "I can think of a better one: Christmas at the Château Debauchery."

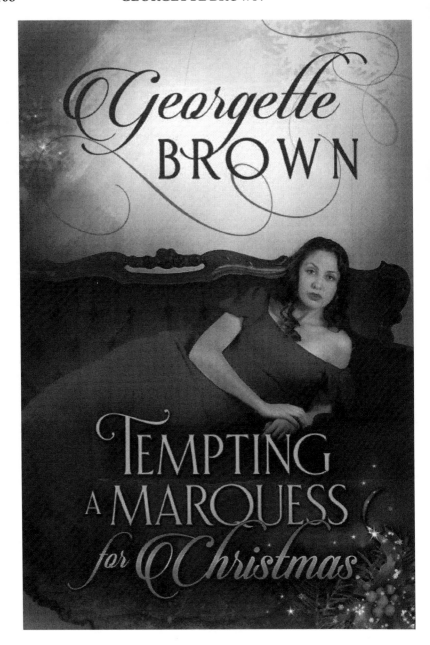

# TEMPTING A MARQUESS FOR CHRISTMAS

## By Georgette Brown

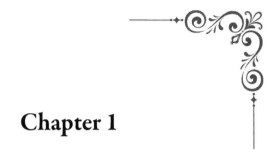

# Chapter 1

MILDRED ABBOTT WINCED as her mother emitted a wail of despair. She had no wish to cause her mother pain, but in this, her relief exceeded her guilt.

"You must speak to Haversham again," Mrs. Abbott insisted.

But Mr. Abbott had settled into his favorite armchair before the hearth, and having done so, was unlikely to rise for some time.

"He has decided to depart for Scotland tomorrow."

"All the more reason to speak to him before it is too late," his wife said, her voice high and shrill with desperation.

Mr. Abbott shook his head. "It would do no good. It is not Haversham who must change his mind. It is Alastair."

Mildred drew in a deep breath. Her cousin had done it. Though he had initially refused to intervene in the matter of her engagement, in the end he had brought about the result she had hoped for. She had erred in accepting Mr. Haversham's proposal, and only the Marquess of Alastair had the position and the influence to alter the arrangement without too much consequence falling upon the formerly engaged couple.

"Surely something can be done," Mrs. Abbott persisted. "Haversham was partial to our Millie. I know it."

"Apparently not enough to acquiesce to the marriage settlements required by Alastair."

Mrs. Abbott wrung her hands. "I know not why the Marquess has decided to concern himself in this matter when he has never concerned himself with us before. Why now?"

"I suppose it is my fault for having approached him with a request for Millie's dowry."

"Nevertheless, he is not the one who need marry Haversham!"

Millie suppressed a smile at the idea of her cousin marrying Haversham. The two men could not be more unalike. The latter was an obsequious dandy who had modest connections, the former was an arrogant and, many deemed, cold-hearted man of quality.

Mr. Abbott reached for his newspaper. "Well, as he is the one providing Millie's dowry, he has a right to interfere."

Mrs. Abbott gave another wail. "Now who will have Millie? It is not as if she has a queue of men wishing to court her!"

Mildred took no offense at this, for it was true. Though there was much she could yet do to improve her appearance, she knew her beauty to be middling. She had neither soft tresses, long lashes nor the slender figure desired by most. She had other qualities that would serve a husband well, but there was a part of her that few would find acceptable.

Beneath her facade of sense and goodness, churned a dark and prurient nature. She had been much ashamed of this part of her until Alastair's aunt, Lady Katherine, had come across her in a compromising way. In agony that she might have ruined her family, Mildred had been greatly astonished when Lady Katherine had comforted her and, later, *encouraged* her.

It had been an immense relief to Mildred to find that she was not alone in her proclivities, and that these were shared by a woman whom she respected and admired.

"Now Millie will never marry!" Mrs. Abbott lamented as she sank to the sofa.

Mildred took a seat beside her mother and passed her a handkerchief to dab her eyes. Spinsterhood was not a prospect that daunted Mildred, save for the grief that her parents might experience. She was their only child, and as they had but the most modest of means despite their connection to Andre d'Aubigne, Marquess of Alastair, their only hope of seeing their daughter provided for was through marriage. For this reason, Mildred had accepted Haversham's hand.

But regret had set in within minutes of her acceptance. That night, she had decided that she would rather face spinsterhood than marry Haversham. If a husband could not be had—she wondered that she could ever find the right man to marry—she would find employment as a governess or lady's companion. She could appeal for assistance to Lady Katherine, who had taken a liking to her. She would secure her own future.

"I feel quite ill," Mrs. Abbott said.

"Shall I assist you to bed, Mama?" Mildred asked.

"No, no. I am too aggrieved to move."

"Millie's dowry is still in place," Mr. Abbott assured his wife without glancing from his paper. "Alastair has even raised the amount to four thousand pounds. I expect we will see more suitors than we care to entertain."

Mrs. Abbott leaped to her feet. "Four thousand pounds! Truly? Why did you not speak of this first? Why, with such a grand sum, Millie can have much better than Haversham."

Mildred sat, stunned. She had not requested this of Alastair, and she doubted that her father, who had been more than pleased with half the amount, would have dared request more than had been initially granted.

Mrs. Abbott practically danced about the drawing room. "I must tell Mrs. Porter of this! She will not believe it! At last, my brother's marriage to a d'Aubigne has produced some benefit for us. I can almost forgive him now for his lack of consideration. He ought to have provided for the rest of us instead of keeping the riches of the d'Aubigne family to himself."

Mildred said nothing, for Richard, Mrs. Abbott's older brother, had passed away many years ago and was thus beyond receiving her clemency. And Mildred believed that her uncle, perhaps ashamed of his humble background, acted to protect the d'Aubignes from clamoring relatives.

"Richard would have us believe that Alastair had not a generous bone in his body, but at four thousand pounds... Well, I suppose it makes up for his lack of attention to us all these years. It amazes me how little he has done for us. Millie is his cousin, after all."

"By marriage, not blood," Mildred reminded her mother.

"Oh! The difference ought not matter. I had hoped the two of you could have formed a bond as you are not so very different in age."

Mildred flushed. Her mother could never know that, for one night, a special bond *of the most intimate nature* had been had between Mildred and Alastair, but not the sort Mrs. Abbott would have ever conceived.

Mildred pressed her legs tighter together as she recalled how delightfully the Marquess had attended to the flesh between her thighs *with his tongue.* And she, in turn, had taken his member into her mouth. How exquisitely naughty it had all been. How amazingly rapturous.

Mildred had tried not to recall too often her night at Château Follet, nee the Château Debauchery, when she had submitted her body to Alastair. But resistance was futile. It had been the most memorable event of her life. She had replayed every moment, and each recollection produced a heat inside of her. In the quiet of her bedchambers, she had fondled herself to the memories. She had found her own touch wanting compared to his, but she dared not dream for an encore. She still marveled that she had managed to harry him into taking her and fulfilling her most wanton desires.

She had resolved, despite Alastair's belief to the contrary, that how they regarded and interacted with each other would be unchanged.

"You think our relationship can remain the same after what happened?" Alastair had challenged her the morning after their congress.

"Why not?"

"Your naivety is charming at best."

"Well, we are not often in each other's company," she had replied. "The night will hold little significance for you after you have had a tumble with Miss Hollingsworth or whomever you choose next. I daresay you will have forgotten the night altogether after your next visit here."

She wondered if he had forgotten, then told herself that of course he had. She was but one of many whom he, a known rake, had taken to bed, and had done so, undoubtedly, with reluctance.

"I wonder if we should invite Mr. Carleton to dinner?" Mrs. Abbott mused aloud. "I think he could be persuaded to take an interest in Millie, now that her dowry is the sum of four thousand pounds."

"Mr. Carleton!" Mildred shuddered. The man was worse than Haversham.

"His family's merchant business does very well, I understand."

"He lobbied *against* the abolition of the slave trade."

"He was not the only one, my girl. And do not suppose that you can disparage such prospects simply because you have a dowry of four thousand. Four thousand!" she cried, her voice shrill this time from glee. "Mrs. Porter had thought her nephew too good for the likes of Millie, but she will have to reconsider now that Millie has *four thousand pounds!*"

Mildred frowned. Mrs. Porter's nephew, a portly fellow afflicted by gout and who disdained of bluestockings and the need for women to display their intelligence, was hardly a better prospect than Carleton. This would not do. This would not do at all. She saw a dinner table full of prospective suitors her mother had invited, hours upon hours of making polite conversation with dull-wits and no end to her mother's efforts at matchmaking.

"But I think Mr. Winslow, her neighbor, may also take an interest in Millie. He had been courting Miss Bennett, but I heard she had taken a fancy to some dandy."

"I thought Winslow to be courting Miss Stephenson," Mr. Abbott commented.

"That was *last* year, shortly after he was courting Miss Drury. Or was it Miss Laney he had been partial to?"

Mildred leaped to her feet. "I think I shall go for a walk."

"Alone?" Mr. Abbott inquired, looking up from his paper, perhaps fearing he would be compelled to keep her company, though it was her custom to take solitary walks.

"I may stop to visit Mrs. Bridges," Mildred replied, regretting the necessity to fib. In truth, she intended to pay a visit to her cousin.

"Do not make it a long visit, as dusk will be upon you before you realize."

"Yes, Papa."

As she exited the drawing room, she heard her mother say, "Perhaps I shall take tea with Mrs. Elliott tomorrow. She has a sea captain staying with her. He is quite a bit older than Mildred, and his complexion reminds me of worn leather, but that is to be expected when one spends as many days beneath the sun as he must..."

Mildred threw on a pelisse, quickly pinned on her bonnet, and slipped on her gloves as she hustled out the door. It was no short distance to Grosvenor Square, where Alastair lived, but she was unafraid of walking.

She could not permit Alastair to increase her dowry to such an amount. It was beyond generous, a trait she—or anyone else—would not have expected to exist in the Marquess. What could have possibly prompted such a gesture from him? She doubted her father, who had been quite nervous at requesting a dowry in the first place and would likely not have done it if not for the prodding of his wife, would have ventured to ask for it.

But why would Alastair have volunteered to raise her dowry? Lest his aunt had persuaded him to? Mildred supposed this must be so. Lady Katherine had a kind heart and was partial to Mildred. She would have to thank her ladyship, but they simply could not accept so generous a dowry. Mildred shuddered to think whom else Mrs. Abbott had in store for her.

Mildred quickened her steps. Though she would rather not make any further requests of her cousin, especially when she had exacted quite a bit from him already, she simply had to convince Alastair to rescind the four thousand pounds.

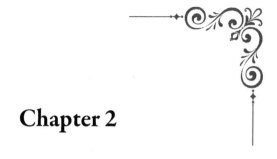

# Chapter 2

MILDRED SCANNED THE gaming hall looking for her cousin. She spotted him at the faro table flanked on either side by two beauties. The flaxen-haired beauty to his right leaned often toward him, her shoulder grazing his every other minute. The woman to his left had wide rouged lips, and the longest lashes Mildred had ever seen. She batted them at Alastair from behind her ivory-handled fan.

The attentions of the two women did not surprise Mildred, for the Marquess of Alastair had a striking, if not imposing, countenance framed by the d'Aubigne curls of ebony and all the qualities desired in form for his sex: a broad chest, square shoulders, and posture that accentuated his height. Though Mildred had not been struck at first by his handsomeness, for his eyes did not glimmer with charm and he did not often smile, since their encounter at Château Follet, she had come to find him compelling in other ways.

"Please let Lord Alastair know that his cousin wishes to speak to him," Mildred informed the footman. She could tell the Marquess was engrossed in his game, for he paid the two women beside him little attention. Mildred would not be surprised if he should choose to ignore her request for an audience. His butler, in informing her of his lordship's whereabouts, had warned her that he would not wish to be disturbed. For that reason, Mildred had kept her bonnet and coat.

She drew in a sharp breath as she watched the footman deliver her message to Alastair. Her cousin glanced up from his cards, he seemed neither pleased nor displeased, and Mildred decided it mattered not if he should see her. If he declined, she could always write him a letter expressing her gratitude. Indeed, she wondered at the necessity in coming to deliver her thanks in person. She wondered at her own eagerness. Had it been simply an excuse to see him?

The footman returned, and Mildred braced herself to receive the news that the Marquess was indisposed, but the servant said, "If it pleases you, miss, you may await his lordship in the parlor down the hall."

She released the breath she had been holding and answered, "Yes, of course."

She followed the footman to the parlor. After he had left her alone, she sauntered about the small but nicely appointed room. She had not the patience to sit upon the sofa in the middle of the room. Why, of a sudden, did she feel nervous? It was silly. She was merely going to thank him.

She had only felt such nerves one other time with her cousin. It was the night she had approached him at his aunt Katherine's birthday to request his assistance in getting out of her engagement with Haversham. She did not often find him as intimidating as others would.

But there was no denying that the nature of their relationship had changed since that fateful night at the Château Debauchery. Not only had she lifted her skirts to him, she had done so in the most wicked and wanton fashion.

To keep her mind from straying into the past, she studied the baroque longcase clock in the corner, wandered to the hearth to warm her gloved hands at the fire, and viewed herself in the looking glass above the mantel. She was glad she was comely enough such that Alastair had capitulated to her desires. She had fancied that perhaps he had even desired her a little, enough to be aroused, though she had heard that his sex required little in the way of arousal and could be titillated by the prospect of congress with any woman, even if she was not the most striking.

"What is amiss?"

She whirled about to face her cousin. Now that he was in closer proximity, he appeared more imposing. She tried not to recall how strong and heavy his body had felt against her.

"Nothing," she answered, gratified that his voice had carried more concern than was his custom.

"Then why are you here, Millie?"

Now he sounded displeased.

"I came first to thank you," she said, refusing to be intimidated by his mood. "Father said that Haversham departs for Scotland on the morrow."

"Good riddance. May I suggest that you pick your next husband more carefully?"

"Of course. I rather think that I shall not be accepting any more proposals for some time."

He made no reply, and she suspected that he desired to return to the card tables, but she could not leave without addressing her other request.

"I would have written a letter to express my heartfelt thanks, but I was uncertain when it would reach you, and I did not think that it would have adequately communicated the sincerity of my gratitude."

"No thanks are necessary."

Knowing the best manner of thanks she could provide at the moment was allowing him to return to his cards, and perhaps the two beauties that awaited him, Mildred could not resist staying him for just a minute. "But you will have it, nonetheless, for it is the proper and polite response to express gratitude where it is due."

"And when have you known me to care for what is proper and polite?"

She grinned. "*I* will do what is right and bestow my thanks. *You* may choose to receive it however you wish."

"Consider yourself acquitted of any further obligation. What is your second reason for coming, and I daresay I hope there is not a third?"

"Worry not. I do not plan to keep you long, and you may return to your vices soon. I have but a simple request."

He raised his brows. "Another request?"

She flushed, realizing she had imposed upon him rather often of late. "It shall be my last."

"I pray it so or it might become a habit."

Ignoring his rudeness, she forged on. "I should dearly appreciate it if you were to return my dowry to the original amount of two thousand pounds—or even less."

He stared at her.

"I know not what my father might have said," she continued, "but two thousand pounds was more than kind."

He crossed his arms. "Never before have I encountered anyone whom it is so difficult to bestow money to. You spoke of what is proper and polite. It would be proper and polite of you to accept my donation and be grateful for it."

"I am grateful for your generosity but would not encroach upon it further."

"Alas, it is not for you to do so. Your father has accepted the new dowry on behalf of your family."

"Well, of course he did!"

"Because anyone of middling intelligence would."

She drew in a sharp breath, then saw a glimmer in his eyes that allowed her to release her breath. "Alastair, you have been more than kind, but four thousand pounds is beyond the pale. I do not merit such a sum."

"There are plenty of unworthy women with far larger dowries than you."

She suppressed a scowl. "But why the need to increase the amount?"

"Because you merit better than Haversham."

"But four thousand pounds will attract every Tom, Dick and Harry."

"That is not my problem, Millie."

"But you—" She forced herself to take a breath. How the man tried her civility!

"You are a clever girl. I expect you will learn the art of rejecting your suitors without badly wounding their hearts—or pride."

"I've no wish to. Dealing with Haversham was enough for me."

"Millie, you have made several requests of me, and I have no desire to encourage further requests from you. Thus, my answer is *no*."

Her mouth hung agape before she landed upon another strategy. "If that is your position, then you shall have to suffer my gratitude and many, many expressions of it—and often—profusely—for such a level of generosity deserves praise and—"

To her surprise, he drew up before her, and the air surrounding them suddenly constricted.

"Are you threatening me?" he growled.

Her heart palpitated rapidly. His proximity left her without words.

"If we were at Château Follet right now..." he began.

She quivered at the unnamed possibilities. Though she had told herself that one too many glasses of wine had contributed to the amorous affect her cousin had upon her, the truth was rather different, as evidenced by the melting sensation she currently felt.

Seeing that he had silenced her, he retreated a pace. "Are we done, Millie?"

Never had gathering words proved so difficult, but she managed a "yes."

Pulling her shawl tighter about her, she made for the doors.

"Wait."

The command sent her hurling back to that night at Château Follett, when she had followed his directives in delicious delight. Her heart still beating rapidly, she dared not look at him, not wanting him to see the effect he had upon her.

"How did you arrive?" he inquired.

She turned around only after she had enough composure in hand. "I walked here by foot."

He looked toward the window. The skies outside had begun to darken. "The hour is late. You should take my carriage."

"Thank you for the offer, but I am not daunted by the distance home."

"Did you come alone?"

"Yes, but—"

"Then you will take my carriage."

"I enjoy walking."

The cool air would help dampen the warmth swirling inside her.

He gave her a penetrating stare, and for a moment, she thought he might finish the thought he'd had earlier and specify a punishment for her refusal. "I will not require my carriage for some time," he said, removing any last obstacle to her acceptance. "Time enough for my driver to take you home and return."

"Very well," she declared. Then, wanting to reclaim a little of her pride, she dared to irk him. "I accept your hospitality. Let it not be said that the Marquess of Alastair lacks kindness."

His countenance darkened, and he grumbled, "Consider yourself fortunate, Millie, that we are *not* at Château Follett."

His words took her breath once more. She wanted a ready retort but could not conjure one. She watched him open the doors and call to a footman to have his carriage ready.

"Good night, Millie," Alastair said before heading back to the card room.

She was glad he did not tarry to keep her company while she waited for his carriage. His presence rattled her more than she liked. Now that he had mentioned Château Follett, there was no holding back from venturing there in her mind.

# Chapter 3

ALASTAIR FAVORED THE BLOND, though it mattered little which of the two lightskirts he selected to fuck in the grounds behind the gaming hall. Miss Woodwin—or perhaps it was Woodwiss; he could not remember nor cared to remember—gasped as he pinned her against the building with his body.

"Your lordship," she breathed, "you are presumptuous."

Despite the dim lighting from a half-clouded moon, he could see the sparkle of desire in her eyes. She had been brushing her body against his all evening; brushing his forearm as she reached for a card; tapping his shoulder to inform him of his turn, though he had known bloody well each time it was his turn; and bumping into his leg beneath the table whenever she shifted in her seat.

"Am I?" he returned, cupping her chin and lifting her gaze to meet his. "Would you rather I take my leave?"

Her lips parted but returned no words. He already knew the answer, and had asked his question to curtail any protests she felt obligated to feign. Her bosom heaved beneath him, and when the silence continued, he lowered his mouth to take her lips. He could taste and smell the three glasses of port she had consumed. A gentleman would have hesitated to press his advantage with an inebriated woman. But she had known precisely what she did, having begun her flirtations before the first glass, the port providing her a ready pretext for her later actions.

And Alastair was no gentleman.

Were it not for his status in polite society and his endowments in form and countenance, no woman of reason would wish to tempt him. And, in general, he found their sex rather wanting in judgment. He had thought his cousin, Millie, whose uncle had married his aunt, to be an exception. But she had surprised him by accepting the proposal of a rather stupid fellow, from which she then suffered buyer's remorse and sought *his* intervention to dissolve the engagement.

Millie surprised him in more ways than one. He remembered how astonished he had been, sitting at one end of the dining table at Château Follet, to see her at the other end. She must have seen him enter the dining room, for she had been in some haste to depart the table, running into a maid carrying a tureen of gravy. He had followed her out and found her, soaked in gravy, hiding behind a sofa in the drawing room.

He had intended to sacrifice his own plans to partake of the carnal merriment at the Château Follet to see her safely away from the den of debauchery, but she had stubbornly refused. He could not believe that his aunt, though she had been the one to introduce him to Château Follet, would have facilitated Mildred's participation. It had been the most confounding night, one in which the proprietress, Madame Follet, in finding him and Millie at odds, dared accuse him of sanctimony. Never before had he been so vexed by their sex. He had implored them to be reasonable:

*"Marguerite, pray be reasonable. You do Miss Abbott no favors by permitting her to stay."*

*"Andre, she is my guest, not yours. Your aunt—"*

*"Katherine is far too enamored with this place and in want of discretion."*

*Marguerite arched her slender brows. "Andre, this is most unlike you. And because we are good friends, I will dare to say that I find your position rather selfish."*

*She astounded him. She deemed him selfish when he was willing to sacrifice his long-awaited weekend at the château to protect his cousin? His look of vexation did not daunt Marguerite. She continued,* "Oui. You have partaken readily of the pleasures here but would deny the opportunity to another?"

*He tried a different approach.* "I ask you, as a friend, I beg of you to see the soundness of my actions."

"Your aunt is my friend as well, and I am loath to disappoint her."

*They had all lost reason, he decided. All three women. Women he had hitherto thought sensible—especially Millie.*

"I do not mean to disparage you or the château, Marguerite," *he said, unrelenting,* "but it is not worth the risk for Miss Abbott."

"Sir, you presume too much on my behalf," *Millie said.*

*Marguerite put a gentle hand upon his arm.* "It is *très* amusing to see you fret in the manner of an old woman, but I assure you that all will be well."

*His vexation trapped all words. If she were not the hostess, he would have a few choice words for her.*

*Marguerite turned to escort Millie from the room, but he stopped them. Addressing Millie, he said,* "Do not be a fool. I am willing to chaperone you home, but I may not be so generously inclined later."

*She straightened.* "I thank you for your kind offer, Alastair, but it is not necessary."

*His nostrils flared. The chit should be grateful for his selfless gesture!*

"Stop such idiocy, Millie. You do not fully comprehend what transpires here."

"I have been well informed by both your aunt and Madame Follet."

"And the wiser course would be for you to reconsider!"

"How is it the wiser course for me but not for you?" *she cried.*

"Are you truly asking such a daft question? I had thought you more sensible than that."

*She flushed with indignation. "I intended to draw attention to your hypocrisy with my question."*

*"It is not my hypocrisy but that of society's. The consequences fall much more harshly upon the female sex."*

*"But here at Château Follet, the sexes are equal," declared Marguerite. "It is a quality you appreciate, mon chéri, and benefit from."*

*"But how will Millie benefit?"*

*"In the same manner you do, but of course."*

*"That is different."*

*"How?"*

*Why were these women asking such ridiculous question? Did they truly require him to state the obvious?*

*"Certain ruin awaits her if she is discovered."*

*"That has yet to happen with a guest."*

*"She won't like it here."*

*Millie breathed in sharply. "Surely that is for me to determine."*

*"I assure you this is no place for you. My dear aunt has not been here in some time and forgets the nature of the acts here would appall you."*

*"I am not easily frightened or appalled."*

*"Millie, don't be a dolt."*

*"I object to your condescension, sir!"*

*"It is for your own good. You know no one here. What man do you expect will pair with you?"*

*He saw her eyes widen and regretted the harshness of his words, but it was warranted if he was to talk sense into her.*

*She looked ready to attack him or cry. "You think no one will desire me?"*

*"That is not what I said."*

*"It is what you meant!"*

*He fumed because her accusation was not entirely untrue. "The men here—their expectations are different."*

*Her bottom lip quivered. "If I am not selected, then I will take plea-sure in watching others."*

*Her response stunned him into silence.*

*"Andre, I protest," Marguerite intervened. "Miss Abbott has a right to be here as much as you do, and I dare say, if you do not leave her be, I shall have to ask you to leave."*

If not for his promise to grant Katherine's birthday wish, in which she, fearing for his loneliness, had requested that he take the concerns of someone in hand, he would have left Millie to her own devices, would have let her suffer the consequences of her foolishness.

Or would he? The memory of the Viscount Devon still made his blood boil. He could not have, in good conscience, allowed Millie to be his prey. Any inaction on his part was tantamount to feeding a defenseless hare to a hawk. Millie had thought the man charming, but Alastair would sooner trust a thief.

And so he had granted Katherine's request and would see to Millie's safety, but she had thwarted his intentions to lock her in her chambers for the night, away from the clutches of Lord Devon.

Alastair had thought he could convince Millie to be reasonable. The pleasures of Château Follet were not worth the risk to her honor. But she had surprised him yet again by revealing that she was no longer in possession of her virtue. He had been flabbergasted at the time, but, upon reflection, he found the revelation rather intriguing. Few people surprised him.

"Something amuses you, your lordship?" Miss Woodwiss asked.

He started.

"I think that the first smile you have displayed all evening," she commented, visibly pleased with the prospect of being the source of his pleasure.

Recalling himself, he gave a half growl and closed her mouth with his. The less she talked, the better. He ground his erection against her. Thinking back on Château Follet had doubled his ardor. A shiver went down his legs as he recalled one of their most memorable exchanges after he had taken her.

*"But I had hoped to take your member,"* she said.

*"Millie, did you think we were engaged in something other than congress?"*

*"Into my mouth."*

*His eyes steeled, and he pressed his lips into a firm line. "I will not degrade you further."*

*"But there is titillation in degradation, is there not? Is it not supremely wanton and wicked to take that man's part and place it where nature had not intended?"*

*"Millie, the hour is late."*

*"Do you not enjoy the act?"*

*"Millie, I will not allow you to browbeat me into this."*

*"Browbeat? No. I merely wish to entice you. I have received some instruction in this and am no novice."*

*He shook his head. "Good God, Millie. When I discover this wretch who has turned you..."*

*"Turned me 'what?' Into you?"*

*He looked a little as if he might like to throttle her. "I will ask no more of you after this,"* she promised.

*"You are asking to—to take me into your mouth..."*

*She gave him a broad smile. "Yes. Please. My lord."*

*He uttered an oath beneath his breath. Before he could answer, she had sunk to her knees before him. She eyed his crotch hungrily.*

*"You might even be pleasantly surprised,"* she said. *"I may be as good as or better than Miss Hollingsworth might have been."*

*She reached a hand to the buttons of his fall, but he caught her wrist.*

*"Millie—"*

*She pouted. "Come. It is not as if we are engaging in sin."*

*"Not engaging in sin?" he exclaimed, incredulous.*

*"Further sin. We have done the worst of it already."*

*With her other hand, she cupped his groin. He groaned. Could she tempt him once more? The prospect that she could, that she was capable of such sway, excited her.*

*"I am not one given to generous doses of conscience," he said, "and you would lay to waste my attempts at goodness."*

*"I never invited you to be what you are not."*

He appreciated this in Millie. Outside the Château Follet, women were constantly trying to change him. His sisters wanted him to end his profligacy. Even Katherine wished he could be more caring of others. And those who set their caps at him...he knew what they were about. They hoped to tempt him into marriage and harbored romantic notions that he would forsake his rakish ways in favor of love. Millie was far too sensible for such silly fancies.

He wondered if Miss Woodwin was as adventurous as Millie. Not knowing the blond well, he would not inquire. Instead, he lifted her skirts and cupped a bare thigh. She sighed against his mouth. The sensation of Millie's mouth about his cock had been nothing short of marvelous. She was not practiced in the art of taking cockmeat, but she had approached it with much vigor.

He moved his hand between Miss Woodwin's thighs and found the moisture of her desire. Her breath became short and shallow as he fondled her. In his mind, he saw Millie moving up and down his shaft, gagging at times when his cock struck the back of her throat, but relentlessly soldiering on.

His groin ready to burst, Alastair could wait no longer. He unbuttoned his fall and, lifting Miss Woodwiss, buried himself inside her. She gave a grunt of satisfaction. He thrust his hips, pinning her to the wall.

He had come close to spending in Millie's mouth but could not bring himself to do so. He had opted to carry her to the bed and return the pleasure he had received. Her quim had tasted fine, her body deliciously responding to every lick and suckle. After she had spent, he had sheathed himself a second time inside her.

His cods boiled, wanting release, but he held off until he sensed Miss Woodwiss approaching her pinnacle.

"Ya, ya, ya," she mumbled as she rode him.

He bucked his hips faster, tightening his hold on her, for Miss Woodwiss was as light as a ragdoll. He remembered how Millie, a quick student, had known to ask his permission before spending. He remembered how she had met his thrusts, how their bodies had formed an easy rhythm.

Miss Woodwiss cried out as her body fell into paroxysms. When she had done shuddering, he pulled himself out of her and set her down. Aiming his shaft away from her, he jerked at his member till his seed shot into the ground. They recovered in silence, she leaning against the wall to catch her breath, and he wiping himself with his handkerchief.

"Will you be here tomorrow evening?" Miss Woodwin asked.

"I think not," he responded as he replaced his fall. It had not been his intention to satisfy his lust with anyone tonight, but the appearance of Millie had changed all that. The memory of her and Château Follet had stayed with him longer than he cared to entertain.

For this reason, he had doubled her dowry. The sooner she found a husband, the better. Of course he would have liked to see her well settled, but it was also best that he be done with his cousin once and for all.

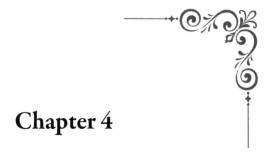

# Chapter 4

SEEING THAT HER MOTHER walked her way with Mr. Carleton beside her, Mildred slipped into the corridor of the Grenville home and went to hide in the music room.

"Your pardon, I did not realize the room was being used," she said to the debonair young man, who seemed equally surprised by the woman who had rushed into the room and swiftly closed the doors behind her. Not wanting to return and risk being found by her mother, she looked about the room, which contained a pianoforte, a harpsichord, two violins, and harp. "Are you musically inclined?"

He looked sheepish. "In truth, I don't play at all. I was seeking refuge—I mean to say, solitude. Do you play?"

"A little, but I must confess that I did not make my way in here in search of an instrument."

He lifted his brows and appeared a little relieved.

"I am not one given to much socializing," she explained further.

"Nor am I."

"You are a friend of the Grenvilles?"

"I am a friend of Mr. Harris, and staying with him, and he is a close friend of Mr. Grenville. I am George Winston."

She returned a curtsy to his bow. "Mildred Abbott. My family and the Grenvilles have known each other for a long time, and I all but grew up with their daughter Jane."

132

They regarded each other for a few seconds in silence before he asked, "Would you care to play?"

She made her way to the pianoforte and sat down. "You may regret your invitation, for my skills are limited."

He went to stand near. "I cannot cast stones, for I do not play at all. Anyone who has taken the time to learn a musical instrument deserves praise."

"That is very kind of you to say," she said as she selected Mozart's 'Fantasy and Sonata in C minor', "but I am quite tolerant of criticism. I know I did not practice as much as my instructor would have liked."

After she had completed the piece, with only a few minor errors, he clapped his hands, saying, "That was marvelous. You were being modest when you said you played only a little."

"I selected a rather easy composition."

"Are you quite difficult to compliment?"

She might have received this question as impertinent, but he spoke in such an easy, gentle manner, that she almost felt guilty for not accepting his praise.

"Your pardon. I did not mean to be rude."

"No offense taken, Miss Abbott. If I played as well as you, I should be deliriously happy with myself. Granted I am no expert at the pianoforte."

"I suppose I do appreciate that my family was able to afford a music instructor for me."

"I imagine you possessed other talents that you deem yourself 'a little' skilled at."

"Lest you think I am all modesty, I will boast that my French is quite good, but I am a horrible dancer. My dance instructor was even more cross with me than my music instructor."

He chuckled. "I would hazard that you are more modesty than not. I expect that if I were to witness you on the dance floor, you would not be nearly as bad as you think."

"Oh, I assure you I am."

He chuckled again, and his eyes seemed to sparkle when he smiled. "I suppose we shall have the chance to ascertain if you are accurate in your assessment or if I am correct that you underestimate yourself."

She shook her head. "I don't often dance."

It was a true statement. She did not often get asked to dance, though that had changed in recent months, thanks to Alastair. She tried not to think of her cousin every time Mr. Carleton or Mr. Porter approached her, but she would not have been in this position if not for Alastair.

"Do you not care for it?"

"I like the activity fine. I would participate more often if I were more skilled at it."

"I suppose I am more selfish in that I consider myself middling in my dancing skills, but my enjoyment of the activity exceeds what guilt I may have from inflicting my inferior abilities upon an unsuspecting partner."

It was Millie's turn to chuckle. "Imagine if we should both take to the dance floor. What havoc we might cause!"

He perked and beamed at her. "What a delightful notion! We should attempt just such a thing!"

She shook her head. "I could not."

"Ah, because you are a better person than I and would not impose upon others that which you believe would be a poor performance."

In truth, Mildred had hoped to remain closeted in the music room till all the dancing had past, but that was rather wishful thinking. She could not disappear for such a length of time without raising brows and appearing rude.

"You think too well of me," she replied to him. "It is because I would rather observe the elegance of those more graceful than I."

"I gather there is little chance, then, that you would accept my request to dance?"

She studied him, wondering if he was sincere in his desire to dance with her. She found herself rather tempted, for he had such an affable manner and the most charming smile.

"Indeed," she answered. "You seem a nice fellow, and I would not subject you to my poor dancing skills."

"If you underestimate your dancing skills as much as you do your skills at the pianoforte, then I should think you a rather good dancer."

"I would not take the chance, were I you. There are enough others here tonight who would assuredly be better than I."

"Even if you are a poor dancer, I would rather have you for a partner because it is quite clear to me that you are a woman of intelligence and wit. And I would sooner have a partner with whom I can converse well than a woman with whom I can dance well."

She shared the same sentiments, and would not mind being in Mr. Winston's company. Certainly, she would prefer dancing with him than the likes of Carleton or Porter. "Very well, but you have been warned."

"Splendid!"

"I shall make your middling abilities appear worse than they are."

"That does not concern me in the least." He glanced toward the door. "I suppose I ought to rejoin the others. I would not wish my host to think I had deserted him."

She drew in a fortifying breath. She was not ready to brave the Carletons and Porters but supposed she had to follow suit with Winston. When he presented his hand to assist her to her feet, she accepted it. He held on to her hand longer than she would have expected.

"I suppose it would not do for us to be seen walking from this room together," he said.

"Most assuredly."

He released her hand, and she felt a little wistful at its loss. "Ladies first, then. I shall follow and find you for a reel—or would you prefer the quadrille?"

"The quadrille, please."

"The quadrille it is."

Mildred took her leave with steps light and happy. The evening no longer presented to be as dreary as she had thought.

# Chapter 5

"WHAT DO YOU KNOW OF Mr. Winston," Jane asked of Mildred as they stood against the wall waiting for the dancing to begin. "The gentleman staying with Mr. Harris. He seemed a handsome fellow."

Mildred scanned the room but did not see him.

"I should say he is the most handsome of bachelors here," added Mary.

"I prefer Mr. Wiggins, but Mr. Winston would certainly be second in my opinion. But I should not be surprised if he takes an interest in Mildred more than anyone."

"In me?" Mildred felt an inner glow as she recalled how her hand had rested in his.

"Yes! All the bachelors seem to have taken an interest in you, now that you have a dowry of four thousand pounds."

Mary heaved an envious sigh. "How lucky you are, Millie, to have such a generous cousin in the Marquess of Alastair."

"She is lucky to have such a cousin, dowry or not."

Perplexed, Mary raised her brows.

"You have not met the Marquess, but you would understand what I mean if you had." Jane gave a mischievous smile.

"He is very handsome then?"

"Oh, he is more than that."

"He has not the best of reputations," said Mildred, feeling a little traitorous in speaking poorly of her cousin, but she spoke to convince herself as much as Mary.

"He cannot be all bad if he granted you such a generous dowry."

"He should despair to hear you speak so well of him," Mildred smiled. She frowned as she saw Mr. Carleton approach. "But I had rather he not be quite so generous."

"Why would you not? I think you must have more suitors now than even Miss Rose."

Yes, and she is none too happy about that," said Mary with a giggle.

"Miss Abbott," greeted Mr. Carleton, a gentleman upon whom grey was not the best of hues. He wore a touch too much pomade in his hair, but was otherwise decent in appearance. "May I have the honor of the first dance?"

Before she could answer, Mr. Porter had arrived and said, "I had thought to ask the same, but I will settle for a reel."

"What say you, Miss Abbott? I think the quartet will begin to play any moment."

Mildred hesitated, wanting to say that she felt too fatigued for dancing, but she was looking forward to taking the floor with Mr. Winston. She supposed she could tolerate one dance each with Mr. Carlton and Mr. Porter.

"Remember you promised the gig to me," a voice behind her said.

Mildred turned her head and perked to see Mr. Winston.

Jane poked her subtly in the ribs as if to say, "I knew it."

"That is correct," Mildred said. "I did reserve the quadrille for Mr. Winston."

"Then I will have the next dance," said Mr. Carleton.

"Or, if I may be presumptuous—" Mr. Porter interjected.

Mildred imagined if Alastair could see the nettled state she was in, he would only be amused that he had produced such a fuss. He would have not an ounce of sympathy.

From across the room, she could see her mother talking to Mrs. Harrington as she pointed first toward Mr. Carleton, then at Mr. Porter. Then into her line of sight came Miss Hannah Rose, dressed in a gown that might have featured in the most recent issue of *The Lady's Magazine.*

"There you are. We wondered where you had gone off to," she addressed Mr. Winston, then noticing Mildred, her smile fell, but she recovered in the presence of others. "Why, Mildred, that gown looks quite charming upon you. I think it my favorite among all your gowns. I can see why you chose to wear it last week at the Westbrook soirée, and the week before that at Mrs. Wilmington's dinner. If I had that gown, I would be tempted to wear it often as well, but then people may think it my *only* gown."

Mildred only smiled, for she was accustomed to these sorts of compliments from Hannah. Miss Rose was not a pretty young woman, though she had large eyes and long lashes. Three of her teeth were crooked, but she did not often smile with open lips. Her complexion was middling, and her lips protruded forward, but she carried herself as if she were a beauty, and that convinced many others that she was just that.

"I wonder that you do not acquire many more gowns, now that you have a dowry of four thousand pounds?" Jane asked.

Mildred looked sharply at her friend. She knew Jane spoke to irritate Hannah, but she would rather Jane did not trumpet the facts of her dowry.

Beside her, Mr. Winston raised a brow.

Jane ignored or did not notice the look from her friend. "How fortunate you are, Millie, that you have the *Marquess* of Alastair for a cousin. Why, you nearly have the connections of Miss Rose here, whom I understand has a great uncle who is an *earl*."

Mildred suppressed a groan. As Hannah often flaunted her family's connections, Jane knew full well whom the Rose family was related to.

Hannah's eyes narrowed before conceding, "It does not compare to being related to a d'Aubigne."

"By marriage only," Mildred said. "My uncle was Lady Katherine's second husband. The d'Aubigne blood does not run in my veins."

"Even if the present Marquess of Alastair has a repute that would make any *decent* person blush and hesitate to boast his name," Hannah finished with a hard stare and a tight-lipped smile directed at Jane.

Jane frowned and visibly struggled for a retort.

"Shall we take to the dance floor?" Mildred asked Mr. Winston.

"Yes," he replied eagerly, perhaps as relieved as she to be departing

Miss Rose appeared startled, but she did not want for a partner and was soon besieged by men asking her to dance. As others followed onto the dance floor, Mildred took her position facing Mr. Winston.

"I beg your pardon," he said.

She gave him a puzzled look.

"It appears you do not look forward to this dance, and I fear I had cajoled you into this earlier."

"No, no, I am fine. I was merely thinking of...less pleasant thoughts. My mind was not on dancing."

He returned a sympathetic smile. "I rather wish I were back in the music room, too."

His statement made her chuckle.

"I should consider myself fortunate to have ensnared the first dance," he went on to say as the music began.

"You are," she said in jest, "for, as I've said, I prefer to watch."

"I was referring to your many suitors."

"Oh. You mistake the men. They are not my suitors."

They took their turn in the first figure.

"No? Then it is commonplace for men to quarrel over a dance with you?"

"They are more interested in my dowry than in dancing with me."

"For a young lady with an impressive dowry, you behave with surprising modesty."

"All ladies of sizable dowries must be overbearing?"

"I suppose I have that prejudice. As you are a d'Aubigne, I admit to having fully expected pretension and condescension."

They awaited the other couple before resuming their discourse.

"I am not a d'Aubigne. My uncle married the aunt of the present Marquess of Alastair."

"That would make the Marquess your cousin."

"By marriage. We are not blood relatives, and our situations in society are quite different. You know the d'Aubigne family?"

"I was at Oxford with Andre d'Aubigne. He was two years my senior, and I do not think he took any notice of me, but I admired him from afar. He was quite the batsman at cricket. Do you see much of the Marquess?"

"No. There are not many occasions for us to meet."

It was a true statement for the most part. Their time at the Château Follet had been an anomaly.

"There are few occasions and little company that merit his tolerance, but, forgive me, I should not speak ill of your cousin. He was that way at Oxford, and he must be a different man now that he is a marquess."

"It would seem not." She nearly added that Alastair tolerated gaming hells better than he tolerated his family.

They moved on to other subjects after that. Mr. Winston danced with sufficient grace despite his prior assertions to the contrary, and when he held her hand, she found his hold warm and comfortable. She was rather sorry to see the dance come to an end.

"I was right," Mr. Winston declared as he led her off the floor. "You are a much better dancer than you give yourself credit for."

"And you as well."

"Not only did we not make fools of ourselves, I think we presented a decent pair."

She smiled and would have accepted a second dance with him if he had asked, but he had not the chance. She was not surprised. A handsome and charming man, his attention was quickly engaged by many others, including Miss Rose. But Millie fancied he glanced her way every now and then. The pleasantness of their exchange lasted the remainder of the evening, and even accepting dances with Mr. Carleton and Mr. Porter was not as insufferable as she would have thought.

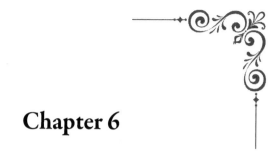

# Chapter 6

WHEN ALASTAIR CAME into his townhouse and received word from his butler that a "lady awaited," he thought it might be Millie. Few women would dare seek him out at his home. But he had not heard from Millie in some time and presumed she had abandoned hopes of persuading him to change her dowry. After their meeting in the gaming hall, she had written him twice with reasoning, threats, cajoling, and pleas.

He had responded by advising her to desist or he should be tempted to double her dowry to *eight* thousand pounds.

He had not heard from her since.

But the woman sitting in his drawing room was not Millie, alas. It was his eldest sister, Louisa, who bore no small resemblance to him. She had the ebony d'Aubigne tresses, sharp eyes, and strong bone structure. She stood taller than the average member of the fair sex, and with her ridiculously large ostrich plume in her bonnet, it appeared she stretched from floor to ceiling.

"Andre," she greeted at his entrance, then wrinkled her nose. "You smell of horse."

Having just arrived, he had not yet changed out of his riding clothes and boots.

"Have you lost all your manners?" she asked with a critical lift of the brow. "I may be your sister, but I am still a lady, and you know perfectly well a gentleman would not receive a lady smelling of horse."

Not bothering to point out that *she* had chosen to call on *him*, and without warning, he returned, "Would you rather I take the time to don a different wardrobe?"

He had no qualms in keeping his sister waiting.

She relented. "I haven't all day. I waited nearly half an hour as it is."

"Then praise the stars, for I nearly chose to ride out to Camden. Your wait then would have lasted hours."

"Your butler assured me you would be home before then, for you are expecting Mr. Kittredge."

"Kittredge does not mind waiting for me as long as he has access to my cellar." He went to pour himself a brandy from the sideboard and nearly considered offering Louisa a glass, though he knew full well she detested the drinks of his sex. She watched him in silence, no doubt waiting for him to inquire into her health or, at the least, the purpose for her visit.

"Do you plan to spend Michaelmas with our aunt?" she blurted when it was plain he had no intention of making an inquiry of any kind.

"No." He set his glass down at his writing table and picked up the letters of the day to review.

"It is not because you have yourself some opera singer here in town for a mistress? Surely you can command better than an opera singer."

Louisa did not approve of his having a mistress at all, but she had voiced this too often to deaf ears and was thus left with criticizing his choice in whom he tumbled.

"Did you come all this way to talk to me of an opera singer?" he asked, opening one of the letters.

She bristled. "Of course not! I asked if you intended to spend Michaelmas in the country with Katherine."

"And I gave you my answer."

"It affords me some refuge but, still, I think I cannot decline. I have not your ability to disregard what is proper. Were she not our only aunt, I should have arrived at some ready excuse to respond with my regrets. I would sooner accept an invitation from our uncle Herbert. Caroline said she can tolerate but a few hours with Katherine, let alone an entire sennight."

Caroline was his other sister, whom Alastair had even less regard for. Louisa could be critical and condescending, but Caroline added vanity to these qualities. She would spare no expense for her carriage, baubles, and lace, but would berate her housekeeper for spending a penny too much on butter.

"I do not think Katherine would care if you accepted her invitation or not," he said, hoping to end their dialogue.

Louisa huffed. "What a thing to say! Is that what she relayed to you?"

"Katherine is far too wise and well-mannered to confide such a thing to me, for she knows all too well that I lack the manners to pretend niceties where none exist."

His sister pursed her lips, not knowing what to make of his statement but wanting to know where Katherine stood in regards to her niece. "Your words imply that Katherine invited us out of obligation and not from a desire to have our company."

"I intended to imply that you should have no reservations in refusing her invitation," he replied without looking up from his letter.

She sniffed, "Well, when I heard that she had also invited the Abbotts, I knew for certain that I had no wish to go."

He paused. Millie had been invited to spend Michaelmas at Edenmoor?

"I shall never understand why she pays such heed to her poor relations."

"They are our relations as well."

Louisa gave a despairing groan. "They are all of such little consequence."

"Richard was a good man."

"I will grant you he was uncommonly decent for a man of his background, but marrying him does not require her to consort with all of his siblings, especially the Abbotts. I wonder that Katherine tolerates them."

"She is partial to the daughter," he said slowly.

"As are you, I take it, for I understand you are providing her a dowry of *four thousand pounds*."

Here was the real reason Louisa had come to see him, he thought to himself.

"Four thousand pounds!" she reiterated when he said nothing. "That is more than that family has seen in their lifetime, I'll wager."

"Probably so."

She huffed again at his indifference. "What possessed you to grant such a sum to Miss Abbott? You realize that all of Richard's poor relations will be making requests of you now."

"They had been doing so long before I underwrote a dowry for Miss Abbott."

"And have you always been this generous?"

"Not at all."

"Then I fail to see the sense in such an extraordinary gift. Why, it is equal to the dowry for my Emily, and that is not as it should be."

"Very little in life is as it should be."

"Then you mean to go through with it?"

"Why would I not?" He immediately regretted his response, for though he meant the question to be rhetorical, he had invited an answer from Louisa.

"Because it is preposterous! Miss Abbott is not the sort of young lady that ought to have a dowry of four thousand pounds."

"It would be bad form for me to withdraw it now."

"Since when do you care about good form?" she cried.

"Withdrawing now would be devastating to the family, and even I am not so cruel."

"But everyone or anyone would understand that it was a grave error on your part. They would not fault you for attempting to correct it."

"Then I have far too much pride to admit I could make so large an error." He was beginning to be more than a little irritated with Louisa. He knew he could provide no answer, short of delivering what she wanted, that would satisfy her.

"Then reduce it to a more sensible amount. I understand you had initially set it at two thousand pounds. Two thousand pounds is perfectly sufficient. Why you saw the necessity to increase it is bewildering."

"You may chalk it up to old age, the onset of madness, or inebriation, I have no intention of retracting."

She twisted her hands in frustration. "Then I suppose, if you are in such a generous mood of late, that I should request an amount for my Emily. A dowry of six or eight thousand pounds would be fair."

"As you pointed out, a dowry of two thousand pounds is 'perfectly sufficient.'"

She bristled. "Sufficient for Miss Abbott. But now that she is at four thousand pounds, it appears all wrong if my Emily, a d'Aubigne, does not have a dowry commensurate with her station."

"If you wish your daughter to have a dowry of six or eight thousand pounds, then talk to your husband and not to me. Your situation allows you to afford that amount."

"Two thousand pounds is no insignificant amount to us, but it is for you. And why should the Abbotts be the recipients of your generosity and not your own sister."

He set his letters down and finished off his brandy. If Louisa stayed much longer, he would require a second glass. "Because you are not in need of the money."

"But you have not granted anyone else in need such a magnanimous gift."

Louisa spoke true, and he had at one time reasoned to himself that he had granted Mr. Abbott's request to avoid having to deal with the man further, but that would not be the whole truth. He met his sister's stare and smiled. "It amused me."

"Amused you?"

"Yes, and I can assure that whatever answer I provide to your questions will not satisfy you, and only serve to exasperate you further. As such, I suggest you curtail this conversation so that you are not completely overwhelmed with vexation."

Affronted, she huffed with her mouth agog. He was a little surprised she was not, by now, accustomed to his impertinence.

"That is all the response I am to receive?" she asked.

"Yes."

She had exhausted his patience, and he was in no mood to entertain her further. He had a preponderance of correspondence to respond to before he left town with Kittredge to go hunting in the country.

"As your sister, I merit better!"

"No doubt you do, Louisa, but as you have often pointed out, I am both ungenerous and impolite."

"And well you deserve those labels!"

He did not bat an eye. Both his sisters had married well and needed naught from him. Louisa's daughters would have no trouble finding husbands of good standing.

"You will regret your actions," she said, "when you are besieged by requests from your relatives and anyone who thinks they may claim a connection to you."

"Madam, I am besieged more by my own sisters than by distant connections."

At that, she threw up her hands and turned on her heels. Before she crossed the threshold, she turned around and waved a finger at him. "If you persist in such heartless disregard for your own family, then I shall wash my hands of you. I will, Andre! And when you are old and alone, you will come to reconsider your youthful recklessness and be sorry that you permitted all this to come to pass!"

Whirling about, she stormed from the room.

When she was gone, Alastair took a relieved breath. Louisa was fortunate he did not voice his true thoughts on her vanity and lack of interest in her relations. The latter, however, he owned he shared with his sister. He could not be certain why he had tolerated Millie. Perhaps because she neither tried to tempt him nor judge him, lest he had provoked her, in which case he had warranted her criticism. He remembered how cross she had been with him at Château Follet. He had been quite overbearing. Yet how easily they had surrendered to each other.

Her soft and supple body had withstood his attentions well. Her lips had yielded deliciously beneath his. Her marvelous heat had welcomed his member. The area of his crotch tightened as he recalled how her body had clenched him as she spent.

In the glow of rapture, she had looked beautiful, though he had not found her striking before. In the morning hours following their night of wicked indulgence, he had had ample time to observe her while she slept and began to appreciate the suppleness of her body. He remembered his concern that she might wake with regrets or have developed an infatuation with him. He had been impressed with her lack of sentimentality. It was not what he expected from her sex.

*"You have no regrets?" he asked.*

*"I am fully content with what has transpired," Millie replied.*

*"You will think differently with time."*

*"You are presumptuous, sir."*

*"There are few who would dare speak to me in such a manner, and fewer who could do so without raising my ire."*

*If they had not resumed their identities as Alastair and Millie, he would have taught her more courtesy. A spanking might do.*

*She lowered her gaze for a few seconds. "Your pardon, but, really, Alastair, you do not know me well enough to make such a claim. In truth, I am quite surprised that you seem to harbor more shame than I."*

*The thought seemed to amuse her, and he bristled. "I was only worried for your sake. My sex can dispense with guilt much more easily than yours, especially over matters of the flesh."*

*She was silent in thought. "Am I more the wanton jade if I harbor no repentance or shame? Am I a...slut?"*

*He groaned, and he felt another unsettling tug at his crotch. He had thought such sensations would not have persisted past the night.*

*"Millie, that is not at all what I intended with my words! I applaud that you honored the natural cravings inside you and sought to fulfill them without fear."*

*"You tried to stop me."*

*"That was before I knew you had already forsaken your virtue!"*

*"Then you have no need to worry of me, though I appreciate your concern. It is quite hopeful that you may not be as unredeemable as society deems you to be."*

*He growled at her teasing smile. Women. If he had had a choice, he would have selected one of his own sex to fulfill Katherine's birthday wish.*

*"My dear cousin,"* Millie said. *"I will forever be grateful to you for last night. My one fear is that you will henceforth be awkward in my presence."*

*"You think our relationship can remain the same after what happened?"*

*"Why not?"*

*"Your naivety is charming at best."*

As he recalled their exchanges at Château Follet, he considered that perhaps he should accept his aunt's invitation to spend Michaelmas at Edenmoor, but he reminded himself that doing so would require him to suffer the company of his sisters and their husbands. Hunting with Kittredge would be much more preferable.

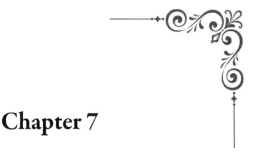

# Chapter 7

ALASTAIR STIFFENED AS he and Kittredge entered the main room of the Dante Club, for he saw, sitting in a tall wingchair beside the hearth, the Viscount Devon. The man had charmed Mildred at the Château Follet, and Alastair shuddered to think what would have happened had he not been present to rescue her from the Viscount's clutches. The man was known to seek virgins and had boasted to an acquaintance of Alastair that he enjoyed their screams and tears of pain when he tore through their maidenheads.

"That fellow must be a new member," Kittredge said, following Alastair's gaze. "You don't appear too pleased to see him."

"I am not," Alastair affirmed.

"Who is he?"

"The Viscount Devon, a cad."

"That would be the pot calling the kettle black," Kittredge laughed.

Mildred had said something similar when he had attempted to raise her doubts of the man.

As if sensing he was the object of their attention, Devon looked toward Alastair. A flicker of recognition passed through his countenance before he returned to his friend.

"Shall we start with brag?" Kittredge inquired. "We can take the table farthest from this Devon fellow. Mr. Thistlewood has acquired some port that he believes to be the best the club has ever purchased."

When they had sat at a card table and saw no signs of the manager, Kittredge rose to find the man. Alastair sat with his back to the fireplace but heard the Viscount approach the table.

"We meet again," Devon said. "Alastair, is it not?"

Alastair returned a silent stare.

"May I?" Devon did not wait for a response before pulling out one of the chairs at the table. He sat down and spotted the cards. "What is your pleasure?"

*To have you depart*, Alastair thought. Aloud, he said, "Kittredge and I were to play brag."

"Ah, I am not the best at that game, but shall we play a few rounds while we wait for your friend's return? I will endeavor my best to give you some measure of challenge."

As he was not interested in encouraging conversation with the man, Alastair started shuffling the cards.

"What is the ante?"

"You wish to bet?"

"Cards are hardly fun if nothing is at stake."

"Name your bet then."

Devon straightened, perhaps not wanting to name an amount too low for fear of appearing miserly or cowardly, nor too high to risk losing. "Will five guineas be sufficient?"

"If it pleases you."

His indifferent response appeared to disappoint the Viscount. Alastair dealt three cards each.

"Have you been back to Château Follet since last we met?" Devon asked as he looked at his cards.

"I have not," Alastair replied blandly.

"Nor have I."

"Place your bet."

"Ah, well, let me add another five guineas then."

Alastair matched the bet.

"But I should like to return before long," Devon continued, his brow furrowing as he pondered whether to bet again or fold. "I did not have the chance to inquire if Miss Abbey—your cousin, is she not?—had enjoyed her stay at Château Follet?"

Alastair clenched his jaw.

"She is a charming creature. How marvelous that you hail from the same family. It was quite the coincidence that you should both be there at the same time."

"You may double the pot if you wish to see the cards."

"Ah, yes, perhaps I shall. That would make it another twenty guineas then."

"Forty."

"Forty it is."

Alastair laid down his cards, a run that edged out Devon's flush.

"I forgot how quickly this game finishes," Devon said as Alastair presented Devon with the cards to shuffle.

After a new pot had been established and the cards dealt, Devon asked, "Will Miss Abbey be returning to Follet?"

"No," Alastair answered quickly.

Devon's brows rose. "No? I pray she was not disappointed in Follet?"

"Her attendance at the château was a rare occasion, and she will not be returning."

"You are in communication with her then? She has confided this to you?"

"You take an interest in Miss Abbey?"

"As you are her cousin, I will admit to you that I found her rather captivating. Say again the reason she will not be returning to Follet?"

"I had not provided a reason."

"If she does not plan on returning, I can only hazard that she had a disappointing experience, and that is a travesty, for no one ought leave Château Follet unsatisfied."

Alastair was tempted to say that she had been more than satisfied with her experience but kept his mouth shut except to say, "Your bet, sir."

"Where does Miss Abbey hail from?"

"Why do you wish to know?"

Devon turned his study from his cards to Alastair. "It would seem you are protective of her."

*She needs protecting from wolves like you,* Alastair thought. "As you are a frequent guest at the Château Follet, you must be aware that discretion is the value most honored."

Devon placed a bet of five guineas and said, "I am more than aware, and during my tenure at Château Follet, I have never once divulged or let slip any indiscretion."

Alastair put in another five. Devon contemplated before doing the same.

"I think I would like the pleasure of seeing Miss Abbey again."

"Do you?"

"Indeed, I thought I might be able to find her here in town."

Alastair felt his body tighten. "I find your interest in her surprising, for she is hardly the most captivating maiden."

"I am not so shallow that a pretty countenance is all that matters to me. While Miss Abbey may not be a beauty in the ordinary sense of the word, I can see she has other lovely qualities to recommend her."

"Such as?" Alastair asked, managing not to grit his teeth.

Devon leaned in. "I suspect, as a fellow guest of Madame Follet, you understand what these qualities are."

"I think my preferences differ from yours."

"They cannot be too different or we would not both find ourselves at Château Follet."

"You had the company of Miss Abbey for but a small amount of time, hardly enough to form a substantive impression of her qualities."

"*Au contraire*, I am quite good at making an assessment in a short amount of time."

Alastair would have liked nothing more than to have Devon lose a sum sizable enough to compel his departure, but he held a poor hand. "I will see your cards."

Devon also held only a high card, but his queen of diamonds beat Alastair's jack of spades.

"Shall we up the ante to augment the excitement?" Devon asked, handing Alastair the deck. "Say, ten guineas?"

"As you wish."

After placing their ante, Alastair shuffled and dealt the cards.

"I wish I had had more time with Miss Abbey. I wondered how she had spent the remainder of the evening at Château Follet?"

"She arrived at Château Follet in error. I kept watch over her till I could see her safely departed in the morning."

"Then she did not have a chance to partake of the château's offerings."

"As I said, she came in error," Alastair said without looking up from his cards, a pair of threes.

Devon placed ten guineas for his bet. "She seemed quite at ease with the activities of the château—and eager to participate."

"Nevertheless, her time with Château Follet is done."

"You are her guardian?"

"I am not—"

"Then how can you be certain?"

Alastair put in ten guineas. "I think your efforts would be better spent attending to other ladies."

"Miss Abbey intrigues me."

"She would not suit your preferences."

"You presume to know me, my lord?"

There was a slight edge in his tone, but Alastair cared little if he should offend the man.

"I have heard of your preferences from my friend, the Baron Rockwell."

Devon frowned at this. "I mean no disregard to your friend, but Rockwell makes a great many presumptions. He is not always right."

"Do you deny you are partial to virgins?"

Devon put in twenty guineas before responding with lifted chin, "I do not. Virgins are delightful, and I consider it an honor to introduce them to the pleasures of the flesh. When you say that Miss Abbey would not suit me, do you mean to say that she is not a virgin?"

"I mean to say that you will stay away from Miss Abbey," Alastair glowered.

"That has the ring of a threat, my lord."

"Then consider it a threat." Alastair folded his cards. "Our game is at an end, sir."

Devon smirked as he displayed his cards, surprising Alastair. He held only an eight for a high card. "It would seem I am better at brag than I thought. I suppose I ought not be underestimated."

He collected his winnings. "I would have provided Miss Abbey an unforgettable experience at Château Follet. It is unfortunate I had not the opportunity to do so. But...perhaps another time."

"You will deem me more presumptuous than Rockwell, but I doubt you are up to the task of satisfying Miss Abbey's expectations." Alastair had the satisfaction of seeing Devon's nostrils flare. "Take care you do not *over*estimate your appeal."

"Your cousin found me appealing enough. Had you not intervened, she would have—"

Alastair had risen, prompting Devon to rise to his feet as well. The two men regarded each other tensely till Kittredge appeared, holding a decanter of wine. "Your pardon. I had not intended to take long..."

"Thank you for the play," Devon said without taking his eyes off Alastair. "And the winnings."

With a bow, the Viscount took his leave.

"What the bloody hell happened?" Kittredge asked Alastair when Devon had left. "You look ready to pummel the man."

Alastair sat back down. "You took a damned long time looking for Thistlewood."

"Found him in the cellar. He wanted my opinion on some Madeira. What the devil happened between you and this Viscount? Did he cheat at cards?"

"No, though I would not put it past him to do so," Alastair answered as he watched Devon across the room.

Kittredge sat down and filled two glasses with wine. "Hm. Then I can't imagine what he could have done to earn your ire. Did he criticize your family? No, that would not trouble you. Is he your competition for the Lady Sophia?"

Alastair turned to his friend.

"He is a handsome fellow, to be sure," Kittredge continued, "but you outrank him, and that is no small matter for the daughter of a duke. The betting book at Brooks's has you in the lead for the fair damsel's hand, though there are just as many bets that you will not marry for at least another five years."

Taking the glass of wine from Kittredge, Alastair drank it without tasting the port. Though he had paid more attention to the woman, Lady Sophia, than was his custom, his mind dwelt at present upon Millie. If Devon knew she was his cousin, he could easily discern that Miss Abbey was none other than Miss Abbott.

"Is that not a fine port?" Kittredge asked, refilling his own glass before it was even done. "I say we drink of it as much as we can and sleep well past the noon hour before we depart for the hunting grounds of Suffolk."

"The grounds at Edenmoor are good for hunting this time of year," Alastair thought aloud.

"Eh?"

"My aunt's estate."

"Not sure your aunt would be pleased to have my company, as she thinks I encourage your vices, but do as you please, Alastair. I will go wherever a good glass of wine can be had."

# Chapter 8

NOT HAVING SEEN Katherine since their trip to Bath, Mildred was overjoyed to see her ladyship. Katherine took her hand in her own and pressed it warmly in reception. Mildred could hardly wait to have a moment alone with the woman.

"You are a welcome sight to these old eyes," Katherine said, taking Mildred's arm in hers, as she led the Abbotts into her house.

"You may describe your eyes as old, but they are sharper than mine," Mildred replied. She never regarded her ladyship as old, despite the appearance of grey in her hair and wrinkles at the corners of her eyes and mouth. Her ladyship was still possessed of impeccable posture and a stout carriage.

"I regret that it has been so long since last we had each other's company, but Harriett required me."

Harriett was Lady Katherine's daughter by her first husband.

"I pray she is in better health?" Mildred asked.

They had a moment of partial solitude, for her father, still drowsy from his nap, walked at a slow pace behind them. Her mother would have been at their side but was busy marveling at her surroundings.

"Yes, but I forbid her to make the trip to Edenmoor till the babe is older."

"You must be overjoyed to have another grandson."

Katherine beamed. "He is quite the rumbustious little babe, as are all the d'Aubigne men."

Mrs. Abbott came up to them. "What a fine entry you have, Lady Katherine! What brightness fills this space! And how nicely appointed all your furnishings and decor are. So light and uplifting to the mood!"

"I must credit Richard for that. My first husband was partial to dark hues, and as all our furniture was made of mahogany then, it all felt rather somber. I pray you will make yourselves comfortable here. You are first arrived and have the run of the place."

"And whom else shall we be delighted to expect?"

"My son, Edward, his wife and sons will arrive today. My nieces, Louisa and Caroline, will come the day before Michaelmas and stay two days."

"What? We shall have the pleasure of their company but two days? It is quite the distance to travel for such a short duration."

"The distance is nothing for the young," Mildred intervened, though her mother's lack of grace had never seemed to bother Katherine. Mildred was secretly relieved that Louisa Wilmington and Caroline Brewster would not stay for the entire sennight. She had met the women sparingly, but neither could hide their disdain that Katherine had chosen a second husband so far beneath her station.

"And when does your nephew arrive?" Mrs. Abbott asked of Katherine.

Mildred stiffened.

"I do not expect him at all," Katherine answered.

"Indeed? He will not spend Michaelmas with his family?"

"Alastair does as Alastair pleases."

Still unsatisfied, Mrs. Abbott inquired, "I hope he is well?"

"I have no reason to believe otherwise. He did not elaborate in his letter to me."

Mrs. Abbott raised her brows. "Oh?"

"Come, Mother, let us see to our chambers," Mildred said.

As they proceeded through the house, Mrs. Abbott had the grandeur of the staircase, the warm and engaging tapestries in the hall, and the very fine paintings upon the walls to distract her. After leaving Mr. and Mrs. Abbott in their chambers, Katherine showed Mildred to her own room. With a window that overlooked the gardens and pastel silk upon the walls, the room was delightful to Mildred.

"I shall have tea ready within the hour," Katherine said, "and hope that is enough time for you to change out of your traveling clothes."

Mildred nodded. "I cannot thank you enough for your invitation to spend Michaelmas with your family. My mother was beyond thrilled, and I think her excitement overwhelms her..."

"Do not fret of that, my dear. While I understand why Richard was hesitant to have me consort with your family, I had told him it troubled me little. I may be a d'Aubigne, but you know that I am not a conventional sort of woman."

The women shared a smile.

"I shall be forever grateful to have had your acquaintance, my lady," Mildred said.

"I require none of your sentimentality, my girl, but I will find a moment for the two of us. I wish to hear how you have fared all this time."

With the appearance of the dressing maid, Lady Katherine took her leave. As Mildred divested her coat, she recalled that the Marquess was not to spend Michaelmas at Edenmoor. She could not help but be a little disappointed, as their last exchange had been unsatisfactory. But she was also relieved that he was to be absent. Though she was determined to maintain their relationship as it had been prior to Château Follet, she knew she would be deceiving herself that it could be perfectly the same.

"ARE YOU DISAPPOINTED?" Lady Katherine asked.

Her ladyship and Mildred strolled the manor after tea. Mrs. Abbott, fatigued from the traveling, had retired to her chambers to rest. Mr. Abbott read the newspaper in the sunroom.

"Disappointed?" Mildred echoed.

"That he will not be here."

"How could I be when I have your company?" Mildred cried.

Katherine smiled. "Nonetheless, you would rather he were joining us."

Mildred shook her head. "For what purpose would I desire to see him? He refused my request to return my dowry to its initial amount, and it is too late now for him to change his mind."

"There need not be a *purpose*. If you take pleasure in seeing him, that stands irrespective of anything else."

Mildred studied her ladyship, wondering if the woman had attempted, as she had with the Château Follet, to put the two of them in each other's way once more? But there could be no reason for a second meeting. Mildred would be forever grateful to Lady Katherine for her introduction to Château Follet, and grateful that she had set it up so that Alastair could be the one to fulfill her desired night of debauchery. Her ladyship knew that if she had revealed her plans to Mildred, Mildred would have balked at the notion of submitting herself to the Marquess.

"My vexation with him has not vanished," Mildred said. "I have been besieged by all manner of unwanted suitors, and my present misery is all due to Alastair."

"Is there none among them that you would consider for a husband?"

Mildred shuddered, but then she considered Mr. Winston. She wondered what sort of husband he might make.

"Ah, there is one," her ladyship discerned. "Who is he?"

"His name is George Winston."

"That name is vaguely familiar, but I do not think I have the pleasure of knowing this man."

"I mention him only because he is more tolerable than the others. His manners are pleasing, and he is both intelligent and articulate."

"That sounds quite promising. Do your parents approve of him?"

"He has a gentleman's income, undoubtedly, but my mother believes there are better prospects to be had. But I am inspired by you, my lady, to place more weight upon the character of a spouse than his riches."

"I did come under much criticism when I married Richard, but then, I had done my duty in my first marriage, and as my children were settled in their marriages, I had more freedom to follow my heart."

Mildred looked out the window. How her life would differ if she had a similar liberty.

"I had thought I would sooner be a spinster than wed a man I did not love or desire," she remarked. "But it is my duty, and I should be considered most ungrateful if I did not choose to marry. Many young women have not the privileges I now have."

"Then be ungrateful. I should hate to see your spirit crushed by the weight of an unhappy marriage."

"There is not a man who could accommodate me, and the fault is entirely my own. I fear I am too fastidious...and too wicked."

"Do not give up hope, my dear. Come, let me show you something."

Lady Katherine led her to the end of the corridor, produced a key, and unlocked a set of double doors. They entered a room of darkness, but her ladyship found the curtains covering the room's lone window and drew them aside.

Mildred's breath stalled as she gazed about the room, decorated with all manner of titillating art from marble nudes to paintings of men and women in congress. At the far end of the chamber, a sumptuous bed draped in brocatelle and clothed in silk beckoned. Mildred walked past a Grecian vase with man holding his impossibly large phallus. Beside it were various pottery with depictions of different positions of coitus. On the walls were replicas of Thomas Rowlandson. The women in his artwork often had their skirts throw up above their waists and their breasts bared.

"You have your own Château Follet," Mildred noted with awe and even envy.

"Richard quite liked how Marguerite styled her château, but traveling to Château Follet is difficult in winter, and we often had not the patience to make the journey. We did our best to replicate Follet"

Mildred looked about the room once more. She would consider herself truly blessed if she should find a man as Lady Katherine had.

"The room gets dusty from want of use," her ladyship said, "but I clean it from time to time, as the servants do not enter. I will not let it fall into disrepair, as it holds too many memories for me."

"You have many fine rooms, my lady," Mildred remarked, "but this one is my favorite."

# Chapter 9

"AND HOW LONG DO YOU intend we stay at Edenmoor?" Kittredge asked as he and Alastair rode on horseback toward Katherine's estate.

"Not more than two days and a night, I think," replied Alastair, who preferred riding over the bumping and jarring of a carriage. The confinement did not suit his temperament, and the autumn air pacified the agitation that had come upon him ever since his encounter with Devon.

"What? All this way for but two days?"

Alastair thought of his sisters and shuddered inside. Katherine's son would be there as well with his family. He did not mind Edward as much but still he had no desire to make conversation with him or his wife, Anne. Their young sons, aged six to twelve, could be quarrelsome with each other and far too boisterous for his taste. He did not think his cousin Harriett and her family would be present, and Mr. and Mrs. Abbott were too intimidated by him to require much of his attention. Nonetheless, he wondered that he could tolerate even two days in such company.

"Is the hunting that superb?" Kittredge inquired.

"It is more than adequate."

"Then say again why we are headed there?"

"I did not say before, but you may content yourself that my aunt keeps a decent cellar."

"Will your niece, Emily, be there? She had her come out last year, did she not? She is quite the tempting armful."

Alastair returned a stern gaze.

"Worry not," Kittredge laughed. "I have no designs upon your family. I prefer you as friend and not kin. Good God, I should hate to have you for a brother-in-law. Will your uncle be there?"

"Traveling aggravates his joints."

"I do like Herbert. And his clarets even more."

Alastair could not bear the company of Katherine's brother any more than he cared for the company of his sisters, whom he would now have to suffer for at least a full day.

He cursed himself. Selecting Millie to fulfill Katherine's birthday request had become a much greater task than he had ever envisioned. He could have waited till Millie returned to London to speak to her, but he worried what Katherine might say or do. He would never have guessed that his aunt would take Millie to the Château Follet, though she had orchestrated the coincidence well. Who knew what other absurdity the two women might attempt?

Having discovered that Millie harbored such wanton and dark desires, he understood why Katherine, who had introduced him to Follet, had brought Millie there. Nevertheless, it was a risky proposition and remained so. He doubted Millie could handle herself with the likes of Devon. He could not chance Millie returning to Château Follet, and he would not now be surprised if Katherine would encourage just such a thing.

"Well! This is a most welcome surprise!" his aunt exclaimed when they had arrived at Edenmoor.

"I pray you had received the notice of our coming?" Alastair asked.

"I did, and have prepared rooms for you, though your notice only said that you *might* come. Where are your valets and baggage?"

"Not far behind. You remember Kittredge."

His friend doffed his hat and bowed.

"I do," Katherine responded. She put aside her reservations. "Welcome, good sir."

"Are my sisters arrived?"

"They come tomorrow, but Edward is here with his family. And the Abbotts." To Kittredge, she explained, "They are relations of my late husband, Richard."

"I look forward to making their acquaintance," Kittredge said.

Alastair looked about, expecting to see the Cheswith boys tearing through the halls. "Where is everyone?"

"Millie is out back playing with the boys."

He found it interesting that she had responded with regards to the one person he had come to see. His gaze came to rest upon a large painting of Richard and Katherine from some years ago. The two had met at Château Follet and fallen in love there. Alastair hoped that was not what Katherine expected for Millie.

Feeling the study of his aunt, he turned to her. "Kittredge and I will greet the others after we have changed out of our riding clothes."

"Let me show you to your rooms then."

She could have had a servant see them to their rooms, but Alastair suspected she offered so that she could speak with him. And he was correct. After seeing Kittredge settled, she walked Alastair down the corridor.

"What prompted your decision to join us for Michaelmas?" she asked.

He had anticipated this question and had no reservations about being candid with her. "Millie."

Katherine's countenance brightened.

"I came across a rogue, one she became acquainted with while at Follet, and I mean to warn the both of you that he may seek her out."

She frowned. "That is against the etiquette of Château Follet."

"He is quite taken with Millie."

"That is hardly a surprise."

"For reasons you should find troubling. He thinks her a virgin."

He turned to face her. "I hope you do not entertain any notions of returning Millie to Château Follet."

"I had not considered it."

"I pray you do not."

"Why not?"

"I cannot always be there to protect her against unsavory characters."

Katherine beamed. "How grand that you take such an interest in her welfare."

"Madam, I bid you consider the matter with seriousness. Do *not* take Millie back to Château Follet."

"Andre, if she desires to return, why should I not facilitate her happiness?"

"Has she expressed a desire to return?"

"Not explicitly. We have not been in each other's company of late, and I hope she and I will have more occasion to speak now."

"You ought to discourage any thoughts of returning."

Katherine sighed.

"You are partial to Millie," he continued, "and if *you* care for her, you will want to see her unharmed. You cannot let your affections for Château Follet cloud your judgment. I bid you be the responsible party."

"Of course I would not wish to place her in harm's way, and because I esteem your display of consideration for another human being, I will honor your request."

He turned to enter his room, but he was only partially satisfied. He would not wager all that he had that Katherine would do exactly as he wanted. And there was also the matter of Millie. He would not be wholly surprised if she dared return to Château Follet without Katherine's participation.

MILLIE WAS WRONG. THOUGH she had protested that the nature of their relationship would not change, it had.

Dressed in fresh clothing, Alastair found her outside playing Blind Man's Bluff with the Cheswith boys and a few servants' children. Millie had the blindfold, and the children scurried around, laughing and calling out to her. Alastair watched for several minutes, but when he saw her headed toward a pit in the ground, he strode over. He was too far to reach her in time, and she seemed not to hear him call out her name. She stumbled to her knees, but he caught her before she tripped on her own skirts in her attempt to rise.

It felt pleasing to hold her.

When he had righted her, she lifted the blindfold, saying, "Goodness, I had not—"

Upon seeing him, her face reddened. She had rarely blushed with him before. He released her with some reluctance.

"M-My lord," she greeted, "you—you're here."

He saw that she had on a much nicer bonnet than he had seen her in last. It suited her.

"Lady Katherine had not said..."

"I had not confirmed my coming with her," he explained.

She seemed to collect herself. "Your presence must please your family greatly."

He wanted to ask it if pleased *her*, but he could ascertain this soon enough. The children complained about the stall. She glanced at her dirt-covered skirts, brushing them off.

He addressed the eldest Cheswith boy. "Thomas, take Miss Abbott's place so that she can tend to her gown."

"That won't be necessary," Millie said. "I can continue. 'Tis but a little dust."

He took the blindfold from her and gave it to Thomas. To Millie, he said, "I will walk you to the house."

"Truly, I am not injured."

He raised a brow. She gave a sigh as if relenting to a persistent child and walked with him. They were silent at first, before he asked, "You do not intend to ask why I am here?"

"Are you inviting me to pry?" she returned with a grin.

"No, but most would be curious to understand my motives."

"You do as you please. It is not my place to question or judge your motives."

He wondered if her reasons were because she knew that he preferred not to be questioned or because she was indifferent to what his answer might be.

"And most would inquire as to how you found the roads, or how your hunting fared," she observed, "but you would disdain these sorts of *tête-à-têtes*."

"You know me well, Millie."

She smiled. "You are not complicated, my lord."

"Nevertheless, I find most people unable to refrain from their own inclinations, regardless of my preferences."

"Does it trouble you that others do not always grant you what you want?"

"As the only son of a marquess, I have been quite spoilt and accustomed to receiving what I want."

She chuckled. "Yes, you are."

He stopped. "I did not seek your agreement of my statement."

"No, but you have it. As I do not think we often agree on anything, I thought it a special occasion to take note of."

He shook his head. His cousin could easily earn both his approbation and his vexation. He wanted to forbid her return to Château Follet, but she would balk at such an arrogant attempt to control her. They resumed walking.

"Whilst in town, I came across your friend, the Viscount Devon," he said.

"Indeed?"

He frowned at her apparent interest. "He is not a man worth your attention, Millie."

"So you have said before."

"I would stay your distance from him."

"I doubt my path will cross with his."

"But if it should, you will heed my cautions?"

She studied him before replying, "You need not worry that I shall lift my skirts upon meeting him."

"And what if he should attempt to seduce you?"

She seemed amused by the idea. "I am certain there are far better conquests for him."

"You need not demean yourself so. You have many qualities to recommend you."

This time, she stopped and looked at him. There was a brightness to her eyes he found quite fetching.

"You are kind, my lord," she said.

He was about to decry being fixed with the trait when Kittredge appeared.

"There you are, Alastair. I have reviewed your aunt's cellar—"

Upon seeing Millie, he bowed. Alastair made the necessary introductions. After a brief dialogue of politeness between Millie and Kittredge, Millie said that she would head to her room.

Alastair had little opportunity to speak alone with Millie, for Edward engaged him next with details of a hunt for the following morning. He could not speak to her during dinner, and she made no effort to seek his company afterward. Quite the contrary, she seemed to stay her distance from him, choosing to speak with Anne mostly. He did see her glance his way, however, when she thought he wasn't looking.

When Anne and the Abbotts chose to retire for the evening, Millie said she would do the same. Alastair stayed with Edward and

Kittredge till the two men had had their fill of sherry and port. In his chambers, Alastair remained awake, considering how he could speak with Millie in private before or after the hunt.

But he need not have waited till the morrow. An hour after everyone had gone to bed, he heard footsteps pass his chambers. Even before he opened his door, he suspected it was Millie.

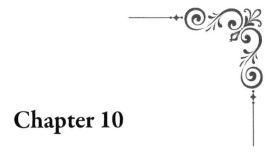

# Chapter 10

MILDRED WANTED ANOTHER look at the room of debauchery. She had not seen Lady Katherine lock the room after showing it to her upon the first day, and when she tried the doors, she found they indeed opened.

She closed the door behind her and, using her own candle, lit a candelabra. She took in a long breath as she gazed about the room a second time. Sauntering to the wall of paintings, she eyed each one again, feeling her body warm with the naughty images. Beneath the one of a woman taking the member of her lover into her mouth was a sideboard. The end of a ribbon poked out from one of the drawers. Opening it, she beheld several satin masks, the sort used to block out light during sleep. Curious as to what the other drawers held, she opened another. The second drawer held jewelry. Many appeared to be earrings, but the tops of them differed. Some had merely string. Others possessed clasps that she recognized but appeared to be fixed at the wrong angles, making the face of the jewelry sit away from the viewer at some 90 degrees. One set of earrings were simply tassels.

The third and final drawer made her gasp.

Nestled atop silk lining were several phalluses of varying size. She picked up one made of glass and admired its smooth finish. The craftsmanship was rather impressive, for the crafter had shaped the top to resemble the flare at the tip of a man's member. Laying down the glass phallus, she picked up a smaller wooden one with ridges.

She wondered that such a hard object could render pleasure. The third and final one was made of a material resembling India rubber. It was quite large both in length and girth. She shuddered to think of taking such a large object. Nevertheless, she picked it up to marvel at its size and instinctively licked her lips. She remembered how delicious Alastair had once tasted.

Looking at the painting above and noticing that the man's shaft was quite wide, she wondered if she could wrap her mouth about this monstrosity she held. Feeling mischievous, she put it to her mouth. She licked its tip, then pushed it between her lips. She took in two inches and felt her lips stretch over the circumference. Desire swirled in her groin.

"Now *that* is a sight worth four thousand pounds."

In her haste to pull the phallus out, she bobbled it several times before dropping it altogether. She felt herself flushing to the roots of her hair. But was somewhat relieved to see it was Alastair at the threshold. How long had he been standing there? Despite the late hour, he still wore his clothes but had his banyan instead of his coat.

"I wondered if Katherine had told you of this room," he said.

She bent down to pick up the dildo. After brushing it off with her robe, she intended to return it to the drawer.

"Not yet," he bid as he walked into the room. "I interrupted your feasting."

Her blushed deepened. "I was merely...it is of such a ridiculous width, I merely wondered..."

"How much of it you could swallow?" He stood in front of her and cupped the hand that held the dildo. "Let us find out."

Her heart drummed in her ears as she allowed his hands to guide the dildo back to her mouth. She parted her lips and relaxed her tongue to permit the behemoth entry. She could take no more than three inches before gagging.

"A little more," he encouraged.

Wanting to please him of a sudden, she did her best to take in more. Her mouth was stretched to capacity, and though she took in air through her nose, breathing felt awkward whilst her mouth was stuffed by the false member. She gazed up at him and the molten lust in his eyes made her throb between the legs. She would stand with her mouth stuffed for hours, mesmerized by the expression of desire in his countenance. It satisfied her to know that he was not immune to her.

"You may release it," he said, drawing the hand with the dildo back down.

She licked her lips and waited to see what he would do next. Did she dare hope he would stay? Releasing her hands, he took a step back. He would now advise her to return to her chambers, she predicted with disappointment. It would be of no use. She could not sleep, not after seeing all that she had, not after he had witnessed her partaking of a phallus into her mouth. Her hands still felt warm from his touch.

"It is hard to imagine her ladyship making use of such implements," she said when she could no longer bear the silence. "Or do you think they are merely for show?"

"My aunt and I do not discuss the particulars of what she and Richard did behind closed doors."

Mildred nodded. Perhaps it was best not to imagine her ladyship engaged in wicked wantonness. She put the large phallus back in its place. Realizing that Alastair would be familiar with the possessions in the room, she steadied the flutters inside of her and asked, "Would you indulge my curiosity?"

He crossed his arms. "No."

"Why not?"

"Because I am not inclined."

"Really, Alastair! You can be quite selfish."

"Only 'quite' selfish? I must be softening in my old age."

Her lower lip dropped for a moment, but then she saw a small glimmer in his eyes and resolved that she would not permit him to rile her.

"At the gaming hall, you had threatened to shower me with praises for my *generosity*," he reminded her.

"Yes, and I did write you several letters to that effect. You responded to none of them."

"I grew weary of receiving them."

"You could have put an end to them if you but acquiesced to my request."

By saying nothing, he seemed to acknowledge her point.

"I merely wondered as to the purpose of a few items," she explained, opening the second drawer once more. She picked up a set of silver earrings with teardrop sapphires dangling from the bottoms. "These earrings, for instance. They are peculiar."

"Katherine encourages your pursuit in such matters. Why do you not ask her?"

"Because she is asleep. And you are...here."

In the dim and flickering light, she thought she saw a corner of his lips turn upward. "I will answer *one* question."

"You refused a far more significant request of mine."

"And because of that I am to grant all other requests of yours?"

"Why do you persist in being difficult? Does it amuse you to trifle with me?"

"The answer to your latter question is yes. As to the former, I will not encourage your prurience."

"Encourage my—" she gasped. "You had me take that—that ridiculously large shaft into my mouth!"

His smile reached both corners of his lips this time.

"How is that not encouraging my prurience?" she threw at him.

"I am at ease with my hypocrisy. If it unsettles *you*—"

She scowled. "You deserve to be turned over the knee and walloped."

"Undoubtedly."

"Very well," she said with a sigh, putting the earrings back, "but I shall divine the uses of these curious objects, if not from Katherine, then..."

He drew a step closer, and all humor had left his tone. "Then what?"

"Perhaps another visit to the Château Follet will—"

He grasped her arm and turned her to him. "You are not returning to the château."

His pronouncement nettled her. "Why not?"

"You have been there already."

"That is no answer at all. There is no reason I should not return there if I wish. And I would favor another visit."

"No reason? You would risk your honor, your family?"

"We have had this discussion before, Alastair."

She attempted to withdraw her arm, but he did not let her go.

"And even if I am ruined," she continued, "I still have a dowry of four thousand pounds for an incentive."

"The sort of man willing to take a compromised woman for four thousand pounds is not the sort of man you wish to marry."

"In truth, I have no wish to marry at all, but *you* and my parents have thrust the matter upon me."

"I will not accompany you to Château Follet."

"I did not expect you would. I certainly would not ask you to."

This seemed to startle him. "Then how—did Katherine offer to take you there?"

"No, she need not, but if I wrote to Madame Follet, I do not think she would deny me an invitation."

"And who would serve as your partner?"

"If you recall, a partner is not required. I can find someone there. And had you not intervened the last time, I might have found myself with the Viscount Devon."

She saw the vein at his temple throb and wondered if she ought not have mentioned Devon.

"You are bloody lucky you escaped his clutches," Alastair growled, his grip on her arm tightening. "I'll be damned if you let my prior efforts go to waste with that bleeder."

"Then satisfy my curiosity! Really, Alastair. I wonder at your sense sometimes."

A muscle along his jaw rippled, but he let her go. "*One* question, Millie. The hour is late."

She rolled her eyes, which she saw raised his ire. She watched him grab the earrings.

"These," he said, opening his hand, "are adornments. Not for the ears but for the nipples."

Her mouth fell open. That explained the angle of the clasps. She wondered how it would feel to have such things affixed to her body. A familiar ache grew between her legs.

"If I am in a decent mood tomorrow, you may ask a second question," Alastair said before turning to put the earrings—nipple rings, rather—back.

"But that was not my question," she protested. "If I am allotted but one question tonight, it would be this...will you take me?"

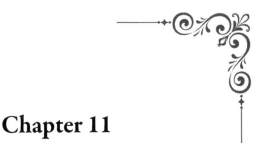

# Chapter 11

"HAVE YOU NO RESTRAINT, woman?" Alastair returned, trying to ignore the tension in his groin. His erection had already stretched when he saw those lovely lips encasing the large dildo.

She lifted her chin and spoke as if she had proposed nothing more than a game of whist. "I thought it was convenient, as I was here, you are here, and there is this room.... It is much more expedient than traveling to Château Follet."

He thought of the Viscount Devon. Once again his cousin had him against a wall, inspiring within him both resentment and awe.

"Millie," he warned.

"What do you care if you encourage my prurience?"

She had challenged him on this before, and he could provide no truly satisfactory response.

"As you are not being reasonable," he replied, "I am obliged to take that role."

"Reasonable? Is offering four thousand pounds for a dowry to a poor relation reasonable?"

"That has nothing to do with here and now."

"You are an odd one, Alastair. I think I liked you better when you were trying not to be reasonable. Your attempts to be good are rather trying."

He could not resist smiling.

"In truth," she contemplated, "it matters not what you do. Whether you encourage me or not, these wicked desires persist inside me. If I am to be shackled by matrimony in the near future, I will indulge my prurience while I can. I asked for your assistance, but if you will not provide it, I will find other ways to address my needs."

He did not doubt that she would.

"Very well, I shall grant this request of yours, and it shall be the last request I ever grant you. On one condition: you promise never to return to Château Follet."

In silence, she weighed his proposition before saying, "I want an experience as fulfilling as that which would occur at Château Follet. You will answer every curiosity of mine, indulge every whim, attend to every desire?"

He groaned as heat churned in his loins. "If you behave yourself."

"I will. I promise."

Blood surged through his cock. There was no turning back now, no matter how strongly his mind might be bent against it. "You will do my every bidding. I shall dictate the particulars. Your role is to submit to my handling. If you contravene me or defy me at any instant, my end of the arrangement may be forfeited."

She nodded before reaching for the nipple adornments.

He closed his hand before she could take them. "I want your word on Château Follet."

"I promise not to return to Château Follet. May I try the earrings—jewelry?"

A series of curses ran through his head, but he opened his hand. She took the sapphires.

He pushed aside the lapels of her robe and loosened the strings of her shift. With a crooked finger, he tugged the décolletage down. Her bosom rose as she inhaled. His knuckle brushed against the softness of her breast as he drew the shift down toward her nipple. The rosebud was already taut with anticipation. He nudged it before trapping it between his thumb and forefinger. He pulled gently. Her back arched subtly, sending her bosom closer to him. He rolled and flicked the nipple, slowly, teasingly, till her breath grew shorter. He pinched the nub, harder and harder, till she yelped. He released it and repeated the treatment on her other nipple. He pinched and twisted this one. She squirmed, not from pain, but from her arousal.

"May I try these now?"

"Not yet." He needed to ensure that her level of arousal was high enough for her to tolerate the discomfort of the clasps. He loosened the sash of her robe and cupped her mons. She gasped in surprise.

"Are you wet?"

"A little, I think."

His hand nestled farther between her thighs. Her dampness began to seep through the fabric to his fingers. She was more than a little wet. He rubbed her shift into her, making her moan. He watched as her lashes fluttered, her breath became uneven, and her mouth remained open, inviting him to kiss her, to force his tongue down into that lovely orifice.

She closed her eyes as he intensified his fondling. His fingers pressed the damp undergarment into her folds, grazing her clitoris. Her every reaction called to the primal in him, from the breaths that filled his ears to the scent of her arousal wafting through his nose.

She gave a small yelp, then giggled.

"Does it hurt?" he asked.

"It is but a slight pinching sensation."

He took her left hand and placed it between her legs. "Stroke yourself."

While she complied, he released her other hand from him and pulled the right side of her robe down her shoulder. The right side of the shift followed, baring the breast now adorned with the sapphire droplet. He stepped back to admire the jewelry dangling from her nipple and had to adjust his crotch. Should he allow her to spend, the more magnanimous part of him wondered?

No. She had not made it easy for him, and he would return the favor. She needed to appreciate the challenges present at Château Follet. The Viscount Devon would have shown her no mercy, and Alastair intended to cast away any chance that she might reconsider her promise to him.

For several minutes he watched her pleasure herself. "Do you wish to spend?"

She nodded. "Please, my lord."

"We should apply the mate."

He slid the left side of her robe off her shoulder, then pulled down the strap of the shift. He eyed her left breast in appreciation of its shape and paleness of skin. He cradled the orb, relishing the weight, the suppleness in his palm, and brushed his thumb over the already erect nipple. She shuddered. He kneaded the flesh, gently at first before manhandling it. She purred her preference. He tugged the nipple to ensure it was at its peak before applying the jewelry.

Her garments, which had fallen about her hips, slid to the floor. She shivered. Though it was a warmer autumn than in past years, the night air was still cool. A fire had not been lit in the room for many years. Her body would warm soon enough and be distracted by other more urgent sensations.

To cultivate her own heat, he cupped her head in both hands and lowered his mouth to hers. He kissed tenderly, teasing her, for she seemed to prefer a harder application of roughness. His tongue grazed her lips, and though she parted them, he did not dwell inside her mouth, taking light mouthfuls of the surface instead. A small whine grumbled low in her throat.

Relenting, to his own ardor as much as hers, he opened her mouth with his and pushed his tongue between her welcoming lips. He heard her sigh before he muffled her breaths. He probed the hot and wet orifice, crushing her lips so she grunted. Rather than yield, she met the assault upon her, her tongue licking at his as she shoved her mouth to him.

Her fervor took him by surprise. Perhaps time, and the suppression of her lust through it, had intensified her desires. Or perhaps it was the jewelry at her nipples that induced the need to release pressure or attention elsewhere. But he liked her passion, liked the dueling of their tongues and the forceful meeting of their mouths. He had a mind to lift her, spear himself into her then and there, but he had developed more patience during his time at Château Follet. He knew the benefits of delaying gratification.

He released her and stepped back to view her naked body. Her hair was tied in a plait behind her. Every part of her was exposed. He took her hand and replaced it at her mound. "Touch yourself again."

In silence, he watched her stroke herself for several minutes.

"Do you pleasure yourself at home?"

"Yes."

"How often?"

"It varies, my lord, but, on average, four or five times a week."

Surprised at the frequency, he said, "You are quite the little wanton, Millie."

She blushed. "How often do others of my sex pleasure themselves?"

"In truth, there are some, even those who have been guests at Château Follet, who do not engage in self-pleasure."

"That is sad, my lord, for though it does not afford me the satisfaction of congress, it is better than naught."

"You prefer to have cock?"

Her blush deepened. "I do, my lord."

His erection throbbed at her candor.

"May I ask a question, my lord?"

"You may."

"Will you take me now?"

All tension collapsed into the area of his groin. He thought his cock might burst through his pants. He took several deep breaths and would have remained silent had she not opened her eyes and looked at him. Of course he would have liked nothing better than to take possession of her, but she had asked for an experience comparable to one at the Château Follet. There were many experiences to be had there, and they were not all as accommodating as that which he had first provided her.

But she had made the promise he wanted to hear. And perhaps, if he satisfied her curiosity, the appeal of Château Follet may be diminished. It meant he would stay at Edenmoor longer than intended, but he found the prospect not quite as dreadful as expected.

# Chapter 12

"WE NEVER DID ATTEMPT the position of *Angelique et Medor*,"
Mildred added. When he made no response, she deduced he had forgotten the art room at Château Follet. She did not fault him. No
doubt it was not as memorable for him as it had been for her. "One
of the engravings from *The Sixteen Pleasures*."

"I recall it," he said, his voice husky.

Seeing the tenting at his crotch, she dared to saunter toward him.
Excitement tingled throughout her. Part of her remained in disbelief that, somehow, she had convinced Alastair to indulge her wanton desires. She was not vain enough to think that her powers of
seduction were so great. His motive was clear: he did not wish her
back at Château Follet. If it was out of regards to her safety, or what
he perceived to be in her best interest, then he was truly capable of
more consideration then she could have ever expected, but she also
suspected that he would rather have the Château to himself, without
having to share it with his cousin of all people.

And perhaps he was bored tonight. Perhaps he had not lain with
a woman in a while. Perhaps the bawdy art roused the carnal in him,
and her availability was more convenience than desirable.

It mattered not what his reasons were. Whatever they were, she
would not pass up the chance to take advantage of this opportunity.
Recalling all the delightful sensations he had once coaxed from her

body, she could have asked for no one better to engage in amorous waltz.

She reached for the sash of his banyan and slowly, as if not to scare a small animal, she loosened it. He said nothing as he allowed her to slip the banyan over his shoulders. She drew the silk robe down his arms and let it fall to the floor. His breath seemed to grow uneven.

He watched her as she attempted to unravel his cravat. Fortunately for her, his valet had styled the neckcloth more simply this evening. She removed his collar next, then kissed the small opening at the top of his shirt. At that, he gripped both her arms, making her gaze meet his.

"Millie, you may call an end to this arrangement whenever you wish."

She began to unbutton his waistcoat. "If I did, you would not have my promise not to return to Château Follet."

His countenance darkened "You expect that Katherine will take you there again?"

"Madame Follett has extended me an open invitation, as I am a good friend of Lady Katherine."

His frown deepened. "I have cautioned my aunt that the guests at Château Follet are less savory than in years past when Katherine and Richard visited."

With his waistcoat unbuttoned, she began to pull his shirt from his pants. When she slid a hand beneath the linen, he took in a sharp breath.

"Without my aunt, you would be hard-pressed to travel to Château Follet."

"If you think so, why make me promise not to return there?" she retorted.

"It is a precaution. You are both far more willful than you are wise."

Unsurprised, she merely replied, "You may be unkind to me as much as you wish, but you ought not speak of your aunt in such a manner. It would break her heart to hear you speak thus."

"It most certainly would not. I have said as much to her already."

She shook her head. Typical Alastair, and yet she had to marvel at his unabashed candor. He did not hide behind shallow pleasantries or fake compliments. She tried to pull his shirt out completely but was hampered by the braces he wore.

"You have never undressed a man, have you?" he asked.

"Pray, show me," she replied. Her pulse had quickened steadily throughout at the prospect of seeing him naked. The heat from between her thighs had spread to the rest of her body, which no longer minded the absence of clothing.

She watched with ravenous eyes as he shed his waistcoat and pulled the braces down his arms. He pulled his shirt over his head. Heat lanced through her as she beheld his chiseled chest, and she was once more reminded of how his features managed to entice her sex despite his poor manners. The Marquess was a handsome figure clothed. Unclothed, he was...exquisite.

"May I?" she asked, wanting to touch him.

Taking his silence, she put her hand to one pectoral. Without warning, he crushed her to him, his mouth descending upon hers. A thrill shot to the tips of her toes as she received his demanding kiss. She had only ever been with the stablehand, and the callow servant had none of the prowess of Alastair. His lips seared hers, hungry, forceful, commanding her mouth to allow him entry. The taste of him, the dance between their tongues as his lips caressed hers over and over all conspired to make her head swim. The throbbing between her legs grew. She ground herself against his hardness. He grunted as he continued exploring the depths of her mouth

His hand roamed her body, pressing the small of her back before cupping a buttock. The other hand went to the nape of her neck as his mouth ravaged her throat next. She shivered, relishing the way he filled her space, her senses. She wrapped her arms about his neck and moved her hips against him. How often had the lustful yearnings surged within her and found no release? She could hardly believe her fortune.

*Thank you, Alastair.*

She dared not speak it aloud for fear of distracting him. Wanting to encourage him, she rubbed herself against his crotch and dropped a hand to the buttons of his fall. She was not skilled enough to unbutton him while locked in his embrace, but he was. He undid the buttons and pulled out his shaft. She felt the smooth skin brush over her belly. If she could have jumped and impaled herself upon him, she would have done it. Her arousal demanded no less.

He wrapped an arm about her and lowered her with him to a nearby chair. Her legs straddled him as he sat down. She found she enjoyed the position as sitting astride his lap made her seem taller. He pulled her head down to his. Their lips met. The kiss began softly, but as the urgency grew between them, she crushed her mouth to his more forcefully. He matched her ardor with his own until their bodies could no longer resist the ultimate joining. He lifted her up by her rump. She dangled above his tip. He teased his hardness against her wet flesh before settling her down upon his shaft. Her lashes fluttered as she sank down and her quim clenched his member.

It felt as if her body had been made for this moment, for him. He made no movement, but his erection pulsed and flexed of its own accord, touching her most intimate places. She imagined being joined to him forever and doubted she would complain once.

He fondled a breast, kneading and rolling the supple flesh, before pinching and toying with the nipple, causing the tension between her thighs to throb. She tried to ease the pressure by kissing him harder.

Slowly, he pulled her hips toward him, grinding her groin to his. She moaned at the delicious sensations fanning through her loins. The yearning of the past several months compressed itself into the heat between her legs, the points of her breasts, the curl of her toes. With a rolling motion, he eased her up and down the length of his desire. When he transferred his hands to her breasts, she took over the motion of pumping herself atop him. His hands cupped her orbs and fondled them, building the pleasure within her. Unaccustomed to the exercise, her legs began to grow sore.

"Do not stop," he murmured against her lips.

She applied herself as best she could. The need inside her demanded her unrelenting effort, but the rhythm of her movements grew shaky. Perspiration covered her brow, her bosom, her legs. She could not recall when she had last made a comparable exertion.

He returned his hands to her hips to assist her, moving her as easily as if she were a ragdoll. With the muscles of her legs receiving relief, she was able to focus on the rapture. His grunting soon joined her moans. Briefly, she wondered if they ought to stop before a reckless accident should occur, but he had withdrawn from her last time. Surely he would do so again. But as she pondered whether or not she should voice the concern, her lust was lifted to a higher plane as he began to move his hips more forcefully, driving himself deeper into her. All thought was drowned out by carnal bliss, by rapture collapsing between her legs. Her mouth slid off his, and she shut her eyes to receive that most sublime euphoria. She cried out as spasms tore through her limbs. She would've fallen off him if not for his hold upon her. Ecstasy spiked through her, making her shudder and tremble and cry and whine. She collapsed against his chest. He held her as she shivered, her quim pulsing madly.

When the fierce thudding of her heart began to recede, she noticed she was still joined to him, could still feel his hardness occasionally flexing inside her.

"Do you wish to, er, finish?" she inquired.

He brushed a strand of hair from her face before easing her off him. She knelt beside him and watched him as he grasped his erection and tugged. His hand pumped rapidly along his shaft, his hips bucked, his muscles tensed, till his arousal flowed from him. His frame shuddered as the ejaculate shot forth. Afterwards, he slumped into the chair.

"How does the satisfaction of spending in this manner compare to other forms?" she asked.

He rolled his gaze to her. "From whence comes such boldness?"

"I am merely curious."

Reaching down to the clothes on the floor, he pulled a handkerchief from his waistcoat and wiped himself before answering, "It is sufficiently satisfying."

She dressed herself. "Is it better than intercourse—of the venereal sort?"

"Not always."

"Do you prefer one to the other?"

He had buttoned his fall and pulled on his shirt. "Damnation, Millie—"

"Does it disconcert you to speak of such matters?"

"It is not discourse I expect to have with my cousin."

"Will you not humor my queries?"

"I have humored you far more than I ought. Now go to bed. I shall leave a few minutes after should there be a servant awake and wandering the corridors."

Deciding not to test his patience, she secured her robe about her and took her leave. She returned to her own chambers with light steps. Once settled in her own bed, she found sleep eluded her. Her mind wanted to recite all that had transpired. What might she dare with Alastair tomorrow?

# Chapter 13

WHEN MILDRED ENTERED the breakfast parlor looking a little fatigued, Alastair felt a modicum of guilty satisfaction that he was the cause of her weariness.

Recalling last night, he felt a tug at his groin and shifted where he sat. Having finished his breakfast, he sat apart from the others with the newspaper and watched as Millie accepted a cup of coffee.

"Did you sleep well, my dear?" Katherine asked. "You appear weary."

Alastair thought he detected a blush in Millie's cheeks, but she kept her gaze lowered. He wondered if she would dare look at him.

"I think I had perhaps too much tea late in the day, and that kept me awake," Millie replied.

"I fear the toast and ham are no longer warm, but I can have fresh toast and eggs brought up."

"That won't be necessary, my lady. I am more than happy with what is here."

After seeing his daughter take but a nibble of the toast, Mr. Abbott said, "You must partake of more, Millie. The bread is freshly baked, and the eggs are but the day-old. You'll not find a finer breakfast."

"But not too much," Mrs. Abbott objected. "A young woman must mind her figure. While a dowry of four thousand pounds may go far, a woman's appearance still is of significant value to the other sex. Though her current form is acceptable, Millie could certainly benefit from losing a little of her weight."

Millie gazed deeper into her cup of coffee.

"I do not think your daughter wants for anything more," said Katherine. "She is lovely as she is."

"That is most generous of you to say, my lady, and we are appreciative of your kindness. A mother wants only what is best for her daughter. Millie benefits from the gowns she wears. The looseness of the skirts hides her form."

As one who had seen her—all of her—without clothing, in bare naked glory, Alastair was a little tempted to respond that Millie's form was more than acceptable. True, it was not perfect, but he had come to appreciate her wider hips and even the roundness of her belly. She was still delightful to the touch.

Sitting at the second table, Thomas asked, "How shall we amuse ourselves today, Papa? May we go hunting?"

"Yes, I think that would be in order," replied Edward. "By all means, let us all have a hunt."

"I think I shall stay inside and read," said Jason.

"What? Not go hunting on such a fine day as this?"

"Would you like to stay and knit purses as well?" Thomas mocked his brother.

"No, no, my boy. We will all take part in the sport."

It was decided then that the men would go hunting, while the women would prepare a picnic to be shared by all at the end of the hunt. But as the men expected to be hunting for a length, Mrs. Abbott deemed she had enough time to sit and rest a while upon the veranda. Mrs. Cheswith would pen a letter to her sister-in-law while Katherine would finalize preparations for the Michaelmas dinner.

"I will keep you company," Katherine offered to Millie when the others left their tables to prepare for the day's activities.

"I would not keep you, my lady," said Millie as she accepted a second cup of coffee. "I know you must have matters to attend."

"Perhaps Alastair can keep you company for a few minutes."

He halted on his way out of the room, and was prepared to decline his aunt's uninvited suggestion, when Millie responded, rather quickly, "I am perfectly at ease in my own company."

At that moment, Kittredge stumbled into the room. He shielded his eyes from the brightness before taking a seat beside Mildred.

"Good morning, Lady Katherine," he greeted.

"Ah, I have company now," Millie remarked. "There is no need for you to stay."

Katherine rose from her seat, but Alastair decided to remain, curious as to why Millie was so eager to be rid of his company. It was she who had insisted that their interactions remain as they were despite what had transpired between them at Château Follet.

"I will stay with my guest," he offered.

"Ha!" Kittredge grumbled. "Since when do you care to extend me such courtesies?"

"Is it not enough I make my cellar available to you?"

"I own it is more than enough."

"As I have finished," said Millie, rising from the table, "I will leave you gentlemen in each other's company."

"Sit," Alastair bid. "You will not want Kittredge to think his presence has driven you away."

She looked at him as if to say "indeed, it is your presence that I wish to avoid." Instead, she gave Kittredge a smile before retaking her seat.

"Finish your toast," he said after noticing she had barely eaten half.

"I am no longer hungry."

"You will require sustenance to see you through the activities of the day—and evening."

"A woman must mind her figure."

He lifted his brows at her resistance. "You are fortunate not to be my daughter, or such *disobedience* would merit *punishment*."

She drew in a sharp breath and pressed her lips together. She knew he had chosen his words with purpose. He stared at her, daring her to continue her defiance. She looked at her toast, applied a little more jam, and took a bite.

"What are to be the day's activities?" Kittredge asked between mouthfuls of ham and toast.

"The men are to go hunting," Millie answered, "and we shall all have a picnic afterwards."

"And what of the evening? What is planned?"

Millie looked to Alastair, but he said nothing, waiting to see how she would reply.

"Nothing as of yet," she said. "Lady Katherine's nieces are expected today, and we shall certainly want their opinion if they are not too tired from their travels."

"I had thought from what Alastair said that something had been decided upon."

A blush crept up her cheeks, but she replied with calm, "I would hazard that Alastair's evening plans entail a hearty round of cards or dice, though I wonder that it will satisfy him, as our play will not rival what he is accustomed to at his gaming hells."

"Not to worry. I take it that is why he brought me along, though I doubt even he would be rude enough to expect that the ladies will match his level of play."

"I absolutely would," said Alastair, as Millie replied, "He absolutely would."

They glanced at each other. Kittredge laughed. "By Jove, she knows you well, Alastair. And dares to show it. Your bravery is impressive, Miss Abbott."

"We shall see where her bravery lands her," Alastair said, his hand itching to deliver a spanking. He had the satisfaction of seeing her disconcerted, but his cousin would not be cowed.

"Surely you are not threatened by what you must own to be an honest assessment of your character? Your candor of your faults is what is impressive."

"Ah, you have redeemed yourself, Miss Abbott," Kittredge praised. "I would be hard-pressed to find a compliment for Alastair. You are clever as well, Miss Abbott."

Alastair gazed upon Millie. She spoke with sincerity and, when she was critical of him, there was not the judgment of how he ought to behave. For that reason, he allowed her remarks to pass. "Finish your toast, Miss Abbott."

"Does he always order you about in such fashion?" Kittredge asked.

"Does he not do the same with everyone? He has quite the high opinion of himself."

That was a jibe. Alastair reconsidered the tolerance he granted his cousin. "Oh, he bullies me about all the time, but I welcome it, for he would only do so if he considered it worth his while. Thus, he considers *you* worth his while. It is quite the compliment, for very few satisfy this criterion for him."

"I think you credit me too much, Mr. Kittredge. He only orders me about because it amuses him to vex me."

"Do you think so? Then subvert his goals and pay no heed to what he says."

Alastair grinned at the difficult place Millie found herself in, though Kittredge had intended his advice to be friendly.

"She disobeys at her peril," Alastair drawled. "Finish your toast, Millie."

"Good God, man, are you her father and she a child?"

She frowned, clearly not wanting to capitulate to his orders before Kittredge, but not wanting the consequences of defying her cousin.

"Surely he jests!" Kittredge said. "What can he do to you?"

"I must be careful, Mr. Kittredge," Millie said. "I am afforded a dowry thanks to his generosity. He can give or take it away as he pleases."

"Or raise it," Alastair said.

"You see, I am at his mercy, Mr. Kittredge."

"No, no, Alastair is not as bad as that," his friend protested. "He would not hold your dowry hostage and cares not about your toast. Finish it only if it pleases you."

"Your attempts to play the white knight are unwarranted here," Alastair said. "Miss Abbott is no maiden in need of rescue. She is quite adroit at getting what she wants."

"And now he means to impugn my character," Millie said, putting her hand to her brow in mock despair.

"You, sir, truly are a blackguard," Kittredge declared.

"Stop. I cannot have you at odds. Alastair has few friends, and I will not have your friendship sullied. I will eat the toast to keep the peace." She took a large bite.

Alastair allowed her the escape she had conjured. He was confident she would have eaten the toast to satisfy him.

"There now," she said when she had finished off the toast. "Are you pleased, my lord?"

"Do not test my patience again," he warned.

Kittredge shook his head. "I hope you do not intend to browbeat your future wife in this manner. I wonder that Lady Sophia would endure such behavior."

Millie sat at attention. "Future wife?"

"If this is how treats the fair sex, I doubt any woman would have him."

Alastair said nothing. He had no doubts that he could train Lady Sophia to be as obedient as his dogs, but, for the present, it was more amusing to compel Millie into obedience.

"Alastair will never want for marital prospects."

"I suppose not. Well, Miss Abbott, accept my condolences for your forced kinship to the man."

"Kittredge," Alastair said, "knows full well that if I bid him eat toast, he would do it."

"I would indeed. I am far too invested in his collection of burgundy—I swear he must purchase his wine from smugglers—to risk losing his friendship over a piece of toast. And I suppose Miss Abbott is indebted to you for her dowry, or such an intelligent woman would not heed you in the least."

Alastair did not dispute his friend, but Millie knew full well that he had other forms of persuasion. Breakfast being at an end, Kittredge offered his arm to Millie. Alastair was content to walk behind them. The silly business with the toast had arisen on a whim, but he was satisfied that he had put Millie on notice and even discomfited her a little. He suspected, however, that Millie would not be easily cowed. He would have to assert himself even more if he were to convince her that she was no match for the Château Follet and its practices.

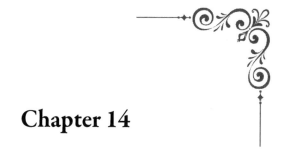

# Chapter 14

THEY HAD NOT AGREED to take their role-playing beyond the night, beyond the doors of the play room, Mildred huffed as she scanned the book titles in Lady Katherine's library. She could only put half her mind, however, to the task of finding a good book for Jason. Her time at breakfast with Alastair and Kittredge still rankled her. If he had made a polite request for her to finish her toast, she might have done so without protest.

No, she would've pointed out that what she ate was no affair of his. She had asked for this, after all, though she had not considered breakfast to be part of the arrangement. Nevertheless, she had invited him to take the role of master, and she had been more than willing to submit to his commands last night.

Last night. Her body flushed at the memories. She could hardly wait for tonight. Should she confess that she had been unable to follow his bidding, unable to withhold herself from spending? But then, what might he do? Would she have lost any chance of experiencing the reward he had promised? Could she, perhaps, find a way to make up for her misstep?

She would have time to think on it while Alastair and the rest of the men were out hunting.

She returned to looking at the books on the bookshelf. There were a good many books she thought Jason would enjoy. She wondered if he had read *Gulliver's Travels* by Jonathan Swift? She pulled the book from the shelf.

"I hope you will not make it a habit to disagree with me?"

She whirled around to find Alastair standing inches from her. His nearness ruffled her more than she liked.

"Perhaps I would not if you were not so overbearing," she replied after she had regained her balance. "I was not aware that our arrangement last night allowed you to order me about at all times."

He took a step closer, and she would have retreated if the bookcase behind her did not block her.

"It most certainly did. Perhaps next time you will be more careful with what you request."

She bristled, though he had a point. "And do you approach me now to order me about some more?"

"I do indeed."

Her pulse surged. She glanced past him to see that they were alone.

"I do not think we shall be discovered, but let that be an incentive for you to comply as swiftly as possible."

She embraced the book she held as if it were a shield that could protect her. She looked up at him. "What is it you wish?"

Instead of answering, he closed the distance between them, bumping her into the bookshelf. He curled his fingers about the back of her neck and pressed her chin up with his thumb. She quivered inside as her breath grew uneven. He gazed down at her, and she saw his pupils dilate. Did he mean to kiss her? She very much hoped he would.

When he lowered his head, she closed her eyes so that all her senses could focus on the touch of his lips upon hers. The kiss was soft and gentle but set off a riot inside her body. Desire flamed anew.

With his hand still wrapped about her neck, he pulled her even closer so that his mouth pressed hard against hers. He parted her lips with his and took mouthfuls of her, sweeping her breath away. The book slid from her grasp, and he grunted when it landed upon his boot.

"Sorry," she mumbled.

He slammed his body into hers, pinning her to the shelves, before resuming his assault upon her mouth.

As much as his kisses thrilled her, she murmured, "Alastair, we must not."

She made a feeble attempt to push him away with a hand, but he pinioned the offending hand to the bookcase. She was trapped. And the possibility that they might be discovered in a compromising way toyed with her ardor.

"Someone might come upon us." She gasped as his mouth trailed to her neck. When his lips caressed her throat, the last of her resistance melted. She wrapped her free arm about him and threaded her fingers through his soft dark locks. She tilted her hips toward him, and she thought she could feel the hardness at his crotch.

He pressed his pelvis into her, making her head whirl. Lust overcame discretion, and she moaned as he kissed whole patches up and down her neck. His hand slid from her neck to cup a breast. She wished she did not have to wear stays so that she could better feel his hand upon her. Nonetheless, she thrilled to his every touch. When he moved his hand to her back, she relished being in his embrace. Truly, there was nothing this man could do that did not excite a response from her body.

Their lips joined once more, and she kissed him back. There was no consideration of what the end would be, for perhaps their actions would only stoke an aggravation that could not be satisfied till later that night. It might even be his intention to set her up for torment, for surely he did not intend to take her here in the library. Yet, knowing this, she could not stay herself from the present temptation. If they were to cease, he would have to initiate it.

He withdrew to give her a chance to catch her breath, and, pressing his forehead to hers, he asked, his own breath a little haggard, "Are you wet?"

"I am not certain. Perhaps."

He took a step back and began unbuttoning his fall. Her eyes widened.

"On your knees, my dear."

"Not *here*. Alastair!"

But his member sprang free. She could not help but stop and admire the stiff and ready pole, but her senses appealed once more. "This is your aunt's home!"

"Katherine would be the least astonished."

She looked to the door.

"If you are worried, I suggest you act quickly."

She was still flustered but sank to the ground. She clasped her hand about his delightful member. A sound in the corridor made her scramble back up to her feet, but the doors to the library remained closed. She looked to Alastair to see if he had changed his mind, but he only waited. Relenting, she settled herself back on her knees, took him in hand, and fitted her mouth over its tip.

*Dear God*, what had she gotten herself into?

Taking her by the back of her head, he guided her mouth farther down his shaft. She licked and sucked, hoping he would not expect a long session. He emitted a low groan. She tried to take all of him, but she could not relax enough to do so. He shifted his hand to the back of her neck so that he would not muss her hair and guided her up and down his shaft.

Surely he did not intend to make her apply herself till he spent? But fearing that he would, she attended to him with as much vigor as she could.

Heat swirled in her loins, for she wished such easy attention could be had for her own body. She enjoyed his shaft, even tasting the saltiness of his seed. She liked knowing that she could arouse him to such hardness. She could sense his desperation in the way he bucked his hips at her.

With a muffled roar, he dispensed his seed.

She had nowhere to turn, for he held the base of her head still. The hairs at his groin nearly tickled her nose. A tangy flavor filled her mouth as she tried not to balk at the load. She swallowed as best she could, gagging a little until he withdrew. Nothing could surpass the wantonness of what she had just done. And she had done it in Lady Katherine's library. It was more than fortunate that no one had come upon them, but there was no denying that the fear of being caught added to the titillation.

"My God," Alastair breathed.

When he fixed a starry gaze upon her face, she returned an impish smile.

He went to his knees and, clasping her head in both hands, crushed his mouth atop hers. The kiss reached into the depths of her mouth, as if he sought to taste himself in her. Heat swirled in her loins, and she knew for certain now that she was wet between the legs.

"I have something for you," he whispered into her ear.

Her pulse quickened. Would he attend her somehow? Her body desperately desired it, but she did not wish to risk them further.

He buttoned his fall first. From inside his coat, he drew out a small box and opened it. Inside, upon the silk cushioning, lay two silver balls, both of which could easily fit in the palm of her hand.

"What are they?"

"Chinese pleasure balls."

He had her sit upon the floor and lift her skirts.

"I think we should—" she hesitated.

"Do not delay, lest you wish to suffer the consequences later tonight."

Reluctantly, she inched her skirts over her bent knees.

"Farther," he commanded.

She bunched the skirts at the tops of her thighs. He spread her knees apart, and the warmth of her body extended to her cheeks at the exposure. He picked up one of the balls between thumb and forefinger and rubbed it against her folds. Pressing deeper, he coated it with her nectar. Closing her eyes, she leaned back and allowed her head to fall against the books. Perhaps she would risk it. At present, he could put anything to her quim, and she would find it pleasurable.

She gasped and sat up when he pushed the ball inside of her. The second ball soon followed. How odd. She had not guessed that this would be their purpose.

He pulled her skirts back over her legs and assisted her to her feet.

"Oh my," she gasped as the balls moved. They even seemed to quiver, as if the tiniest hammer were striking her most intimate areas.

"The balls have small weights inside them," Alastair explained.

"Ah." She knit her brows till the balls settled in place.

"They will stay till I remove them."

She stared at him in stunned silence.

"Do your best to keep them. You will not want to constantly replace them."

"I am to walk in these?"

"Till I remove them."

He backed away from her to give her room. She took a small step and immediately felt the movement of the balls. Worried that they might fall out, she clenched her cunnie.

"It is not possible," she murmured.

"I gave you the lightest pair I could find."

She tried another step. "No, no, this is too awkward."

If she were walking in private, she might enjoy these delightful balls. But to have them inside her as she went about the day was too much. And what if she should lose one?

"How long am I to have these pleasure balls?"

"As I said, till I have them removed."

"And when will that be?" She looked to the long case clock at the corner of the room. Would he make her wear these for ten minutes? Half an hour? One hour?

"I have not yet decided. Perhaps all day."

"All day!" she cried.

He bent down and picked up her book, handing it back to her before making his way to the doors.

"Alastair!"

"Be grateful, Millie. If we were at Château Follet, I could make you wear a chastity belt of iron."

He turned back to the doors and unlocked them.

Her mouth fell open. "They were locked all this time?"

He grinned. "They were."

She would have liked to have thrown *Gulliver's Travels* at him.

"After you, my lady," he said, opening a door.

She trembled with anger but sauntered toward him. She moaned as the balls rolled and bumped each other, sending ripples throughout her nether region. Seeing his look of amusement, she suppressed the urge to glare at him. She would show him instead her poise, and that she was worthy of the experience she had requested of him.

"Thank you, my lord," she said as she swept by him.

"There you are," exclaimed Kittredge. "Mrs. Cheswith asked if I was to join the hunt, and I thought of passing since Alastair and I have been at it for a few days already. She suggested a ride, and I think it a capital idea. Would you care to join us, Miss Abbott?"

"Thank you, but I think I shall spend a quiet morning reading," she answered. The last thing she wanted, with these balls inside of her, was to be bounced about on the back of a horse.

"But we may never see such pleasant weather again till the spring," said Alastair.

She tried not to scowl at him. "I am a poor rider and would slow the party."

"I doubt Mrs. Cheswith will want to ride fast or break into gallop."

Millie frowned at the thought of the balls bouncing madly inside of her if she were to ride at full gallop.

"I think I shall read, then assist with the picnic preparations."

"My aunt and the servants can attend to the picnic," said Alastair. "You should ride, Millie."

He meant it as a command. What a treacherous man her cousin could be!

"Then let it be a short ride."

Kittredge turned to Alastair. "And will you join us?

"I think I shall."

Her heart plummeted. With Alastair along, there would be no relief for her. The faintest regret began to creep into her. Perhaps it had been unwise to submit her request to Alastair. She eyed him, wondering why he was being so vexing. Was this truly how men were at Château Follet? She thought of the Viscount Devon. Would he have made her carry Chinese pleasure balls inside her cunnie while horseback riding? Or was such cruelty unique to her cousin?

She believed the latter.

# Chapter 15

THOUGH IT MIGHT NOT have been clear to the others, Alastair could tell when the jostling discomfited her and knew that the blush in her cheeks was not the result of the occasional breeze that blew their way. Nonetheless, Millie bore the riding well and even appeared to bond with Kittredge over their observations of *him*.

"Alastair has more virtues than is credited to him," Millie said. "For example, he is quite equal and fair in his treatment of compliments and criticism directed at him. He pays neither any heed."

"How true," Kittredge acknowledged. "I had never considered that Alastair possessed any virtues."

"Beyond his wine cellar?"

Kittredge laughed. "Yes, yes. Perhaps most of us do not see his virtues because they are dwarfed by his failings."

"We all have failings, Mr. Kittredge."

"And you are kind to grant your cousin an allowance for his."

Accustomed to Kittredge's mockeries, Alastair said nothing. As he watched Millie stumble off her horse despite Kittredge assisting her, he reminded himself that *she* had requested her situation. Soon enough she would deem that the debauchery of Château Follet was too much for her.

But he had thought the same before, and she had surprised him. Just as she had surprised him with how well she had taken his member in the library. He had not intended to spend, but she had gained in skill somehow. Her hot, wet mouth wrapped about his member had been absolutely divine, and he had approached his climax with stunning speed.

"Are you well, Miss Abbott?" Kittredge asked, holding her arm to steady her. "If you will not mind my saying, you appear rather flushed."

"It is merely from the exercise. I am not much accustomed to riding," she had answered.

"The coloring in your cheeks becomes you."

Alastair, having just dismounted, raised his brows, for Kittredge spoke with uncharacteristic sincerity. He observed the two sharing a smile while he handed his horse to the stable hand.

"Come, Millie," Anne beckoned, "let us exchange these riding garments for more fitting attire for the picnic."

From Millie's expression, Alastair gathered her "more fitting" attire differed little from what she currently wore, but she followed Anne into the house. The men had to change as well, and Alastair decided he would give Millie a reprieve from the Chinese pleasure balls. Stopping her before she entered her chambers, he handed her the box that the balls had come in.

"You may remove them," he told her.

Relief flooded her countenance. "Thank you, my lord. They are wrongly named."

"They brought you no pleasure?"

"Can you imagine being bounced about with two balls inside you? They were the worst possible distraction. I could hardly keep my mind off them."

"You seemed to do just fine, but if they did not arouse you, then they failed in their purpose."

The blush in her cheeks deepened, and he had to agree that the rosiness became her.

"That is precisely the difficulty! I should not be put in such a state when in the company of others."

"Take heart. Perhaps you shall be rewarded for your sufferings."

He took pleasure in considering the many ways he could reward her, provided that she had followed his directive not to spend.

"HOW LONG DO YOU STAY, Alastair? Alastair!"

Louisa's voice broke through his reverie. She had arrived with her husband and daughter a few hours ago. Caroline and her husband were also there.

"Kittredge and I depart the morning after Michaelmas," he answered.

"Why such a short stay?"

Alastair was tempted to quip that it was a longer stay than he had intended, but decided to make an attempt to be civil to his sister at his aunt's table. "I had agreed to meet with Mr. Farnsworth regarding a bill he hopes I will support in the House of Lords."

This seemed to perk Millie's interest. She asked, "What is it Mr. Farnsworth proposes?"

He regretted his answer now, for he had no interest to bring about a discussion of a political nature. He returned to cutting the venison on his plate, but answered, "To raise the destruction of stocking frames to a capital felony."

"And punishable by death?" she exclaimed.

He chewed his venison without looking at her, but she would not leave the subject alone.

"That is unnecessarily excessive! Is the punishment of transportation not harsh enough?"

"Alas, it seems not," said Charles, Louisa's husband. "I understand that more of our soldiers are fighting Luddites than are fighting Napoleon on the Iberian Peninsula."

"We cannot afford to war with our own citizens till the threat of Napoleon is eliminated," added Mr. Abbott.

"But surely there is a better solution than executing our own citizens, men who are merely fearing for their livelihoods," Millie persisted.

"*Merely* fearing?" Louisa asked. "I would hesitate to condone the willful destruction of property."

"I do not condone it, but how does the destruction of property merit the taking of a life?"

Clearly not wanting a divisive discussion involving her daughter, Mrs. Abbott interjected, "Lady Katherine, I cannot compliment your chef enough. I have never tasted venison prepared with such rich flavors! You say you have a French chef?"

"I do, but he does wonders with English puddings," Katherine replied.

Alastair could see that Millie was not satisfied with the end of the conversation, but she took her mother's intimation and returned to eating her dinner. Later, Alastair overheard her ask Kittredge what he thought of the Farnsworth proposal.

"Oh, I never have an opinion on political topics," Kittredge returned. "It is an area that will win you many more enemies than friends."

"I thought perhaps it was the Lady Sophia who compels your return to London more than Farnsworth," Louisa voiced.

"Will you never cease to take an interest in my affairs?" Alastair returned. He knew Louisa favored a match between him and the Duke of Wakecastle.

She huffed. "I *am* your sister."

"While that entitles you to have opinions of my affairs, I am under no obligation to heed them."

Her jaw dropped, though she was hardly new to his rudeness.

"I say, Alastair," Edward tried, "I think my dear cousin merely wishes to understand that all is well with you."

"You are too generous, Edward. What you deem a polite interest is little more than prying." He pushed himself away from the table and rose to his feet.

"I do not deserve such criticism!" Louisa objected.

"Perhaps not," Katherine said, "but you should know by now not to tempt the devil."

"Your pardon, my lady," he said to his aunt, "I will excuse myself before I offend further."

Knowing her nephew well, Katherine waved a dismissive hand. An awkward silence fell upon the table while Louisa continued to fume. This was precisely why he had not wished to attend the gathering for Michaelmas, and he decided then and there that he would refuse any invitation for Christmas.

He would depart Edenmoor on the morrow if he could, but first he had to deal with Millie. It was one event he looked forward to during his stay here, and he had much in store for her.

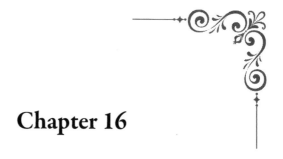

# Chapter 16

"I THINK ANDRE DELIGHTS in abusing me!" Louisa lamented after dinner as they gathered for cards in the drawing room.

"That is what comes of being the first and only son. He was far too pampered in his upbringing," Caroline consoled. Then, realizing that Lady Katherine stood near, she added, "I know not what villainy he would have fallen into if not for the influence of our kind aunt."

Their husbands, not knowing whether to fear their wives or Alastair more, remained silent.

The Abbotts, Lady Katherine, and her son formed one table. Mrs. Cheswith opted not to play. The rest of the men formed another table, leaving Millie to play with Alastair's sisters and Emily. Millie had been grateful not to have had many words with Louisa or Caroline. She had felt the former's study upon her since the lady arrived. But now she would be forced to interact with Alastair's sisters.

"Whist," Louisa declared. "I will play nothing else."

She looked to Millie as if daring her to disagree.

"If it pleases you, Mrs. Wilmington," Millie said in friendly way.

"Now then, Miss Abbott, it seems you have many a political opinion?" Louisa asked as Caroline shuffled the cards.

Millie withheld from saying that she had thus far offered an opinion on one subject only, but replied that she did.

"If I were you, I would not offer them frequently," Louisa contin-ued. "Men may regard you a *bluestocking*, and even a dowry of four thousand pounds may not influence them to think otherwise."

"I should not hold such men in much esteem if they allowed money to sway their true opinions of me, but I am sorry that I spoke when I did. It was perhaps not the best subject for discourse at din-ner."

"Indeed. I mean only to provide the advice of a sister. A young woman who is too outspoken risks being deemed a conceit, and you have no wish to challenge my brother on such matters. Surely you do not expect a member of the House of Lords to consider the thoughts of one less practiced in the affairs of the kingdom?"

"I am not equal to his station," Millie conceded, certain that is what Louisa meant, "but I have not given up hope that his lordship is so dismissive of his fellow men that he will hear nothing of what they have to say."

"Oh, but he is!" Caroline cried. She finished dealing the cards.

Louisa narrowed her eyes. "There are not many in this world who would come to Andre's defense. Most would say he is arrogant, dismissive and discourteous. Boorish, even. No one is spared his dis-dain, not even his family."

"Especially his family," Caroline added.

"Would you not agree with this assessment of my brother, Miss Abbott?"

Alastair sat at the table beside theirs and could undoubtedly hear many a word.

"I am far too indebted to your family to speak ill of anyone," Millie replied. She could not disagree with Louisa without offending her, nor agree with her without offending the Marquess.

"Is Alastair as generous with others in your family as he is with you?"

"I am not aware of all that he does, but he is better equipped to answer your question."

Millie lost many a hand at whist, for, having to attend to Louisa's questioning with carefully crafted responses, she could not concentrate on her play. When they finally called an end to cards, Millie felt as if she had survived several jousting matches. She knew not what Louisa wished she would say. On the matter of the dowry, she told Louisa, "I would his lordship were not so generous. I certainly do not deserve such charity."

Louisa sniffed. "It is almost unseemly and raises many questions."

"I would his lordship could be persuaded to adjust the amount to a more appropriate sum."

That had seemed to appease Louisa a little. She turned to Caroline. "Have you spoken with him?"

"He has even less regard for me," Caroline replied.

After the card tables were put away, the Abbotts and Lady Katherine declared the hour well past their bedtimes. The Wilmingtons and Brewsters also retired, as the day's traveling had fatigued them. Mrs. Cheswith went to look in on her children, for Henry would often experience nightmares. Edward chose a book to read, and Kittredge had settled himself on the sofa and closed his eyes.

Millie, too agitated with the prospect of meeting with Alastair later, had no wish for the solitude of her chambers.

"Do you come to rebuke me for my treatment of my sisters?" Alastair asked when she approached the sideboard where he stood.

"I came to pour myself a glass of port," she answered, "and your relationship with your sisters is none of my affair."

"Would you agree they merit my insolence?"

"Even if they should deserve it on the grandest scale, and I do not mean to say that they do, must you respond with insolence?"

He returned a wry grin. "You suffered them with grace. I heard their every word."

Millie sipped the port she had poured.

"You may speak your mind freely with me, Millie. I am well acquainted with the nature of overbearing."

"I had much rather discuss this bill for the destruction of stocking frames."

"And I do not."

"But what think you of his proposal?"

"I am inclined to support Mr. Farnsworth."

"Death ought to be reserved for the worst of crimes."

"The destruction of property is a severe crime, and you pursue this discussion at your peril."

She hesitated, not knowing what he intended, but she could not resign the topic. "Have you no sympathy for the plight of these men?"

He narrowed his eyes at her.

"I do not say that they should go unpunished for their crimes, but it is out of fear for their livelihoods that they resort to such actions."

"What of the mill owners and the laborers who work the stocking frames? Would you stop industry and the progress of technology?"

"Perhaps the weavers and others of their trade would feel less threatened if they had other resources, such as the ability to combine and negotiate with their employers as a collective."

"Such actions are illegal."

"Then repeal the Combination Acts and permit workers to form such societies. What they seek—wages that will prevail with the rising cost of goods—is not unreasonable. But they are rendered unable to help themselves, and the balance of power lies with the mill owners."

"Now is not the time to encourage Jacobinism."

"Is it wrong to want better wages and better working conditions?"

Alastair leaned in toward her and spoke softly so that no one else would hear. "Is your backside prepared to take the consequences of your colloquy?"

Her cheeks burned and she finished the rest of her port in one gulp. "Forgive me if I did not think you so heartless that you would acquiesce to hanging a man without consideration for the arguments against such judgments."

"Such arguments will undoubtedly be made by the likes of Burdett."

"And the likes of me ought have no opinion of value." Vexed, she turned to pour herself another glass of Madeira.

He stayed her hand. "One glass will do for you."

She opened her mouth to protest, but she had no wish to make a scene over an inconsequential glass of wine. Perhaps it was best she retire to her own chambers.

"I will bid you good night, Alastair," she said, setting down her glass and turning on her heels.

"Midnight," he told her. "And not a minute late."

Her heart palpitated. She dared not look back.

Midnight could not come soon enough.

# Chapter 17

ALASTAIR WAS WAITING for her when she entered the room. Her body's senses heightened at the mere sight of him. He sat in an armchair in his banyan, open to reveal his shirtsleeves. She hoped he would disrobe and treat her to the vision of his naked body.

"What shall we attempt tonight?" she inquired, try not to appear too eager.

"The engraving of *Angelique et Medor* was your favorite among the *I Modi*, was it not?"

She was surprised he remembered that it was her favorite. She felt almost giddy. "Yes."

"Are you certain your legs have the stamina for the position depicted in that engraving?"

"I should like to try."

"I will grant your desire if you behave."

"Have I not done your bidding today? I took those dreadful balls, did I not?"

He smiled. "Indeed. How were they dreadful?"

"I think you must know."

He rose from the chair. "I wish to hear your explanation."

He was taunting her, but she would indulge him for she wanted to experience *Angelique et Medor*.

"I said earlier that they were distracting."

"How so?"

217

She tried not to glare at him. "Because my attention was between my legs the whole time, and it was more than devilish of you to make me ride with those things inside of me."

"I could have made you wear them through dinner."

She paled at the thought. *That* would have been horrendous.

"You have no wish to try them again?"

"Heavens no!"

"Why not?"

"Not only were they an awful distraction, they produced a most inconvenient agitation."

"They aroused you."

Heat traveled up her cheeks. The area between her legs pulsed with the memory. She nodded.

"They produced such wetness, I had to send the dressing maid away."

His eyes dilated, and his breath deepened. "Surely you did not undress yourself."

"I told the maid I was much fatigued from riding and would take a nap before I changed."

"And did you?"

His gaze traversed her body, seeming to take in the swell of her breasts and the thin shift she wore beneath her robe. She grew warm beneath his stare. "I did not."

"What did you do instead?"

She pursed her lips before replying, "I relieved the agitation caused by those bloody balls."

A muscle rippled along his jaw. "Show me."

She hesitated. Given all that had transpired between them, perhaps she should be comfortable rather than awkward at the prospect of displaying herself before him.

"I was in bed."

"We have a bed."

He glanced in its direction, and she knew he meant for her to lie upon it. Reluctantly, she sauntered over and sat down.

"Did you remove your skirts first?"

"No, I was in too much haste to release the balls. Once they were out..."

She took in a slow breath, seeking to tame her quickened pulse.

"Once they were out," he prompted.

"I laid down and pleasured myself."

"Demonstrate precisely what you did."

She lay back upon the bed and drew the shift past her knees. She paused. "You have a purpose in this?"

"Perhaps. Perhaps not. But the sooner you apply yourself, the sooner you may realize the role of Angelique."

She thrust her hand beneath her shift and sought that nub of desire between her folds. She stroked the flesh with her forefinger. He pulled her shift past her hips so that he could see everything. She hoped that he would not make her caress herself for long as she much preferred intercourse to self-pleasure. He undid the sash of her robe, which he then opened. He palmed a breast through her shift.

"Do you ever fondle your own breasts?"

"At times."

Pushing the shift down, he pulled out an orb. "Why not more often? They are such beauties."

He took her left hand and placed it upon her left breast. She groped and kneaded herself, hardly believing she was splayed upon the bed, arousing herself in such wanton display. Despite the embarrassment, her middle finger continued to coax the hunger budding between her legs.

"How many times did you bring yourself to spend?"

"Twice."

He attended to her other breast, gripping it, squeezing it, and rolling it over her chest. He pinched the nipple and pulled it lightly.

"You have quite the carnal appetite, Millie."

"I would rather I did not."

"Why, when the rewards are so delightful?"

"Because the satiation of it is no easy task. I must deal with the likes of you as there is no obliging stablehand about."

His jaw tightened, and she wished she had not given in to her impudence, a quality she did not often display save in the company of her cousin.

"Forgive me," she said. "I was impertinent."

He narrowed his eyes. "Is there anyone you would *not* consider lifting your skirts to? The stablehand at Edenmoor is near sixty years of age and suffers from rheumatism, but would you consider seducing him?"

"I protest. Aside from you and Lady Katherine's former stablehand, I have not lain with anyone."

"Is that by choice or want of opportunity?"

"Now you are impertinent," she huffed.

"By choice or not?" he insisted.

"Yes, by choice," she snapped, then wondered why she allowed him to perturb her so. Without antagonism, she said, "But you may judge me a harlot if you wish, my lord."

Attempting to ease his vexation, she added, "I would be the harlot with *you,* Alastair, if it pleases you."

She started, surprised by her own words. Dear God, was she flirting with the man?

He growled and said nothing, perhaps unsure if it pleased him or not.

Unaccustomed to playing the coquette with any man, let alone Alastair, she sat up. "May we attempt *Angelique et Medor* now?"

"Lay down and continue your caresses."

He went to stand at the foot of the bed so that he had a better view up her legs. She obliged, wishing they could replicate the easy corporal rapport from last night. For several minutes she stroked herself. A slow but steady arousal built within her.

"How long do you wish me to pleasure myself?" she asked, noticing his pupils had dilated.

"As long as I wish."

She moaned as he dipped his thumb toward her slit and caressed the edge of it. She hoped he would enter her. She craved to be filled. He rubbed the outside of her slit before sliding two digits into her wet heat. She gasped when he struck a particularly sensitive part inside of her. He knew it, and brushed it over and over.

"*My God,*" she managed to exhale.

She shivered and writhed, unsure if she could withstand the acute pleasure, yet wanting the torment. Desire, a humble fire before, burst into vibrant flames. She gripped the bedclothes beneath as her body rode the most beautiful waves, hoping it would never end. A world of sensation exploded deep within her before sending ripples of rapture to every extremity of her body. She cried and laughed in the same breath.

When at last it seemed her body had peeled itself from the rafters above and settled back upon the bed, the blood still pulsing madly in her loins, her breath was shallow and her head light. She stared into nothingness, waiting for the remaining tremors to fade, before taking a deep breath, in awe of the ecstasy her body was capable of.

After withdrawing his fingers, Alastair began to disrobe, removing his banyan first, then pulling down his braces to free his shirt. She drank in his chiseled chest and torso before dropping her gaze to the tenting at his crotch.

"You should undress as well," he said as he unbuttoned his pants.

Her slippers had already fallen to the floor and she had but to remove her robe and shift, which she did while seated on the bed. After discarding his shoes, stockings, and trousers, he stood in glorious nakedness. Her breath catching in her throat, she tried not to gape too openly. He retrieved from the pocket of his banyan a linen sheath, then climbed into bed beside her and lay upon his back, stroking the hardness between his legs.

"*Angelique et Medor?*" she asked.

He nodded as he tied the sheath over his member. "But bend your knees. You will find movement much easier that way."

With her back to him, she straddled his hips, her knees on either side of his legs. He held her by the hip with one hand as he pointed his member with the other. Slowly, she lowered herself onto him. Her copious amount of wetness allowed him easy entry. With a luscious groan, she sank down his length. Closing her eyes, she relished the fullness.

"Are you able to move?"

In response, she pushed herself up his shaft and shivered when it stroked the area his fingers had caressed earlier. He gripped her hips and assisted in pumping her body up and down. She had found such bliss in her previous climax and was surprised to find the craving returned. She truly was a glutton.

As with the previous night, her legs grew sore, but her need for release was greater. Alastair bucked his hips, slapping his pelvis into her rump. Their grunts and groans filled the room as they pushed their bodies toward the finish line. She wished she could see his countenance, her arousal reflected in him, his muscles tensed in exertion, his perspiration matching hers, but she could not deny the position provided his entry a wondrous angle. Once more the prospect of rapture loomed, the achievement made more worthy by the effort needed to acquire it. Her body exploded into paroxysm, and she was only mildly aware of Alastair spearing himself into her with rapid thrusts until he roared and his body fell into spasms.

She collapsed atop him. He helped her stretch her legs out. For several minutes they lay together, gulping air, waiting for their bodies to return to normalcy. She rolled off his chest and nestled into the crook of his arm. Turning his head, he kissed her brow.

She had never felt more content.

# Chapter 18

THE FOLLOWING MORNING, Alastair went fishing with Edward, Thomas and Henry. Thus, he was not present to see Millie after she had come down for breakfast. He was glad for the reprieve from her company but would have preferred a more strenuous activity than fishing for his mind would wonder back to the prior night when she lay curled into him in bed.

"I knew I would like the position of Angelique," she had murmured into his shoulder as he held her. "May we do it again tomorrow night?"

He turned to stare at her. "Have I granted there will be a third night?"

With bright eyes, she returned his gaze. "Why not? Was it not pleasurable for you?"

As one of the male species, he would be a fool to decline the prospect, but he was wary of giving in to Millie too much. He sat up and reached for her garments to hand to her.

"You spent," she pointed out as she accepted her robe and shift, "so it could not have been terrible for you."

He got off the bed to remove the sheath and retrieve his own clothes. "Perhaps."

"Please."

The plea stalled him. Standing less than two feet from her, he was tempted to take her into his arms and kiss her. The sparkle in her eyes, the anticipation in her countenance, caused feelings to swell in his bosom. But he stayed himself.

Instead, he cupped her chin and brushed his thumb over her bottom lip. She was not the woman he had thought her to be upon first meeting her. He had found her polite and intelligent but also plain and uninteresting. Her initial timidity had waned surprisingly quickly, and thereafter she had adopted a nonchalance toward him that he found more acceptable than the receptions he more commonly received from others.

"If you behave yourself, you shall be rewarded," he relented. "But there will be no questioning of my directives and no talk of stocking frames."

Her whole countenance radiated with joy. "Thank you, Alastair."

The simple words undid his resistance, and he lowered his head to sweep his lips over hers. His arm circled her waist, and he crushed her to him. He could feel his hardness reviving as his senses took in the scent of her arousal, the sound of her breaths, and the pressure of her lips and body. He could take her again, wanted to take her again, but he would be a poor example if he could not retain the discipline he required from her. Letting her go, he stepped away before desire overcame him.

"That's two you've let get away," Thomas remarked.

Snapping out of his reverie, Alastair realized he had not attended to the tugging of his fishing pole. But a more troubling realization took hold: he was looking forward to his night with Millie. He wondered if he could provide her body even greater ecstasy.

The women were all having tea in the parlor when they returned. Henry went immediately to his grandmother to tell how he caught the largest fish of anyone, and Thomas was quick to point out that the fish would have gotten away if not for him. Mr. Abbott dozed in a chair beside the fireplace. Wilmington read the paper while Brewster penned a letter at the writing table. Kittredge sat beside Millie as she and Jason appeared to be discussing *Gulliver's Travels.*

"I am glad to hear that Farnsworth is proposing a bill to discourage the destruction of textile machines," said Wilmington. "This paper says that more of our military have been deployed to Lancashire following an attack on Burton's Mill. The Luddites there have threatened the local magistrates with death if they attempt to interfere. Something must be done. Your meeting with Farnsworth is timely and commendable."

Alastair scanned the room. His niece, Emily, occupied the settee nearest Millie. When Emily met his gaze, she blushed and quickly looked down at her embroidery. She had been casting glances at him since her arrival. He would not normally sit for tea, but he wanted to see how Millie would do in his company. He decided he would take his tea standing.

Millie had looked up when Wilmington spoke, and it seemed she had contemplated speaking, but when she saw Alastair, she remained mute.

"Are you well acquainted with Farnsworth?" Wilmington asked.

"I am not," Alastair replied. "Millie, I will have a cup of tea, if you please."

A few heads turned her way, for she was not sitting nearest to the tea table, but she rose and dutifully poured him a cup.

"But he asked you to meet with him on this important matter?"

"I have little interest in the subject, or in Farnsworth, and agreed to meet with him only because he once granted a favor to my father. I have very little to do with Parliament."

Millie approached with his tea. "Alas, it is a duty you cannot eschew."

"Why not?"

She seemed taken aback. "Because you sit in the House of Lords."

"Not by choice."

"It is both a responsibility and a privilege of the peerage."

"I hardly deem it a privilege. You would not either if you had to sit through a session of Parliament."

"I have read the speeches given by various members. It is a privilege no matter how tedious the task. Your decisions have repercussions on all the citizens—and even creatures—of the crown."

"There are other men who delight in such responsibilities. I am not one of them."

She furrowed her brow. "Have you no sense of *noblesse oblige*, my lord?"

He gave her a stern look. Did she not wish to earn her reward tonight?

"Millie!" Mrs. Abbott exclaimed, bewildered that her daughter dared to speak to him in such a manner. "Lord Alastair, your pardon. Millie, whatever are you on about?"

"Ha! Alastair? *Noblesse oblige?*" cried Louisa. "Clearly you know him little, Millie."

"Louisa is right," he said to Millie. "The care of the citizens is best left to others more capable than I."

But Millie was not prepared to relent, and he found the depth with which she stared at him to be unsettling.

"You delight in being seen as heartless," she said, "but I think we would be gravely mistaken to despair of you so easily."

He returned her stare. "You pay too much heed to my aunt and her opinions of me. She is prejudiced in my favor."

"And do you suggest that her hand in your upbringing was a failure?"

Someone in the room gasped. His jaw tightened but he managed to say, "Thank you for the tea, Millie. You may sit down."

She blinked several times, unaccustomed to taking such direct commands.

"Millie, come!" her mother bade.

She did as told and went to sit beside her mother and Mrs. Cheswith, but she did not appear pacified.

"Millie is right to question you, Andre," Katherine said after setting Henry off her lap. "It would seem you have no regard for my influence in your life."

"If not for you, m'lady, I would be an even worse scoundrel."

"Scoundrel or not," said Wilmington, "it is right of you to meet with Farnsworth and support his proposal. An act of Parliament is required to repress machine-breaking and other violent acts against commerce."

Alastair waited to see if Millie would speak, and she seemed to contemplate it.

"These rebels are as terrible as the colonists in America," offered Caroline. "Who knows what other atrocities they, if unchecked, will commit?"

Millie could not resist. "Perhaps they would not resort to desperate measures if they could find the means to support themselves and their families."

He could hardly believe his ears. Last night, she had sounded so eager to earn his approval. Had she forgotten that he had forbid further talk of this very subject? "By desperate measures, you mean the destruction of *stocking frames?*"

"Yes. If Parliament could see fit to repeal the Combination Acts or consider setting minimum wages, these workers would have more hope."

He stared at her. There was both defiance and fear in her countenance. She had not forgotten. She had simply chosen to disregard him.

"It is not for Parliament to interfere with the economy's natural order," Wilmington responded.

"Workers are part of the economy as well, but our laws prevent them from seeking the most basic necessities. Costs have risen, but wages have not. These workers—and, yes, the Luddites among them—are being denied an ability to seek what every Englishman has a right to: life, liberty and the pursuit of happiness."

Seeing that everyone was staring at her, she withdrew and said nothing more.

"Where does it say every man has such a right?" Wilmington asked.

"My dear Millie, you have an eloquence to your speech," Katherine voiced, "and it is clear you have much charity in your heart. It is easy for our society to overlook the toils and sufferings of the lower classes."

"She has always had much compassion for the poor," Mrs. Abbott said gratefully.

Louisa shared a smirk with Caroline. No doubt they thought that Millie held such an affinity for the less well-off because her family was among them.

Millie avoided his gaze the rest of the time. Kittredge, who had witnessed the scene in silent amusement, approached him to inquire how the fishing went. Louisa persuaded Emily to play her best sonata on the pianoforte. Afforded some of the finest instructors, Emily played extremely well.

"Do you play, Miss Abbott?" Louisa asked when Emily had finished both a sonata and a prelude.

"Not well," Millie replied. "We would benefit from having Miss Wilmington play another piece."

"As well as Emily plays, she is happy to share the instrument. Though her instructor says he has no student who can accomplish a piece as well, and in so short a time as Emily, she is no glutton for attention. I bid you play a little, Miss Abbott."

"Do play, Miss Abbott," Alastair seconded when it was clear that Millie had rather not.

Millie glanced at him. After her earlier defiance, he did not expect that she would disobey him again. She went to the pianoforte and chose to play one of Mozart's simpler sonatinas. Her fingers had not the agility of Emily's, but she performed more than adequately.

"I think I shall collect some of the Michaelmas daisies for our dinner table tonight," said Anne.

"May I join you?" Millie quickly asked.

"Mr. Kittredge, you have not seen the gardens," said Katherine. "Perhaps you would care to assist the ladies?"

Kittredge bowed. "Certainly, my lady."

Caroline, Emily and Mrs. Abbott decided to join Anne and Millie. Edward decided to take his boys out for a walk with the hounds, to be joined by Wilmington and Brewster. Louisa said she would rest a while in her room. Mr. Abbott continued to slumber beside the hearth.

"You could be kinder to Millie," Katherine told him as they took their leave after all the others.

"Gifting her a dowry of four thousand pounds is not kind enough?" he returned.

"She would rather not have such a gift."

"Am I to blame if she chooses not to appreciate it?"

"Is that why you seem cross with her?"

He nearly replied that it was because Millie had contravened him when he had required her obedience as part of *acquiescing to her desires*. Katherine would understand then. But, lest Millie had already confessed their nightly activities, he would not reveal them.

"She may not have the finest manners," Katherine continued as they walked down the corridor, "but she means no disrespect."

"Madam, perhaps you had not heard all that she had said, but she dared upbraid me for my lack of *noblesse oblige* before mine own family."

*And against my orders*, he added silently.

"And that perturbs you, Andre?"

He said nothing at first, for he cared very little what others might say or think of his actions, but Millie's words had rankled him. Feeling his aunt's keen study upon him, he asked, "And you feel I deserve just such a scolding?"

"I do."

"I receive enough from my sisters and you. Louisa, in particular, is fortunate I do not throw her out of my house."

"And do you pay us any heed?"

"No, and you would now add Millie to your party. As a result of our encounter at Château Follet, she now thinks herself entitled to speak to me as she does."

"She was never terribly afraid of you, and I think she will continue so, despite your best efforts to intimidate her."

Ready to end the conversation, he said, "I know you have a fondness for Millie, but I would take care what thoughts and actions you encourage in her."

"You promised, for my birthday, to look after someone."

"And I have done so, but once Millie is married, my responsibility ends."

"No wonder you gave her such a grand dowry."

"Precisely."

He bowed and took his leave. He had to consider what he would do with Millie tonight.

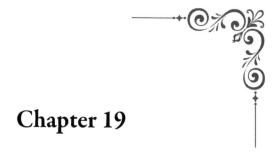

# Chapter 19

"IN FRONT OF HER LADYSHIP, our host!" Mrs. Abbott cried for the third time as Mildred dressed for dinner in her chambers. Her mother had already reproached her after the tea, and again when they had finished collecting flowers. "Have you gone mad, Millie? Truly, I think there was not one who was not in horror at your behavior."

Mildred hung her head. She regretted challenging Alastair before his family and had no excuse for her lack of manners. The morning had come with promise, for she had succeeded in not spending the night before, but she had ruined her prospects for a reward. His displeasure at her defiance had been obvious.

"I cannot fathom why you would assume such familiarity with the Marquess?" Mrs. Abbott wrung her hands. "I fear for your dowry and should not be surprised at all if he retracted the endowment. Oh, Millie, what were you thinking? How will you atone for what you did? You will have to ask his forgiveness. How I hope he shall forgive you! We must not lose the dowry."

But not everyone had been horrified by her display during tea. During the walk in the garden following, Kittredge had approached her. "Miss Abbott, I must say I am in some admiration at your courage to speak with such frankness to Alastair."

"It is not courage but foolhardiness," she had replied.

"Nonetheless, there are few who would have dared question him as you did."

"I regard the subject with some passion, but I should not have allowed my sentiments to overrule common courtesy."

Before the dinner, Mildred had apologized to Lady Katherine, but her ladyship had dismissed her apology. "Goodness knows Alastair could use a little scolding."

That Lady Katherine had taken no offense did little to cheer Mildred. When she saw Alastair enter the anteroom, her breath caught. But she could not pass the dinner without speaking to him beforehand. Collecting herself, she went to where he stood, conscious that many in the room were gazing upon her.

"My lord, I must ask your forgiveness for my earlier rudeness," she began. "I ought not have spoken in the manner that I did, and my wrong is worse for having done so before your family."

She would apologize for another reason as well, but she could not speak it before company. She hoped that her eyes conveyed what she could not say.

"I accept your apology, Miss Abbott," he said after staring down at her for far too long than was comfortable for her. "I hope that you consider the discussion of stocking frames at an end?"

She hesitated but replied in the affirmative. She curtsied and returned to the other side of the room. Though he had sounded sincere in forgiving her, she thought she had best not put herself in his way.

A footman entered to announce that dinner was ready. Alastair presented his arm to his aunt, but Lady Katherine had hooked her arm through Thomas's.

"It is not often I have the pleasure of having my grandson escort me to dinner," her ladyship declared.

There was a brief moment of awkwardness as the others wondered how to proceed, as Lady Katherine had upended the proper order.

Alastair, unruffled, turned to Mildred. "Miss Abbott."

Surprised, she could only stare at his proffered arm. Louisa's eyes widened. Mildred was tempted to protest that he ought to escort Miss Wilmington, who had more standing, to dinner but that would only call further attention to the situation. She accepted Alastair's arm, and Kittredge was left to escort Miss Wilmington.

Fortunately she did not have to sit near Alastair during the dinner and was near enough to Kittredge that she could hear his easy, affable talk of the theater and how Charles Kemble was to perform in a production of *Hamlet*. But Mildred could enjoy little else of the goose, baked turnips and pie. After dinner, she declined to join the rest in cards and chose to read in the corner of the drawing room, but the words blurred often. She wanted to ask Alastair's and Lady Katherine's pardons once more, though she knew the former would abhor the necessity of exchanging more words and the latter would deem it unnecessary.

"Papa, I have been the rudest of guests," she said when her father had approached. The card tables were put away, and Miss Wilmington was to play the pianoforte again.

"Your mother told me what had transpired. As it cannot be undone, all that you can hope to do is ask their pardon, which you have done."

"I must ask your pardon as well, for my want of manners must reflect poorly on our family."

"You could not do worse than your Uncle Stephen."

Her mother's younger brother had run off with a married woman, but this offered little consolation to Mildred.

"I doubt Lady Katherine was much troubled by it."

"Even if she were, she is too kind to speak of it."

"Are you certain? She strikes me as a woman who is most comfortable with speaking her mind."

Mildred had to agree that she saw and heard little from her ladyship that indicated she thought less of Mildred for what had happened. Nevertheless, she would not permit herself any leeway. "But I criticized her nephew before her family!"

"As for the Marquess, I doubt he heeds what anyone says of or to him. You could call him a blackguard or worse, and I doubt he would be disturbed in the least."

"I think I would like a cordial," Mildred started before her father could complete his sentence, for Alastair stood behind him

Mr. Abbott, seeing her widened eyes, turned about, colored, and stuttered, "Cordial, yes—yes, you, er, wished for a glass of—of cordial?"

With a curt bow to Alastair, Mr. Abbott hurried away. Mildred felt her heart sink. How many more times would her family offend Alastair? She found solace in the fact that the Marquess was to depart on the morrow.

"You may find page ninety-one instructional for your situation," Alastair said, handing her a book before walking away.

She turned to the page he'd named and saw a note:

*Midnight.*

*Your redemption awaits.*

Her redemption. She both welcomed and dreaded it. But she would suffer whatever he intended. Closing the book, she looked at the clock. It was just past nine o'clock. She would pass the next few hours in anxious anticipation.

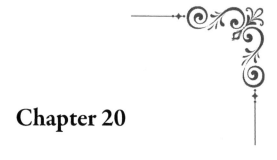

# Chapter 20

A VIBRANT FIRE GREETED her as she entered the chambers at the appointed hour. Alastair, in his nightshirt and banyan, stood with his arms crossed before him. Without forethought, she knelt at his feet.

"Forgive me, my lord."

"I accepted your apology already, Millie," he said.

"That was for speaking before your family. I now ask your pardon for having defied your wishes."

"You will atone for that tonight. And I had thought you intended to earn a reward."

"I did have such intentions. But...I should have waited to voice my opinions to you in private."

"Then you do not regret what you said? Only that it was said in company?"

She kept her gaze lowered. "My thoughts on the topic have not changed, my lord, and needed to be voiced."

"Then why ask my pardon now?" He sounded slightly baffled.

"Because I had not wanted to disappoint you. In hindsight, I should not have agreed to a command I could not follow. When you were so dismissive of your duties—well, I will accept whatever actions you intend, my lord."

He threaded his hand in her hair and eased her head back so that she could meet his gaze. "It will be a long night if you do not."

Despite the threat, warmth pooled between her thighs.

"On your feet."

She rose from the floor and stood, waiting for his instruction.

"Remove the robe," he said.

She slid out of the garment. With a masterful stride, he stood behind her, close enough to make her every nerve come to life. Reaching an arm around her, he cupped a breast through her shift. He rolled the orb against her chest as he hardened and released his grip.

"You were very wet between the legs last night."

She let out a ragged sigh.

"Did you enjoy being in such a state?"

She gasped when he pinched her nipple through her shift. "Yes, my lord."

He pulled her shift down one shoulder and kneaded the exposed breast. He pulled her into him. "Your body will want to spend desperately tonight."

She moaned at the thought, relishing the hardness of his body at her back.

"Do you deserve to spend?" he asked, his other arm snaking around her hip to clasp her mound.

"Perhaps not."

He rubbed her between the thighs. It did not take long for the wetness to flow. Feeling him harden behind her, she wanted her body to meld with his, for the hand at her breast to become a permanent part of her. The fabric he rubbed into her folds, though damp now, created a pleasurable friction. He lightly pinched her nipple before moving his hand to her throat. Her head fell back to his chest as the rest of her writhed against him. She panted and slipped further into the pool of desire.

Her backside brushed against him as he pulled her closer, his caresses pushing her arousal higher and higher. She arched into him, ground herself into him, straining for that imminent release. How easily she could spend for him! But he lightened his caress, and when he withdrew his hand, she felt bereft. Her body trembled, dangling over an unseen precipice.

He pulled the sleeves of her shift down her shoulders and allowed the garment to drop to the floor. Once more she stood naked before him, and once more arousal triumphed over modesty. His hands roamed her body, gripping, grasping, caressing. She relished every touch but wished he would return to fondling her between the legs.

Stepping away, he instructed her to lie down upon the bed. Eagerly, she obliged. But he puzzled her when, instead of coming to her in bed, he took the newspaper he had left upon a nearby table and sat down in a chair several feet away. She watched him read the paper for several minutes before sitting up and clearing her throat.

"Am I to watch you read all night?" she asked.

"If that is my desire," he replied blandly.

This, then, was part of her redemption—or punishment, rather. Did he truly intend to read the newspaper? He could not be without lust himself. She had felt the thickness of his desire. She wondered what she could do to entice him. Or did he expect her to patiently wait while her body vibrated with need?

She supposed she had brought this upon herself. Seeking to relieve her agitation, she touched herself, but his voice stopped her.

"I did not allow you could pleasure yourself."

Reluctantly, she stilled her hand. He set down the newspaper and approached the bed. Her pulse quickened in an instant. Instinctively, she licked her lips.

He began to untie his cravat and undress at a leisurely pace.

"May I assist you?" she asked when she thought she might go mad from his slowness. Her body remained on edge, yearning to be taken. But he had only removed his neckcloth and collar.

"No," he replied, undoing the buttons of his waistcoat one by one.

She ground her teeth in impatience as he removed his waistcoat, his braces, and finally his shirt. The sight of his fine form caused the heat within to surge. She urged him on with silent words and practically cried out in joy when he stood as naked as she, his hardened arousal bared to her.

"Are you still wet?" he asked.

"Need you ask?" she returned.

A faint grin tugged at one corner of his mouth. "Lay back."

She did as he bid. He widened the distance between her bent legs and studied the intimacy between her thighs.

*Touch me*, she willed him.

When he did, her body could have leaped off the bed. He resumed where he had left off, his strokes increasing the agitation so that she could scale the mountain of pleasure. He curled two fingers inside her, sending waves of delight reverberating throughout her. She moaned her appreciation and grasped the bedclothes as tension mounted.

And waned.

Her breath caught in her throat as he withdrew. He attended his own center of arousal, rubbing her moisture onto his shaft. She hoped he intended to sink himself into her waiting heat. Instead, he leaned against the bedpost and continued to fondle himself. With anticipation and envy, she watched him stroke his member. She wanted to touch him but dared not without his command. His body tensed, the veins in his neck visible, as he thrust himself into his hand. A flush spread across his chest, and he gave a fierce grunt as he attained the pinnacle she craved.

Heat swirled angrily in her loins as she watched him spend, and she looked longingly upon the evidence of his rapture upon the bed.

Having achieved his end, he would not now take her as she had hoped. She began to fear that the night would prove long indeed.

# Chapter 21

ALASTAIR SHOOK OFF the shivers of his climax. He found his handkerchief and wiped himself. Millie stared at his crotch, lust still sparkling in her eyes, but a frown graced her lips. He felt some guilt for having tormented her so, but she needed to learn that he was not to be trifled with.

"Your patience may yet be rewarded," he told her.

"I hope so," she quietly replied. "May I pleasure myself to completion?"

"Is that what you prefer?"

"You have dispensed with what I prefer."

She gave him a wry smile that was uncharacteristic of her. He found himself captivated.

His gaze fell to her breasts. They were a lovely pair. They protruded nicely from her chest and were large enough to spill from his hands when he cupped them. He envisioned sliding his member between them, hardening between those supple spheres He shook his head and reminded himself that this was to be their last time together.

He cupped a swollen mound. Her brows shot up, indicating how sensitive her breasts had become. Lowering his head, he licked a nipple. She whimpered.

"You may pleasure yourself now."

She reached an eager hand between her thighs and stroked herself. He watched for several minutes, feeling the blood course hot and strong through his veins. Her body begged to be taken, made his. He passed his hand over her belly, then threaded his fingers through the hairs at her mound.

With his forefinger, he teased the swollen bud beneath her curls. Her lashes fluttered, and she moaned when he sank an inch of his digit into her sodden slit. His cock throbbed with renewed need, surprising him with how quickly it had recovered.

He slid his finger along her clitoris, drawing from her moans filled with urgency, swelling with need. Her body quivered. He lifted his hand a little higher, and her pelvis followed, seeking his touch. He played with her clitoris, rubbing it, pinching it.

With both hands, he caressed her belly, her hips, her thighs, spreading the moisture over her soft skin. He bent over and encased a nipple with his mouth. She cried out loudly, her body tensing and twisting with desire He brushed a tendril of hair that had matted to her forehead. When she had calmed sufficiently, she turned to meet his gaze. Her eyes appeared particularly expressive and luminescent. At the moment, they were the loveliest eyes he had ever beheld.

*My God*, she was beautiful.

He had waited long enough. He straddled her body. He eyed her lush breasts and thought again of positioning his shaft between them. Though there was not a part of Millie he did not relish, he had to take her, feel himself in her warm, wet depths.

"Do you wish to spend?" he tempted.

"I have a greater wish."

Perplexed, he paused. What could she possibly wish for more at the moment?

She closed her eyes and drew in a shaky breath. "I would rather you not give your ready support to Farnsworth till you have thoroughly examined the arguments against his bill."

He stared at her, stunned. Was this truly what she preferred? It was unexpected. Outlandish, even.

"Millie, our carnal pursuits do not involve politics."

"Why not? You forbade me to talk of stocking frames as part of our arrangement. It would seem there is nothing that *you* cannot involve."

He had to acknowledge her reasoning, but still he could not completely believe what she was asking. After all that her body had endured, it surely needed release. She deserved to spend.

"Are you certain this is what you want?" he asked.

She nodded.

A strange emotion overwhelmed him. Of awe and even shame. She was unlike any woman he had ever known.

"I will consider it," he said finally. "I do not owe Farnsworth my support. Nevertheless, I will only promise to delay my decision."

"That is all I ask."

His hand was between her legs, an area too much a temptation. He stroked her nub with his middle finger. She moaned softly.

"Pray do not tease me further, my lord."

"Shhhh."

He continued to fondle her. She bit her lower lip but eventually released a moan when his fingers found the spot of greatest sensitivity.

"Alastair, you will make me spend. Oh, G—no." She gripped the bed with both hands. "*Please.*"

He was accustomed to hearing women begging to spend, but Millie begged *not* to spend. He intended she should.

"Alas—ah—ah!"

After having her desire caged, her body could not resist the temptation.

"Spend, Millie.".

Her body fell into convulsions, shaking the bed. Her hips bucked a few times before settling back down when he eased his strokes. She panted for a different purpose now.

"I was sincere in my request for a different reward," she bemoaned when the trembling had quieted.

"And you will have it."

Lowering himself, he licked at her pleasure bud. He applied his tongue to her in earnest.

"Oh, God. What is it you wish, my lord? You cannot..."

Encasing her nub of desire, he sucked, liking the taste of her. The scent of her arousal caused his lust to swell.

"You will make me spend again," she managed through clenched teeth.

He continued to assault her with his mouth. Her body quivered.

He released her long enough to give his encouragement. "Spend, Millie."

Her response was immediate. Her body bowed off the bed. Her legs kicked out. It was exhilarating to see, hear, and feel her body succumb to euphoria.

He kept her aloft at the apex till she cried for him to cease. She sobbed for breath. His arousal stretched, yearning to mate to her with an intensity he had never expected. It was as if she had cast a spell upon him, and he had no wish to shake it off.

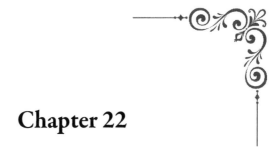

# Chapter 22

THE CEILING STILL BLURRED before her eyes. Mildred marveled that her body had survived the second orgasm. Alastair had applied his mouth *there* and encouraged her to spend, despite her willingness not to. Whatever his motives, it did not matter. This was their last night together. Ever. She closed her eyes and drank in the splendor still waving through her body.

"Thank you, my lord. Thank you."

His lips crushed down upon hers, and it was as if she had not spent twice already. Her arousal never tired in his presence. Despite her shaky legs, she tried to press herself to him as she wrapped her hands about his neck to help hold herself up. He eased her legs open and enclosed her in his arms .

Laying himself over her, he resumed kissing her, taking her mouth with delicious fervor. She gripped his hair in one hand and his shoulder in the other. Her hips met his body, seeking his erection. She was overcome with impatience and wanted his body to meld into hers. He ground himself against her as his mouth ravaged hers.

"I should search for French letters," he uttered against her lips.

Not bearing to be parted from him, she wrapped a leg over his and tightened her embrace. "Take me, my lord. Take me."

It was an invitation he could not refuse. He positioned his cock at her opening and plunged in. His cock felt grand—the angle and

245

shape of his shaft provoked much more pleasure. She pushed herself into him, wanting every inch.

"My God, Millie," he breathed, groping one of her breasts.

Gradually, they came to a rhythm with their bodies. Holding the bottom of her thigh, he lifted the leg to gain deeper penetration. Lust surged within her, and she shoved herself up at him. He met her fervor and rolled his hips into her, sending waves of delight fanning from between her legs. She grunted and babbled half words, trying to resist the tide of pleasure threatening to drown her.

"Spend. As you please, my lord," she managed, digging her fingers into his muscular arms.

"Ladies first," he replied.

At this, her body shattered. He kissed her again, dampening her cries. Her body bucked of its own accord. He quickened his pace, hammering himself into her till his own release became imminent. He pulled from her and his seed shot into the mattress below. To her consternation and slight trepidation, she would rather he had spent inside her. Several shivers went through his frame.

She wished he would remain where he was, the weight of his body resting partially upon her, but he pushed himself up and held out his hand to her. Their evening had come to an end.

"Thank you, Alastair. Thank you for the past three nights."

"I pray they met your expectations?"

"Mmmmm. Exceeded expectations."

"Good. The pleasure was mine."

She hoped he spoke sincerely and not merely from courtesy. She reminded herself that he was not a man compelled by obligations of the latter. In silence they tidied the room and stripped the bedclothes to put in the laundry. "Good night, Millie," he said when they were done.

She almost wished she could stay in his company longer but replied, "Good night."

As she shakily strolled down the corridor toward the stairs, a mix of feelings beset her. She felt both a euphoria and guilt, shame at what she had done, what she had asked of her cousin, but gratitude that he had acquiesced in taking her to such sublime carnal heights that all future attempts must surely disappoint.

Thus, she wondered at the wisdom of her actions. However, if she had to do it all again, she would not have asked differently. She was amazed when Alastair had brought her to spend thrice.

And, additionally, he had agreed to reserve his support of the Farnsworth bill. It was entirely possible his delay of support would be of minimal duration, even a day at most, for she had required no particular timing to her request. But while Alastair often held the expectations of polite society with contempt, she had never known him to go back on his word. He did not trifle with tricks, artifice, or even insincerity.

He was a different man than she had known before. There was no one like him, and she felt privileged to know a side of him few others saw.

# Chapter 23

MILDRED WINCED AS SHE took a seat before the vanity the following morning.

"Are you all right, miss?" asked the dressing maid.

"Yes," Mildred answered as she positioned her rump to avoid the tenderest spots and not aggravate the soreness between her thighs. Her cheeks warmed as the memories of the prior night flooded her. She observed her reflection in the looking glass and noticed her plaits had come undone. She had slept soundly last night, but there were faint half circles beneath her eyes. Nonetheless, she felt buoyed by all that had transpired.

When she was dressed and went downstairs, she found that everyone else had already finished breakfast except for Edward's boys. Alastair and Kittredge were already in their riding clothes.

"Miss Abbott," said Kittredge, approaching her, "I had hoped to have the chance to bid farewell. I quite enjoyed meeting you and your family. Perhaps our paths will cross back in London."

She smiled and expressed a similar sentiment. Alastair did not approach her, and she was partially glad for it. She had protested what awkwardness may come of their affair at Château Follet. But this time felt different. She wished she had not slept quite so late that she might have more of his company before he and Kittredge departed.

As Alastair accepted the well wishes from his family, Millie felt his gaze upon her often.

"I mean to host Christmas dinner," said Lady Katherine. "You will come, will you not, Andre?"

He frowned.

"Of course I will not expect you," she said, "but you are welcome, nonetheless."

Everyone moved outside to watch the two men out to their horses. Mildred assumed the appearance of indifference but found herself grappling with a sadness as she observed them depart. And when everyone returned indoors, she was the last to follow.

During what felt like a somber breakfast, she tried to rid herself of the strange sentiments that had settled upon her. She told herself that she might not see Alastair again, not for some time. And it ought not matter to her. He had gifted her three nights of ecstasy; she should expect no more from him. He was probably relieved to be done with her.

After breakfast, she declared that she would go out and enjoy the weather before winter made such outings difficult.

"I will join you for a stroll about the grounds, Miss Abbott."

Mildred turned around in surprise, for it was Mrs. Wilmington who spoke. Though she would have preferred the chance to be alone with her thoughts and feelings, she gave a short curtsy and waited till Mrs. Wilmington had donned her coat, bonnet and gloves.

They walked in silence until they were far enough from the house not to be beset by anyone. From Mrs. Wilmington's demeanor, Mildred suspected she had not joined her for friendly conversation.

"Though your standing in society differs greatly from ours," Mrs. Wilmington began, "you are, nonetheless, joined to the d'Aubigne name, which has generations of breeding."

"It is an illustrious name," Mildred acknowledged.

"You must know the importance, therefore, of acting in proper accordance with your family's elevated position. You must now adhere to higher standards."

"I shall strive to, madam, and am most sorry that my recent behavior was not in concert with expectations."

Mrs. Wilmington narrowed her eyes. "You took great liberties in your speech."

"And I am most sorry for it."

"Andre ought to have put you in your place with the harshest of words."

"Yes, I wish he had."

"The Andre I know would have spared nothing, regardless of your sex. That he did not is curious. But when you pair that with the excessive dowry he has granted you, I can only conclude that you have influenced him as only a jezebel could."

Mildred stopped in her tracks.

Mrs. Wilmington looked at her squarely. "I know what you are about, Miss Abbott."

Mildred felt her color rise. Her voice quivered when she spoke. "Madam?"

"I mean to warn you that you will only ruin yourself if you continue in the manner of a trollop. Imagine the shame your mother and father would face. It would not matter then that your uncle had married our aunt. A d'Aubigne can weather scandal, but the same cannot be said for an Abbott. Whatever your designs upon my brother—"

"I must protest, madam! I have no designs upon your brother."

"No? It was merely coincidence that you returned to your chambers shortly before Alastair did? It is more than curious that you two were both awake at such an ungodly hour."

Stunned, Mildred could make no reply. Her legs trembled beneath her skirts. When she finally found her voice, she said, "It would seem that *three* of us were awake, and perhaps it is thus not so curious."

"Your breeding shows in your impudence, Miss Abbott. I know that I suffer from insomnia. Can you say the same?"

"It was a coincidence."

"That you would attempt to deny it only sinks you further in my estimation."

Mildred looked away. What was she to do? What could she say?

"But I will keep your dirty secret if you can assure me that you will cease this jezebel business. I have long deplored Andre's profligacy, but with Lady Sophia, there is hope that his indulgent ways will finally come to an end."

"Madam, I can assure you that you need have no worries. You are mistaken in your presumptions. There is nothing between Alastair and I."

Mrs. Wilmington raised a single brow. "I presume that you are a light-skirt, and that Andre, being the man that he is, does not hesitate to make use of such easy virtue. If you were not in Katherine's good graces, you should be no different than a whore that he would take to bed before casting back into the streets."

The constriction in her chest made responding difficult.

"If I were you," Mrs. Wilmington continued, "I would make use of your dowry whilst you have it, and marry the first man who offers. Perhaps he will never discover the doxy that you are. Andre will succumb to his obligations. He has enough pride in the d'Aubigne name that he will not shirk his duties. He may continue his dalliances even after marrying Lady Sophia, as many men are wont to do, but if you have any fanciful notions that he will favor you, you have but to look at his pattern of behavior. I could let you descend into disgrace—it is a fate you most assuredly deserve—but you have the chance to save yourself and your family from utter ruin. If you have any decency in you, you will take my advice."

Without another word, she turned and headed back to the house.

Still in shock, Mildred stood without moving. When Mrs. Wilmington was no longer in view, Mildred reached for the nearest tree and sank to the ground beside it. Her chest hurt, the pain exceeding any she had experienced last night at Alastair's hands.

It ought not matter what Mrs. Wilmington thought of her, but it did. Because she was Alastair's sister and Lady Katherine's niece. But Mildred knew there was little she could do to earn the good graces of Mrs. Wilmington. She did not doubt that the woman could carry out her threat, though she need not have worried. Mildred would not have wanted to harm the d'Aubigne family in any way. She respected Lady Katherine too much.

And she loved Alastair.

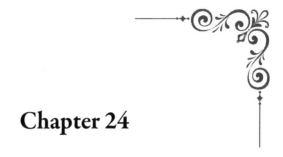

# Chapter 24

"AS LONG AS SLAVERY is safe in the colonies, the economies there need not collapse," Mr. Carleton explained at the dinner table. "It was more economical to import slaves than to encourage them to breed. A slave's first five years are useless and a burdensome cost to the slave owner, but now that the slave trade has been abolished, we have little choice. That is why you have seen the price of sugar rise, Mrs. Abbott."

Mildred bit her tongue to keep from speaking, telling herself that doing so would only prolong the conversation. She kept her attention upon the partridge on her plate.

"And are you quite certain you must travel to the West Indies in December?" her mother asked. "Why, you will likely have to spend Christmas aboard a ship!"

"Alas, our plantation manager is gravely ill, and quite possibly dead as we speak. I would, of course, much rather spend Christmas here in England."

Mildred felt his gaze upon her.

"Well, when you are returned, we shall certainly have to have you over once more for a proper welcoming dinner."

"I hope you will spend Christmas more enjoyably than I?"

"We will have Christmas dinner with Lady Katherine, the aunt of the Marquess of Alastair. We spent Michaelmas with her at her country estate."

"I remember. What a fine family are the d'Aubignes. They have an illustrious history."

"Yes, and they will soon join with the equally exalted family, the Strathingtons, for we expect a betrothal between the Marquess of Alastair and Lady Sophia."

"Indeed? Felicitations on such a grand union for your families."

This was not the first that Mildred had heard of Alastair and Lady Sophia recently, and she was determined not to be forlorn.

Since Michaelmas, her mother had redoubled her efforts to obtain an offer of marriage for Mildred, and Mildred had considered choosing one simply so that she would no longer have to entertain Mr. Carleton and Mr. Porter. The one gentleman whose company she did welcome was that of George Winston. If not for him, she would've found herself thinking too often of Alastair in the months since Michaelmas. She had kept herself busy and spent much more time with friends than she used to do. Though for several weeks after, she could not pass the day without thinking of him, and at night, her body burned for his touch. She hoped eventually she could face the memory of him without the pain of sadness. She had even declined two invitations from Lady Katherine, for his aunt would remind her too much of him.

"ARE YOU QUITE CERTAIN you don't want to go to the club for cards?" Kittredge asked as he and Alastair guided their horses past the trees in the fields outside of London. "The manager had me sample some Russian spirits. I know they are not quite the gentlemanly drink, but I rather liked their potency."

Alastair observed the gray clouds in the sky. There was likely to be rain, and if they rode much longer, they might be caught in a shower, but part of him would not mind. Ever since returning from Edenmoor, he had wanted to be out of doors as often as possible.

The brisk autumn air helped to calm his ardor whenever his thoughts turned to Millie.

He had erred in agreeing to her proposition yet again. Only this time, it would be harder to shake the spell she had cast upon him. He appreciated that she had made no effort to contact him in the fortnights following Michaelmas. Too many women entertained hopes that he would renew their acquaintance despite his advice to the contrary. Millie was far too practical for such fancies. She knew that if he wanted her company, he would seek her out, and not expect to receive a letter or visit from her.

And yet, when his butler brought him each day's mail, Alastair found himself looking for a letter from Millie. At night especially, and even during the day when there were far more distractions to be had, his mind would wander back to Edenmoor. To the bright crimson of her ass after the paddling. To the triumph shining in her eyes when she had caused him to spend in her mouth. To the glow of rapture upon her countenance after her body had succumbed to his ministrations. There was no better triumph or accomplishment than making a woman spend. Millie especially. He often considered what more he could do with her. The possibilities were endless.

"Then perhaps you will join me at the club tomorrow evening," offered Kittredge.

"Alas, I am to escort the Duchess and Lady Sophia to a pantomime tomorrow," Alastair replied.

"Ah, I had meant to ask about Lady Sophia. You have been seen in her company more often, and I have been asked by our friend, Sir Carrie, how he should bet at Brooks's. When is an announcement expected?"

Alastair had thought that spending more time with Lady Sophia would help to ease away the memories of Millie, but he only found himself comparing the two women. Without doubt, Lady Sophia, with her golden curls, long thick lashes, and alabaster complexion, was a beauty none could rival. And she was perfectly aware of this; thus, she carried herself with a regal confidence that Millie would never have. Their stations in life could not be more different. The daughter of a Duke, Lady Sophia had all the connections anyone could want in society. Millie clearly had not, yet she still had much compassion in her heart. He was still astounded that, when given the chance to enjoy her much deserved euphoria, she had chosen instead to ask for his consideration on behalf of weavers. What woman would propose such nonsense? It had been clear her body needed and desired to spend. Her request was tangential, even if admirably selfless. It was not the sort of proposition he would ever had made, which explained his surprise and awe.

Realizing that he had been silent, and that his silence had earned the careful study of his friend, Alastair said, "And did you advise Sir Carrie how he should place his bet?"

"I told Carrie that I am not privy to your innermost thoughts. We share wine and cards, but not women. I did say, however, that you have had more than ample time to ask for Lady Sophia's hand, and despite your reputation, His Grace is amenable to you for a son-in-law. That an announcement has not been forthcoming marks some hesitation on your part, I think. But Carrie responded that you are loath to do what others expect of you, and I had to agree there was much truth in that. Would you consider my assessment a fair one?"

"It is as Carrie says: my actions are not guided by what others wish to see from me. When I am ready to propose to Lady Sophia, you may be assured that you will be the first to know."

As he spoke, he wondered if he would ever be ready to ask for her hand in marriage.

"Will I know far enough in advance to place a bet myself?" Kittredge asked.

As Kittredge spoke in jest, Alastair made no answer, though he would not put it above Kittredge to use his position of friendship to monetary advantage.

They rode in silence for a spell before Kittredge said, "Shall I have the pleasure of meeting your cousin again?"

Alastair stiffened. "My cousin?"

"Miss Abbott. She is quite the interesting creature. She seems so deferential to the likes of your aunt, your sisters, and her parents. I would almost say she is a shy young woman, but she speaks to you with a daring few women would."

Millie did address him with much more ease than she did others, which was odd because she ought to have found him far more intimidating than the individuals Kittredge had named. Alastair found her audacity both vexing and impressive.

"Perhaps she does not hold you in much esteem," Kittredge mused, "and that is why she finds such courage to address you as she does."

Alastair would have to agree that that was likely how it started for Millie, but he hoped that she had come to find more reason to value his thoughts and opinions despite their disagreements.

"My aunt no doubt encourages her boldness," Alastair replied dryly.

"I can fathom why your aunt might be partial to her. She is not much to look at upon first glance and not the cleverest in conversation, but there is definitely a quality to her that compels, the more one is acquainted with her."

"And what is your purpose in talking of Miss Abbott?"

"No purpose at all. She merely popped into my mind by happenstance."

Alastair let that be the end of their dialogue and started his horse into a full gallop.

# Chapter 25

MRS. ABBOTT LOOKED out the window of the drawing room and frowned. She sniffed, "It's that George Winston fellow again."

Mildred tied her bonnet in place and smiled to herself. It was the one name her mother had recently uttered that did not cause her to cringe.

"Why is he so often with the Grenvilles? And they have Harold Wiggins with them," Mrs. Abbott continued. "I wonder that Wiggins has a farthing to his name? His family is practically penniless if you take into account all the debts his father has. No doubt four thousand pounds would mean a great deal to him."

"No doubt," agreed Mildred, "but despite that, he is most interested in Jane. I could have a dowry of ten thousand pounds, and he would not look my way."

Mrs. Abbot sniffed again. "Well, that simply shows that he lacks sense as well! And what of Winston? What do we know of his situation?"

"I gather he is well situated enough, but it hardly matters. I do not think him overly partial to me. Not when he has the attentions of Miss Hannah Rose."

That piece of intelligence seemed to appease Mrs. Abbott a little. She knew that Mr. and Mrs. Rose would never permit their daughter to favor a man with no standing.

"Nevertheless, it would be more worth your while to keep the company of some others. Mr. Carleton, for example, has requested to speak with your father on his return. I expect the topic of conversation will be a *proposal*."

"Mr. Carleton reeks of tobacco and has a propensity to pick his teeth when he thinks no one is looking."

"What does that matter? He is a far better prospect than someone like Winston."

"It is not only income that makes for a good husband."

"We are of a family with the d'Aubignes. It is your obligation to wed well or your dowry is gone to waste."

Mrs. Abbott had been in particular good spirits ever since Michaelmas. An invitation to dine with Lady Katherine for Christmas had only added to her glee.

"Take care you do not give Winston any encouragement," her mother advised after Mildred bid her adieu.

Although modesty had prompted Mildred to say to her mother that Mr. Winston took only a cursory interest in her, she suspected it was not the case. And if he should show greater interest, she did not think she would discourage him as her mother wanted.

"I saw this pantomime last year," said Jane after they had entered the Theatre Royal, "and I thought it quite amusing, especially Clown."

"What of you, Miss Abbott?" asked Mr. Winston. "Do you enjoy pantomimes?"

"I do," Mildred answered.

"Look there," Jane whispered to Mildred. "There is Miss Rose. She sees us, and is not at all happy to see Mr. Winston is in our company. You should vex her further by flirting with Mr. Winston."

Mildred opened her mouth to object, but the words never came out, for she saw Alastair across the room. He had on his arm a most beautiful woman, with golden locks framing a sweet face comprising a charming nose and dainty, rosy lips.

"See there," said Mr. Grenville, "is that your cousin, Miss Abbott?"

"And I think the woman to be Lady Sophia, daughter of a Duke," added Mrs. Grenville.

"How lovely she is!" said Jane.

"Are they betrothed yet?" asked Mrs. Grenville.

"I know not," replied Millie after a difficult swallow. "But I think there is much talk of it."

"What a grand wedding they must have! How lucky you are, Millie, for certainly you will receive an invitation."

Alastair and the woman were headed to the boxes and did not seem to see her. Mildred tried not to look up at the balconies where they would be sitting, but during the entire performance, her mind traveled to where her gaze avoided. She pretended to enjoy the pantomime far more than she did. At one point, she gasped in surprise when Clown surprised Harlequin from a trap door. She inadvertently grabbed for the arm of her chair, only to land her hand upon Mr. Winston's. She blushed. He returned a warm smile.

"I once saw an actor, in the role of Clown, leap from a platform above the stage, rotate in the air, and land on his feet," Mr. Winston said.

They talked about some of the most daring and comic stunts they had seen, but Mildred admitted that as much as she enjoyed the pantomime, she favored dramas much more.

"Tragedies or comedies?" he asked.

She considered the answer. "What think you?"

"Tragedies."

"You know me well, Mr. Winston.

"Given I had but two choices, the odds were pretty good for me."

They shared a laugh.

During the interval, Mr. Winston and Mr. Wiggins offered to purchase lemonade and confections for the women. Shortly after they returned, Jane bid them fetch some fruits, for she wanted to speak with Mildred while they strolled the lobby.

"I think my father would approve of Mr. Wiggins," Jane confided. "He is a good sort of man, though he is not so rich as my family would wish, but they desire my happiness."

"How fortunate for you, Jane! I agree that Mr. Wiggins is a fine man, and I would that more parents thought as liberally as your father," Mildred replied.

"What thinks your father of Mr. Winston?"

"My mother does not consider him—"

"Miss Abbott."

Mildred felt her heart stop in mid-beat. She turned around to face the Marquess. He bowed coolly to Jane before saying, "May I have a word, Miss Abbott?"

Seeing that the Marquess appeared unhappy, Jane did a quick curtsy and scurried away as if fleeing for her life. Mildred looked for Lady Sophia but did not see her.

"My lord," Mildred said, "how are you enjoying the—"

He interrupted, "What are you doing in the company of that man?"

Taken aback by his brusque tone, she asked, "What man?"

"That Winston fellow. I knew him at Oxford."

"He is a friend of the Grenville family."

"You should avoid his company."

"Why? He is an amiable and thoughtful gentleman."

"You thought the same of the Viscount Devon."

"And I still have no evidence to think otherwise."

"You have my advice."

"And why do you advise against Mr. Winston?"

"I do not recall the specifics, but there was some sort of affair involving him and a young woman of little standing."

"I did not think you easily persuaded by rumors."

"This was no rumor."

"It would seem a common accusation of young men at Oxford to have had dalliances, and whatever happened, this was many years ago."

"I somewhat doubt that he is significantly changed for the better. What transpired spoke to a serious flaw of character."

"And what was it that transpired?"

"He was not of my year, and I spared it little heed, but as wretched as I am, I did not think highly of him after what I had heard."

"When you have recalled what had happened or what you had heard, I will hear what you have to say. Till then—"

"Till then, you will not entertain his company."

She bristled. "You are not my father."

"I am the one providing your dowry."

"Which you can dispense with at any time."

She saw a muscle in his jaw tighten.

"Are you often in his company?"

"You are impertinent, Alastair."

"He must be attracted to your dowry if he seeks your company."

She fumed that he would suggest her company was not worth seeking if not for her dowry. "Then he would be no different than every man who seeks me out! And it is your fault for granting me such a dowry."

He pressed his lips into a grim line before saying, "You invited my involvement with that Haversham fellow. I will approve whomever you wish to marry."

"And what if I wish to marry Mr. Winston?"

"I would sooner you wed Kittredge, and he is no good for any woman."

At that moment, the orchestra began, indicating the performance was about to resume.

"There you are, Miss Abbott." Mr. Winston had approached. Upon seeing Alastair, he made a stiff bow. "Lord Alastair, you may not recall but we were at Oxford together."

"I do recall, Mr. Winston," Alastair responded, his face darkening.

A brief and awkward silence followed.

"I think we should take our seats," Mildred said to Mr. Winston. She made a curtsy to Alastair.

As she and Mr. Winston returned to their seats with the Grenvilles and Wiggins, he observed, "I do not think your cousin pleased to see me."

"He is cross with everyone," Mildred answered, her mind half turned to what Alastair had said.

"Perhaps he recalls the less encouraging moments of my time at Oxford. I was more foolish then, frequented one too many taverns and fell in love far too often. There was one young woman in particular. She and I had become exceedingly fond of one another, but, alas, she had no connections, and my family would not approve our marriage. It broke my heart to tell her that we could not marry, and I considered it all quite my fault. She was younger and more naive. The tragedy of it is that she took her own life not long after, and I shall carry the burden of my actions to my grave."

He lowered his head.

"I am sorry to hear it," Mildred said, moved by his sadness.

"I should have known better, and been the party of greater responsibility, but I have learned from my mistakes. I am much more careful of falling in love now."

"That you place the blame upon yourself shows tremendous character," she praised, and put a hand upon his arm.

He looked at her with gratitude. "I do not deserve your compliments, Miss Abbott. Not on this matter."

Her heart ached for his pain. Alastair had merely assumed the worst of Mr. Winston, and, given his own shortcomings, he ought not cast stones so readily at others.

Alastair's attempts to interfere in her life suddenly, when he had made no attempt to see her after Michaelmas, rankled her for reasons she knew not why. She certainly did not appreciate his overbearing manner in forbidding her continued acquaintance with Mr. Winston.

At the end of the performance, as he was with Lady Sophia, Millie was, to her relief, spared from having to speak with the Marquess again. As her party stood outside awaiting their carriage, Mildred and Mr. Winston chanced to stand a little ways from Wiggins, Jane, and her parents.

"Mr. Winston, Miss Abbott," greeted Hannah Rose, who had ventured a few steps from her family to greet them. "Miss Abbott, I rarely see you at the theater. What brings you here tonight?"

"The Grenvilles have made it a tradition to see the pantomime at Christmas each year," Mildred replied. "I am a guest of theirs."

Miss Rose showed no interest in her answer and had already begun addressing Mr. Winston. "Did you enjoy the pantomime?"

"I did," Mr. Winston replied politely.

"The view is much better from the boxes. My family has an annual subscription. Perhaps I can persuade my father to extend you an invitation."

Mr. Winston made no reply. Miss Rose was recalled by her family, for their carriage had arrived.

"Am I ungrateful if I feel relieved that her family has not extended such an invitation?" Mr. Winston asked quietly.

"There may be men who would call you that, for the attentions of Miss Rose are quite coveted," Mildred said.

"I suppose, but I seek more in a woman than wealth or beauty. My family wishes I were not so particular. They are quite anxious for me to wed."

"As are mine," Mildred sighed.

"I think I cannot forbear them longer. At times I have been tempted to simply marry the first woman I see, but I cannot be content with a woman lest I hold her in regard. She must be easy to converse with, like you, and of an easy disposition."

Mildred was struck with an inspiration. "I dare say, and you may find this presumptuous—ridiculous even—and I will take no offense if you should think it precisely that. But, as you and I are in similar situations, perhaps we could find a solution that would eliminate the pressures we both face."

His countenance brightened. "I am intrigued, Miss Abbott."

"As we seem to find each other's company pleasurable, have no dearth of topics to converse on, share similar sensibilities, perhaps it would not be so farfetched a notion if we were to wed one another."

"Do you truly think so, Miss Abbott?" he cried.

"I do."

"And I think we should deal with each other famously! Should I drop to bended knee here?"

"Oh no! That would not do. You ought to speak to my father first."

"Will he give his consent?"

"He might, if he is not too persuaded by my mother. She wishes me to wed a man of great income."

"As she should. She wants security for her daughter. But I will have my family write to her to explain that I am more than capable of providing for all that you need and more."

Mildred felt giddy. She had not expected to find a man as handsome and charming as Mr. Winston who might also be partial to her. Alastair, if he maintained his opinion of Mr. Winston, would not approve the match, but the worst he could do was revoke her dowry, which she had never truly desired from him in the first place.

"I shall come by to speak to your father on Thursday, shall I?"

"Yes, yes."

Jane called to them then. As they rode the carriage home, Mr. Winston sat opposite Mildred. They exchanged several smiles. The carriage stopped at Mildred's house first, and Mr. Winston insisted upon walking her to the door.

"Till Thursday," he said, kissing her hand as a servant opened the door.

"Yes, Thursday," said Mildred, a little breathless. "Good night, Mr. Winston."

"How was the pantomime?" Mr. Abbott asked when the Grenville carriage had departed.

"Amusing,"

"Is that all?"

"The costumes were brilliantly colorful, and the actress playing Columbine was quite talented in her role."

She spoke with calm, but inside she was hardly serene. Alastair may not approve of Mr. Winston, but Mr. Winston was her best chance for matrimonial bliss. Mr. Winston could have wooed the willing Miss Rose, but he had always chosen different company, and Mildred believed the man had a genuine interest for her. She could hardly wait for Thursday.

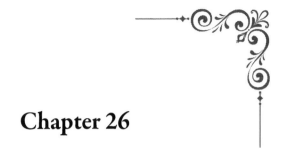

# Chapter 26

"I KNEW GEORGE WINSTON well during our time at Oxford," said the gentleman, Henry Stanton. He and Alastair stood at the billiard table at one of the gentlemen's clubs on the Strand. "But I have not been in contact with him since then."

"If you do not deem it too prying, I should like to hear all that you know of him," said Alastair.

Stanton aimed his cue stick at one of the billiard balls. "I considered him a good friend at the time, but we parted ways after an unfortunate affair."

"I recall some matter with a young woman, Miss Jones. I would say he took her maidenhead, but I think his involvement entailed far worse."

"Yes. There was quite the scene, for she had come to the campus in search of him and, finding him on one of the lawns, proceeded to speak to him before no small number of persons. She was not a person of much consequence but very pretty. George had lain with her a few times, and it led to her being with child. She came to plead for his assistance, for her family had thrown her out."

Alastair watched the ball strike a skittle. "Was it certain the child was his?"

"The lass was a virgin. George complained of the copious amount of blood she shed when he took her maidenhead. She fan-

267

cied herself in love with him, and he with her. I doubt she would have lain with another."

"I understand that Winston received her rather coldly."

Stanton nodded and stood aside as Alastair took his turn. "He was, in my humble opinion, surprisingly callous. He responded that she was mistaken. And how dare she impugn his character. It seemed he could not rid himself of her presence fast enough. He spoke with such vitriol, and the poor thing looked so devastated, I would have intervened had I no loyalty to George at the time. I approached her afterward and offered what money I had on me. I implored George to take some pity upon the creature. He need not marry her, but perhaps he could provide some funding for her. He would not, and claimed that she had entrapped him. Her misery evoked no sympathy from him. A few days later, she leaped off the edge of a cliff to her death."

"Did he show any remorse for what happened?"

"I cannot say for certain. After I had expressed my disappointment in his actions, he no longer desired my company. I regret that I had not cautioned the young lady against George. He had always talked of marrying an heiress, and I knew his dalliance with the young woman was nothing more than a lark to him."

"I hope he is a changed man, and that the years have afforded him more wisdom and charity."

"What I had heard gives me little hope. A mutual acquaintance had mentioned his attempts to woo the daughter of a nabob, but the father deemed him unworthy, for he had no income and lived off an inheritance from his uncle. George had then attempted to seduce the girl into a compromising situation, forcing the father's hand, but when the family got wind of it, they sent her off to a nunnery. George is charming, to be sure, and amiable company for both sexes. But, upon examination of our time together, there had always been evidence of a selfishness that I had failed to see. Even if he has improved in the years since I have known, had I a daughter, I would not permit her within several yards of him."

When they had finished the round of billiards, Alastair thanked the man for the game and his time. He left the club and ordered his driver to Cheapside, where the Abbotts lived. If they were not at home, he would wait for them. What he had observed of Millie and Winston last night at the theater did not bode well. And once again she had seemed dismissive of his cautions.

Alastair found the Abbotts at home, and the most surprised and flustered Mrs. Abbott was the first to greet him. She said that Mr. Abbott would be down shortly, as he was just waking from his nap. When Mildred appeared, equally surprised as her mother to see him, Mrs. Abbott snapped at her daughter to bring tea as quickly as she could.

"Pray, have a seat, your lordship," Mrs. Abbott bid. "Oh, no! This settee is much more comfortable. I mean to dispose of that one there and replace it."

Mildred gave him a curious look as she returned with the tea.

"Oh, surely we have better biscuits than these!" Mrs. Abbott exclaimed.

"Alas, we do not," Mildred replied.

Mrs. Abbott colored. "Well, we shall be sure to add biscuits to our list. Perhaps we have some fruits we can offer his lordship?"

"I require no refreshments. The tea is sufficient," he said.

Mr. Abbott appeared just as Mildred had finished pouring the tea. When she handed Alastair his cup, their fingers brushed. A blush seemed to rise in her cheeks and she quickly retreated.

"Your lordship," greeted Mr. Abbott, "you are most welcome in our home, always, but is there something I can assist you with?"

Alastair stared at Mildred as she busied herself adding sugar and milk to her tea. The sugar surprised him, for he had noticed at Edenmoor, she did not take sugar, possibly in protest of the slavery used to provide it.

"Indeed, your presence honors us," added Mrs. Abbott. "Were you in the neighborhood then?"

Mildred glanced at her mother as if to say that no business would bring the Marquess to Cheapside.

"Forgive my unannounced appearance," Alastair said, "but I had thought to inquire if the dowry I am bequeathing your daughter will be needed this year?"

"Oh, we had hoped so!" Mrs. Abbott replied. "But Mr. Carleton may not return till spring of next year."

Alastair noticed Mildred was only half successful in suppressing a grimace. "Mr. Carleton?"

"He is a gentleman engaged in much trade in the West Indies, and alas, he is required there to oversee some troubles." She looked to her husband. "But we expect that a proposal will be coming upon his return."

Mildred did not seem to share the excitement of her mother.

"I shall have to look into this Mr. Carleton," he said. "As the provider of Miss Abbott's dowry, it is in my interest to see the funds bestowed upon a worthy man."

"Yes, of course, and we cannot thank you enough for your generosity. Indeed, it is beyond generous. I should say it were saintly—"

Mildred coughed, and even Mr. Abbott, aware that Alastair found verbosity tiresome, attempted to gesture for his wife to cease.

"I would hazard, however, that Miss Abbott has many suitors?" Alastair asked.

Mildred met his stare. "Is it Mr. Winston that concerns you?"

He appreciated her bluntness. "He does, Miss Abbott. Mr. Winston has a suspect past, and I think it wise to stay your distance from him."

"I knew it!" Mrs. Abbott cried. "I knew he was not worthy of Millie."

"He is a friend of the Grenvilles, Mama, and I do not think they would associate themselves with someone of questionable character."

"He is staying with Mr. Harris, who is a friend of the Grenvilles. That is different."

Mildred turned to Alastair. "What do you have to support your judgment?"

"Sufficient details exist to warrant my disapproval. The death of a young woman may be placed on his conscience."

Mrs. Abbott gasped.

"I know of this already," Mildred declared.

Alastair stared at her in disbelief while Mrs. Abbott made another gasp.

"And you are not troubled by this?" he asked.

"He admitted full responsibility to me, and perhaps if you had granted him the opportunity to speak his side of the matter—"

"It would not alter my opinion of him."

"But are you certain you do not form your opinions too quickly?"

"Millie!" Mrs. Abbott cried. "I doubt his lordship would speak ill of anyone lest he had reason. I am certain you are a great judge of character, my lord."

"Miss Abbott, on the matter of Mr. Winston, I will not support any suit of his."

"What if he were to convince you that he could make a good husband?"

"How would he do so?"

She furrowed her brow. "He could have married any number of eligible women from families of means."

"Perhaps, but are you certain they would have him?"

"Millie, why are we discussing Mr. Winston?" Mrs. Abbott asked. "His lordship has made known his opinion."

"His opinion may be misplaced," Mildred replied. "Perhaps if he took the time to better acquaint himself with Mr. Winston—"

"You may save your breath, Miss Abbott. I have no desire to better acquaint myself with Mr. Winston."

"But then how will he prove himself to you?"

"That is not a concern that troubles me. But there is one way to prove his intentions. Let us remove the dowry and see if his interests remain true."

Mildred straightened in indignation. "I am certain it shall! Despite what you may think of him, avarice is not a prevailing trait."

Her ready defense of Winston vexed him, and he made no reply.

"There, that is the wisdom of Solomon," Mrs. Abbott praised.

"Mr. Carleton began to take an interest only after my dowry had been raised," Millie said, "yet you do not condemn him."

"I will look into the character of Mr. Carleton," Alastair voiced, "but Mr. Winston will not have a penny of your dowry."

"It will not matter to him!"

Alastair tightened his grip on his teacup. This was madness. Why was she so stalwart in her defense of the man, especially if she knew his past?

"You would marry without a dowry?"

"I would."

Mrs. Abbott looked horrified. "Millie! Stop this nonsense! Mr. Abbott, you have heard his lordship. You would not approve a proposal from Mr. Winston."

"No, of course not," Mr. Abbott answered. "I have the highest regard for Lord Alastair. And as he is the benefactor, his opinion prevails."

Alastair looked back to Mildred. He saw a stubborn set to her jaw, but she made no further objections. Having made himself clear, he indicated he would take his leave. Mrs. Abbott attempted to persuade him to stay, till Mr. Abbott told her that surely his lordship had more important matters than to while away the time with them, to which Mrs. Abbott then heartily agreed and said that they would not detain him further.

Mildred bid him farewell with a silent curtsy, but he noticed the frown upon her countenance had not left her. As the carriage took him back to Mayfair, Alastair considered if he should have divulged more details of Winston's past. He should not have had to. Millie's parents had given no objections. But Millie had remained steadfast in her own opinions of Winston. Perhaps the reason she was blind to the man's possible faults was because she had fallen in love with him. The thought made Alastair grind his teeth.

Her reactions concerned him greatly. More needed to be done to address the situation.

# Chapter 27

"THIS IS MOST UNFORTUNATE," Mrs. Abbott declared. "What will her ladyship think?"

"Millie does look pale," Mr. Abbott said. "Come, we had best depart soon or we shall be late."

"Give my regards and, of course, my regrets to Lady Katherine," Mildred said weakly from her bed.

"How is it you should fall ill on Christmas!" Mrs. Abbott lamented for the fourth time, but, with many sighs, she followed her husband.

When Mildred heard the sound of their carriage pull away, she leaped out of her bed and dressed in better traveling clothes. She pulled out the valise she had packed earlier. It was a small one and could only fit a few of her garments, but a larger one would prove too cumbersome. She had a few hours to make her way to the designated posting inn outside London. From there, she and Mr. Winston would make their way to Gretna Green.

"Elope?" Mr. Winston had echoed in great surprise when she had intercepted him a few blocks from the Abbott home earlier that day. "Am I not to ask your father for your hand in marriage?".

"It is the only way," she had explained. "Father will not give his consent. Not after Alastair threatened to retract the dowry."

"Retract the dowry? Are you certain?"

"He came to tea yesterday and spoke quite forcibly. He claims he heard complaints of your character in your time at Oxford, but when I pressed him for specifics, he provided none and admitted he has no direct knowledge of you."

"That is distressing to hear," Winston had said, appearing deep in thought. "I own I was hardly perfect in my youth, but what he had heard must have been quite serious for him to make such a declaration."

"Well, it matters not. I asserted that you were not the sort to marry for money. Alastair deserves a proper scolding, but it is useless, he pays little heed to anyone."

"There must be some way to convince him that I have only honorable intentions toward you."

"He believes that removing the dowry is the only way to prove you truly care for me."

Troubled, he furrowed his brow. "But eloping will not improve matters. We had better attempt to reason with your cousin."

"In truth, I have no desire to. I had asked him to retract the dowry long ago. I've no wish for his money. It only affords him the opportunity to interfere in my affairs. You say you have sufficient income for a modest living, and I have no wish for more. I am quite accustomed and content with a humble life, and making economies does not frighten me."

"Millie, eloping is no small matter and will greatly upset your family."

"The sort of man they wish me to marry would certainly make me unhappy. I could not do it. It is my hope that, in time, my mother and father will love me enough to forgive me."

George had continued to make other arguments against eloping, but she was determined and eventually wore him down. She appreciated that he was concerned for her welfare and her honor, but the sooner she set upon her new path in life, the better.

"We could be wed within the day at Hyde Park Corner..." she suggested.

"No, no, if we are to elope, we ought to—perhaps—well, let us make it a grand adventure and make for Gretna Green."

"Gretna Green? Is that necessary?"

"We should go where we cannot be found till after we are wed."

Mildred nodded. "Very well. I do not require much packing."

"And we should meet outside of London so that we are not seen by anyone known to us. There is an inn on the road to Scotland, the Boar's Head."

They agreed to meet on Christmas, when her family would be with Lady Katherine and not notice her absence for many hours. That night at dinner, Mildred could barely eat as she considered how much she would miss her mother and father, and what their reactions must be when they discovered what she had done. She trusted her father would not disown her, but it might be some time before she would be admitted into their house.

Lady Katherine, too, would be wounded that she had not been brought into Mildred's confidence, but Mildred feared her ladyship's discouragement. Though Lady Katherine might form a favorable opinion of Mr. Winston, and Mildred suspected she would, her ladyship would undoubtedly urge patience, perhaps even offering to speak to Alastair.

But Mildred wanted an end to the tormenting feelings that gripped her whenever she thought of her cousin. In truth, she had fallen a little in love with him at Château Follet. She had not wanted to acknowledge it, and their time at Edenmoor had only deepened her feelings for him.

Mildred slept fitfully that night. Christmas morning could not arrive soon enough.

"IT IS CHRISTMAS DAY, my lord," said Alastair's housekeeper.

"Food and money, then," Alastair replied to her inquiry as to what should be given to the wassail before dismissing her. He remained seated behind his writing table but retained a view of the gentleman who sat opposite on the sofa. "Do you love her?"

"I have a great fondness for Miss Abbott," Winston replied after a pause.

Alastair stared at the man as if he could see past the façade and into his heart.

"I care for her greatly and would endeavor to make her happy to the best of my effort," Winston added. "That would seem sufficient to qualify for love."

Alastair felt his body tighten. His next question was the more difficult one. "And does she love you?"

Winston was more quick to answer this one. "Yes, and I am grateful and honored to receive her affections."

If the quill he held had been made of sturdier material, it would've snapped beneath Alastair's grip.

"A man of your charms could have a woman of superior qualities."

"You flatter me, my lord, but I am more than content with Miss Abbott. She is an intelligent creature, and her company quite enjoyable."

"She is of middling beauty, her figure imperfect."

"I do not see that to be the case, my lord. She may not have the loveliest of countenances and her form is perhaps not so slender, but I would not say she is not comely."

"Her family is of inferior breeding."

"My family is not so superior that I would criticize her background. She is fortunate, however, to be connected to your family."

"The benefits are not as great as they may seem. I erred in my generosity with her, and thus have reconsidered the dowry I was to provide her."

"May I ask what has prompted this decision?"

"It has come to my attention that her dowry has attracted unsavory suitors. If the dowry is lacking, then we may be assured that the man who still wishes to marry her is sincere in his affections."

"What of her happiness?"

A muscle rippled along Alastair's jaw. Of all men, why had she chosen Winston?

"I am willing to care for her as well as any man can care for his wife. And if she would be happy with me, I fail to see the wrong in this."

"Then you would wed her without a dowry?"

Winston said nothing and would not meet his eye. "I do not think it wise for us to marry in that case."

"Without a dowry, she no longer holds your interest. I think I see the extent of your affections, sir."

Winston looked up at him. "You would punish a member of your own family in so harsh a manner?"

"She is a cousin by marriage only, and marrying you, sir, would be the greater punishment."

Winston drew in a sharp breath. "Does her happiness mean so little to you?"

"Are you so certain she will be happy with you?"

"She loves me."

"You are certain of this?"

"She does not care for your dowry. She will have me without it. Indeed, we plan to elope. Today, in fact."

Alastair leaped to his feet. "Elope? On Christmas? I find it hard to believe that Miss Abbott would disrespect her family in this manner."

"Perhaps you underestimate her affections for me."

Alastair wanted to wring the man's neck.

"It was her idea. I tried to dissuade her from it. I had thought it would be more reasonable to attempt to persuade you of the virtues of our marriage, but she was adamant."

"And you mean to see this elopement through?"

Winston straightened. "I may yet convince her to abandon her impulsive suggestion."

Alastair narrowed his eyes. "You have no desire to marry Miss Abbott without her dowry."

Winston lifted his chin. "Perhaps I will elope with her."

"I think not, for if it is funds you seek, I will make it worth your while to stay your distance from her: an annuity of a hundred pounds a year. Marry her and you will have nothing."

"That is a paltry sum, especially for a man of your means."

"It is more than you're worth, but marry Millie, and you receive nothing. Or would you prefer that I bring all my resources to bear against you? If I choose to, I can see you turned out of every door in polite society."

Winston's bottom lip quivered. "I accept your proposal, Lord Alastair, and will let Miss Abbott's happiness fall upon *your* conscience."

Alastair drew the note he had prepared and thrust it into Winston's hands. "That is your first installment. You may communicate with my solicitor hereafter. Now get out before I throw you out."

Winston did not need to be told twice and strode out with as much dignity as a man of his character could bear.

Alastair fisted his hand, regretting he had not been given a provocation to box the man's ears in. He went to sit at his table but was too restless to remain seated.

*Damnation.*

Though he was glad to have rid Millie of Winston, he doubted she would be pleased at his intrusion. She did not understand that he acted for her benefit.

Her commitment to Winston still stunned him. Mildred was not the sort of silly young woman to fall in love with a handsome face and charming manners. Only one explanation remained for why she would disregard what he had done in his time at Oxford: she was deeply in love with the man.

His chest constricted at the thought, and he felt an ache surge in his groin. Winston was the last man he would see Millie with. Though he doubted this Mr. Carleton would be any worthier, if he had earned her contempt. He could think of no man he would be content to see her marry, but, for her sake, he would make an effort to see the better qualities in her other suitors. He did not wish to see her unhappy. If she knew the sincerity of his intentions, she might better be able to forgive him.

He rang for his hat and gloves. The Abbotts would be with Katherine for Christmas dinner.

# Chapter 28

KATHERINE HAD DECORATED her home in holly, rosemary and ivy. As he took notice of the greenery, Alastair wondered why Katherine had chosen to celebrate Christmas with more fanfare this year rather than confine the holiday to the customary acts of charity.

"What a pleasant surprise," Katherine remarked. "I have hopes that perhaps you mean to amend your strained relations with your family."

"Such efforts are better aided by my absence rather than my presence," he replied.

He greeted the family members already present: Edward, his wife and sons; Harriet, her husband and newborn babe; his sisters and their husbands.

When he came to the Abbotts, he inquired, "Where is Miss Abbott?"

"Alas, she took ill after the Christmas service," answered Mrs. Abbott.

Guilt twisted in his bosom. Had she fallen ill from a broken heart after learning that she was not to wed Mr. Winston?

"She seemed weak during the service, "Mr. Abbott said to his wife. "I hope it is nothing serious."

Alastair frowned. "When did your service conclude?"

"I would say eleven o'clock."

"And she was already ill?"

"She was slow in her steps and put her hand often to her brow."

"She would have made every effort to come," said Mrs. Abbott, "if she were not feeling so poorly."

Alastair recalled that he had met with Mr. Winston about one o'clock. Her illness then was not due to the news Mr. Winston had to break to her.

This provided no solace to Alastair, for something seemed amiss. Millie and Winston had planned to elope today. Would Winston still intend to do so despite the offer he had accepted?

Alastair pulled his aunt aside. "Have you heard from Millie?"

"Not in some time, though I had invited her to tea several times."

"She has not written you? Or spoken of a man named George Winston?"

"I have heard nothing from her. In truth, I'm quite surprised that I have not, but I understand from her mother that she has been busy entertaining various suitors. Who is this gentleman you speak of?"

"A man not worthy of being called a gentleman." A sense of urgency haunted him. "They had planned to elope today."

Katherine blinked in surprise. "Elope? Millie? This is unlike her. And not to have said a word to me. I am astonished."

"Are you? But you were not astonished that she would go to the Château Debauchery with you?"

"That is different. An elopement will alter her life. How do you know of this Winston fellow and their elopement?"

"Because I had expressly forbid her continued acquaintance with him and threatened to revoke the dowry if they married."

"You said this to her?"

"And to her parents. Winston is a dangerous fellow."

Katherine furrowed her brow. "In what manner?"

"In the severest of manners."

"Millie is unaware of this?"

"She is not, but would have him nonetheless." His whole body tensed. "She must be quite in love with him."

His aunt stared at him keenly. "And that vexes you?"

"That she would disregard my advice and elope with a man who will most certainly cause her ruin or grief? That she would fail to appreciate my generosity in providing for her dowry by running off with Winston?"

"And is that all that troubles you?"

"What do you imply, madam?"

"You think I do not know what happened during Michaelmas?"

He started. He was in disbelief until she smiled.

"I had hoped to speak to Millie about what transpired. She had seemed dispirited after you left Edenmoor. I thought perhaps she had fallen in love with you."

"Millie? With me?"

"And you with her."

He straightened. "Madam, you are a romantic."

"Do you deny it?"

"Even if true, it is of no consequence. Millie is in love with Winston, and I fear they may carry out this elopement. "

"If he is as bad as you say, you must stop them."

He nodded. "But speak not of this to Mr. and Mrs. Abbott. I do not wish to alarm them unnecessarily. I will take my leave without bidding adieu to the others."

"Of course. Godspeed, Alastair."

He could not receive his garrick, hat and gloves fast enough. When his carriage pulled up before the Abbott residence, he was out the vehicle before it had come to a complete stop.

"Where is Miss Abbott?" he asked the maid who answered the door.

"In her room resting," the surprised woman replied.

He whisked past the servant. "I will see her—in her room, if she is too ill to leave it."

"Shall I take your hat and gloves, sir?"

"No, but please inform her that her cousin is here."

The maid nodded and went upstairs. He paced the vestibule while he waited. If Millie was asleep, he would wait until she wakened.

But what he had feared was true.

"She is not in her room," the maid said when she had returned.

Alarm gripped him. "Where are the other servants? Have they seen her?"

"I am the only one. There is a laundry maid who comes once a week, but as it is Christmas, she will come tomorrow."

Wanting to confirm for himself, he took the stairs three steps at a time and went into the room with the open door.

It was empty. She had left. With Winston.

Alastair was stunned. Had Winston played him for a fool and only pretended to accept the offer of the annuity? Had he underestimated what partiality the man may have had for Millie? Or perhaps Millie had convinced him that the better course still lay in elopement. Millie was surprisingly persuasive. He ought not have underestimated *her*.

"Have you searched the rest of the house?" he asked the maid as she came up behind him.

"I have not. Should I? I don't understand. Miss Abbott was too ill to leave her bed."

"Where does she keep her coat?"

"Her coat, sir?"

Alastair opened the doors of an armoire.

"Oh!" the maid gasped in surprise. "It is not there."

"Are all her bonnets and shoes accounted for?"

The maid examined the rest of the armoire's contents. "How strange! Perhaps the laundry maid had come early this week?"

Alastair needed no further evidence. Millie was gone.

As disbelief faded, a sense of loss took its place. If she succeeded in marrying Winston, she was gone for *him*.

It was what he wanted, Alastair reminded himself. He had doubled her dowry so that she could easily find a husband and he would be done with her, but she had been right. Her dowry had attracted too many suitors, including undesirable ones.

He could not let her marry Winston. If he should find her before they married, he vowed he would make finding the best man he could for Millie his utmost priority. Or he could—

An object upon the floor caught his eye. The maid had missed the note that had perhaps fallen off the bed. Bending down, he picked up the note and unfolded it.

*My Dearest Parents,*

*Please know first and foremost that I hold you in much regard and love. My present actions may appear to contradict this assertion, and perhaps it is my selfishness, and not a lack of esteem or love for you, that wins the day. I wish I could be a better daughter. I wish I could envision myself married to Mr. Carleton or any of the other men you would deem in my interest to marry. Alas, I cannot. I expect my greatest chance for matrimonial happiness lies with Mr. Winston. He is a good man whose disposition matches my own. I hope you will one day come to forgive the actions I feel compelled to take. I do so with a heavy heart at the pain this must cause you.*

*I will send word when Mr. Winston and I are married. He assures me that his situation is more than capable of sustaining a modest living. I have never wanted much more. Thus, you need not worry of providing for me. I hope that you will consider welcoming us into your house as Mr. and Mrs. Winston.*

*With love,*

*Mildred*

Pocketing the note, he asked, "Mr. Harris. He is a friend of the Grenvilles. Do you know where he might live?"

"I know not, but the Grenvilles live at Cavendish Square."

He cursed, for he would have preferred to go straight to Mr. Harris'. After telling the maid that there was naught to worry and that he knew where Millie was—it was only a temporary fib, as he fully intended to find Millie—he hurried back to his carriage and made for Cavendish Square.

He found the Grenville residence, and, to his fortune and immense relief, Mr. Harris and Mr. Winston. Upon setting eyes on the latter, he found it hard not to stride over and deck the man.

"Lord Alastair—" Mr. Grenville began.

"I will have a private word with Mr. Winston," he growled.

Mr. Grenville showed them into the library. As soon as the doors were closed, Alastair shoved Winston to the wall, closing his hand about the man's throat.

"Where is she?" he demanded.

Winston gripped his arm, attempting to keep it from crushing his neck to the wall. "What do you mean, sir?"

"Millie. Where did she go after you spoke with her?"

"I didn't."

Alastair felt the veins at this temple throb. "What? You did not speak with her?"

"I did not wish to make a scene."

"If you did not speak with her, then she still thought you were to elope?"

"I sent a note to her."

Millie must not have received it. "Where? When?"

"At the Boar's Head Inn off the main posting road to Gretna Green."

"Gretna Green! Why the devil would you travel that far? You are both of age. Why not marry at Hyde Park Corner or even Fleet?"

"It was her idea! Their sex thrives on romanticism!"

Alastair tightened his grip before throwing Winston to the ground in disgust. If he had the luxury of time, he would throttle the man. But he wanted to get to Millie.

"You will not speak of this to anyone, save that you and I had a disagreement to settle. If you wish to demand satisfaction, name your seconds," he said to Winston, who remained on hands and knees.

When Winston only stared at him as if he were mad, Alastair threw open the doors and stalked past the surprised host. When in his carriage, Alastair let out an oath that even startled his driver. He could not believe that Winston had not spoken or, at the least, written a letter to Millie at her home. Instead, he had allowed her to travel to a posting inn on her own.

*The damned bleeder.*

The carriage could not arrive at the posting inn fast enough. As few people traveled on Christmas, the innkeeper was properly astonished to see Alastair.

"I seek a young woman," he informed the elderly keeper when he did not see Millie.

"I had a young woman here earlier. She was alone and sat for several hours, till a letter arrived by messenger for her."

"Do you have the letter?"

"It is with her. I saw her place it in her reticule."

"What happened then?"

"After readings its contents, she asked if there would be a coach today. I said not likely, as it was Christmas. My son was visiting and had himself a wagon. I offered that he could take her where she wished to go for the right price."

"And where did she wish to go?"

The man furrowed his brow. "Can't remember, as I never heard the name before."

Alastair drew in a breath to calm his patience. He was ready to wring the innkeeper if it would do any good.

"They took the road that leads to Surrey."

Surrey. Why would Millie head in that direction? Alastair understood that she no longer needed to head north to Gretna Green if the letter the innkeeper referenced was the one that Winston had written, but what lay to the southeast?

He stiffened as the answer came to him.

Château Follet.

# Chapter 29

"YOU ARE NO IMPOSITION, *ma cheri*. Of course you must stay," Madame Follet said, greeting Mildred in the salon. As always, the hostess appeared radiant in her white draped muslin, a vibrantly hued Turkish shawl, and golden jewelry. She carried herself with the vivacity of a young woman of twenty, despite being twice that in years.

"I could think of nowhere else to go," Mildred said, abashed.

"I am flattered you would choose to spend Noel at Château Follet. I have a number of guests here, and they would more than welcome an addition."

"A place to spend the night is more than sufficient."

"Nonsense! You cannot come here and not take part in the revelry. I have even prepared a special midnight feast, a *Le Reveillon* if you will, but of a much more wicked nature."

Gratitude filled Mildred. Madame Follet had not even inquired into why Mildred should have traveled here on her own.

"I cannot thank you enough, Madame Follet."

"I will have a room prepared for you, and mind the kissing boughs."

"Kissing boughs?"

Madame Follet pointed at the ivy with white berries that hung above the threshold. "It is a quaint practice, from the peasantry I believe. If you wish for more than kisses, do not hesitate to inform me if you are desirous of a partner. I would be happy to provide you one."

Mildred blushed. She had not considered participating and doubted she could be in the proper mood. Once settled in her own room—the very same she had stayed in her first time at Château Follet—she drew out the letter from Mr. Winston.

*Dear Miss Abbott,*

*I regret that you shall be reading this, but I could not forgive myself if our marriage earned you the disdain of your family and, in particular, your cousin, the Marquess of Alastair. I would Lord Alastair had not threatened to take away your dowry, but you are deserving of a man who can both make you happy and keep your dowry.*

*G.W.*

She sighed at the brevity of the letter and how it had made no mention of his affections. Yet, the letter had not caught her completely by surprise. The look in his eyes when she had informed him that Alastair intended to revoke her dowry, and his hesitant reception of her idea to marry regardless of Alastair's approval, had been evidence of his true intentions, but she had failed to give them their due. Did he truly decide not to marry because he thought she would be better without him? Or had she misjudged his partiality for her?

Tearing the letter in twain, she cast it into the hearth.

Since Christmas service this morning, she had vacillated between heartache and anticipation. Perhaps she could have made it back to London before her parents had returned from Christmas dinner with Lady Katherine, but, at the time, she had had no desire to return home in defeat. She realized now that she was given to impulsiveness, and perhaps, as with accepting Haversham's proposal, she had been rash. She had wanted to be the good daughter, but in the end, she had not the fortitude to see it through. Disgrace and shame certainly awaited her now.

And she had thought she could not commit a worse mistake than accepting Haversham's proposal.

Looking about, she found comfort in the familiarity of her surroundings. She had liked this room during her first visit, though she had not spent a great deal of time in it. The same pastoral paintings with but hints of lasciviousness graced its walls of rose-colored silk. She remembered how cheerfully the afternoon sun shone into the room, brightening the mahogany furnishings.

Bhadra, the comely Indian maid who had served her last time, appeared to assist her from her traveling clothes. When selecting a gown for the evening, Mildred hesitated at the ivory muslin she had thought she might wear when she wed Mr. Winston.

"You'll look lovely in this gown," Bhadra said, running her hand through the delicate top layer with burgundy embroidery at the hem. "You must wear it, miss."

"I suppose it is festive in appearance," Mildred contemplated.

To the gown, Bhadra added the pearls she had unpacked from the valise and did Mildred's hair in a loose coiffure. "Oh, miss, you do look lovely."

Mildred gave her reflection in the vanity looking glass a half smile. She could not look much better than she did.

"Will you be joining Madame downstairs? She said she would save you a seat beside hers."

Straightening, Mildred replied, "I think I shall."

She had no desire to nurse her sorrow alone in her chambers. As she was here at the Château Debauchery, why not benefit from some of its aspects?

Madame Follet was in a drawing room downstairs sitting on a sofa against the wall. With tapestries of gold, red, and turquoise, and pillows and rugs of equally vivid coloring, Mildred was reminded of a painting she had seen here at the château of a Turkish harem. In the center of the room, lounging upon the pillows, were a couple. The woman wore only pantaloons of the sheerest fabric. The man had on nothing. He languidly caressed the full breasts of the woman while a half dozen other occupants looked on.

"How wonderful that you could join us," Madame greeted Mildred. "And how ravishing you look!"

Mildred blushed, trying to appear nonchalant despite the brazen scene. "It is Christmas."

"Sit with me a while. Would you like a ratafia or negus?"

Mildred opted for the latter, which had a strong taste of cinnamon and nutmeg. She sat and glanced to see the woman in the pantaloons pull upon the man's erection.

"Have you had the pairing already?" Mildred asked of the ritual in which the guests who had come alone would seek their partners.

"Are you interested?"

"No, no," Mildred quickly replied.

"Because Francois, one of my footmen, would be more than happy to have the company of a lady tonight. Or Laroutte, my brother, said he would make himself available."

"Monsieur Laroutte?"

"You seem surprised."

"I thought him partial—well, I mean, I..."

"Thought him partial to men? He is. But on occasion he enjoys the fair sex. He remembers you."

Mildred flushed deeper. "You are a gracious hostess, but I am content to sit a while."

She watched as the man stroked the woman through her pantaloons and was reminded of how Alastair had fondled her through her shift. Finding the area beneath her waist stirring with sensation, Mildred tried to put the memory out her mind. But every caress the man made, every groan the woman made, returned her to Edenmoor

A young man with a woman on his arm approached, providing a welcome interruption. "Madame Follet, my wife and I wish to thank you for your hospitality. Christmas is not a holiday we observe with great festivity, but thanks to Château Follet, it is now our favorite holiday."

"I am pleased to hear it, Mr. Cornell. I wondered that you would attend this year, given how busy you have been with Parliament. May I congratulate you on your election."

He bowed.

"He is a newly elected MP from Middlesex," Madame explained after the couple had left, "and a proud—what do you term them—Foxite?"

"He does not worry that he will be discovered here?"

"He could not be more notorious than Fox himself was."

Mildred could not imagine any man with a career in the public realm would dare consider the debauchery of Château Follet. Nonetheless, she was intrigued, but as Mr. and Mrs. Cornell had left the room, Mildred returned to watching the couple, their lips locked to one another as hands roamed over, under, and in between There was no denying the warmth that spread through Mildred.

Madame Follet leaned toward her. "Are you quite certain you would not wish to pass the evening in the company of Francois or Monsieur Laroutte?"

Mildred felt her pulse quicken. "I suppose...if Monsieur Laroutte is amenable..."

AS SHE WAITED FOR LAROUTTE, Mildred scanned the chamber and found it elegant, not as provocative as the chamber she and Alastair had once made love in, but the four post bed was inviting with its velvet curtains, plush pillows, and fine bedclothes. After spending over half an hour observing the couple fondle each other lust had warmed her own body. She was pleased with her decision to partake of the activities at the château. It would relieve her mind of Winston...and memories of Alastair.

Hearing someone enter, she turned around—and nearly died. She would have preferred to die. For upon the threshold, closing the door behind him, stood not Laroutte but Alastair.

Her mind reeled. How could such a coincidence occur *twice?* She ought not be surprised that he would spend Christmas at Château Follet—it was a more probable destination than any other—but she still could not refrain from disbelief.

They regarded each other in silence for what felt like an eternity before she managed to swallow her trepidation and ask him, "What do you do here?"

He crossed his arms before his chest, his stare unrelenting. "I could ask the same of you?"

"Why—You are not at Christmas dinner with Lady Katherine?" she stalled. Her mind searched for a plausible answer, for she knew that he would not allow his question to go unanswered for long, but came up wanting.

"Why are *you* not?"

Of course he would ask the same of her. There was nothing left but to confess.

"You may be pleased to know that we need not concern ourselves any longer with Mr. Winston. You are correct. I think he wanted only my dowry."

Fearing that her voice would crack, she said no more.

His expression softened. "I would rather have been wrong."

She nodded, comforted a little by his remark, though she could not recall a more dreadful moment than this: facing her cousin after a failed elopement with a man he had advised against. If he gave her a set down for her silliness, or triumphed that he had been the wiser of the two, she would not fault him. She supposed she should have known that Alastair would be right, that he would have an intuition for these sorts of things, especially as he claimed to be a cad himself.

"I will not disturb your visit here," she assured him, hoping he would leave soon to tend to his own pursuits for the evening. When he did not move, she added, "As I am no longer a novice here, you need not concern yourself with me and may forget my presence entirely to enjoy the revelry."

"I did not come to Château Follet for the revelry."

She blinked several times. Had her family, upon discovering her note, sent him to fetch her?

"I came for *you*," he confirmed.

He sounded displeased. This would not do. She had no wish to return. Not now. Not until she had nursed her wounds by indulging in a night of debauchery.

"How did you know to find me here?"

"An educated supposition based on the information I obtained at the posting inn."

"The posting inn? How did you know...?"

"Winston told me of your ridiculous notion to go to Gretna Green."

"You—you spoke with him?"

"He came to see me in hopes of persuading me to reinstate your dowry."

Her heart sank further. Of course he did. She wondered if he had ever truly entertained the notion of marrying her sans a dowry or if it had all been a charade?

"I should have known my dowry was my finest quality," she murmured.

"Millie, you are worth far more than Winston."

The earnestness in his tone surprised her, and she was able to rally her spirits a little and proclaim, "I think after this, I am determined to remain a spinster."

She expected him to chuckle, and his crossness did appear to thaw a little. She wondered where Monsieur Laroutte had gone to?

"I suppose my family must be discouraged?" she asked after another spell of silence.

"Perhaps, as they will likely have discovered your absence by now."

"You did not...? You did not come at their bidding?"

"When I found you were not at Christmas dinner with my aunt, I suspected what was afoot, but I had no wish to alarm your parents. If I had arrived at the posting inn before you left, we could have returned back to London before your family was the wiser. But you chose to run off to Château Follet."

His tone made her flush.

"Why?" he demanded.

"Why not?" she returned.

"You promised not to return."

"It was a rather inane promise to make."

"Nevertheless, you made it."

She found it difficult to swallow. His pupils had constricted.

"And you will now pay the consequences of breaking your promise," he finished.

# Chapter 30

ALASTAIR COULD SEE her quiver. She looked exceptionally lovely tonight. The gown suited her. The décolletage did not dip particularly low; still, her breasts swelled nicely above it. He felt a wave of jealousy as he considered that it might have been Winston who had inspired her to appear this alluring.

He continued to seek in her countenance evidence of the extent of her grief, but she appeared, at present, to weather the devastating blow that Winston had dealt her with poise.

"She appeared a little downtrodden," Madame Follet had said when he had pressed the hostess for any insights Millie might have confided to her, "but far from despondent."

"Millie is too practical for melancholy," Alastair had replied, feeling some measure of assurance. Though he knew he had spared Millie a life of misery with Winston, he could not bear the sorrow he must have caused her.

"If she was taken with this Mr. Winston, I would have expected her to be much more disconsolate."

"Perhaps the shock of it has not dissipated."

"Or perhaps she does not love this man as much as you think."

He would have liked that to be the case, but why else would Millie have risked her reputation and disappointed her family?

As he stared at Millie, he was determined to drive out all thoughts of Winston.

"I will agree to no such thing," Millie declared.

"You broke a promise."

"You may exact another consequence, such as the revocation of my dowry."

"That has already been done," he said more harshly than he intended, but he was cross with her, despite his sadness for the wounds she had suffered both to her pride and her heart. Nonetheless, he would rather she had not sought to comfort her grief by coming to Follet to lay with another man. Bloody hell. Who would this woman not lift her skirts to?

And yet, he had to admire this similarity between them. He would have done no less had he been in her situation.

"You agreed not to return to Château Follet within the context of certain circumstances," he reminded her. "You will therefore uphold the arrangement under which you made the promise."

"I am expecting Monsieur Laroutte."

"He is engaged with another now."

Distress flared in her eyes. Trembling, she backed away from him as he advanced toward her. He had a dual purpose in what he did. He wanted her never to break a promise with him again, and her apprehension would take her mind off her broken heart. Removing his coat, he tossed it aside. He uncuffed his sleeves and rolled them up to his elbows.

Coming upon an armchair, she stepped behind it, though it would offer her little protection. When he reached for her, she slid from behind the chair toward the doors, but he caught her easily enough. Stumbling, she would have fallen to the ground if not for his grasp about her arm. She struggled to free herself and clawed him with her free arm. He dragged her over to a chair. When she had regained her footing, she yanked harder, but he pulled her down onto the chair as he sat. "Alastair!" she cried.

"Behave yourself."

Laying face down over his lap, she attempted to wriggle herself free, but he pinned her in place with a hand on her back. Her motions caused her pelvis to grind against him. Heat flared through him, pounding in his head.

"Alastair!" she protested again.

The sound of his name only fueled his ardor. He palmed the arch of her rump, ripe for what he was about to do.

"What do you—?!"

*Smack!*

His hand landed upon a cheek. She yelped, mostly in surprise. He struck the delightful half-sphere harder. Desire throbbed in his groin at the contact.

"Stop!" she pleaded with equal parts indignation and desperation.

"I am convinced you were not properly disciplined as a child," he said before whacking her derriere. His hand itched to do more.

"This is monstrous!"

"You deserve far worse."

*Smack!*

"I will tell Lady Katherine," she threatened.

"And you think I am daunted by this?"

*Smack, smack!*

She sucked in her breath at the harder blows. "Madame Follet then. She will throw you out."

"She may, but I am willing to risk it."

Wanting to see her bared, he reached to throw up her skirts. Realizing what he intended, she intensified her struggles till he gave her a harsh slap upon a buttock. His arousal lengthened at the sight of her beautiful backside. He caressed the soft curves before groping the supple flesh. Then he reached between her thighs to find the beginnings of wetness.

She cried out. "Alastair!

"Is this not what you sought in coming here?"

"Not with you." The blood drained from him. No. She had expected Laroutte, or would have had some other bleeder. Devon if he were here.

But he would not let any other man have her. She belonged to him.

"You will have me all the same," he told her, attempting to stay his anger.

"You're the most abominable man ever! If you have revoked my dowry, you have no standing to interfere in my affairs."

"*You* invited my interference first."

"Which has become the greatest regret of my life!"

"Has it?" He nestled his fingers into her folds. She shivered. "Your body might disagree."

She renewed her struggles and managed to bend far enough to bite him on the calf. She tumbled from him as he leaped to his feet, but he grabbed her before she could flee. Hauling her to her feet, he pulled her over to the four-post bed, yanked a tasseled rope from the bed curtains and, ignoring the kicks she delivered to his shins, bound her to the bedpost as he had their first night at Château Follet.

"Alastair, this is madness!"

He cupped her chin and stared his passion into the depths of her eyes.

"When I am through with you, you'll not think to break a promise to me ever again."

# Chapter 31

MILDRED COULD NOT SWALLOW. The intensity of his stare stalled her words. This was *not* what she wanted, because she knew her body would betray her, would yield to his touch. And then she would be left yearning in body and heart.

But with her wrists pinioned to the bed, how was she to escape? What could she do? Though she would agree that she had to atone for breaking her promise, his imposition infuriated her. Did he not have the slightest pity for her situation? Or did it only matter to him that he was in the right? How had she even come to love this man?

Drawing upon her indignation helped to ease her fears. But, due to the turmoil inside her, her body was on edge in an all too familiar manner. When he released her jaw and brushed the backs of his fingers along her arm, she shivered. His hand came to cup a breast, and she had to close her eyes to refrain from being overwhelmed by the sensation, from wishing he could palm her naked instead. Standing behind her, he covered her bosom with his hands and squeezed the flesh through her stays. She grunted and tried not to let his touch excite her.

His hands roamed her body, caressing her midsection, gripping her hips, pressing her belly, and eventually fondling her between the thighs. She had worn but two layers of petticoats beneath, and she could easily feel his fingers pressing into her through the fabric. She squirmed to loosen his access, but he stilled her with his other arm. One hand clamped down upon a breast; the other rubbed her folds.

No matter how tightly she kept her thighs together she could not stay his penetration. The spanking had, to her surprise, aroused her, though she had called upon every ounce of outrage to quell her reaction to his touch. Resistance, however, was futile. The firmness of his grasp, his ability to alternate between light and heavy caresses, called to her desire in a manner she had only ever experienced with him.

He pulled up her skirts and grazed her bare thigh, causing the blood to throb in her extremities. She both relished and wanted to evade his touch. It was madness wanting such contradictions, as if her mind was at war with her body.

Gradually, he released her and went about removing the pins from her gown. She closed her eyes. *Dear God.* She was to be naked before him. The skirt of her gown pooled below her. He then proceeded to untie her petticoats. The bodice of her gown, however, was a challenge, for, with her arms tied above, it could not be slipped off of her. He stepped in front of her, and seeing the fire in his eyes made her melt. There was nothing more titillating than seeing the desire there.

His gaze dropped from hers to the bodice. Undaunted, he gripped the décolletage in both hands and proceeded to rip the gown in half. She squealed. Was he mad? She could not believe he would destroy her finest muslin. The fabric ripped easily beneath his efforts and hung in tatters at her shoulders. Her stays laced in front, so he had but to undo the ribbon.

"This is unnecessary," she tried as he unlaced her stays. "I will suffer what penance you deem appropriate, but not this."

He looked into her eyes. "For one whose body is as wanton as yours, this is the proper penance."

She groaned. The spanking had warmed her body, and his nearness heated it more.

"You may arrange it with Madame Follet that I am no longer welcome here," she offered.

"That is insufficient."

The shift went the way of her gown. Tearing it open, he exposed her breasts, midsection and pelvis. Her pulse leaped and her breath quickened. His hand went between her thighs. She shuddered as he rubbed her. For several minutes, he fondled her, nudging the bud that swelled with desire. His gaze did not leave her face, and she succumbed to the look in his countenance, the smolder in his eyes, the firm set of his jaw. The wetness of her arousal coated his fingers.

She searched for threats, temptations, or taunts that might persuade him to stop, but her body warred with her mind. Her body wanted him to continue, to pursue whatever devilry he intended.

In the looking glass across the room, she caught the reflection of herself, her body stretched toward the rafters, her tattered clothing hanging from her. Only her garters, stockings, slippers, and pearls remained intact.

He grasped a breast, his fingers slowly digging into the ample flesh. Lowering his head, he captured the nipple in his mouth, sending currents to shoot from that bud to the heat collecting between her thighs. She ached within as he licked and sucked. He performed the same attention upon the other nipple. Soon, she was fit to burst. She wanted his hand back between her legs—no, she wanted *him* between her legs.

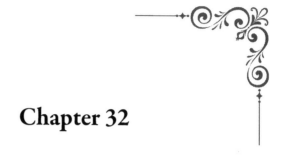

# Chapter 32

REACHING BETWEEN HER thighs once more, he returned to stroking her. Her arousal hardened his already stiff cock. He wished he knew that he was the sole cause of her desire, that she would not be so aroused by anyone else. Her breath grew more haggard still. He fondled her till she squirmed, but she was not done resisting.

"Is your time not better spent in other pursuits?" she asked, her voice husky of its own accord.

"Are you so eager to rid yourself of my company?" he returned, teasing the bud, now engorged with need, that made her gasp. "Perhaps you regret having solicited my attentions?"

"Yes," she whispered. "Had I known you could be so overbearing..."

"Overbearing? You are fortunate I do not attempt what I truly think would be a worthy punishment of your broken promise."

"I own I made a mistake. I was...lost and a little beside myself. I knew not where to turn."

Her words tugged at his sympathy. He stepped into her. A mere half inch separated their bodies. His member throbbed. He wanted her more than he had ever wanted a woman before. But he wanted her to feel the same intensity. How could she consider marrying a man like Winston? Could Winston take her body to such heights, catapult her body into euphoria?

"I suppose Château Follet a proper place to forget one's intended," he said wryly.

Anger flared in her eyes. "Accuse me if you wish but would you have done differently? Would you rather I wallow in self-pity alone?"

He could make her forget Winston. As if to prove it, he curled two fingers inside her slit. Her lashes fluttered as rapture bloomed in her countenance.

"Then it would seem you ought to welcome my presence," he said, stroking the sensitivity behind her mound.

She trembled and lowered her gaze. "Yes, but...I did not expect you. I expected Monsieur Laroutte."

"Do you still wish for Laroutte?"

"Yes."

He stopped his fingers.

"I mean...perhaps," she amended.

He pressed himself into her, making her meet his gaze.

Looking into her eyes, he was lost momentarily in their brightness, and this time he felt his bosom swell. She looked ravishing in her current position, and he was tempted to wrap her legs about him and take her against the bedpost. But he wanted to hear her surrender. Hearing her need, her desire for him, excited him to the depths of his loins.

"Perhaps?" he echoed. He resumed his stroking. Her moan was long and low. "Your body would indicate it is more than 'perhaps.'"

"My body is incongruent with my better judgment."

For now, he would be content with victory of the flesh. He strummed his two fingers against her as his thumb circled her clitoris. She clenched her hands and shut her eyes. She looked exquisite with her lips parted and the flush of arousal coloring her features. He could hardly wait to see her spend. The furrow of her brow indicated she was ascending that peak. He crushed his mouth atop hers, to take in every breath, every pant. Her body trembled beneath him, her back arched, she murmured against his lips—prayers or curses, he knew not, nor cared not. His only aim was to wrest from her that sublime carnal euphoria.

With a muffled cry, she succumbed to his ministrations, her body bucking and quaking as tension erupted into bliss. He pressed himself into her, his own need flaring, demanding release. After wringing the last of the spasms from her body, he gently slowed his fondling. He could feel her flex about his fingers and throb about his hand, her wet heat calling to the lust in his groin.

He withdrew his hand to untie her wrists. Before her legs buckled and she crumbled to the ground, he swept her into his arms and carried her to the bed. After laying her down, he pulled her arms through her torn garments. He had not intended to rip her clothing, though his ardor had appreciated the outlet. He silently promised her that he would purchase an even finer gown, shift and stays. Indeed, he would gift her anything she desired.

To his satisfaction, he found her staring at his crotch and the bulge there. He remembered all too vividly how well she had swallowed cock at Edenmoor. But tonight was about her pleasure. If he could rain such ecstasy upon her, she would not think to seek satisfaction with another man. Certainly not Winston or the Viscount Devon. Alastair shuddered at the possibility the latter could cross paths with her at Château Follet.

He did not want to think of Millie with another man—any man, let alone the Devon bastard. Millie belonged to *him*. She was his.

And the only way he could assure that she would be his, and his alone, was to marry her.

# Chapter 33

MILDRED SILENTLY CURSED.

Conscious of how wantonly she was splayed upon the bed, she stared up at the ceiling instead of meeting his eye. What was she to do now? What would *he* do?

She shut her eyes at the emotions, the truth, threatening to overwhelm her. Though her body had received what it most desired, the pain of it was that she could not keep such pleasure. Alastair could never be hers.

She gasped when she felt his touch at her mons. Looking down, she saw that it was his cock. Anticipation surged within her. He had undressed and now stroked the head of his member against her. She wondered that her body could be aroused after it had spent so gloriously but a moment ago. Her moan wavered as delicious sensations rippled between her legs. He teased her with light brushes of his length along her, touching his tip to her clitoris, pushing the crown of his shaft at her folds but not enough to enter.

"Oh, God, Alastair," she whispered when she thought she could endure no more. "Please take me."

"Look at me, Millie."

She gazed at him. He had a hard set to his jaw, and she did not know if it was from displeasure with her or merely the tension of lust.

"Do not break a promise to me again."

She nodded. "I promise to never break a promise to you again."

His shaft was at her slit, and she tried to wriggle herself onto him. "And I expect you'll never return here without my assent."

"Yes, yes," she replied, straining for penetration. She would go mad if she had to endure the vacancy in her quim much longer. "I will uphold my promise this time. Truly."

In response, he flipped her onto her stomach. Grabbing the pillows, he pulled them beneath her hips. She flushed at how her derriere was raised in the air, but she was soon distracted by the length rubbing her folds, tantalizing her desires. She groaned, rapture swelling within her. Then, finally, he sank himself into her.

At that moment, there was nothing more exquisite than being impaled upon his member. Her quim clutched at his shaft, eliciting a groan from him. He pressed himself farther into her. The angle of her body allowed him to penetrate deeply, and he buried himself to the hilt, till she could feel the hairs of his pelvis against her rump. It was marvelous, even grander than the position of *Angelique et Medor*. Each thrust, each withdrawal was more delectable than the last. With his thumb, he strummed her clitoris as he bucked his hips. It was more than she could bear. All sensation hurled her toward that carnal purpose. Her orgasm erupted with the violence of cannon fire. A blinding white glory flashed through her, followed by much quaking and shaking, the intensity of which left her in a state of quasi-delirium.

Bracing himself over her, he pounded himself fast and furious into her to achieve his own end. The bed rocked beneath the force of his motions and thumped against the wall. She would have cautioned him to pull out before he spilled his seed, but the words remained lodged in her throat. In truth, a part of her wanted to have his essence inside her. She could feel the heat of his mettle, mixing with her own fluids.

"My God, Millie," he breathed before a final shudder went through his limbs. He collapsed onto the bed and pulled her to him.

His satisfaction gratified her. She wished she could remain joined to him forever, and for the time being, she would refrain from considering the grim truth that awaited her and relish the weight of his body against her and pretend that he was hers.

# Chapter 34

HE WOULD HAVE PULLED out of her, but the temptation to mark her for his own, to leave a part of him in the deepest part of her, prevailed. He had already decided upon marrying her; thus, if there should be consequences to their congress, she would be safe.

Safe. He liked the certainty that marriage to Millie afforded. Liked that he would have many more opportunities to take her as he just had. It was the most brilliant paroxysm he had ever had. He hoped she had spent with equal glory, and he vowed to bring her to rapture as often as she wished. And more.

Settling back into bed, he wrapped her in his arms as they lay upon their sides. He could see that she was weary. She pushed aside the pieces of her torn garments

"I will replace the gown," he assured her.

She nestled into his embrace. "Thank you, but it is unnecessary. My portmanteau is here with my effects."

"You will have a finer gown—and shifts and stays—whatever you wish to spend your pin money upon."

"Pin money?"

He breathed in the scent of her hair. "Though I suspect you are as likely to donate your pin money to Luddites and the like."

She sat up, leaving his arms, to his regret. "Pray, it is not necessary to substitute my dowry with pin money. I am quite pleased you have revoked my dowry. I assure you that, despite what my parents may say, I am better off without one."

He pulled her back down. "A dowry is unnecessary, but as the Marchioness of Alastair, you will want pin money."

She sat back up. "The what?"

"The Marchioness of Alastair."

She looked horrified. "My lord? I mean, Alastair—my lord—what is this jest?"

"Have you ever known me to jest?"

Her horror grew, and she scrambled from the bed. "Why would I marry you? I mean, why would you marry *me*?"

He could not help feeling a little insulted by the intensity of her reaction. He allowed she was in love with Winston, but the Marquess of Alastair was hardly rubbish.

"You have no need to salvage my honor, Alastair."

"Then who will? Your journey to Château Follet has made it impossible to return home at a reasonable time. You will have to pass the night here. Have you considered what explanation you can offer your family?"

"I have not, but that is not your concern."

He could not believe what he was hearing. She would not take his dowry. Now she would not take his hand in marriage. It could not be because she found him repulsive—her body had given him plenty of evidence to the contrary.

"Millie, I may be far from a saint," he said, "but I am more worthy of you than Winston. He is not even deserving of the hundred pounds I gave him."

"What hundred pounds?"

"I offered him an annuity to stay his distance from you."

Her mouth fell open. "You *bribed* him?"

"I should have simply threatened him, but I knew money would move him."

"You're the reason he didn't come!"

"Do not delude yourself. He never had any intention of marrying you without a dowry."

She gasped, made a face, then began angrily collecting her garments.

"Millie, he accepted the annuity without hesitating a second. Why are you not vexed with him?"

He grasped her by the arm as she turned toward her petticoats on the floor.

"You flatter me once again, Alastair. I am pleased to know I could be forsaken for as little as a hundred pounds a year."

"I would have offered more if I thought the bloody bastard deserved it. Devil take it, I would have offered a thousand pounds a year, but I think it quite telling that he accepted my offer as it was."

Her shoulders sagged, but he still heard vexation in her voice. "You're right, Alastair. I hope it pleases you to know that you are right."

She wrested her arm from him and, taking up her petticoats, she tied them about her.

"I care nothing of that," he protested. "I wanted to see you safe from him. Though you are of a stronger constitution, I would not want what happened to Miss Jones to befall you."

"Who is Miss Jones?"

He started. "I thought you knew? She is the young woman he cast aside after getting her with child. She took her life afterwards."

Millie paused. "That was not how he had told it."

"That surprises me little, but he lost a good friend, Mr. Stanton, over the affair."

"I suppose I owe you an apology, then, and my gratitude for rescuing me."

She looked at her garments and realized they were too torn to wear. He gave her his shirt and began to dress as well.

"I do not require your apology or your gratitude," he told her, relieved that she sounded less angry. "However, I would that my generosity was not wasted upon you."

"I must seem an ungrateful wretch, and perhaps I am. You have been good to me, Alastair, even though I have not always deserved it."

He liked the look of his shirt over her. Her coiffure had come undone, but the blush in her cheeks remained. "You deserve far more than you allow for yourself, Millie."

A grateful smile tugged at the corners of her lips.

"And while you deserve better than a rogue such as myself," he continued as he slipped into his braces and reached for his waistcoat, "I hope you will find some comfort in being married to me. I daresay your parents and Katherine would be happy."

Her eyes widened, and the dread returned. She shook her head. "Alastair, you are far kinder and more munificent than anyone could have imagined, but your offer is unnecessary."

To his surprise, she turned on her heel and, carrying her garments in her arms, made for the doors.

"That may be, but—" He took several long and quick strides to catch her. "Millie!"

"You need not concern yourself with my wellbeing. I am certain I can find a situation to support me till my family has forgiven me."

She opened the doors and hurried down the corridor. In her haste, as she turned the corner, she bumped into a couple. Her articles of clothing fell to the floor.

"Your pardon!" the various parties cried.

Alastair bent down to assist Millie.

"Lord Alastair, is it not?" the man asked. When Alastair made no reply, the man offered his hand. "Mr. Cornell, at your service. I represent Middlesex, and must say I was most pleased to hear that you had rejected the Farnsworth proposal regarding stocking frames.

I think he may present a bill next year, but at least we were spared its consideration this year."

Her garments returned to her arms, Millie stood and stared at him.

"I look forward to serving in Parliament with you, your lordship," Cornell added before he and his companion continued on their way.

Alastair turned to Millie. Her eyes swam with emotion. "You did not support Farnsworth?"

"We had an agreement, you and I, did we not?"

"Yes, but I had bid you only to consider the subject more than you had."

"And I did. I went to Nottinghamshire and observed the conditions of croppers and weavers. Their numbers in the poor houses have grown. You inspired me to consider their cause with more compassion. The Farnsworth proposal provides no solution for their suffering. I still consider machine-breaking a wrong, but I could not send a man to his death for it."

Her countenance brightened with what he thought might be affection. Encouraged, he took her hand. "Millie, you could make me a better man."

"You are far better than you credit yourself."

"If you believe that, then there is hope in our marriage. If you think I will always assume the role of master as your husband and lord over you, I assure you that will not be the case." Even if he did, he doubted she would submit to it. She tried to pull away, but he kept his hold of her. "You have my permission to give me a proper set-down when I am found to be overbearing."

"Alastair, stop such talk. I don't understand—"

"You may love Winston today, but I will earn your affections."

"Alastair, you...Winston is..."

His face darkened. "You do not still harbor hopes that he will have you?"

"Not at all. I don't love him. I never truly loved him because I loved..." Distraught, she continued to yank her hand from him. "*We* can't marry!"

"Why not?"

"Because you're the Marquess of Alastair."

"I do not fear the consequences."

"But—"

He pulled her into his arms. "If you do not love Winston, why will you not have me?"

Caught in his gaze, she seemed not to be able to speak. When she did, her voice was small and trembled. "Because I love you."

Relief flooded him. He wanted to shake her a little for the unnecessary distress she had incited. "And I thought you had a proper reason for refusing me."

"It *is* a proper reason! I will not allow you to make such a sacrifice on my behalf."

"It is no sacrifice."

"How is it not a sacrifice?" she persisted in arguing.

"Because *I* love *you*."

She started, then returned a doubtful look.

"And I mean it," he said, cupping her chin. Then, daring her to refute him, added, "As sincerely as you meant it when you claimed never to break a promise to me again."

Her bottom lip quivered. "Alastair..."

"Say that you will have me, Millie, and then we may enjoy what remains of Christmas day."

She followed his gaze up toward the ceiling, where a kissing bough hung.

Before she could say another word, he claimed her mouth, impressing his love through his kiss. Her lips parted willingly for him, and in that moment, he sensed the last of her resistance had given way, just as her body had submitted to him earlier. He kissed her with tenderness, with vigor and passion.

He never would have thought, when Katherine first orchestrated their encounter at Château Follet, that their path together would have ended in marriage. Perhaps Katherine had suspected its possibility, and though he did not appreciate her meddling, he would forgive her this one time. For he had in his arms a woman worthy of worship and whose body he would take great pleasure in exalting in all manner of delicious wantonness.

When he parted to give her a chance to collect her breath, he felt a familiar tug at his groin. He saw the same lust in her eyes, as well as affection.

"Merry Christmas, Alastair."

He smiled and crushed her to him in another forceful kiss before bidding her a Merry Christmas, too.

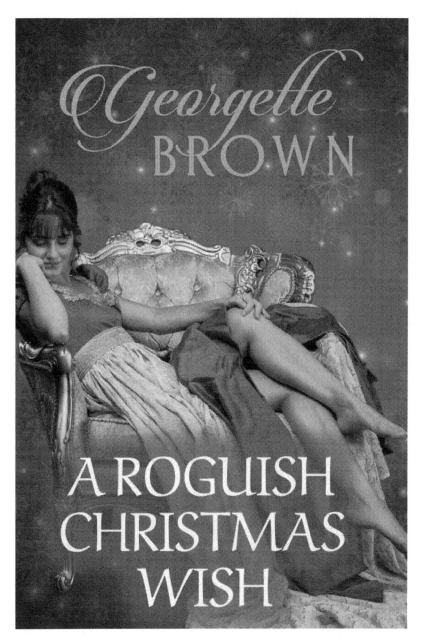

# A ROGUISH CHRISTMAS WISH

## By Georgette Brown

# Chapter One

IT WAS FOOLISH to have come.

As Sir Rowan Hubert attempted to find a comfortable position upon the stiff wooden chair in the corner of the room, he contemplated that he could not have squandered a hundred guineas in worse fashion had he chosen to wager a lame horse could win at Ascot.

But he could not resist.

He adjusted the mask that covered his face. When first Sir Arthur had hinted to him that Sarah had been seen at Madame Devereux's inn, a suspected bordello, Rowan had feigned disinterest. He had washed his hands of the woman. Given that a jury had found her guilty of criminal congress, despite the vociferous protests of innocence from both her and her lover, it was only a matter of time before the petition of divorce succeeded. She would be his wife no longer.

A fortnight later, however, Rowan had decided to pass by the inn. After the *crim con*, he had heard that her lover had taken himself to Bristol. Rowan had been surprised to learn that Sarah had not left with her paramour and remained in London. Perhaps, accustomed to a life of quality, she had decided that the living provided by a poor barrister was not up to snuff for her. She should have considered this before lifting her skirts to the man.

Rowan shifted in discomfort. He would have offered his wife anything she desired. She would have wanted for nothing. Instead, disowned by her family for her infidelity, she been reduced to whoring. Though the proprietress of the Inn denied it, he saw the establishment as a bawdy house.

Dismissing the unsettling remorse he felt in regards to the demise of his wife—for it was not *he* who had broken their vows—Rowan rose to his feet. Naught but the satisfaction of curiosity was to be gained by bearing witness to the depraved deeds Sarah now engaged in. But before he could take a step, the door to the room opened. Not wanting to draw attention to himself, Rowan quickly sat back down in the shadows, away from the single lamp that lighted the room. He stiffened at the entry of a man, stalwart in build, his skin darkened and made rough by the sun. Captain Gracechurch, Rowan presumed. His heart swelled with jealousy.

"Come in, my dear," said Gracechurch after sauntering into the room with an off-putting swagger, as if he owned the place. The man might have done well for himself as a merchantman, but, unlike Rowan, he would never be welcomed by finer society.

Rowan would have continued his deprecating assessment of the captain, but the appearance of Sarah took all his attention. She wore only a banyan. Her thick dark curls cascaded loosely over her shoulders. Rowan had always found her hair most beautiful when undone from its coiffure.

"Tonight," said Gracechurch, "we have ourselves a guest."

Rowan clenched his hand. He had arranged to be anonymous.

"He is here to watch only," Gracechurch continued. "We must provide him a worthy performance. Is that understood, my dear?"

"Yes, sir," she replied.

*Bloody scoundrel.* Rowan wondered that he would be able to stay his desire to throttle the man, but he was, in part, distracted by the sight of his wife. He had not seen her in some time. She looked more slender but no less lovely. His chest constricted with the pain of past sentimentalities. To keep them at bay, he imagined he would have been satisfied to see her decrepit and homely.

"You may disrobe," Gracechurch told her.

It took all his forbearance for Rowan to remain seated. A man of Gracechurch's station issuing commands to a woman of superior breeding was unacceptable.

But Rowan reminded himself that the woman was an adulteress, a lightskirt. She no longer deserved consideration.

She loosened the sash and slid the banyan off. Rowan became rooted to the chair as he drank in the curvature of her body. He had often thought her proportions perfect. She had trim ankles and wrists, but full hips and ripe breasts. No woman could possess a more pleasing figure. That she had shared this treasure with another man had driven him mad. He dared not think how many hands she had allowed upon her during her time here at the inn.

Feeling warm, Rowan pulled at his cravat.

"Turn around, my dear, that our guest may see all of you," Gracechurch instructed.

She did as he bid, offering the sight of her deliciously rounded rump. Rowan felt his breath stripped from him. He would never have thought to witness his wife being displayed like wares for sale, but his lust responded at seeing her naked beauty. He pulled at his cravat again.

"Delectable," Gracechurch murmured before groping her.

Rowan wanted to look away but couldn't. He took in the darkened hands grasping her breasts, her buttocks, wandering over her belly and her legs, the dark rough flesh a contrast to her silken paleness. Gracechurch slapped the sides of her breasts, making them wobble. The orbs appeared larger than Rowan remembered, and he wondered if she still nursed her son.

Standing before her, Gracechurch pushed her breasts up, lowered his head and suckled the nipples. She yelped and grunted. When he squeezed a breast, white liquid dripped from the nipple.

"Did you enjoy that, my dear?" Gracechurch asked with a salacious grin that Rowan would have offered money to smack off the man's face.

A frown creased her brow, but she replied, "Yes, sir."

Gracechurch smiled and returned to suckling her breasts more. She wriggled and strained. To Rowan, she did *not* seem to enjoy the suckling.

"Please," she gasped after a few moments.

Gracechurch lifted his head and wiped the moisture from his lips. "Let us have a look at your arse, m'dear."

He turned her around and ogled her rump before giving it a slap. He spanked her several times, rather harshly. Rowan searched her countenance for evidence that she was in greater discomfort than she revealed. He had paid a hundred guineas to bear witness to this. Surely that gave him the right to put an end to it.

"Let us assess your arousal," Gracechurch said in a tone that Rowan found among the most detestable sounds to fall upon his ears.

His head swam with what followed. Gracechurch put his grubby paw between her thighs and rubbed her *there,* a place only a husband should know. Her lips parted in a low and shaky moan.

He knew this moan. Had relished the sound all the times he had taken her to bed. Now she gave it freely. Did she know who touched her? Did she not care?

For several minutes Gracechurch fondled her between the legs. Her moans grew haggard, her breath uneven. Rowan recognized the impending climax that would erupt through her body. Looking to the captain, he noticed a visible tenting at the man's crotch. His own erection pushed against his trousers. It had not been this hard in some time.

Gracechurch undid his fall first, and Rowan smirked at the relatively small length that was revealed. The captain grabbed the back of her thighs and hoisted her legs up about his hips. Rowan felt his chest constrict. Sarah gasped loudly. She knit her brows and groaned as Gracehurch slid into her.

Rowan imagined breaking the man's neck in twain.

"Feel good, m'dear?" inquired Gracechurch.

It seemed she required much effort to steady her breath. Yet she managed to reply, "Very good, sir."

Gracechurch began to thrust. Rowan shifted in his chair. He crossed his legs, uncrossed them, and crossed them again. The worst sort of jealousy twisted in Rowan's groin. This was what he had dreaded to see. Why had he subjected himself to this?

Sarah moaned as Gracechurch bucked his hips at her. "What a lascivious harlot you are."

Rowan ground his teeth together. He had uttered similar words about her after learning of her affair. But he had little tolerance to hear her so described by another man.

She trembled. Little beads of perspiration glistened upon her brow.

After a while, Gracechurch seemed to tire a little and sat down upon the edge of the bed with Sarah straddled over him. He tilted up her chin and covered her mouth with his. To Rowan, the captain's kiss looked like a dog shoving his face into food. The man had no finesse and all but slobbered over her. This Rowan could not watch. He looked back, however, when he heard her emit a grunting groan. He could not decide if she found any pleasure in her experience. Gracechurch had begun to thrust in and out of her, his motions slow for when he did attempt to move faster, his member would pop out and he would have to re-insert himself.

"Are you enjoying this, my dear?" Gracechurch asked after one particularly forceful thrust.

She gasped, then replied, "Yes, sir."

Rowan could not believe the depths of wantonness to which Sarah had sunk. And even if she had not spoken true, that she would participate in such devilry spoke to a most bawdy nature, one that Rowan had never suspected his wife to possess. Instead of being disgusted, however, he found himself intrigued.

"My dear, what a fine quim you have."

The veins at Rowan's temples throbbed. His ardor stretched painfully to the hilt. Gracechurch began grunting in earnest, sounding like a rutting pig.

"Oh, oh," Sarah cried, her teeth chattering.

Did she enjoy this? Rowan wondered. The lascivious harlot.

Sweat trickled down the sides of Gracechurch's face as he pummeled himself into her. It did not take long for him to spend, spilling his seed on her belly. Rowan felt sick. Sarah slid off him and crumpled onto the bed. Gracechurch slumped against the bedpost in some manner of stupor.

Rowan silently cursed the man every with every invective he could think of. He dared not touch his own member for fear that if he did, he would not stop until he too had spent. He had no desire to give evidence that what he had witnessed had aroused him in the least.

Quietly, he stood up and let himself out. Once he had closed the door behind him, he leaned against the wall and took in a haggard breath. His mind aflame, he knew he would never forget the vision of his wife impaled upon that seaman. He wanted to spend badly, to release the immense tension at his groin. He did not think he could bear witness to the scene ever again, but this would not be his last appearance at Madame Devereux's inn.

# Chapter Two

T he next evening, Rowan pumped himself inside her, his eyes closed. Sarah, he thought to himself, imagining her tied to his bed, writhing beneath him. But it was not her delectable form prone under him but that of his sometimes-mistress, Caroline. She had flattered him and been loyal to him, when his Sarah had betrayed him.

Yet it was Sarah whom he imagined beneath him. Her curves, her dark curls, her moans.

By all accounts, he had wed well when he had chosen Sarah. She had come from a good family and considered lovely in form and manners. At first he had found her a bit of a blue-stocking and prone to having opinions on matters best left to men, but in time, he had come to appreciate that she was not as silly or stupid as others of her sex. He had found her particularly pleasing on their wedding night. He had taken his time undressing her, caressing the different parts of her body previously hidden beneath her garments. She had received his attentions with less timidity than he would have expected, but he found he liked her curiosity and enjoyed her touch.

Kissing and groping each other, they had made their way to the bed, where she had lain under him, her supple form ripe for his taking. And take her he had. First, kissing his way down to that lovely mound, tasting of her wet heat. She had spent for him, and hearing her moans for the first time had made his member stretch painfully toward her. While she still writhed in her carnal delights, he had slid up her beautiful body, pressed himself to her, and watched her a moment. There had never been a more beautiful sight.

He had entered her then, with more patience than he thought he had, glorying in her tightness, pausing only when she cried out at the breaching of her maidenhead. When it seemed the pain had subsided, he had thrust as tenderly as he could. The brightness of her eyes had almost blinded him with their beauty.

Rowan grunted and forced himself home. He spent. But when he opened his eyes, it was not Sarah he beheld, but a thin, sallow Caroline.

He shook himself and eased off Caroline. Laying on her side, she watched him as he began readying himself—he would be late for the theatre.

"That picture is misplaced, is it not?" she asked, observing the wall opposite the bed. "It does not fit the space. You ought find a larger work of art."

His jaw clenched. The small painting of a vase of flowers had replaced a portrait of Sarah painted shortly after they had wed. "Did I ask for your advice on how to decorate my chambers?"

"There is no need to be short with me, Rowan. I could be elsewhere just now, you know. Sir Richard has expressed his interest in me."

"Pray do not let me stop you from enjoying his favors."

His response surprised her, and she changed her demeanor.

"But he has not nearly the qualities you have," she said with a flattering smile. A false smile. Not like Sarah, whom he had thought the sincerest of persons till she betrayed him.

When he had made no response, she pouted. "Or perhaps I have overlooked Sir Richard's assets."

Having buttoned his fall, he proceeded to adjust his cravat. "He is a wealthy man, to be sure."

She narrowed her eyes. "Are you suggesting that I *should* entertain Sir Richard over you?"

"I understand Sir Richard treats his mistresses well."

She sucked in her breath sharply, rose from the bed, smoothed her gown and gave him a scowl.

"Well, if that is how you feel, then perhaps you shall see no more of me."

Grabbing her shawl off the bed, she strode from the chambers.

It was just as well, Rowan thought to himself. They had never been suited, and what he had to pay in gifts for her favors, he might as well spend at Madame Devereux's inn. Yes, he would enjoy himself much better there, as Caroline would be happier with the likes of Sir Richard.

He sank into a chair, then rose again and rang for his valet. His mother would be in a pique were he any later in joining them at the theater.

While he readied himself, he recalled getting ready to meet Sarah for the first time, those three years ago, also at Christmastide. She and her parents had come to a ball where his mother had introduced him to her. He and Sarah had fallen into easy discourse, and he found her not nearly as dull to converse with as others of superior beauty. She had grace when she danced, and he liked that she never seemed bored or lacked for activity. Yet beneath her fine façade, she was a whore.

His jaw tightened as he did his cravat. He waved away his valet and donned his hat and gloves on the way out.

He had taken Sarah on a stroll through the bedecked halls that evening, her parents at a slight distance. He had not expected to be drawn to a woman such as her. She seemed to possess a maturity beyond her years, and he would have thought such a quality to be tedious or remind him too much of his mother, but she had a quiet confidence he found soothing. The women that tended to giggle or flirt overly much excited but also agitated him.

That very night, he had asked to court her, and both she and her father had consented. Perhaps they had wed too soon. Perhaps he would have then come to discover a side of her he had not noticed before. Perhaps she had never loved him.

The chill night wind snapped him from his thoughts. He hopped into the waiting carriage, which wound through the streets to the theater. But he saw only Sarah, from that first fateful night, to the last he had seen her, impaled upon that bloody Gracerhuch.

That roil of revulsion and desire coursed through him, causing his groin to stir. Desire would not win out. At least not tonight. He disembarked and walked into the crowded building. Making his way to their box, he steadied himself for the battle to come. It could not be any worse than the turmoil within him.

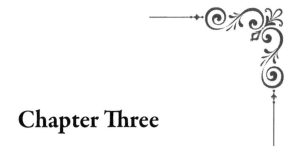

# Chapter Three

"Why were you late again?" his mother hissed at the intermission. He escorted her to the crush of the lobby, where they would be on parade. That is how it felt and was in a sense. No doubt his mother would have a march of wealthy women to pass before him, in hopes he would marry again.

"I have apologized. No more can I do."

"You could attend church. Surely you will for Christmas. Your absence has become an embarrassment. We have surely suffered enough on that score, have we not?"

He bit back a rejoinder. "I shall be there for Christmas."

"Good. Look, there is Lady Chilton. Doesn't she look lovely this evening? What taste she has. And what a loyal wife she was to her poor departed husband."

He closed his eyes briefly to stop himself from rolling his eyes at his mother's obvious tactic. However, she was correct that Lady Chilton was lovely. Her blonde coiffure was set off by her peachy skin and the sapphire color of her well-trimmed gown. She had quite a pleasing figure, too, still youthful and curvaceous.

His mother made introductions. He had heard of Lady Chilton and had once met her staid, steady husband, a viscount. Rowan knew little of Lord Chilton, save that the man had left his wife a wealthy widow.

"Isn't the theatre a crush?" Lady Chilton said in an almost vicious tone that did not match her ready smile. She paused, but his only response was a nod. Were Sarah here, she would be more concerned with the play itself, and whether they should buy extra treats to give to any urchins they might come across outside. She had too soft a heart, his Sarah.

"Have you seen Mrs. Vale?" Lady Chilten addressed his mother.

"Oh, yes." His mother's tone dripped with disdain.

"She ought hire someone to advise what suits her rather than employ those cast-offs as she does. Really, her home is like a house for wayward women."

Sarah would have lauded Mrs. Vale for such practices. She had given much time to such causes, to those less fortunate. Rowan had thought her efforts rather excessive. Perhaps that should have been a warning to him of her proclivities. Or perhaps it had been his indifference toward her ideals that had driven her to the arms of another...

"I shall forward an invitation to my soiree then?" Lady Chilton was asking his mother.

He had lost part of their conversation, absorbed in his thoughts—thoughts he needed to drive from his mind, as he had Sarah from his life and heart.

"Thank you, I should be pleased to receive it," his mother replied.

Lady Chilton turned her eye to Rowan with veiled yet potent interest. He gave the expected bow. "We would be much honored to attend your soiree, your ladyship."

Lady Chilton preened at his compliment. She was nothing like... No, she was nothing like Sarah. But at least Lady Chilton knew how to be a faithful wife.

She gave a slight curtsey to him. "Sir Arthur will be in attendance as well. He speaks very highly of you."

Sir Arthur, dubbed a *nabob* for he owed his extensive fortune to the East India Company, had taken a liking to Rowan, and his interest in Rowan had doubled after Sarah's infidelity had come to light. It had been rumored that Sir Arthur's wife had been less than faithful.

She had died tragically after giving birth to their son. Some speculated that the son was not Sir Arthur's.

"Yes, Sir Arthur has been a good friend to us," his mother answered for him.

Sarah had never warmed to Sir Arthur, and Rowan had to concede he also found the man rather unsettling, though he could not state specifics and merely attributed his unease to his awe of the man. Nor would Rowan speak ill of a man whose guidance and profitable opportunities could make Rowan a very wealthy man.

"Ladies, would you care for some refreshment?" he asked.

They assented and he went about his task, his mind still half in the past. He had been home less and less frequently as a result of his relationship with Sir Arthur, and yet Sarah had not complained. He thought it had been because she understood that opportunities such as the ones presented by Sir Arthur did not come by often or easily. The fortune he was creating with the help of Sir Arthur would afford them anything they wanted and secure the livelihoods of their children and their children's children. But she had deceived him well and taken the opportunity of his absence to entertain that bloody lover of hers, a penniless barrister whom Sir Arthur had derided as a mockery of the judicial system with his belief that criminals ought to have rights to representation and other such delusions.

Rowan did not understand why Sarah's paramour had left her. Now she had no one to support her and that bastard child of hers. But it was all her own doing. She did not merit the pangs of pity that threatened to form within him.

"Rowan?" his mother touched his arm. He had not been attending to them, again.

Still, he knew enough to bow to Lady Chilton—it was time to go back into the theatre. "We look forward to seeing you at your soiree, Lady Chilton."

"Delighted." She offered him her hand, which he kissed. When he met her gaze, he saw from her parted lips and the hungry glaze of her eyes that she had more in mind than capturing another husband—she wanted also a lover.

Lady Chilton walked away, and he escorted his mother back into the box. He did not attend to the play—rather, his mind returned to the scenes of his past.

What if he had been more philanthropic, as Sarah had wanted? He was not opposed to philanthropy and would have been happy to donate to her causes once he had amassed more wealth. But what if he had not ignored her in favor of his pursuit of his fortune? Would Sarah be his? Her delectable body writhing beneath him, his to caress and hold. Not given to a damned sailor.

He could not shake the vision of her with Gracechurch. Did she enjoy his attentions more than she had enjoyed those of her husband? Surely he could command her pleasure as much as Gracechurch. But he would never know. He would never get to taste of her again, never claim what was supposed to only be his to claim.

Or could he?

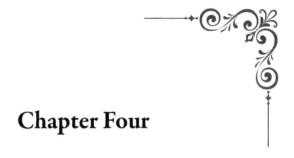

# Chapter Four

He sat sipping his port in the office of the inn's proprietress, Joan Devereux, a mature woman who was undoubtedly a beauty in her youth.

"Really, Sir Rowan, your request is most...unexpected. I believe some other woman here would suit you better."

Yes, no doubt someone she believed would keep him returning to her Inn, a regular patron as Sir Arthur seemed to be. It was Sir Arthur who had first informed him of where his wife was.

"I think I offered you a worthy price."

She tapped her fingers upon her writing table as she contemplated. "Very well, Sir Rowan. I do like my guests to be pleased. The price you named will be sufficient for one night with Sarah. She is much valued here, you know, and quite popular."

He bowed slightly. "Much obliged, Madame Devereux. I would have Miss Sarah brought to me blindfolded. She must not know my identity."

"That can certainly be arranged. My footman will show you to your room. Sarah will attend you there, as you have requested."

He bowed once more, his throat suddenly constricting at the thought of seeing Sarah again. Of having her again. Would she be pleased with him?

Following the footman, he traversed the halls, smelling of carnal pleasures and spices. Rowan entered a chamber lit by candles, a large bed the predominant feature. It was fitting, he supposed, as that bed would be the stage upon which this night's play would be performed.

Aside from the bed, there was a fireplace, with a low fire crackling; a settee and an occasional table; and a sideboard with a tray of decanters and glasses on top.

The familiar roil in him began, over his desire to be pleasured by Sarah one last time and the impulse to punish her, to see her suffer, as her betrayal had done to him. To know he was to be a father had completed his joy in their marriage. And then...it had all been ripped from him, a loss more profound than any he had ever known.

He tugged off his cravat and divested himself of his boots and coat. Sometimes, Sarah would assist him with such mundane tasks. His skin warmed at the remembrance of her supple fingers touching him, the slow anticipation of where her hands might go next. Yet she, unlike his mistress, had a certain demureness about her, even in the throes of passion, that was lovely. A knock sounded. He threw the silken ties he'd selected onto the bed and paced a moment.

"Enter."

Footsteps padded into the room. He turned. A maid, young and lithe, accompanied Sarah, who was blindfolded, as he had instructed. And Sarah, in a shift, her dark curls free and caressing her shoulders, took his very breath from him. Her full lips begged to be kissed, her breasts causing the fabric of her garment to strain, and her fulsome hips ready for gripping as he rammed his way home.

He stepped closer and breathed in her scent, infused with some seductive hint of jasmine and sunlight.

"Sir?" the maid enquired. She had been given no further instructions, at least not from him, other than to bring Sarah here in a shift and blindfold. He had wanted her in a shift, as she had sometimes been at home with him, and as she had been when she had first told him of the happy news that she carried their child.

He clenched his jaw and paced again. That news had been a lie. Perhaps this had been a mistake.

"Do you wish me to undress her, sir?" the maid asked after several minutes of his troubled perambulation.

Sarah remained still and silent, her arms at her sides. She licked her lips, a mere flick of her tongue, but it was enough to stop him mid-step and make his ardor quiver.

"No." He waved her away.

With a curtsy, she moved to the door. "If you need assistance, sir, please ring and someone will attend you. Madame Devereux hopes you enjoy your visit."

He did not respond. He stared at the woman before him. A whore selling her body to the highest bidder. Never would he have thought Sarah could have fallen so far, and guilt reared its head once more. He drank it down with his wine. Before hearing that she resided at Madame Devereux's inn, he had thought for certain that she lived with her lover. But he was not to blame if her lover had decided to cast her aside.

With a disgusted snort, he went to the sideboard, poured himself a glass of port, and gulped it down. Yet despite his revulsion, his ardor continued its march upwards. There had been titillation in seeing Sarah engaged in congress, some satisfaction that she had been his, that he had been fortunate to have her maidenhead, freely given by her to him. How much more inciting to have her for his own, though. He moved to the other side of the room to better admire her backside, a shadowy form under her shift.

Whore or not, she was still a lovely sight to behold. She kept herself well groomed. But he had to remind himself that she was no different than the dirty strumpets that walked the streets about Covent Garden. Not only was Sarah now a whore, she was a whore engaged in the most wicked forms of carnal depravity.

And enjoyed it. Surely that spoke to how much of a strumpet she was. If only he had known, if only she had shown her true colors before they had married...

His anger rising once more, he set aside his glass of wine, grabbed her arm, and dragged her to the bed. She gasped when he threw her forward against the bedpost. Yanking off one of the cords to the bed curtains, he used it to tie her wrists above her to the bedpost. He did not want her to remove her blindfold, purposefully or by accident.

Her bottom lip hung down, and he stared at its fullness. Here at Madam Devereux's inn, it seemed the women could not afford rouge. But her lips looked supple and inviting nevertheless. As if knowing that he stared, she closed her mouth. He touched her lips, parting them slightly. She shivered. From cold or excitement? he wondered.

He dropped his hand to her collar, then to the swell of her breasts. He gasped one through the shift, sinking his fingers into the soft flesh. He rolled the orb, then brushed his thumb over the nipple. Her lips parted once more. He toyed with the nipple, tugging and pinching, before dropping his hand to cup her mound. As his wife, she had enjoyed being petted there. Was she still partial to being fondled in that manner, or did she now seek more wanton forms of pleasure?

He rubbed the shift against her, and it seemed a timid moan escaped her mouth. Gently and slowly, he caressed her through her shift. When she seemed to move her hips to grind herself into his hand, heat rushed through him. He used to marvel that she enjoyed the venereal as much as his sex did. He had many friends who lamented that their wives had little interest in being ravished.

But she knew not whose hand was betwixt her legs. How could she find pleasure from a stranger? An honest woman would only wish to be touched by her husband.

He withdrew his hand. Deciding that he wanted to see her naked, he pulled her shift over up and over her head. With her wrists pinioned to the bedpost, the garment remained caught upon arms, draped over her head and bunched about the shoulders.

Taking a step back, he admired what he had laid bare. Blindfolded and bound, she was at his mercy. His groin tightened. He could take her now, make quick work of the tension coiled in his pelvis.

Instead, he returned his hand between her thighs. Finding her slightly damp, he continued to fondle her till her moans grew louder, the delicious sounds ringing in his ears and throbbing in his hardened arousal.

But did she deserve to be pleasured? Did she merit the euphoria of spending? He withdrew his hand. She was the whore. It was her duty to pleasure him. He untied her wrists and yanked the shift from her. She stood in naked glory before him. He drank in the sight of her full hips and ripe breasts before pushing her down to her knees.

He undid his fall. His member sprang free, a rod she used to enjoy stroking. He rubbed the tip of his shaft over her lips, and she knew to kneel and open her mouth. His lip quirked at her ready obedience. It pleased him, and his shaft stiffened further as he pointed his member between her lips. Her breathing quickened, and he felt the warmth of it on his tip. He pushed himself into her orifice.

*My God.*

Her quick tongue lavished his tip then danced down his hard length. A fire went off in his head. In all their years of marriage, he had never made her take his member into her mouth before. In his eagerness, he would have sank himself completely into her, but he restrained himself and instead crushed his hand into her dark curls. She was adept at using a pacing that elicited a long groan from him. Then she took him into her hot, wet mouth, sucking and licking with abandon. His breathing hollowed. She was divine. His tip hit the soft back of her throat. Though she choked, she did not release him, and he pumped harder in her, wanting to possess her in this most wicked fashion. He would use her, as other men had.

Wondering how many men had invaded her mouth, he began to pump his hips more vigorously. She struggled to keep pace but found no reprieve as his hand pushed her further down his length. She sputtered and gagged. He allowed her to come off him to collect herself before urging her back down. She grabbed the base of his shaft to keep his shaft at a more predictable angle. Her other hand cradled his cods.

*Damnation.*

Desire coiled in his groin. The wet heat of her mouth sliding up and down his member was beyond exquisite. Caroline was more adept in the art of swallowing a man's shaft, but the fact that it was Sarah taking him was far more titillating.

His climax burst forth with unexpected force. He bucked his hips in quick succession, using her mouth to milk the last drop of seed. Shuddering, he stumbled back, holding his pulsing member.

*Glorious. Bloody glorious.*

He stared, his eyes half glazed with lust still, at his mettle dripping from one corner of her mouth as she coughed.

He felt ashamed at having used her in such a manner. He wanted to shake her. Why had she committed adultery and brought such ruin upon herself? A small, weaker part of him wanted to collapse, to lament the tragedy of their broken marriage. In recalling the wanton manner in which she had ridden Gracehurch, however, he allowed his anger to rule.

"Are we finished, sir?" she asked after wiping her face.

He wasn't ready to leave her. Disguising his voice, he said hoarsely, "No."

"Then how may I please you next?"

"You are eager to please, are you?"

"Indeed I am, sir."

"Are you sincere or do you merely play a part, as an actor would upon the stage?"

A ripple went through his jaw as he awaited her response. She furrowed her brow, perhaps wondering at the terseness of his tone.

"I am sincere, sir."

His jaw clenched before he responded, "Is that because you are truly a whore to your core?"

She paused as she perhaps strained to understand the purpose of his query. "If that is what you seek, sir."

"Yes," he choked, "why else would one come to this bloody inn?"

"I serve at your pleasure, sir."

Pulling her up by her arm, he threw her onto the bed.

"Tell me, do you grow wet for every rogue that you lift your skirts beneath?"

She was quiet before replying, "No."

"Then why are you wet now?"

"I know not. There is something familiar about you, sir. Have you been here before?"

He could not answer. "Do you spend for all your patrons?"

"I do not."

Of a sudden, he needed her to spend. His pride could not abide it if she found more carnal pleasure with a merchant captain.

"Pleasure yourself," he told her.

She tentatively moved a hand between her thighs. To his surprise, he found his member stirring to life once more. She stroked herself with a finger, circling the nub of pleasure hiding between her folds. With her other hand, she groped her own breast.

What a wanton creature, he thought to himself with equal parts awe and disgust. Walking over to the bed, he grabbed her other breast. Leaning over, he captured a nipple in his mouth. She groaned, and he was reminded of the many times in the past when he would suckle her nipples till her fingers dug into his flesh.

The unexpected liquid, light and sweet, that dripped from her nipple startled him. He quickly came off and straightened.

"Your pardon," she said.

He realized it must be from nursing. Had she been faithful and born his son, she would have had a nursing maid at her disposal. Now she had to nurse her own child.

He turned his attention to the area between her thighs. He pulled her legs wider apart that he could improve the view. While she fondled herself, he undressed fully. His desire had hardened, and he would have her once more.

Situating himself between her legs, he joined his hand with hers. The rosebud between her folds had become engorged from her ministrations. He slid a finger over it.

"Ohhh," she moaned as her lashes fluttered.

Her cunnie slicked his fingers with its sweet juices. He caressed her till she dug her hands into the bedclothes.

"Beg me." He did not know where the words had originated, but a new heat invigorated him, making his lip quirk again. "Beg me to spend."

"Yes, sir," she panted out as he increased the friction of his fingers around her bud.

He stroked himself with his free hand, encouraging his member to stiffen further.

"Please, sir..."

"Please, what?"

"Please, may I spend?"

"And why should I grant you this privilege?"

"Because you are kind, because you take pity upon a whore."

He sank a digit, then two, into her slit.

She began to squirm. "Ohhh...please, sir, please..."

"You beg quite prettily. Perhaps I shall let you spend."

"Yes. Please, sir."

"Spend."

She contracted around his fingers as he pushed them in deeper. She raised her hips to meet his movements while her body thrashed upon the bed, breasts bouncing. Seeing her in the throes of ecstasy, hearing her cries of delight, he was ready to sink himself into her.

But he would not take her as he would have as husband and wife. He flipped her onto her stomach and pulled her onto all fours. Kneeling behind her, he aimed his shaft at her folds. She was dripping wet. Inch by inch, he sank himself into her. Putting a hand upon her lower back to hold her in place, he began a slow and steady thrust till she began to moan anew.

The wantonness of taking her in such a position and the magnificence of her proved too much for his patience, and soon he began to buck his hips more vigorously, slapping against her rump. Closing his eyes, he buried himself as deeply into her as possible, listening to her squeal in a mix of pleasure and pain. He continued to pump into her over and over until all the tension, all the anger found release.

After emptying himself, he collapsed onto the bed, pulling her into his arms. She seemed surprised but lay against him without word.

He felt as if he had had somehow ascended the heavens again...but a voice within cautioned that therein also contained a hell.

# Chapter Five

The next evening, he met his parents at Lady Chilton's soiree. After being greeted by the hostess, his father went straight to the card room, and his mother found more biddy hens to squawk with.

Rowan had little patience for women's talk and moved away in search of solitude, especially as his mind was still aflame with thoughts of Sarah. His evening with her had been more than he had imagined it could be. More pleasure, more pain, both scorching into one fire that consumed him.

"Rowan, there you are," Sir Arthur said. He leant on his jeweled cane. Rowan found himself wondering if Sir Arthur made other uses, besides aiding him in walking, with his cane? He suddenly had an ill thought. Had Sir Arthur ever availed himself of Sarah's charms? He received Sir Arthur less warmly.

"I see you merited an invitation from Lady Chilton," Sir Arthur said. "A fine woman and much sought after as she would undoubtedly make a good match in many respects."

"She has many assets," Rowan agreed.

"You seem less than impressed, but I will grant your right to be skeptical. Women can be devilishly deceitful. Our only consolation is that when they are discovered, they are properly cast out from good society."

Rowan could not help but note that men were not similarly castigated for their indiscretions and licentiousness.

"Yet the Good Book does preach forgiveness."

Sir Arthur raised a brow. "So it does, and it speaks well of your Christian values to speak to it. I suppose there is no harm in harboring Christian charity, but I would not dwell upon it at the expense of better opportunities. I would think you and Lady Chilton well-suited. And she is still young enough to bear you an heir."

"Yes, I should be fortunate indeed to have her favors," Rowan replied. He did not find he could disagree with Sir Arthur, the man to whom he owed his growing fortune, but Sarah's reservations began to find new resonation. Had Sir Arthur's eyes held such a cold gleam?

Another guest approached Sir Arthur, and Rowan was glad to part with the man. Excusing himself, he went in search of solitude but instead came across Sarah's parents, Mr. and Mrs. Merryton, whom he had not thought to have known Lady Chilton, though her guests included just about anyone of importance in polite society.

He stiffened. He knew they had suffered, and he could not help but feel partially responsible, though all the fault ought to lay with Sarah. Her parents had rightfully cast out their daughter for the shame she had brought upon the family and the Merryton name, but he knew it had not been easy for them.

He gave them a stiff bow. Mrs. Merryton had the same dark tresses, albeit streaked with strands of grey, that Sarah possessed.

"Sir Rowan, it has been some time since last we met," Mrs. Merryton greeted. "Not since..."

Not since the trial, she undoubtedly meant to say.

"I hope you both have been in good health," Rowan returned.

He bowed again, ready to escape this awkward moment, but Mrs. Merryton spoke again.

"Have you—have you seen Sarah of late?"

Rowan stared at them, frozen in place.

"The soft heart of a mother, you understand," Mr. Merryton said.

"I merely wondered what had become of her. We have not heard from her since we..." Her lashes lowered, and her voice quivered. "Since we turned her away."

"As was necessary," her husband reminded her. "We could not condone her behavior."

Mrs. Merryton spoke softly. "Of course."

Even if he knew what to speak, Rowan doubted the words would come to him. He could indeed tell them, but the truth would only serve to devastate them. Mr. and Mrs. Merryton were good people and did not deserve the further humiliation of a daughter who had prostituted herself. The way Mrs. Merryton looked and sounded just now, it might break her heart irreparably.

"If I should hear or come across your daughter," Rowan began. "I will send word."

"Thank you," Mrs. Merryton replied.

He bowed once more and was determined this time to leave. He could not bear seeing the sadness in Mrs. Merryton's eyes.

They allowed him to depart, and he wondered that perhaps he could have found something to say that might offer them some comfort. Perhaps he could mention that he had seen Sarah in passing while out and about on the streets of London, but then they might try to pin him down on specifics: what part of town and how did she appear? He would find himself with more lies than one of omission.

He found his way to the library, where he assumed he could be alone. It was not to be. He had only a minute to himself before he heard skirts rustle into the lowly lit room.

"Lady Chilton." He bowed slightly.

Lady Chilton closed the door behind her before approaching, that predatory smile upon her cool, beautiful countenance.

"I thought I saw you enter," she said. "You must find my soiree wanting if you prefer the loneliness of my library."

"I sought only a respite, my lady," he replied.

She closed the distance between them. She was a beauty, and were his mind not recently upon Sarah, he might have taken advantage of the moment.

"Indeed?" she questioned as she drew nearer. "You need not flatter me, Sir Rowan. I—"

Her foot catching the edge of the rug, she tripped into his arms. To steady her and prevent her from sliding to the floor, he held onto her. She gazed up at him through long lashes.

"Thank you, Sir Rowan," she said in a low and husky voice. "I am much obliged."

"Of course," he said, still holding her for she seemed uninterested in moving.

*Kiss her, you fool.*

But he could not help but notice how Lady Chilton, being quite slender, felt less supple in his arms than Sarah. He remembered the last time he had wrapped his arms about Sarah as husband and wife, he had felt the swell of her belly, heavy with child. She had appeared no less beautiful.

Yet Lady Chilton was the superior woman, a respected widow whereas Sarah was a disgraced adulterer.

"I was beginning to wonder if it was my company you eschewed," she said.

"Of course not," he replied, gazing at her lips, not so far from his own.

She straightened, but her hand remained upon his waistcoat.

"Are you quite certain of that?"

He raised his brows at her challenge. The air between them had grown tense and warm. Her hand slid over his waistcoat, a subtle invitation.

He should find her alluring. Certainly she was beautiful, light where Sarah was dark. Damn Sarah. He would blot her out. He wrapped his arm around Lady Chilton's waist, pulling her flush to him.

She let out a pretty gasp. Her lips parted. He crushed his mouth to hers. His lips roamed over hers, tasting of her rouge. She did not taste like Sarah, did not smell like Sarah. He pressed down harder.

But to no avail. He eased off her mouth and drew apart.

Her eyes glimmered when she looked up at him. She batted her eyelashes. "My, you are forceful, Sir Rowan."

He thought of trying again, but he knew it would make little difference. He supposed if he had a drink or two in him, he could make love to her, woo her. Perhaps if he gave himself more time, Lady Chilton's charms would grow. But for tonight, he was not prepared to press his advantage.

"Forgive me," he said, releasing her. "I ought not have taken such a liberty."

"Perhaps. Perhaps not," she said.

"You are too kind, Lady Chilton."

"I am rarely unnecessarily so."

Silence followed.

"I keep you from your guests," he said.

"But I am looking after a guest right now."

"I could not, in good conscience, monopolize you all for myself. Especially when you have so many guests that undoubtedly wish for your attentions."

She reluctantly accepted the truth of his statement. "Your mother had extended me an invitation to Christmas dinner. Perhaps we could...further our acquittance then."

"Indeed," he acknowledged and offered his arm.

She received it, and they walked from the library. Christmas was a sennight away. That should provide him enough time to train his mind away from Sarah and toward Lady Chilton. The latter represented his future, the former a past that was best forgotten.

# Chapter Six

B ut try as he might, Rowan could not keep Sarah from his mind. Two nights before Christmas, he sat in his bedchamber, idly stroking his half-erect member. He had tried to keep Sarah's image locked away, as he had done to her portrait. He had failed. Maybe he could see her again...maybe he could even take her as a mistress. He imagined taking Sarah in so many ways indulge in every inch of her body. He had thought of little else recently. He went about his business as if in a daze, not seeing what was there, seeing instead visions of Sarah, of what had been, of what might have been.

His gaze wandered to the painting of his mother and himself as a child. His innocent face, unknowing where this life would take him, unwrit upon. He may need to release this tension within him, indulge the carnal, but his duty was to his family, the life he had planned. He needed an heir. A little boy who would look like the one in the painting before him, a pleasant little lad, the pride of his parents' hearts. He would not fail that boy—the one he had been, the one who would be.

But before that duty commenced, he would slake his thirst for Sarah.

Stowing away his erection, he prepared himself for what he vowed would be one final night with Sarah.

The footman at the inn showed him into a gathering room, where various couples sat or stood together. Some were in locked embraces, kissing and groping one another, others appeared to be awaiting something. In a low voice, he told the footman his business.

"I will deliver your request to Madame," the young buck said. "If you will wait here, sir."

Rowan found a vacant chair in a shadowed corner near the door. Better to be close by for his answer. He needed to see Sarah again. Soon. His lust already tented his trousers slightly at witnessing the women in various states of undress.

For a spell, Rowan watched a man and woman engaged in deep and loud kissing. When the woman straddled the man, Rowan could take no more. He had to have Sarah, now.

He turned and strode from the room. In the hall, he almost ran into the footman.

"Excuse me, sir. Miss Sarah is with another guest this evening. But Miss Lucy—"

He shook his head. "I will have no other. Where is Madame Devereux?"

"She is with other guests, sir. She assures you, you will find Miss Lucy most satisfactory."

The thought of Sarah with yet another man was too much to bear. He had to leave before he burst a nerve.

"My hat and gloves," he barked.

As soon as the footman returned with his belongings, Rowan grabbed them from the man and did not wait to don them before stalking out into the corridor. He realized then that he had not requested a cab be called. Part of him wondered that he could wait. He was distraught enough to consider walking all the way home, but it was unwise to traverse the streets alone at this hour. With a grunt of exasperation, he turned about to go in search of the footman when a woman passing the corridor caught his eye. She held a small swaddled babe of golden brown hair.

Rowan felt a chill come over him. The face of the child was his own—the replica of the portrait he had pondered in his study earlier.

He quickly followed the pair. The woman headed down a slight of stairs.

"Come, George, let us find you some milk, shall we?" she asked the little boy, who sucked upon his thumb.

Realizing she was being followed, the woman turned to face him. "Are you in need of assistance, sir?" she asked.

He looked to her, then stared once more at the boy. Trying to find breath and words, he managed, "I...May I have a word, Miss?"

She looked him over from head to toe, and her features relaxed after taking in his fine clothes. "Indeed, sir. What do you wish to speak of?"

"Is—Is this your child?" he ventured, unsure what he hoped the answer to be.

"No, no, I am merely watching him. His mama is...occupied."

Rowan grimaced inside. "He is a delightful looking child. I, er, had a cousin whose boy looks quite similar. Pray, who is the mother of such a fine looking boy?"

"That would be Miss Sarah."

He nearly reached for the rails to the stairs, but there were none. He swallowed with difficulty.

"Could we speak in private, Miss—er, might I have your name?"

She appraised him once before responding, "Meredith. I be Miss Meredeith. And what would we be speaking of?"

"Please...I would pay for the privilege."

She smiled coyly. "But I would need to find someone to watch George."

Realizing she misunderstood him, he said, "That is unnecessary. I mean only to talk of—I mean only to ask you of this Sarah you know."

"I know few men who would pay to merely *talk*."

"I am in earnest." He pulled out his coin purse and gave her a crown.

She accepted the coin. "George needs milk. We can talk after."

He nodded. His heart beat rapidly, sensing that tonight, his world would be upended.

# Chapter Seven

"Your life could be forever changed in a night."

Rowan, fixed upon the clock on the mantle above the fireplace of his drawing room, did not hear his mother. He needed to be at Madame Devereux's inn in less than an hour, but his mother, having visited with Mrs. Appleton around the corner, had stopped in unexpectedly.

"Your father came across Sir Arthur," his mother continued, "who remarked how much he admired Lady Chilton. You already know that she has accepted my invitation to Christmas dinner. A few months ago, I would have thought all that had happened with Sarah to be a great misfortune, but now I rather think it good fortune. Your prospects, dear Rowan, look bright indeed."

He pretended to yawn. "I am feeling rather tired, mother. It has been a rather busy day. Without Sarah, my housekeeper has had to seek my counsel on what to give the wassailers and arrange for the boxes and perquisites for the servants. Sarah used to handle all such matters."

"Then the sooner you find a wife, the sooner you can free yourself of such obligations."

"Yes, yes, well, I shall retire early for the night and should be quite awake tomorrow for Christmas service."

His mother nodded her approval and prepared to take her leave while he called for her carriage. To Rowan, everyone and everything, save time itself, moved far too slowly. Once his mother had departed, he threw on his garrick and called for his horse. He rode as quickly as he could to the inn, threw on a mask before entering, deposited his hat and gloves with the butler and made his way up the stairs to where Miss Meredith said she quartered with Sarah.

As directed, Miss Meredith had left the door to their room slightly ajar. He eased closer as quietly as he could. He nearly held his breath, pausing to make sure no one was about, and no one had heard his approach. Nothing appeared, and no one made alarm. He leaned closer to the door to better hear.

"He's slept like an angel, Sarah," Miss Meredith ws saying.

"Yes, he sleeps as soundly as his father," Sarah commented.

He sucked in a breath.

"A tree could fall upon the house, and he would barely stir," Sarah continued.

"George or his father?"

"Both."

"Do you mind my asking where be the babe's father?"

There was silence before Sarah finally said, "I believe him in town."

"Then why are you not with him? Did the louse throw you out? Did you flee from him?"

Again, there was a pause that seemed unending to him.

"My husband and I have a *divortium a mensa et thoro, a separation from bed and board,*" Sarah replied, *"though I expect my husband is pursuing a petition for divorce."*

"Indeed? How cruel! To cast out a woman and his own son."

"Oh, he had cause as I was found guilty of criminal conversation, and he believes George not to be his."

"Then your lover is most cruel, if you not mind my saying, Miss Sarah, to abandon you and George."

"He is far from cruel and among the most compassionate of men."

Rowan clenched his jaw and fisted both hands.

"But, you see, he was wrongly convicted."

"How so?"

"I admit I harbored affection toward him, and we were seen often in each other's company. Even my own family believed me an adulteress. I think I found myself rather alone when Sir Rowan was so often busy, but I never broke my marital vows. Not even for a kiss, though I will not say I was innocent of temptation."

"Then George *is* your husband's? Are you certain?"

"Of course I am certain. How can he not be when I have never lifted my skirts to anyone but my husband?"

Of a sudden, Rowan found it hard to breathe. A strange void twisted his guts. Was this true? But how could everyone else, himself included, have been so wrong?

"Oh, my," Miss Meredith cried. "I'm that sorry for you, Miss Sarah. You and George. 'Tis like a Greek tragedy."

"Well, I nearly fell in love with a man not my husband. In that sense, I was guilty. I may not have betrayed Sir Rowan in body, but I had in my heart. And though my supposed lover is a worthy man, and I wish him well, I would that I had made more of an effort to make my marriage a happy one. I think I had given up too easily. But wallowing in the past will hardly aid me now. I must build a new future for my son."

Silence ensued, and it seemed that the women had finished talked. Feeling as if his legs might give way, Rowan stumbled down the stairs all the way to the scullery where he had arranged for Miss Meredith to purposefully seek answers about the babe.

He gasped for breath in the dank, dim space. Then he pulled on his boots and exited from the servants' entry.

His head spun with the possibility that her criminality had been misplaced, that the crime might have been his, that he was guilty of false accusation. Against his own wife. He fisted his hand in front of his chest, where an indescribable pain churned.

He knew not how he found his way home. He was not aware of the passage of time. He did, however, upon arriving home, find his brandy and drank himself into a stupor.

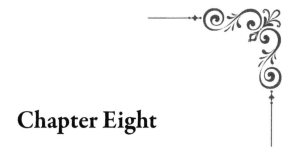

# Chapter Eight

Lying in bed, his head throbbing, Rowan stared at the wall where Sarah's portrait had been. How could he have made such a mistake? But all of polite society, the jury at the crim con trial—everyone had believed Sarah guilty. Yet, in replaying all the facts that had been presented, Rowan realized there had been no actual evidence. Yes, many had seen Sarah and her supposed lover in the corner of a corridor or conversing in Hyde Park, often in close proximity, but no one had actually attested to seeing them kiss, let alone engage on congress.

She was innocent. The boy was *his son*. And in seeking the crim con and now a divorce, he had condemned both to a life of hardship. He had reduced his wife to a whore, and now his son was being raised in a brothel. His wretchedness cut him to the marrow. He was too miserable even for tears.

"Leave me be," he grumbled upon hearing a knock at his door.

"Do you not wish to prepare for service, sir?" asked his valet.

Rowan emitted groan. It was Christmas Day. Cursing, he roused himself from bed. His head throbbed in protest, but he made his way to the basin and pitcher of water. After pouring water into the basin, he washed himself.

His valet knocked once more. "Sir?"

"Enter," Rowan replied.

He managed to dress, then had his breakfast, which included four cups of coffee. Stepping out of his townhome, he had to pull his hat low over his eyes for the glare of day proved too bright.

During the whole of the service, he thought of nothing but Sarah. He tried to convince himself that perhaps she had lied to Miss Meredith. But the boy was his. Of that he was certain. And as the divorce had not yet come to pass, the boy was his legitimate heir. Even if he were to secure the divorce, marry Lady Chilton, and have a child with her, his properties were entailed to George.

The thought pleased him. For certain his son could not be raised in a brothel. The child must come home. But what of Sarah?

He was inclined to believe her. Indeed, aside from her protests that she had not had an affair, he had never known her to speak false. It made sense to him now. She had always been truthful.

"What have I done?" he murmured and looked upon the cross. He wondered that anyone save Jesus could forgive him.

"Five o'clock," his mother reminded him after the service had concluded, "or you could come earlier. Perhaps it would be nice for you to receive Lady Chilton and the other guests with your father and me."

He grunted, his mind elsewhere. Arriving home, he found he could not sit still. He had to see her. He had to see the child again.

The inn was relatively quiet, though it seemed the place always bore the scent of lust. Madame Devereux received him and explained that most of their guests were with their families on this day.

"Is Miss Sarah disposed?" he asked.

"I grant my members a reprieve on Christmas," Madame Devereux replied, "but I can see if she would be willing to make herself available."

He waited several long minutes before the maidservant returned to inform him that Sarah would receive him.

"Shall I have her ready as before?" the maid asked.

He leaped from his chair eagerly. "Please."

After waiting several minutes, the maid informed him that Sarah was ready in one of the rooms upstairs. He found Sarah in her undergarments, a blindfold over her eyes. His breath caught. A part of him wanted to throw himself upon his knees and prostrate himself at her mercy, but he had not the courage to do so just yet. He had treated her as a whore their last time, intent on his pleasure above hers, not caring how roughly he handled her. Tonight he wanted the chance to reverse course and show he was capable of more, that he was worthy of her.

Sensing his presence, she said, "Good evening, sir."

He walked over to her, drinking in her beauty. She stood still and silent as he unlaced her stays. After she had stepped from them, he pulled her shift down her shoulders, revealing smooth pale skin. He caressed a shoulder and kissed it lightly. He slid the garment lower. Her breasts came into view, full and heavier. Perhaps she had not yet nursed. His member stiffened as he cupped an orb and gently kneaded it. He grazed his thumb over the nipple till it protruded. She let out an audible breath when he took the nipple into his mouth, lightly licking it but retreating before she started to drip.

He pushed the shift down her body. It pooled at her feet. He caressed all the parts he had laid bare, letting his hands roam and grasp waist, hips, buttocks. He trailed kisses from her back, over her delightful rump, across her thigh, and to her mound.

"How do you wish me to pleasure you, sir?" she asked.

Did she ask because she wished a sooner end to their encounter? He stood before her and swirled a digit in the curls at her pelvis.

"It is your pleasure I seek," he whispered, slipping his hand below her mound.

She gave a small gasp when he slid his finger between her folds, rousing the nub between. He fondled her till she moaned and moisture collected upon his hand. Sweeping her into his arms, he carried her to the bed. After laying her down, he once more took in her nakedness. He wanted to crush her supple lips beneath his but did not feel he merited a kiss yet. He returned his hand between her thighs. Her breath quickened as he tenderly played with her nub of pleasure. The heat in his body rose as he felt her growing wetter, saw her bosom rise and fall with uneven breaths.

His fingers moved in and out of her, curling as they retreated. Her legs twisted below her, and she tightened her fingers into the bedclothes below. Her groans grew louder as he continued at a steady pace. Her back arched up off the bed as she began to climax. Color flooded her cheeks.

"My God," she cried out as spasms racked her body.

His gaze did not leave her till the last of her shivers had left.

She drew in a long breath before saying, "Thank you, sir. May I now attend you?"

His shaft was as hard as a maypole, and he unbuttoned his fall to release the tense member. He stroked himself. She felt for him and found his shaft. Embracing it with both hands, she sat up on her knees next to him. He watched as she bent her head down, blindfold still in place, and guided his length into her mouth. Her tongue slid down his length, swallowing half of him inside of her. He had thought to attend her once more, but the sensation of her mouth upon his flesh was too much to resist. Laying back as she sucked him in and out of her mouth, he curled his hand into her hair, cradling the back of her head. He lifted his hips to meet her each time she bore down on him.

Sarah licked him from his base to the tip of the head, swallowing as much of him as she could. Her free hand reached under him, massaging his cods, working the saliva that spilled from her mouth into his skin.

When he pressed against her throat, she gagged and pulled him out, stroking his hard shaft, pulling the skin up over the head. He could have easily allowed himself to spend at her hand or in her mouth, but he wanted a deeper connection.

"I will have you atop me," he said.

Obliging, she straddled his hips and positioned his hardened desire at her quim. She slid it through her wet lips. He closed his eyes, savoring the sensation of his skin rubbing against her. They both cried out at the same time as he sank deep inside her warm tunnel. He pushed past her soft muscles, pressing against all of her internal nerves as he parted her insides and slid deeper still. Gradually, she had taken in his entire length, her folds settled against his pubis. Grabbing her hips, he slowly lifted her up and down. She emitted a groan of pleasure.

She felt amazing, and he wanted to release her from the blindfold so that she could see who pleasured her, whose staff penetrated her and whose shaft she would ride to glory. She began to work with him, timing her motions with his thrusts. She ground herself against his pelvis before lifting herself up then back down, swallowing him whole. When she tried to rise again, a loud moan escaping her, he held her there and then gently lifted her, slowly sliding her up before lowering her down on him again, smacking flesh to flesh.

He felt his member open her up inch by inch and then felt her muscles contract over him as he withdrew. Her breathing shifted, and her cries increased each time he slid her down on him. He stared at her bright nipples, and then up at her beautiful mouth, the one that had swallowed his member deep inside earlier. He wondered how he could have ever let her go. Even if she been truly unfaithful, in any manner, she was worth keeping.

He watched as her mouth twisted. She covered his hands with her own as his shaft pierced deeper still. He watched as her breasts bounced and her brow furrowed. He could sense her arousal building to that sought-for peak.

"Spend for me, my love," he said, quickening his thrusts.

She grunted and groaned before crying out and erupting into rapturous paroxysm. He bucked himself into her, seeking his own climax as heat washed over him. With a roar, he released the desire within him, spilling himself into the depths of her wet heat. Shivers surged through his body from head to toe in the most glorious carnal bliss he had ever known.

When he had stopped thrusting, she fell atop him. They lay, still joined, breathing hard. And in that moment, he wished that time could stand still so that they could forever be entangled in the glow of ecstasy.

Alas, he would have to depart soon to make it to Christmas dinner on time, but he could not leave her. She should be joining him for dinner. And their son, too. His son. His son should not be spending Christmas in a brothel.

"Where is your boy?" he asked her.

She started. "You know I have a son?"

"I have seen him about."

"He is with Miss Meredith, with whom I quarter."

"Have you no reservations raising your son in a place such as this?"

"I have a great many, but at present, my options are few."

He grimaced. "Your pardon. I did not mean to accuse you. It merely seemed—on such a day as this—surely there is some other place to spend Christmas?"

"We have been invited to dinner."

He frowned. The wretched sea captain had invited her to Christmas dinner?

"Indeed? By whom?" he asked.

"A woman who once resided here and with whom I quartered before Miss Meredith came. She was a dear friend of mine."

He could not help but feel a little jealous. Who was this woman that his Sarah was spending Christmas with? She must be of dubious quality if she came from Madame Devereux's.

"And you, sir? Will you be spending the rest of Christmas day with your family?"

He gazed down at her. She was family.

"Yes, that is the plan," he answered. What more should he say? How was he going to go about undoing all that had happened?

"Did you attend service today?" he asked of a sudden, recalling that Sarah attended church for more often than he had cared to, though she had never harried him about his inconstancy.

"I did not," she admitted. "Alas, I have neglected the church since...for some time. But I must not delay you from your plans."

She started to rise, but he held onto her.

"The priest read from Matthew today and spoke of forgiveness as one of the greatest gifts man could give to his brother. Do you abide by such a belief?"

"Jesus told Peter that one must forgive thy brother not up to seven times, but seventy times seven."

"That is a lot of forgiveness to comprehend."

"Yes, but we must strive toward it."

"If you were wronged, could you find it in yourself to forgive your transgressor?"

"Ter—the woman with whom I quartered survived the most atrocious acts against her and her kind. What I suffer pales in comparison to the brutality she has had to endure, yet she does not allow resentment or anger to weigh down upon her."

"Then she is a better Christian than most."

"Perhaps, though I wonder that she has ever set foot in a church, but she inspired me greatly. I would expect one who has seen as much cruelty as she to have a heart occupied too much by bitterness and cynicism for love and generosity. And yet she is capable of much love and sacrifice."

"Do you think yourself capable of the same?"

"I believe that forgiveness is a gift we grant ourselves as much as we grant to another."

He found a lump rising in his throat but managed to force out words nonetheless. "Have you forgiven, then, those who wronged you?"

"Of whom do you speak?"

"Your family...your husband? Have they not reduced you to whoring? Forced your son into poverty?"

"They acted in accordance to what society expected."

"It is a society that hardly sounds Christian."

"Society is formed by men, and we are imperfect beings."

"Do you not bear anger toward your family and husband?"

"What anger I had is long gone. I worried that my husband would try to take my son from me, and I live in gratitude every day that I am able to hold him in my arms."

He choked back his emotions and said hoarsely, "You have a generous spirit—more than is deserved..."

"Are you well, sir?"

Needing space to breathe, he rose from the bed and walked a few paces to stare at the door.

"I have wronged someone," he said after he was able to collect himself. "Someone dear to me. I have wronged two innocent persons. And all this time, I wondered that I could ever forgive the person who wronged me, when it was I who am guilty, who need be forgiven."

"And have you sought forgiveness?"

"I have not. Not yet. I cannot conceive that she would ever forgive me, though I believe her to be far superior than I in embodying the teachings of Christ."

"I think she would forgive you."

"How can you be certain?"

Her statement had struck him as rather preposterous, but he realized her tone had changed. He turned around.

She had removed her blindfold.

He froze, waiting for disgust, mortification, or fury to light her countenance, but though her eyes were wide, and the whole of her body trembled, she exhibited none of the emotions he had expected.

"Sarah..." He could barely choke out her name.

"It was you this whole time?" she asked.

Overcome with guilt, he could not respond. He should apologize, but words seemed too paltry for the task.

"Why did you not come forth?" she inquired.

"Would you wish to be with a man who had cast you out of his home, who had reduced the mother of his son to a whore?"

She lowered her gaze. Her bottom lip quivered, and it seemed she might cry. All manner of emotions tore at his heart, and he flew to her, kneeling before the bed.

"Sarah, I am a most wretched man! I could not begin to ask for your forgiveness for my sins are too great."

She bit her bottom lip and could not meet his gaze. "For Jesus, no sin is too great for forgiveness."

"Hang Jesus," he blasphemed, and at this she looked at him. "It is your forgiveness that I care for."

She stared at him in agonizing silence.

"But I shall not hold it against you should you choose not to forgive me," he said. "Only I must—and I will—make amends. I cannot have my son—our son—spend Christmas night in a brothel. If you do not care to return home with me, you shall stay in a respectable inn till I have secured a worthy residence for you."

"What of George? Do you mean to take my son from me?"

He stared at her. A boy belonged with his father. George was his heir. But how could he wrest from Sarah the one being she cherished above all others?

"He will stay with you," he answered, "and then we should discuss his future. But what else do you desire, my love? What can I grant you to atone for all that you have lost? A new wardrobe, pinmoney, a carriage of your own?"

"I have no desire for such things. I have lived all this time without them, and I think I was rather silly to place value in such items before."

"But you must let me earn your forgiveness in every way that I can," he exclaimed.

She shook her head. "You have my forgiveness."

Stunned, he looked at her wordlessly.

"I forgive you, Rowan."

He continued to stare, then rising from his knees, he swept her into his arms and crushed her to him. "Oh God, my God. Sarah, my love."

She held him tight, and he felt a tear where their cheeks met. He continued to hold her as if at any moment some unknown force would tear her away from him forever. The pressure of so many sentiments threatened to burst his chest, and only the feel of her in his arms kept it at bay.

He turned his head and took her mouth in his. Her lips had never tasted so sweet. She returned his kiss, and he nearly cried at such undeserved happiness. He wanted to make love to her once more, without her blindfold, with her knowing it was her husband who worshipped her, who brought her pleasure.

But Sarah pulled away. "Should you not prepare for dinner with your family?"

"I will send word that I cannot attend."

Her eyes widened. "You must not!"

"I will spend Christmas with you. And with George."

"But..."

"Do you feel obligated to attend the dinner with your friend?"

"No, she will be disappointed for she is fond of both me and George, but she will want what makes me happy."

He grasped her hand in his and held it to his bosom. "Will it make you happy to have Christmas dinner with me, my dear?"

She smiled, her eyes bright with moisture. "It would."

His heart swelled. Eagerly he rang the servant bell. After fitting a robe over Sarah, he penned a note to his mother, and she penned a note to her friend. They then went to retrieve George together.

Rowan wanted to take them home, but he had given most of the servants, including the cook, the day off, so he and Sarah took what foods had been prepared at the inn to her room. With his son on his lap, they partook of Christmas dinner on the floor.

It was the finest of Christmases, and he could not have wished for better.

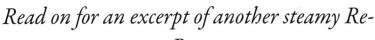

*Read on for an excerpt of another steamy Regency Romance:*

# EXCERPT: THAT WICKED HARLOT

## By Georgette Brown

# Chapter One

**T**HE BEAUTIFUL WOMAN wrapped in the arms of Radcliff M. Barrington, the fourth Baron Broadmoor, sighed into a wide smile as she nestled her body between his nakedness and the bed sheets. Gazing down at Lady Penelope Robbins, his mistress of nearly a twelvemonth, Broadmoor allowed her a moment to indulge in the afterglow of her third orgasm though he had yet to satisfy his own hardened arousal. He brushed his lips against her brow and happened to glance toward the corner of her bed chamber, where a man's waistcoat was draped over the back of a chair. He did not recognize it as his own. The fineness of the garment suggested that neither did it belong to one of her male servants.

Penelope was entertaining another lover, he concluded even as she murmured compliments regarding his skills as a lover. The realization came as no surprise to him. Indeed, he had suspected for some time. What surprised him was that he cared not overmuch. Nor had he the faintest curiosity as to who her other lover might be. He wondered, idly rather than seriously, why he continued to seek her company. Or she his. They had very little in common. He knew that from the start and yet had allowed her to seduce him into her bed.

He was possessed of enough breeding, wealth, and countenance to be able to command any number of women as his mistress. With black hair that waved above an ample brow and softened the square lines of his jaw, charcoal eyes that sparkled despite the dark hue, and an impeccable posture that made him taller than most of his peers, Broadmoor presented an impressive appearance. He had no shortage of women setting their caps at him. A number of his friends kept dancers or opera singers, but he had never been partial to breaking the hearts of those young things. In contrast, Penelope was a seasoned widow and had little expectation of him, having been married once before to a wealthy but vastly older baronet, and scorning a return to that institution, preferred instead to indulge in the freedoms of widowhood.

Pulling the sheets off her, he decided it was his turn to spend. She purred her approval when he covered her slender body with his muscular one. Angling his hips, he prepared to thrust himself into her when a shrill and familiar voice pierced his ears.

"I care not that he is indisposed! If the Baron is here, I *will* speak to him!"

The voice was imperial. Haughty. Broadmoor recognized it in an instant.

Penelope's eyes flew open. "Surely that is not your aunt I hear?"

His aunt, Lady Anne Barrington, was not wont to visit him in his own home at Grosvenor Square, let alone that of his mistress. He knew Anne found him cold, heartless, and arrogant. He had a dreadful habit of refusing to encourage her histrionics, and in the role of the indulgent nephew, he was a miserable failure.

"Let us pretend we do not hear her," Penelope added, wrapping her arms about him.

It would be easier to silence a skewered pig, Broadmoor thought to himself.

A timid but anxious knock sounded at the door.

"What is it?" Penelope snapped at the maid who entered and apologized profusely for the interruption, informing them that a most insistent woman waited in the drawing room and had threatened, if she was not attended to with the utmost haste, to take herself up the stairs in search of his lordship herself.

"I fear there is no immediate escape," Broadmoor said, kissing the frown on his mistress' brow before donning his shirt and pants and wrapping a robe about himself. "But I shall return."

Before descending the stairs, he took a moment for his arousal to settle.

*Whatever had compelled his aunt to come to the home of his mistress had better be of damned importance.*

"Anne. To what do I owe this unexpected visit?" he asked of his uncle's wife when he strode into the room.

He discerned Anne to be in quite a state of disconcertion for she only sported two long strands of pearls—far fewer than the five or so he was accustomed to seeing upon her. Her pale pink gown did not suit her complexion and made her pallor all the more grey in his eyes.

"Radcliff! Praise the heavens I have found you!" she cried upon seeing him.

He refrained from raising an inquisitive brow. Undaunted by the lack of response from her nephew, Anne continued, "We are *undone*, Radcliff! Undone! Ruined!"

His first thought was of her daughter, Juliana, who recently had had her come-out last Season. Had the girl run off to Gretna Green with some irascible young blood? He would not hesitate to give chase, but Juliana had always impressed him as a sensible young woman with an agreeable disposition—despite whom she had for a mother.

"I can scarce breathe with the thought!" Anne bemoaned. "And you know my nerves to be fragile! Oh, the treachery of it all!"

She began to pace the room while furiously waving the fan she clutched in her hand.

"I could never show my face after this," she continued. "How fortunate your uncle is not alive to bear witness to the most disgraceful ruin ever to befall a Barrington! Though I would that he had not left me to bear the burden all alone. The strain that has been put upon me—who else, I ask, has had to suffer not only the loss of her husband and now this—this unspeakable *disgrace*? I have no wish to speak ill of your uncle, but now I think it selfish of him to have gone off to the Continent with Wellington when he *knew* he would be put in harm's way. And for what end? What end?"

Broadmoor did not reveal his suspicions that his uncle had taken himself to the Continent as much as a means to relieve himself from being hen-pecked by his wife as for military glory. Instead, he walked over to the sideboard to pour her a glass of ratafia in the hopes that it would calm the incessant fluttering of her fan.

"And what is the nature of this ruin?" he prompted.

"The *worst imaginable!*" Anne emphasized in response to his complacent tenor. "Never in my life could I have conceived such misfortune! And to think we must suffer at *her* hands. That—that unspeakable wench. That *wicked harlot*."

So it was the son and not the daughter, Broadmoor thought to himself. He should have expected it would be Edward, who was four years Juliana's senior but who possessed four fewer years to her maturity.

"You cannot conceive what torment I have endured these past days! And I have had no one, not a soul, to comfort me," Anne lamented, bypassing the ratafia as she worried the floor beneath her feet.

"The engagement to Miss Trindle has been called off?" Broadmoor guessed, slightly relieved for he did not think Edward up to the task of matrimony, even with the dowry of Miss Trindle serving as a handsome incentive. But it displeased him that Edward had not changed his ways.

"Heavens, no! Though it may well happen when the Trindles hear how we have been undone! Oh, but it is the fault of that devil-woman! My poor Edward, to have fallen victim to such a villainous lot."

Broadmoor suppressed a yawn.

"No greater ruin has *ever* befallen a Barrington," Anne added, sensing her nephew did not share her distress.

"Madam, my hostess awaits my attention," he informed her, looking towards the stairs.

Anne burned red as she remembered where she was. "As this was a calamity—yes, a calamity—of the highest order, I could not wait. If your uncle were here, there would have been no need...well, perhaps. His disquiet could often worsen my state. But your presence, Radcliff, affords me hope. I have nowhere else to turn. And you were always quite sensible. I wish that you would learn Edward your ways. You were his trustee and have fifteen more years of wisdom than he. You might take him under your wing."

He raised an eyebrow at the suggestion. "Edward came of age last year when he turned twenty-one. He is master of his own fortune and free to ruin himself as he sees fit."

"How can you speak so?"

"I have intervened once already in Edward's life and have no wish to make a practice of it," Broadmoor replied coolly.

"But..."

He placed the ratafia in her hand before she sank into the nearest sofa, bereft of words in a rare moment for Anne Barrington.

"But that *darkie* is a hundred times worse than her sister!" Anne said upon rallying herself. "Oh, are we never to rid ourselves of this cursed family and their treachery?"

Broadmoor watched in dismay as she set down her glass and began agitating her fan before her as if it alone could save her from a fainting spell. He went to pour himself a glass of brandy, his hopes of a short visit waning.

"What will become of us?" Anne moaned. "What will become of Juliana? I had hopes that she would make a match this year! Did you know that the banns might be read for Miss Helen next month and she has not nearly the countenance that Juliana has!"

"What could Edward have done to place Juliana's matrimonial prospects in jeopardy?" he asked. "Juliana has breeding and beauty and one of the most desirable assets a young woman could have: an inheritance of fifty thousand pounds."

His aunt gave an indignant gasp. Her mouth opened to utter a retort or to comment on her nephew's insensitivity but thought better of it.

"But what are we to do without Brayten?" she asked with such despondency that Broadmoor almost felt sorry for her.

"I beg your pardon?"

"The thought overwhelms me. Indeed, I can scarcely speak, the nature of it is so dreadful…"

He refrained from pointing out the irony in her statement.

"Edward has lost Brayten."

It was Broadmoor's turn to be rendered speechless, but he quickly collected himself and said in a dark voice. "Lost Brayten? Are you sure of this?"

"When I think of the care and attention I lavished upon him—and to be repaid in such a fashion! To be undone in such a manner. And by that wretched harlot. What sort of odious person would prey upon an innocent boy like Edward?"

"Edward is far from innocent," he informed her wryly, "but how is it he could have lost Brayten?"

The boy was reckless, Broadmoor knew, but Brayten was the sole source of income for Edward. The estate had been in the Barrington family for generations and boasted an impressive house in addition to its extensive lands. Surely the boy could not have been so careless as to jeopardize his livelihood.

"It is that witch, that hussy and devil-woman. They say she works magic with the cards. Witchcraft, I say!"

"Do you mean to tell me that Edward lost Brayten in a game of cards?" Broadmoor demanded.

"I had it from Mr. Thornsdale, who came to me at once after it had happened. I would that he had gone to you instead! Apparently, Edward had to wager Brayten to win back his obligation of eighty thousand pounds."

"Eighty thousand pounds!" Broadmoor exclaimed. "He is a bigger fool than I feared."

"I wish you would not speak so harshly of your cousin."

"Madam, I shall have far harsher words when I see him!"

"It is the work of that *harlot*." Anne shook her fan as if to fend off an imaginary foe. "A sorceress, that one. The blood of pagans runs in her veins. Her kind practice the black arts. Yes, that is how she swindled my Edward. She ought to be run out of England!"

He narrowed his eyes. "Of whom do you speak?"

"*Darcy Sherwood*." Anne shuddered. "Her sister and stepmother are the most common of common, but Miss Sherwood is the worst of them all! I hear the Sherwoods are in no small way of debt. No doubt they are only too happy to put their greedy hands upon our precious estate! I wonder that the darkie, that wench, had orchestrated the entire episode to avenge herself for what Edward had done to her sister—as if a gentleman of his stature could possibly look upon such a common young woman with *any* interest."

It had been five years, but Broadmoor remembered the Sherwood name. Only it had been Priscilla Sherwood that had posed the problem then. He had not thought the young lady a suitable match for Edward, who had formed an unexpected attachment to her, and severed the relationship between the two lovebirds by removing his cousin to Paris, where Edward had promptly forgotten about Priscilla in favor of the pretty French girls with their charming accents.

But Broadmoor had only vague recollections of Miss Darcy Sherwood, the elder of the Sherwood sisters.

"Oh, wretched, wretched is our lot!" Anne continued. "To think that we could be turned out of our own home by that piece of jade."

"That will not happen," Broadmoor pronounced, setting down his glass. Perhaps Anne was right and he should have taken more of an interest in Edward's affairs.

Relief washed over Anne. "How grand you are, Radcliff! If anyone can save our family, it is you! Your father and mother, bless their souls, would have been proud of you."

His thoughts turned to the woman upstairs. Penelope would not be pleased, but he meant to have his horse saddled immediately. His first visit would be to Mr. Thornsdale, a trusted friend of the family, to confirm the facts of what Anne had relayed to him.

And if Anne had the truth, his second visit would be to Miss Darcy Sherwood.

*That wicked harlot.*

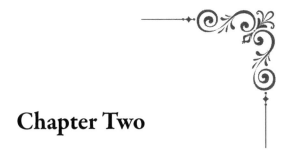

# Chapter Two

NO ONE NOTICED the gentleman sitting in the dark corner of Mrs. Tillinghast's modest card-room. If they had, they would have immediately discerned him to be a man of distinction, possibly a member of the *ton*. His attire was simple but elegant, his cravat sharply tied, his black leather boots polished to perfection. On his right hand, he wore a signet bearing the seal of his title, the Baron Broadmoor.

Upon closer inspection, they would have found the edition of *The Times* that he held before him and pretended to read was over two days old. Why he should be reading the paper instead of participating in the revelry at the card tables was a mystery unto itself. No one came to Mrs. Tillinghast's gaming house to *read*. They came for three distinct reasons: the friendly tables, the surprisingly good burgundy, and a young woman named Miss Darcy Sherwood.

*That wicked harlot.*

Somewhere in the room a clock chimed the midnight hour, but the wine had been flowing freely for hours, making her partakers deaf to anything but the merriment immediately surrounding them. From the free manner in which the men and women interacted—one woman seemed to have her arse permanently affixed to the lap of her beaux while another boasted a décolletage so low her nipples peered above its lace trim—the Baron wondered that the gaming house might not be better deemed a brothel.

The only person to eventually take notice of Radcliff Barrington was a flaxen-haired beauty, but after providing a curt answer to her greeting without even setting down his paper, he was rewarded with an indignant snort and a return to his solitude. He rubbed his temple as he recalled how he had left the hysterics of his aunt only to be met upstairs with a tirade from his mistress about the impolitesse and hauteur of Anne Barrington to come calling at the residence of a woman she had hitherto acknowledged with the barest of civilities. After noting that the waistcoat upon the chair had disappeared upon his return, Broadmoor had turned the full weight of his stare upon Penelope, who instantly cowered and, upon hearing that he was to take his leave, professed that naturally he must attend to the affairs of his family with due speed.

A lyrical laughter transcending the steady murmur of conversation and merrymaking broke into his reverie. It was followed by a cacophony of men exclaiming "Miss Sherwood! Miss Sherwood!" and begging of said personage to grace their gaming table of faro or piquet. Peering over his paper, Broadmoor paused. For a moment, he could not reconcile the woman he beheld to the devil incarnate his aunt had described.

Miss Darcy Sherwood had a distinct loveliness born of her mixed heritage. The gown of fashion, with its empire waist and diaphanous skirt, accentuated her curves. The pale yellow dress, which Broadmoor noted was wearing thin with wear, would have looked unexceptional on most Englishwomen, but against her caramel toned skin, it radiated like sunshine.

Her hair lacked shine or vibrancy in color, but the abundance of tight full curls framed her countenance with both softness and an alluring unruliness. However, it was her bright brown eyes, fringed with long curved lashes, and her luminous smile that struck Broadmoor the most. It was unlike the demure turn at the corners of the lips that he was accustomed to seeing.

He felt an odd desire to whisk her away from the cads and hounds that descended upon her like vultures about a kill. But this protective instinct was shortlived when he saw her choice of companions was one James Newcastle.

Miss Sherwood could not have been much more than twenty-five years of age. Newcastle was nearly twice that, and it was all but common knowledge that he buggered his female servants, most of whom were former slaves before the British court finally banned the practice from the Isles. But then, the man was worth a hefty sum, having benefitted tremendously from his business in the American slave trade.

"A song, Miss Sherwood!" cried Mr. Rutgers. "I offer twenty quid for the chance to win a song."

"Offer fifty and I shall make it a *private performance*," responded Miss Sherwood gaily as she settled at the card table.

She was no better than a common trollop, Broadmoor decided, trading her favors for money. He felt his blood race to think that the fate of his family rested in the hands of such a hussy. He could tell from the swiftness with which she shuffled, cut, and then dealt the cards that she spent many hours at the tables. Her hands plied the cards like those of an expert pianist over the ivories. He was surprised that her hands could retain such deftness after watching her consume two glasses of wine within the hour and welcome a third. He shook his head.

*Shameless.*

Broadmoor felt as if he had seen enough of her unrefined behavior, but something about her compelled him to stay. Miss Sherwood, who had begun slurring her words and laughing at unwarranted moments as the night wore on, seemed to enjoy the attentions, but despite her obvious inebriation, her laughter sounded forced. There were instances when he thought he saw sadness in her eyes, but they were fleeting, like illusions taunting the fevered brain.

It was foolhardy for a woman to let down her guard in such company. She would require more than the assistance of the aging butler and scrawny page he had noticed earlier to keep these hounds at bay. Could it possibly be a sense of chivalry that obliged him to stay even as he believed that a woman of her sort deserved the fate that she was recklessly enticing? His family and friends would have been astounded to think it possible.

"My word, but Lady Luck has favored you tonight!" Rutgers exclaimed to Miss Sherwood, who had won her fourth hand in a row.

"Miss Sherwood has been in Her Company the whole week," remarked Mr. Wempole, a local banker, "since winning the deed to Brayten. I daresay you may soon pay off your debts to me."

Broadmoor ground his teeth at the mention of his late uncle's estate and barely noticed the flush that had crept up Miss Sherwood's face.

"It was quite unexpected," Miss Sherwood responded. "I rather think that I might—"

"That were no luck but pure skill!" declared Viscount Wyndham, the future Earl of Brent.

"Alas, I have lost my final pound tonight and have no hope of winning a song from Miss Sherwood," lamented Rutgers.

"I would play one final round," said Miss Sherwood as she shuffled the deck, the cards falling from her slender fingers with a contented sigh, "but brag is best played with at least a fourth."

"Permit me," said Broadmoor, emerging from the shadows. He reasoned to himself that he very much desired to put the chit in her place, but that could only partly explain why he was drawn to her table.

She raised an eyebrow before appraising him with a gaze that swept from the top of his head to the bottom of his gleaming boots. "We welcome all manner of strangers—especially those with ample purses."

*Brazen jade,* Broadmoor thought to himself as he took a seat opposite her and pulled out his money.

"S'blood," the schoolboy groused immediately after the cards were dealt and reached for a bottle of burgundy to refill his glass.

Glancing up from the three cards he held, Broadmoor found Miss Sherwood staring at him with an intensity that pinned him to his chair. The corners of her mouth turned upward as her head tilted ever so slightly to the side. Looking at her sensuously full lips, Broadmoor could easily see how she had all the men here in the palm of her hand. He wondered, briefly, how those lips would feel under his.

"Our cards are known to be friendly to newcomers," she informed him. "I hope they do not fail to disappoint."

He gave only a small smile. She thought him a naïve novice if she expected him to reveal anything of the hand that he held.

Darcy turned her watchful eye to Newcastle, whose brow was furrowed in deep concentration. She leaned towards him—her breasts nearly grazing the top of the table—and playfully tapped him on the forearm. "Lady Luck can pass you by no longer for surely your patience will warrant her good graces."

Radcliff tried not to notice the two lush orbs pushed and separated above her bodice. He shifted uncomfortably in his seat for despite his inclination to find himself at odds with anything Anne said, he was beginning to believe his aunt. Miss Sherwood possessed a beauty and aura that was like the call of Sirens, luring men to their doom. His own cock stirred with a mind of its own.

His slight movement seemed to catch her eye instantly, but she responded only by reaching for her glass of wine. After taking a long drink, she slammed the glass down upon the table. "Shall we make our last round for the evening the most dramatic, my dears? I shall offer a song—and a kiss..."

A murmur of excitement mixed with hooting and hollering waved over the room.

"...worth a hundred quid," she finished.

"S'blood," the schoolboy grumbled again after opening his purse to find he did not have the requisite amount. He threw his cards onto the table with disgust and grabbed the burgundy for consolation.

Newcastle pulled at his cravat, looked at his cards several times, before finally shaking his head sadly. Miss Sherwood fixed her gaze upon Radcliff next. He returned her stare and fancied that she actually seemed unsettled for the briefest of moments.

Almond brown. Her eyes were almond brown. And despite their piercing gaze, they seemed to be filled with warmth—like the comforting flame of a hearth in winter. Broadmoor decided it must be the wine that leant such an effect to her eyes. How like the Ironies in Life that she should possess such loveliness to cover a black soul.

"Shall we put an end to the game?" Miss Sherwood asked.

"As you please," Broadmoor replied without emotion. Her Siren's call would not work on him. "I will see your cards."

He pulled out two additional hundreds, placing the money on the table with a solemn deliberation that belied his eagerness.

Smiling triumphantly, Miss Sherwood displayed an ace of hearts, a king of diamonds, and a queen of diamonds.

"Though I would have welcomed a win, the joy was in the game," Newcastle said. "I could not derive more pleasure than in losing to you, Miss Sherwood."

Miss Sherwood smiled. "Nor could I ask for a more gallant opponent."

She reached for the money in the middle of the table, but Broadmoor caught her hand.

"It is as you say, Miss Sherwood," he said and revealed a running flush of spades. "Your cards are indeed friendly to newcomers."

For the first time that evening, Broadmoor saw her frown, but she recovered quickly. "Then I presume you will hence no longer be a stranger to our tables?"

Broadmoor was quiet as he collected the money.

"Beginner's luck," the schoolboy muttered.

Newcastle turned his attention to Broadmoor for the first time. "Good sir, I congratulate you on a most remarkable win. I am James Newcastle of Newcastle and Holmes Trading. Our offices are in Liverpool, but you may have heard of the company nonetheless. I should very much like to increase your winnings for the evening by offering you fifty pounds in exchange for Miss Sherwood's song and, er, kiss."

"I believe the song went for fifty and the kiss a hundred," Broadmoor responded.

"Er—yes. A hundred. That would make it a, er, hundred and fifty."

"I am quite content with what I have won. Indeed, I should like to delay no longer my claim to the first of my winnings."

"Very well," said Miss Sherwood cheerfully as she rose. "I but hope you will not regret that you declined the generous offer by Mr. Newcastle."

She headed towards the pianoforte in the corner of the room, but Broadmoor stopped her with his words.

"In *private*, Miss Sherwood."

In contrast to her confident manners all evening, Miss Sherwood seemed to hesitate before flashing him one of her most brilliant smiles. "Of course. But would you not care for a supper first? Or a glass of port in our dining room?"

"No."

"Very well. Then I shall escort you to our humble drawing room."

Broadmoor rose from his chair to follow her. From the corner of his eye, he saw Newcastle looking after them with both longing and consternation. As he passed out of the gaming room, he heard Rutgers mutter, "Lucky bloody bastard."

For a moment Broadmoor felt pleased with having won the game and the image of his mouth claiming hers flashed in his mind.

What would her body feel like pressed to his? Those hips and breasts of hers were made to be grabbed...

But hers was a well traversed territory, he reminded himself. Based on his inquiries into Miss Sherwood, the woman changed lovers as frequently as if they were French fashion, and her skills at the card table were matched only by her skills in the bedchamber. The men spoke in almost wistful, tortured tones regarding the latter and often with an odd flush in the cheeks that Broadmoor found strange—and curious.

As with the card-room, the drawing room was modestly furnished. Various pieces were covered with black lacquer to disguise the ordinary quality of their components. A couple giggling in the corner took their leave upon the entry of Miss Sherwood, who closed the door behind him. Sitting down on a sofa that looked as if it might have been an expensive piece at one time but that age had rendered ragged in appearance, he crossed one long leg over another and watched as she went to sit down at the spinet.

Good God, even the way she walked made him warm in the loins. The movement accentuated the flare of her hips and the curve of her rump, neither of which her gown could hide. And yet she possessed a grace on par with the most seasoned ladies at Almack's. She did not walk as much as *glide* towards the spinet.

"Do you care for Mozart?" she asked.

"As you wish," he replied.

She chose an aria from *Le Nozze di Figaro*. The opera buffa with its subject of infidelity and its satirical underpinnings regarding the aristocracy seemed a fitting choice for her. Save for her middling pronunciation of Italian, Miss Sherwood might have done well as an opera singer. She sang with force, unrestrained. The room seemed too small to hold the voice wafting above the chords of the spinet. And she sang with surprising clarity, her fingers striking the keys with precision, undisturbed by the wine he had seen her consume. Despite her earlier displays of inebriation, she now held herself well, and he could not help but wonder if the intoxication had not all been an act.

"My compliments," he said when she had finished. "Though one could have had the entire opera performed for much less than fifty pounds, I can understand why one would easily wager such an amount for this privilege."

"Thank you, but you did so without ever having heard me sing," she pointed out.

She wanted to know why, but he said simply, "I knew I would win."

Her brows rose at the challenge in his tone. The work of the devil could not always prevail. He ought bestir himself now to broach the matter that had compelled him here, but he found himself wanting to collect on the second part of his winnings: the kiss.

She rose from her bench, and his pulse pounded a faster beat. She smiled with the satisfaction of a cat that had sprung its trap on a mouse. "Would you care to test your confidence at our tables some more?"

"Are the bets here always this intriguing?" he returned.

"If you wish," she purred as she stood behind a small decorative table, a safe distance from him.

She began rearranging the flowers in a vase atop the table. "How is it you have not been here before?"

The teasing jade. If she did not kiss him soon, he would have to extract it for himself.

"I did not know its existence until today."

She studied him from above the flowers with a candor and length that no proper young woman would dare, but he did not mind her attempts to appraise him.

"You are new to London?"

Feeling restless, he stood up. He did not understand her hesitation. In the card room she had flaunted herself unabashed to any number of men, but now she chose to play coy with him?

"My preference is for Brooks's," he stated simply. "Tell me, Miss Sherwood, do your kisses always command a hundred pounds?"

Her lower lip dropped. His loins throbbed, and he found he could not tear his gaze from the maddening allure of her mouth.

"Do the stakes frighten you?" she returned.

"I find it difficult to fathom any kiss to be worth that price."

"Then why did you ante?"

"As I've said, I knew I would win."

He could tell she was disconcerted, and when he took a step towards her, she glanced around herself as if in search of an escape.

Finding little room to maneuver, she lifted her chin and smiled. "Then care to double the wager?"

"Frankly, Miss Sherwood, for a hundred pounds, you ought to be offering far more than a kiss."

*As I am sure you have done*, he added silently. He was standing at the table and could easily have reached across it for her.

Her eyes narrowed at him. No doubt she was more accustomed to men who became simpering puppies at her feet. Perhaps she was affronted by his tone. But he little cared. She was too close to him, her aura more inviting than the scent of the flowers that separated them. He was about to avail himself of his prize when a knock sounded at the door.

"Yes?" Miss Sherwood called with too much relief.

The page popped his head into the room. "Mistress Tillinghast requested a word with you, Miss Sherwood."

Miss Sherwood excused herself and walked past him. The room became dreary without her presence. Though at first he felt greatly agitated by the intrusion of the page, he now felt relieved. He had a purpose in coming here. And instead he was falling under her spell.

Shaking off the warmth that she had engendered in his body, he forced his mind to the task at hand. Now that he had gathered his wits about him, he shook his head at himself. Was it because he had not completed bedding his mistress that he found himself so easily captivated by Miss Sherwood?

He could see how this place could retain so many patrons and ensnare those of lesser fortitude and prudence like Edward. Even Mr. Thornsdale, whom Broadmoor would have thought more at home at White's than a common gaming hall such as this, revealed that he had known of Edward's increasing losses to Miss Sherwood because he himself was an occasional patron. Mr. Thornsdale had also offered, unsolicited, that he thought Miss Sherwood to be rather charming.

But Broadmoor doubted that he would find her as charming. The fourth Baron Broadmoor had a single objective in seeking out Miss Darcy Sherwood: to wrest from the wicked harlot what rightfully belonged to his family. And he meant to do so at any cost.

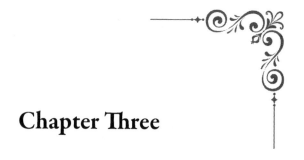

# Chapter Three

"NOW WHO DO you suppose that tasty morsel of a stranger be?" wondered Mathilda Tillinghast—dubbed 'Mrs. T' by her gaming hall patrons—as she observed Darcy staring into the vanity mirror. Once a beauty who could summon a dozen men to her feet with a simple drop of her nosegay, Mathilda was now content to use Darcy as the main attraction of the gaming hall. "I find the air of mystery about him quite alluring."

"I thought for certain that I had correctly appraised his position," Darcy said, still wondering how she had lost that hand of brag. She had begun working at the gaming hall ever since her father, Jonathan Sherwood, had passed away ten years ago and left the family the remains of a sizeable debt, and rarely misjudged an opponent. What was it about the stranger that had sent her thoughts scattering like those of a schoolgirl?

She was both intrigued and unsettled by him. Instead of luring him into more rounds at the card tables—and the kiss would have been a perfect bait with any other man—she found herself *timid*. Mathilda would have found it incomprehensible that she, Darcy Sherwood, who had taken many a man to her bed in more ways than most women could imagine, should be afraid of a simple kiss. When the page had appeared, she could not wait to escape and was now reluctant to leave the refuge of Mathilda's boudoir.

"How could I have lost?" she wondered aloud.

Mathilda snorted. "You sound as if you were in mourning, m'dear. Tisn't as if you lost any money. Wouldn't mind taking your place, in fact. Would that I were your age again. Give you a run for your money I would, 'cept for Newcastle maybe—you can have him."

Darcy shuddered. "If he had not boasted of how well his former slaves were treated—'better than courtesans,' were his words—and then to say that these women ought to be grateful for his kindness—I might have developed a conscience towards him. But knowing that his wealth comes from that horrible trade that ought to be outlawed if only Parliament would listen to Sir Wilberforce, I have no remorse of relieving him of some of that money."

"He can easily afford it, m'dear. They all deserve what they get if they are fool enough to fall for a pretty face."

"Who deserves it?" blurted Henry Perceville, Viscount Wyndham, as he entered the room unannounced and threw himself on the rickety bed. Despite his slender build, the mattress promptly sank beneath his weight. His golden locks fell across a pair of eyes that sparkled with merriment.

"Men," Mathilda answered.

"Nonetheless," said Darcy as she tucked an unruly curl behind her ear, "I should be relieved to give up the charade and restore what little dignity is left for me. Never to have to counterfeit another interested smile or to feign enjoyment at being fondled by every Dick and Harry...to be free..."

"You have the means to end the charade this instant—you have the deed to Brayten!" protested Henry.

"Which I mean to return. I feel as if I have fleeced a babe."

Henry rolled his eyes. "What a ninny you are. Edward Barrington is no innocent, as evidenced by what he did to your sister."

Darcy pressed her lips into a firm line. It had been five years, but the wound flared as strong as ever. She adored her sister Priscilla, her junior by four years, and whom she had always sought to protect. Edward had not only wronged Priscilla, but in so doing, had wronged Nathan, an innocent boy born without a father.

"How you can have the slightest sympathy for that pup confounds me," agreed Mathilda.

"I will never forgive the Barringtons for their mistreatment of Priscilla," Darcy acknowledged. "But I could not send a man and his family to ruin in such a fashion."

"That folly were his own creation. It was not your idea to offer up his own estate for a wager."

"If I offer to return Brayten in exchange for what Edward had initially lost to me, I could pay off our debts to Mr. Wempole and have enough to live comfortably for many years. Eighty thousand pounds were no paltry sum."

Henry threw his legs off the bed and sat up to face Darcy. "I am your oldest and dearest friend, and I must say that if you dare return Brayten to that Barrington fellow, I will never speak to you again. At the very least, wait a sennight before making your mind."

"Make the rascal squirm a might," agreed Mathilda. "I had meant to tell you that Mr. Reynolds has returned, and I think he is willing to open his purse a great deal more tonight—with the appropriate persuasion, of course. But this delectable stranger is far more promising."

Darcy blushed, turning away but not before Henry noticed.

"Do my eyes deceive?" he inquired. "Are you interested in this fellow?"

"He is different," Darcy admitted, recalling the most intense pair of eyes she had ever seen.

"Simply because a man refrains from ogling you or pawing you does not make him different from the others, darling. Oldest trick in the book."

"Am I not old enough to know all manner of tricks?" Darcy replied. "It amuses me how often men overestimate the appeal of their sex."

"They serve their purpose," added Mathilda with an almost sentimental wistfulness before taking a practical tone, "but like a banquet, one must sample a variety. Our Darcy will not be turned by one man alone, no matter how appetizing he appears."

"The only use I have of men, save you, dear Harry, is their pocketbooks," said Darcy firmly before taking her leave.

Despite her parting words, however, before returning to the drawing room where *he* waited, Darcy stopped at a mirror in the hallway to consider her appearance. She found herself concerned with how the stranger might perceive her. An entirely silly feeling more appropriate to a chit out of the schoolroom than an experienced woman such as herself. She wasn't even sure that the man liked her. Indeed, she rather suspicioned that he did not, despite his having wagered for her kiss. Nonetheless, she confirmed that the sleeves of her gown were even and that her hair was tucked more or less in place.

"Never thought to find you here, Lord Broadmoor."

It was the voice of Cavin Richards, a notorious rake known among women for his seductive grin and among men for his many female conquests.

Broadmoor, Darcy repeated to herself. The name was vaguely familiar.

"And your presence here surprises me none at all," was the uninterested response from the stranger in the drawing room.

Not put off, Cavin replied, "Yes, I find White's and Brooks's rather dull in comparison to Mrs. T's. Care for a round of hazard?"

"I came not for cards or dice but to see Miss Sherwood."

"Ahhhh, of course, *Miss Sherwood.*"

Darcy was familiar with the suggestive smile that Cavin was no doubt casting at the stranger. She held herself against the wall but inched closer towards the open doors.

"Quite pleasurable to the eye, is she not?" Cavin drawled.

"She is tolerable."

"Tolerable? My friend, you are either blind in an eye or have odd standards of beauty."

"While I find her appearance does no offense, it cannot hide the vulgarity of her nature."

Darcy bit her bottom lip. She supposed she had played the flirt quite heavily tonight, but had she been that offensive?

"Vulgarity of nature?" Cavin echoed. "I agree Miss Sherwood is no candidate for Almack's but that's playing it up strong. Or is it her vulgarity what draws you? I must say, I never saw that side of you, Broadmoor. I own that I thought you rather a bore, but now you intrigue me!"

The irritation in his voice was evident as Broadmoor responded, "It is clear to me that you know little of me, Richards, and perhaps less of Miss Sherwood or even you would not be so ready to consort in her company. I know your standards to be *pliant,* but I did not think they would extend to the lowest forms of humankind. Indeed, I would barely put Miss Sherwood above the snail or any other creature that crawls with its belly to the earth. For beauty or not, I would rather be seen with a carnival animal than in her company. It is with the greatest displeasure that circumstances have compelled—nay, forced—me to call upon her. I would that I had nothing to do with her, her family, or any of her ilk."

"Then what extraordinary occasion would bring my lordship from his Olympus to consort with us lower mortals?" Darcy asked upon her appearance in the drawing room, relieved that her voice did not quiver quite as much as she had feared it would for it was difficult to contain the anger that flared within her.

The Baron seemed taken aback but quickly collected himself. His bow to her was exceedingly low, but the ice in his tone would have sent shivers down the most stalwart man. "Miss Sherwood, I have matters to dispense that I trust will not require much of your time or mine."

He turned to Cavin and added, "In private."

Darcy could tell from his eager expression that her former lover desired very much to stay, but she had no interest in his presence either.

"My invitation to hazard remains open should you decide to stay," Cavin told Broadmoor as he picked up his hat and gloves, winking at Darcy before departing.

With Cavin gone, Darcy placed the full weight of her gaze upon the Baron. She lifted her chin as if that alone gave her height enough to match his.

"I think you know why I have come to call," Broadmoor said without a wasted second.

"It was not for my song?" She hoped her flippant tone covered how much his earlier words had stung her.

"Do not play your games with me, my child."

Games? What was he getting at?

"Then what game do you wish to play, sir, brag apparently not being sufficient for you?"

Her response seemed to ignite flames in his eyes. He took a menacing step towards her, his lips pressed into a thin line. "It would be unwise of you to incur my wrath."

"And you mine," she responded before thinking. She was not about to allow him browbeat her.

He looked surprised, then amused to the point of laughter. She took that moment to move towards the sideboard for despite her desire to challenge him word for word and gaze for gaze, his nearness was beginning to intimidate her.

"I am prepared to offer a great sum for the return of the deed to Brayten," he announced. "I am told that the circumstances of the wager between you and my cousin were fair. For that reason alone, I offer recompense."

It was then that Darcy recognized the eyes—the same color of coal as Edward Barrington, who sported much lighter hair and whose lanky form did not match his cousin's imposing physique. Her mind sank into the recesses of her mind to connect the name of Broadmoor with one Radcliff Barrington.

She had heard only that his manner tended towards the aloof. She should not be surprised that, like his cousin, he tended towards the arrogant as well, but nothing had quite prepared her for the condescension that overflowed with each deliberate word of his.

"Pray, what great sum are you offering?" she asked with nonchalance as she poured herself a glass of burgundy.

"The proposal of a monetary recompense interests you, I see," he noted.

How she wished she could turn the lout into stone with her glare. Instead, she feigned a sweet smile and said, "Yes, we lower creatures of the earth prefer the petty and base interests."

"I am prepared to offer one hundred thousand pounds, Miss Sherwood."

Darcy began choking on the wine she had tried to imbibe just then. After coughing and sputtering and feeling as if her face must have matched her beverage in color, she straightened herself.

One hundred thousand pounds...it was enough to discharge the debts and provide a decent living for her family. By returning Brayten, her intention from the start, she could have done with the gaming house. She was tempted to take his offer without a second thought, but various words he had said rang in her head. Had he called her a child earlier?

"Your cousin was in debt to me for eighty thousand pounds before he lost Brayten," she said, stalling. "One could say you are offering me only twenty thousand pounds for Brayten. I think the estate to be worth far more than that, surely?"

His eyes were flint, and her heart beat faster as she tried to ignore the way his stare bored into her.

"What sum would you find more appropriate?"

The question stumped Darcy. She had no impression of what Brayten could actually be worth.

"Two hundred thousand pounds?" she guessed.

This time it was Broadmoor's turn to choke and turn color. "You are refreshingly forthright of your greed. I have known many indulgent people in the course of my life, but you, Miss Sherwood, are the epitome of cupidity!"

"And you, sir, are the epitome of insolence!" she returned.

As if sensing that the gloves had come off, Broadmoor sneered, "I am relieved to discard our pretenses of civility. My courtesy is wasted on a wanton jade."

"If you think your impertinence will aid your efforts to reclaim Brayten at a lower sum, you are a poor negotiator!"

"My offer stems from my generosity. I could easily consult my barristers and find another means of retrieving what is mine."

"Then speak to your barristers and do not misuse my time!"

The words flew from her mouth before she had a chance to consider them. She wondered for a moment if she were being unwise but then decided she didn't care.

In his displeasure, he clenched his jaw, causing a muscle in his face to ripple. "You may find my cousin easy prey, but I assure you that I am no fool."

"How comforting," Darcy could not resist.

"Impudent trollop! I have a mind to drag you into the street for a public whipping!"

Unable to fend off her anger, Darcy glared at him and declared, "You have persuaded me that to part with Brayten for anything less than three hundred thousand pounds would be folly."

"Jezebel! Are there no limits to your wickedness?"

Darcy shrugged and looked away. Her heart was pounding madly.

"I see plainly what is afoot," Broadmoor observed. "You mean to punish me for taking Edward from your sister."

She glanced sharply at him. "You! You took Edward?"

"A most wise decision on my part, for I would rather see him in hell than attached to a family such as yours!"

Her heart grew heavy as she remembered Priscilla's pain and thought of the life that should have been afforded to Nathan had Edward done right by them both.

And it was apparently the doing of Edward's arrogant cousin!

"I would not return Brayten to you for the world!" Darcy cried. "If I were a man, I should throw you from the house. You are a lout and a mucker!"

He took a furious step towards her. "You ought consider yourself fortunate, Miss Sherwood, not to be a man else I would not hesitate to box your ears in. You do not deserve the decency afforded to a trull..."

A trull was she? A Jezebel. A jade. She had heard worse, but coming from him, the words were fuel to a fire already burning out of control. What else was it that he had said? *For beauty or not, I would rather be seen with a carnival animal than in her company...*

"I will consider your exchange under one condition," she said. "You will submit to being my suitor—*an ardent suitor*—for a period of six months. You will tend to my every wish and command. Only then, upon your satisfactory and unconditional submission, will I relinquish the deed to Brayten."

He stared at her in disbelief before smirking. "You suffer delusions of grandeur. I am not in the habit of courting sluts."

"Then I suggest you begin practicing," she replied, feeling triumphant to see the veins in his neck pulsing rapidly. "You will appear no later than ten o'clock each evening and await my directions. You will speak not a word of this arrangement to anyone or I am sure to find Brayten beautiful this time of year."

Broadmoor was beyond livid. He grabbed her with both of his hands. "Damnable doxy! I shall see you thrown in gaol for your treachery and have no remorse if you perished there."

He was holding her so close that she could feel his angry breath upon her cheek. She tried to ignore the rapid beating of her heart and the painful manner in which her arms were locked in his vice. He looked as if he desired to snap her in twain—and could no doubt accomplish it rather easily in his current state of wrath. It took all her courage to force out words.

"Unhand me, Baron—lest you wish to pay for the privilege of your touch."

At first he drew her closer. Darcy held her breath. But then he threw her from him in disgust as if she possessed a contagion. Grabbing his gloves and cane, he strode out of the room. Darcy watched his anger with pleasure, but a small voice inside warned her that she had just awoken a sleeping tiger.

1

---

1. https://www.amazon.com/gp/product/B071XNH3BD

Manufactured by Amazon.ca
Bolton, ON

31163697R00219